Books by George Sklar

THE IDENTITY OF DR. FRAZIER
(1961)

THE HOUSEWARMING
(1953)

THE PROMISING YOUNG MEN
(1951)

THE TWO WORLDS OF JOHNNY TRURO
(1947)

The IDENTITY of *Dr. Frazier*

The IDENTITY of *Dr. Frazier*

GEORGE SKLAR

ALFRED · A · KNOPF NEW YORK

1961

L. C. catalog card number: 61–13491

THIS IS A BORZOI BOOK,
PUBLISHED BY ALFRED A. KNOPF, INC.

Manufactured in the United States of America.
Published simultaneously in Canada by
McClelland & Stewart, Ltd.

FIRST EDITION

To Angus

With a bow to

Vera, Guy, Mary, Walt

AUTHOR'S NOTE

Although there are many Mexican seaboard towns which bear a resemblance to it, the village of San Vicente does not exist. This is a work of fiction; the characters and situations are imaginary. There has been no intention to portray any actual persons or incidents.

"My devil has long been caged;
it came out roaring."

Robert Louis Stevenson

Book · I

I

ALEX was back home, on the streets of Meriden, a child again and running. It was getting darker and darker. The power must have gone out because the streetlights weren't on. Then he heard the clatter of machinery, the whirring of buffers, and the BAM! of drop hammers and he knew he must be near the silver shop. An eerie green light flooded the long stretches of window. It was reflected in the broken panes of glass in the charred black, skeletal remains of the haunted house across the street. The shards of glass, like jagged witches' teeth, grinned malevolently down on him, and he was sure he heard the wail of old Mrs. Kennisher's ghost.

He streaked down the street, a yipping dog at his heels. At the corner, in front of Minnery's Saloon, stood a bunch of drunks. He tried to avoid them, but they stepped in front of him. Among them, as usual, was his father, red-faced and loud. He grabbed hold of Alex and pulled him close in a boozy embrace, smothering him in the stench of sweat and beer. Somehow, Alex squirmed free. His father's voice shouted after him as he ran. It kept echoing in his ears as he rushed over Brookside Bridge, his pounding feet making a terrifying rataplan on the wooden planking.

Alex kept running, past the cut-glass factory, up the old railroad, past the lumberyard and toward the big trestle. He had started across, picking his way over the precarious ties, listening to the frightening roar of the waters underneath, when the train whistle hooted in his ear. He turned to run back, but his father was lurching up the ties toward him waving his belt in his hands like a madman, and the train was already rounding the curve, the big, black locomotive bearing down on him, blinding him with the glare from its headlight.

Alex let out a strangled cry—and suddenly he was awake, his eyes blinking into the glaring sun that shone in through the window. The sound of water continued, though it was an irregular sound, like the lapping of waves.

He raised his head. A sudden looping sensation made him fall back. His eyes closed to shut out the dizziness. When he opened them again the ache in his temples was palpable. Dull and oppressive, it seemed to batten down all attempts at thought. He had no idea of where he was. His senses, struggling to grasp at identifying marks, were caught in blanketing layers of fuzz.

Feverishly he tried to break through. When his mind finally meshed, he realized he was some forty years and three thousand odd miles from Meriden. He certainly wasn't in the master bedroom of his Beverly Hills home. The ceiling was too low. He noticed the broken dome fixture and smashed bulb. Then the rectangle of broken plaster and the overturned chest. The room was a shambles. The window was smashed. Hunks of plaster lay scattered or pulverized into a white dust tracked and ground into the floor boards and serapes.

The ghastly pink and purple of the serapes told him where he was. Heavy and hung-over, he had an odd identification with a drugged Gulliver waking in the land of the Lilliputians. A swarm of tiny tormentors with minuscule pneumatic drills seemed to be boring into his skull. And he felt so stiff in every muscle and bone that he might as well have been tied down. Looking down, he was surprised to find that he was stretched out on one of the outdoor chaises. Which made no sense at all.

He tried to think back to last night and was alarmed to discover that he couldn't summon up one single moment. It was as if last night hadn't existed. Nor much of the day. All he could recall was that he'd been out fishing. And he had a dim memory of coming back to the motel room and having an argument with Peggy.

Where was Peggy? He looked at the empty bed. Then he noticed a cot near the door. There had been no cot in the room when they'd come down. And no stupid outdoor chaise, either. Why in hell should he be waking up on the lumpy thing when his place was in that bed, with Peg warm and soft beside him?

Peg's absence bothered him. He turned toward the open bathroom door, called her name. There was no answer. From the angle of the sun, it was quite early. Much too early for Peg to be up and out. Not on a holiday week-end, in this remote village, two hundred miles south of the Mexican border. "I'll sleep around the clock," Peg had announced on the way. "Wild horses won't be able to get me up." Why, then, should he wake to find himself alone and abandoned in this wreck of a room? Why, in God's name, was she up this early? And on New Year's morning, come to think of it, after what must have been something of an Eve of celebration. There must have been a party. Not a glimmer, not an echo of it in his mind.

He hit his temple with the palm of his hand as if to jar loose those maddening few hours of amnesia. It didn't help.

His eyes ranged over the wreckage of the room, fastened on the gas heater, which lay incongruously on its side in the middle of the room, far removed from its outlet. Four dots of shiny red, lying in a white spattering of plaster dust, caught his attention. He stared at them in fascination until they began to take shape. They were capsules, Seconal.

Weird. The whole thing was weird.

The party—if party it was—had turned into a brawl. The questions of who, why, and what buzzed and darted around in his mind. What part had he played in it? Considerable, he was beginning to feel. The over-all ache and torpor was now taking on shadings. Specific pains were registering on his awakening sentience. The burning sensation of a scraped knee, the bone ache in his jaw, and, most curious of all, he was aware of that special ache in the buttock which is the aftermath of a shot from a hypodermic needle.

A shudder of apprehension shook him. He was suddenly frightened—and cold. Leaning over on his side, he reached down and pulled a serape from the floor. Covering himself with it, he lay still, content not to probe or conjecture, seeking only the elementary comfort of body warmth.

A line of sunlight cut across his lids. He heard the grating squeal of a heel on glass and opened his eyes. Peg was standing over him, her face impassive.

"Are you all right?" she asked.

He groaned. "Where were you?"

"In the restaurant. I went for some coffee."

"Oh . . ." He touched his hand to the raw spot on his face. "What happened?"

"You fell. You took a lot of falls."

"Sounds like I had myself a time," he said, a little too lightly. Then, looking up at her, "What was it all about, Peg?"

"You had yourself a time," she said sardonically.

"Seriously," he said, disturbed by her tone.

"It was your party. You ought to know."

"I don't. I don't remember a thing."

"Perhaps it's just as well."

The apprehension seeped down, spreading through him. "Tell me. There was a brawl. I want to know."

He looked at her in all earnestness, anxious, willing her to answer. Peggy averted her eyes, said, "Later. Why don't you take a shower? I'll get you some black coffee."

"Now. Please!" he pressed.

She drew in her breath, said, "All right," but kept her eyes averted. "It wasn't brawl. There was only one person fighting. The others were trying to quiet him."

There was a pause, then Alex, as if stating rather than asking, said, "Me."

She didn't say anything. There was no need.

He shook his head in awe. An unknown fear settled queasily in him stomach. "Why?" It was a cry of despair.

She shook her head. "You were drunk."

"It's not like me, is it?"

"For a man who measures his drinks to the half ounce, no."

He was silent; his mind fought for balance against an encroaching panic. "Did I hurt anyone?" he finally asked.

"You broke someone's nose."

"Oh, Christ . . . Whose?"

"A stranger's."

"Anything else?" he asked after a pause.

"Frank's black and blue."

He shook his head, incredulous. "I didn't throw a punch at Mr. Press, I hope."

"That wouldn't have been very politic, would it?"

Again he caught the sardonic note in her voice and looked up. For the first time he noticed the darkened area around her cheekbone. Not Peg, he told himself. He couldn't have thrown a punch at her. It was inconceivable.

"What's that?" he managed to say, his fingers reaching toward the sensitive area.

She drew back sharply, as if she didn't want to be touched, almost, he felt, as if she were repelled.

"Oh, God, Peg." It didn't make sense. To have hit Peg! "It just doesn't seem possible."

"You did and said a lot of things I didn't think were possible."

She said it quietly, with deliberation. The implications were so frightening he didn't dare ask what. Not this moment. He didn't know whether he could take it.

She turned, started toward the door. "I'll go get that coffee."

"Peg," he called.

She paused.

"Don't be angry with me."

"I wish it were as simple as that."

A heavy silence hung over the room. She seemed to sense his hurt. Her shoe grated on a piece of glass as she turned. "Oh God, don't look at me as though I slapped you! I suppose I should be more considerate. But I've been up all night! I'm tired!"

"I'm sorry," he said, in an abject voice.

"So am I." The heavy silence again. "Suppose you get up and take your shower."

He tried to sit up, fell back. "You'll have to give me a hand," he said.

She held it out to help him but turned away the moment he got up. Taking hold of her arm, he said, "Forgive me."

"For what? For keeping me up all night?"

"For everything."

"Everything's a pretty large order," she said and pulled free of his touch. Her heels made a brisk tattoo across the floor.

He watched her walk out the door. She couldn't seem to get away fast enough.

II

THOUGH the wounds smarted and stung, Alex forced himself to stay under the shower, turning the spray from hot to blasting cold in the hope that it would clear his head. He emerged in a state bordering on numbness.

Surveying himself in the mirror, he was shocked by the unhealthy tokens of debauch: in his puffy, bloodshot eyes, in the brown mottling of the pouches beneath, in the angry calligraphy of lines. He looked with distaste at the swollen lip, the welts and contusions. Alex had an almost narcissistic preoccupation with bodily fitness. He'd played football in his day, and the training habit had never lapsed.

He didn't like what he saw now. The red veins mocked the blueness of his eyes, and the webbing of lines gave him the graven look of a man prematurely old. All of which was beside the point of what had happened and how deeply it might have affected his relationship with Peg. The flutter of fear was back again, the deepening disquiet. Oh, Christ, what was it he'd done!

If only he hadn't insisted on taking Peg along on the trip! She hadn't really wanted to go. Ironically, he'd persuaded her because she was in such need of a rest. The responsibilities of her job as merchandise manager of Black's-Beverly, especially during the Christmas rush, were as strenuous as the load of surgery cases he was carrying at Memorial. Actually they needed a longer break than the week-end, which he'd hoped to extend by another day. Well, that was out now. He sighed.

Rest, he reflected wryly. Poor Peg . . . Besides, whom was he kidding? That wasn't what he'd come down for.

Angrily, he picked his way through the rubble of the room,

found some clean shorts, a plaid shirt, and a pair of slacks. After he was dressed, he moved to the door, pausing a moment when he heard Ted's voice, blurred at first, then the distinct phrase: "No one's going to say a thing."

Alex opened the door, intending to say, "I wish they would." But Ted, who was sitting on the edge of the chaise beside Peg, jumped up, said, "Hi," and walked abruptly away. Alex looked uncertainly to Peg, but she refused to meet his eyes.

"There's your coffee." Peg's hand indicated a tray on the metal table.

"Thanks for getting it."

"Thank Ted."

"I'd like to—if he hadn't been in such an all-fired hurry to get away."

"He was anxious to get to bed. He was up all night, too."

"What did I do, keep everyone up?"

"Till four-thirty. Ted stayed to keep me company."

"I'm glad he did." Slowly he sipped the coffee, watching Peggy as she stretched out on the chaise.

The slanting rays highlighted her close-cropped blonde hair and brought out the flecks of gold in her hazel eyes. Her features, which were normally angular, had in the past weeks begun to fill in, giving a rounded softness to her cheeks and a becoming fullness to her lips. The faces of some women become puffy with pregnancy. Peggy's gentled and glowed.

The black and blue mark was all too evident in the glare of the sun. The sight of it was a rebuke to Alex. After all the times he'd seen his mother slapped around by his father! After all the mortification of watching the neighbors intervene and the police elbow their way in, oh so many times! That he should give way to the violence he abhorred! That he should have abused Peg, who kidded him for living by the code of the Round Table.

He felt sick.

The trip to San Vicente was a mistake, and he certainly had no right to bring Peggy. Not four hundred miles. Not in her fourth month. Oh, he'd vowed he wouldn't drive over fifty an hour. But he was he, and a Ferrari was a Ferrari. The adrenalin flowed faster when he found himself on top of all that power. And the speedometer had a way of sneaking up. It read ninety-three when Peg had called his attention to it.

The worst thing was that he'd coaxed her into it under false pretenses. So unnecessary with Peg. Why couldn't he have been frank and told her about Ike Press?

The fact that she was so understanding about it made him feel all the guiltier. It was probably what set him off on that drinking bout. Though it was a little more complicated than that. Why, for instance, had he felt the terrible urgency to come down here? And why and to what end was he driving himself?

It had all seemed so clear and necessary at one point. After last night nothing seemed important, nothing but the desire to straighten this out, to bring back the frankness in Peg's eyes.

He heard a door open and looked up to find Finch, the friendly fisherman from Orange, staring at him. Alex raised his hand in tentative greeting. As if he hadn't seen him, Finch turned and walked toward the restaurant. Had he, too, been witness to last night?

And witness to what, in God's name?

Peg wasn't telling, that was clear. And she was usually so forthright. They'd had a certain honesty between them. This had vitiated it.

If the question of the appointment hadn't come up out of nowhere to needle his ambitions, none of this would have happened. They wouldn't have come down to San Vicente; there would have been no drunken tear, no blackout, no question mark pointing at him like a threatening dagger. Life would have flowed on quite smoothly.

The idea of the appointment hadn't even occurred to him. So much was accident, the conjunction of chance and circumstance which precipitated a situation, and, because you were handily around, you were suddenly thrust into it, willessly, without forethought, plan, or wish. It was as simple a matter as Dan Simon's being in Rome on a sabbatical on the particular day that Doc

Trattner, who had had no previous history of heart trouble, dropped dead of a massive coronary occlusion.

Alex had been called into the office of Arthur Portugal, the executive director of Memorial, and told that he was to function as acting surgeon-in-chief, on a temporary basis, of course. When Dan returned from his sabbatical he'd naturally take over. His appointment was a matter of course. Except that Arthur was one of those abnormally sensitive men, with his own ideas of protocol, and when Dan had continued on his sabbatical without volunteering to come back if needed, he'd taken it as a personal slight.

Three weeks before the board meeting set for the appointment, just as Alex was emerging from Surgery, depleted after a drastic, touch-and-go arterial scraping, he was again called into Arthur's office.

"I'm putting your name up along with Dan's," Arthur announced brusquely, without introduction or formality.

Alex objected. Dan was his friend; he was in line for the job.

"And he'll probably get it, boards being what they are. Seniority, tradition, and all that hoorah! But I'm putting your name up anyway."

"What's the point?"

"One: You're a better surgeon. Not technically. But you have ten times the imagination, ingenuity, and boldness. Two: You're a better administrator. I've watched you these past two months. Three: Devotion to calling and to this hospital. You've been carrying the full administrative load and enough operative cases to tax any two men, including Dan Simon. . . . I shouldn't be telling you this, but that's the way I feel about it and that's the way I'm voting. Don't let it go to your head."

"I won't. Not that I'm not flattered," he hastened to add. "But Dan's an old friend, and I wouldn't want to jeopardize—"

"It's not your doing," said Arthur. "I'll carry the ball."

He didn't like it. He'd roomed with Dan when they were undergraduates at New Haven. It was Dan who was largely responsible for his switch from research to surgery. Not wholly, of course. Because the army, which needed surgeons more than parasitologists, had given him his training. But when the war was over and he was debating about going back to research, it was Dan who had offered him a start in his practice. He'd gone on from there, but he owed much to Dan. And coming out of Arthur Portugal's office that day, he felt uneasy.

Before he took his shower, he put in a transatlantic call to Rome to tell Dan what had happened. He didn't want him getting ideas there was any skulduggery involved.

Dan understood. "If I'm not upset, why should you be?" he asked, chuckling. "If Arthur wants a scrap at his board meeting, why shouldn't he have one? It'd be pretty dull if there were no contest. Besides you might get it."

"I don't want it."

"Don't be a sap. You think I'd hold it against you? You think I'd care? I'm in Italy, the living's easy, and I like it, man."

The uneasiness washed off with the shower. He was glad he'd called Dan. Once he had it off his mind, he could appreciate Arthur's gesture. Especially since he was one of the few gentiles in this essentially Jewish hospital. It might be that Arthur actually believed he was the better man. In any case, it was nice to hear him say so, nice to linger over the phrase: "You have ten times the ingenuity, imagination, boldness."

Dan was as sound a technician as they came, but he was fundamentally conservative in his surgery. Alex, on the other hand, prided himself on his alertness to every innovation, on his perfectionist search for newer and better techniques. He was one of the very first surgeons to reroute the blood stream. He'd had extraordinary success in his work in coarctation, had invented a special device to clamp off the aorta while removing the diseased section. It was his idea to set up an artery bank.

Knowing that Peggy would get a boot out of the conversation, he called her at the store and persuaded her to meet him for dinner at Perino's.

He loved the place, the muted elegance, the service, the food, the "Ah, Dr. Frazier!" with which he was always greeted by the maître de, the table always available whether he'd called or not.

His excitement was so evident that Peggy said, "You're bursting with it. Tell me."

When he finished, she said, "Do you want it?"

He looked up startled, ready to protest, then realized she'd cut to the heart of what he'd been too embarrassed to admit to himself.

"You do, don't you?"

"You don't approve," he said.

"I couldn't very well approve of anything that would shorten your life, could I?" she said wryly. "You're a good surgeon, Alex, not an administrator."

"And I was a good research man, not a surgeon. That was the argument then."

"I was wrong. But I still prefer research. Perhaps because I like to think of medicine as divorced from the grubby trappings of business. Maybe it's idealism, maybe it's arrested development."

It was all very well for Peggy to say she preferred research. Perhaps he had, too. But grants were unstable and unrewarding in the depression thirties. Which wouldn't have mattered—until he discovered that Joe Strauss, his father-in-law, was supplying Peg's wardrobe, and that on Friday nights, when Peg had dinner with her folks, she invariably came home with enough food to last the week. None of which he could take from in-laws who refused to recognize her marriage to a gentile.

"The trouble," he told her, "is that you're so used to having a rich family, you forget that we're not."

"We're not exactly lacking, either."

True. He netted forty thousand a year—and, unfortunately, spent it. But it took plenty to keep up their establishment and to afford all the extra niceties which so readily became a way of life. He didn't *have* to have them; there was no law, as Peggy put it, that they had to live on the north side of Beverly Hills, or that he had to be seduced by art auctions and expensive Italian sports cars.

Peg was as indifferent to these things as only a girl brought up on Park Avenue could be. Alex, who came from the other extreme, where the rats were two feet long, wasn't as ready to surrender what he'd learned to enjoy. You had to be without to appreciate it. All the childhood years when a penny was passage to the rare pleasure in a jawbreaker or licorice stick! All the adolescent years after the genteel but parsimonious Fraziers had adopted him, when a dime meant admission to the Poli's Palace peanut gallery, to heavenly communion with the sultry images of Alice Terry and Barbara La Marr, with the fantastic adventures of Valentino, Fairbanks, and Chaplin! He still had dreams about that time, as he had about his father, dreams in which he was forever running, always to be lost in desolate gray corridors, listening to the mocking hoot of pleasure-bound trains highballing by.

No, he'd led too starved and Spartan a life to be casual about money. And he didn't see anything reprehensible in earning more by taking on something he really wanted to do.

He'd never regretted the change to surgery. Not that he'd lost interest in research. Those first years when his practice was small he spent more time in Memorial's research wing than in the hospital proper. Whenever he operated on a cancer case he brought in a tissue specimen for virus study. His work on tissue cultures with his old classmate, Dick Lerner, had eventually resulted in a joint paper titled "Isolation of X-19 from Cervical Carcinoma." He had a pride in that paper, a nostalgia for his own work in parasitology. But that was a closed chapter.

He liked what he was doing. Perhaps Peg was right and it was crazy to think of carrying that extra administrative burden, but he couldn't deny he was tempted by Arthur's notion. Then he decided that attractive as it seemed, that's all it was. Quite firmly he decided to put it out of his mind—until Dan came flying back from Rome the very next day—after all his professed unconcern.

He didn't blame Dan. He had his seniority to protect, and Alex certainly wasn't going to combat it. He stood by with a considerable cynicism and amusement as Dan tried to mend his fences with

Arthur. Kay, the model doctor's wife, was doing her bit at the Hillcrest Country Club, where she socialized with the wives of Memorial board members.

A few days before New Year's, Arthur called him into the office again. "Do you want that appointment?" he asked, with his customary abruptness.

"I'd like it, but I feel uneasy about Dan."

"Dan doesn't feel uneasy about you. He's been working at it. You haven't."

"I can't."

"And I haven't asked you to. I told you I'd carry the ball and I've made fair headway. So has Dan. The decisive man is, of course, Ike Press. I've invited him to my New Year's Eve party. You'll be there, and I don't think it'd be difficult to find a moment with him."

"Forget it," said Alex. "I can just see myself—"

"I'm not asking you to say a word about the appointment or bring up anything remotely connected with the hospital. Talk fishing."

"Fishing!"

"You're a fisherman. So is he. Nothing could endear anyone to Ike more than to give him a chance to sound off about the last marlin he caught."

The next morning Alex learned that Ike Press wasn't going to be at Arthur's party after all. Frank Meyers had invited Press to come along on a fishing trip to San Vicente. Alex had the sudden sinking sensation that with the trip went his last chance at the appointment. He'd been above the battle, hadn't lifted a finger. But now that it was slipping out of his grasp he realized how strongly he wanted it.

"Do you mind if I go along?" he found himself asking.

"That's precisely why I've been telling you," said Frank. "Bring Peg, too."

He called her at the office. "How'd you like to go to Mexico?" he said.

"If you could wish me there."

"I can. In six hours. You need the break and so do I."

"I need sleep—and I don't know a better place for it than bed."

"There are beds at San Vicente. And fine, white sand. And a hot sun. And blue water warm enough to swim in. And me—out of reach of good old Memorial."

He gave her every reason but the true one.

III

Before they left for San Vicente, before they got into the car he promised himself that he'd tell her about Ike Press. But Peg was in a talkative mood. She'd had a hectic morning. A teamster's strike had tied up a big shipment of garments from the East. They'd been especially ordered for the January Sale, and she had to fill in with numbers from local factories and from San Francisco. It was a piecemeal operation, involving much phoning, a rejuggling of specials and prices, a recasting of ad copy and layouts. So he put off telling her until they were on their way. Then she'd suddenly said, "I don't know why I go on jabbering when I'm so exhausted," and calmly slumped down, her head against the back of the seat, and dozed off.

They were approaching Indio when she awoke, and it seemed odd to blurt out a piece of information which he should properly have told her when he first broached the question of the trip. The longer he put it off, the harder it got. She presented him with a perfect opening by asking who was in Frank's fishing party.

"Bert Krantz," he started to enumerate. "Ted Crisler—"

"Ted Crisler!" she said in an incredulous voice.

"Not your Ted Crisler." He paused. "At least, I don't think so. Funny, it hadn't occurred to me. He's in pediatrics. Came out from New York about six months ago."

"And you didn't say anything . . . Ted Crisler."

"I must have mentioned his name. He was the doctor in the Amster case. The one who diagnosed the—"

He lapsed into silence. He couldn't talk about it, didn't even want to think about it. He'd promised himself he wouldn't, but there it was like a burr in his brain. For days he'd lived with it, brooding with Ted over the imponderables which made the decision for surgery so difficult, emotionally involved, as Ted was and as Alex so rarely allowed himself to be, with the frightened parents and the infant whose huge eyes seemed to take over her face as she wasted away.

Inevitably he'd performed an exploratory—and found nothing. A second seemed called for, but in a situation where the X rays failed to confirm the clinical diagnosis and with the infant in so weakened a condition, he'd decided to put it off for seventy-two hours in the hope that she'd gain a little strength. Though Dan, whom he consulted, seemed to agree with Ted that postponement might be just as dangerous. The next day the baby had died, and he couldn't forgive himself because the fistula which the X rays had failed to reveal had been exposed in the post-mortem. He'd received a call from Pathology just before they left, and it was he who'd have to tell Ted. He didn't look forward to it.

He'd learned to face mortality. But each time he had to harden himself, to face his self-questioning. He'd allowed himself to get too involved in this case. Ironic that this one time when he'd played it more conservatively than Dan, he'd been so wrong. He felt answerable to him and to Ted and to the bereft Amsters. It was a heavy weight and he carried it with him for the rest of the drive, forgetting completely about Ike Press.

It was evening when they arrived and he hadn't said a word.

Frank, who had an old maid's fussiness about reservations, had obviously checked and rechecked to see that they'd have a room. The boy at the desk recognized the name immediately. For *el doctor* Frazier, there was a room, *seguro*. He flicked the key out of the cubby hole and led the way. It was, he confessed apologetically, one of their smaller rooms but the motel, they would understand, was crowded on the holiday week-end. There were, for instance, four in the room of their *amigo, el doctor* Meyers.

"Four," Peggy said weakly. "We seem to be growing."

"At least we've got our own room," he said uneasily.

"And very jolly, too," said Peggy, as the boy opened the door on the rather dank-looking interior.

There was a purple serape on the concrete floor and a set of matching drapes on the one window. An oak-stained chair, a chest of Monterey maple, a gas heater, and the bed comprised the room's furniture. The bed had a pink and orange spread.

"They certainly did a decorating job on this," said Alex, after the boy was gone.

"Very cozy. One chair, no closet, no curtain on the shower—and that ten-watt bulb's just made for reading. God, I'm dead." She sank down on the bed. "At least there's a firm mattress. Light a cigarette for me will you, darling."

He picked up a paper bag containing a bottle of tequila and a dozen packs of *Delicados,* which he'd bought in Mexicali. The taste and aroma of the cigarettes recalled the time, place, and circumstances of their first meeting in Mexico City, evoking an old nostalgia.

"I suppose we ought to let them know we're here," he said finally, torn between a reluctance to face the situation and a desire to get it over with.

"Let's not," she said. "We'll be up half the night if we do."

"I suppose."

The sweet-scented smoke curled lazily to the ceiling. After a moment Alex opened the window which looked out over the bay. "That air," he said, taking a deep breath. "Am I going to sleep tonight!"

"And wake to the sound of waves. I just love it."

"Want to go down and take a look?"

"Mm," she said, speculatively.

He took her hands, pulled her up to her feet. Her body rested against his a moment. He put his arm around her waist, and they walked silently out on the patio.

"*Número once,*" he said, glancing at the doors. "Their light's on."

"No, Alex," she said.

"Just to tell them we're here. We won't even go in. I'll say we're tired and want to hit the sack."

"And they'll say: 'Come in and have a nightcap,' and before we know it, it'll be three o'clock in the morning."

"Okay," he said, half-relieved.

"Of course, if you want to go without me and make a night of it with the boys—"

He stopped, said, "Whatever gave you that idea?"

She shrugged. "You've made such a to-do about letting them know we're—" She broke off suddenly. "I don't know why I'm arguing with you. Maybe it's just being pregnant and jumpy and overwrought. All I know is we've been driving all day and I'm tired and just self-centered enough to be very uncivil and want you all to myself."

He turned her to him, his hands gripping her arms. "There's no argument, Peg."

Her shoulders started to tremble, and she slumped against him, unable to check her weeping.

"I don't know what brought that on," she said when she was quiet again. "I guess I'm frightened."

"Nonsense."

"A first child at my age is something to be frightened of."

"You know better," he said with gentle reassurance. But something of her mood had communicated itself to him, and he found himself thinking of the Amster child again, unable to shut out the image of her appealing eyes.

"I'm being foolish, I know," Peg was saying.

"I think the job's too much for you," he said. "You should have quit before the Christmas rush."

"I couldn't . . ." She took a tremulous breath. When she spoke again, her voice was calmer. "This isn't like me. Me, the imperturbable executive."

"There's no one you have to prove that to. I won't tell—and neither will the stars."

She looked up. "I've never seen so many stars."

Neither had he. Unless it was the first night he'd spent at that camp the Child Welfare had sent him to. He was all of eight and everything looked so awesome: the campfire and the big firs and the dark, glossy lake and the sky, not just a patch hemmed in by tall buildings, but everywhere, with the stars spattered about as thickly as they were now, and the shadows, especially his own, moving ahead and growing bigger as he walked, frightened, toward the tent with the other boys. . . .

Peggy was leaning against him. "I'm taking off my shoes." She dug her toes into the sand. "Feels good," she said.

"I'll bet it's cold as hell."

"It's cool and squooshy and doesn't feel a bit different from Short Beach, Connecticut, on an August night." She had the ability to make an adventure out of the slightest experience.

He bent down to take off his shoes and socks and roll up his trousers. "October, not August," he said, as his bare feet touched the sand.

"You're a softie." She took his hand, "Come on," she urged, and they ran down the sloping beach, stopping short of the water-line.

They could see the dark outlines of the fishing boats, the crescent curve of the beach, the somber mass of mountains at either end, the few spots of light from the dormant village.

"This is prettier than Short Beach," she said.

An occasional breeze stirred the air; a salty mist brushed their faces. They savored it on their lips and in their nostrils, taking deep breaths. The wash of a wave caught them unawares and overran their feet. They gasped from the cold, and Alex tried to pull her back, but she held on to his hand, saying, "Let's wade in. Let's dunk our knees."

"You're crazy," he shouted. "It's ice."

"Dare you!" She tugged at his hand, urging him forward with her, letting out an "Ai!" as the icy shock of the unrushing water caught them halfway up their calves. They tried to turn and run back, but it was all they could do to hold still as the undertow of back-rushing water sucked at them.

As soon as they were clear of it, they scampered back to the safety of dry sand.

"I'm numb," he said.

"I feel perfectly wonderful. What you need is a shot of that tequila." She put her arm around his waist, and together they plodded back to the motel, coming to a halt as they neared the patio. A group of men, laughing as if at some bawdy joke, was coming out of a lighted doorway. "Don't tell me," she groaned.

"We can't very well avoid them."

"Why not?" she said, pulling him into the shadow of the wall. "We can duck around the building."

"Too late . . . They've spotted the Ferrari."

"Remind me to have you trade it in for a Chevvy," she muttered. Then, "Isn't that Ike Press next to Frank?"

His heart stopped. "Looks like it," he mumbled.

"Damn," she said. "Now I'll have to be at my best."

"Forget it," he said gruffly.

"Oh, well." She straightened up and walked out into the light with the same aplomb with which she'd greet a familiar grouping at a Beverly Hills party.

"Hi," Alex found himself saying as Frank Meyers came forward to greet them. He was a big man with a flourishing mustache and a courtly manner, an internist with a teddy bear charm attractive to old ladies. It had built the biggest practice in Beverly Hills. Though Alex felt it a little too cultivated, he considered himself fortunate to be sharing his suite of offices.

"Welcome to San Vicente," he said to Peggy, taking both her hands in his. "You know Mr. Press, of course."

"I'm so glad you and Dr. Frazier could come," said Mr. Press, bowing slightly as he took her hand. "I've been looking forward to a chat with the doctor."

"Be delighted," said Alex.

"And how are your dear father and mother, my girl?"

"Fine. They just got back from a trip to Israel."

"Didn't know you knew them, Ike," said Frank.

"I know everybody who ever made a contribution to Memorial, and Joe Strauss's are sizable enough for even a poor memory. Yes, a very civic-minded and philanthropic man." Slight of stature, measuring five-feet-four in built-in heels, Ike Press was given to character pronouncements which, by virtue of his position as president of the Fidelity-First National Bank of California, gained the authority which his deliberate syllable-by-syllable enunciation might not alone have carried. "He has also the distinction of being a good pinochle player," he added. "Which reminds me that I must arrange a session when he comes to town." He turned to the others. "You know Bert, naturally."

"Hi, Peg," said Bert Krantz, the blunt-speaking, powerfully built surgeon who had once won a weight-lifting title at Muscle Beach.

"Hi," she answered.

Her attention was really directed toward the ascetic-faced man with wavy brown hair whose deep-set blue eyes wavered between the warmth of recognition and a secret reserve.

"I don't believe you've met Dr. Crisler," Frank started to say, but they were already moving toward each other. Alex caught the rise of emotion which swept them together in an involuntary embrace.

"I guess that introduction was rather unnecessary," Frank remarked, fingering his mustache.

"We've known each other since we played in the same playpens," said Ted.

"And haven't seen each other for twenty years."

"Is it that long? It can't be. You don't look twenty years older. Or five, for that matter. You're still as ravishing as ever." He shook his head incredulously. "Peg," he said, "Peggy Strauss."

"You're thinner, Ted, but more distinguished looking."

"You mean I'm getting gray," he said, indicating his temples. Then, after a pause, "I've been meaning to call."

"You know how delighted I would have been to see Jean and you. How *is* Jean?"

His voice was suddenly constricted: "Haven't you heard?"

She shook her head, a premonitory look in her eye.

"Jean was killed in a car crash eight months ago."

Alex noted the wince in her eyes. A strangled rasp of sound, half moan, half breath, cut harshly into the quiet. She was trembling when he took hold of her arm. She mumbled something about being terrible sorry.

"I can talk about it now," Ted said. "But at the time, it knocked me off my pins. I couldn't stay back East where everything reminded me of her. That's why I moved to L.A."

"And a most valuable addition to our pediatrics staff he is, I assure you," said Ike Press. "He has a way with the youngsters that makes this bribery with the balloons and lollipops a bunch of tommyrot."

"I'm way behind," said Peggy. "The last I heard you were in Europe studying with Anna Freud."

He shook his head. "I found out *I* was neurotic."

"Well, if I'm ever in the market—" She started glibly, then broke off.

"Leave it to my wife!" said Bert. "She's uncanny! You are, aren't you?"

"Are what?"

"Did I put my big foot in?" he asked, then bumbled on. "I wouldn't have said anything, but that remark about being in the market for a—"

"We might as well tell them, Peg."

Startled, Peggy turned to Alex, who put his arm through hers.

"Anne was quite right," he said with an abashed smile. "I'll be passing out cigars in July."

"Congratulations, my girl," said Ike Press, coming forward to take Peggy's hand. "Joe Strauss is going to be a happy man."

"Fathers don't count, apparently."

"Forgive me, doctor, if I react as a grandfather first." He pumped Alex's hand. "No one, of course is happier and prouder than the father. . . . My congratulations, Alex."

"This calls for a celebration," said Frank, as the others echoed their congratulations. "We were on our way to the *cantina*, anyway."

"To the *cantina!*" said Bert. "And am I going to get loaded!"

"Why don't you boys go on ahead, and Alex and I'll follow after we freshen up a bit."

"On second thought," said Ike Press, "maybe we should skip the *cantina*. After all, a Mexican *cantina*, full of rough fishermen, is hardly the place for a lady."

"I'm not. Besides, I'm not missing any fun if I can help it. That is, unless I'm cramping anyone's style."

"I hate to disabuse you, Peg," said Frank, "but we really did come down to fish. Aside from drinking, I don't think this place is set up for dissipation."

"Unless Alex is interested in some 'rough trade,'" said Bert. "The *cantina*'s hopping with them. You should have seen this boy Carlos make a play for Ted."

"Something tells me you're going to have to fight for your honor tonight, boy," said Frank with something of a leer.

"Gentlemen, gentlemen," chided Ike Press. "What kind of talk is this?"

"Are we shocking you, Ike?" asked Frank.

"Me? The world is too depraved, and I'm too old to be shocked by anything. But, after all, there is a—"

"No, there isn't," said Peggy. "After listening to stylish stouts try on dresses for ten years I'm completely shock-proof. Anyway I'm going to wash the sand off and put on my face. Get the directions, Alex. We'll be along shortly."

Alex listened to Frank's directions and, as the men drifted toward the car, managed to take Ted aside.

"I finally heard from Pathology," he said.

Ted looked up, his eyes somber and alert.

"You were right. There was a fistula. And if I hadn't put it off—"

"We still don't know whether she would have survived," Ted said quietly.

"There would have been a chance. This way—" He shook his head.

"You had your point of view and you might just as well have been right. It isn't as if I didn't have doubts—or Dan. You can't blame yourself."

"I do."

Ted put his hand on Alex's arm. "Don't. If I'd been sure, I'd have insisted. I wasn't." Frank was honking the horn. "It was one of those things," he added. "I think we can both use a drink."

He hurried off.

Alex watched the car pull out and turn down the dirt road, then walked slowly back to the room.

Peg, who was in her robe, started toward the bathroom. "I'm taking a quick shower," she said.

"Actually, we don't have to go," he remarked wearily.

"I want to."

"Five minutes ago you didn't want to see anyone. Now you're off to the races."

"That's what you were after, weren't you?" She turned. "Why'd you make that announcement, Alex? You were the one who wanted it quiet."

He didn't answer, didn't know, really.

"Did you think it would soften up Ike Press?" she said, walking into the bathroom and turning on the shower.

For a moment he was roiled with anger, then realized that it was he who was at fault and that she had every reason to strike out at him. He'd taken advantage of her, and she probably felt she was being used—as, in a sense, she was. The urgency to go to the *cantina,* be near Ike Press, was gone.

Undressing, he waited for the shower to stop. Peg was drying herself when he opened the bathroom door. Standing in a cloud of steam, a pink glow on her face, her breasts round and full, the slight bulge of her belly beginning to show, she looked like something by Botticelli.

"I've decided I don't want to go," he said.

"Don't be silly, Alex. I know you do. And I told them we'd be along."

"Let's not," he said, stepping forward, his arms going around her, his chest aware of the weight of her breasts. "I mean it, Peg." His lips touched hers.

"You came here for a purpose," she said. "Don't make up to me by pretending you don't care."

"At the moment I don't." He kissed her again.

She pulled gently away, said, "No, Alex, we did promise, and I think we'd better."

When he came back from his shower she was standing in a skirt before the mirror. "What do you think I ought to wear?" she asked. "A sweater or blouse?"

"Sweater," he said, without thinking.

She picked out a white cashmere, slipped it on. "I really fill one these days," she remarked, then added archly, "You think Mr. Press likes sweater girls?"

"I'm not asking you to seduce the man."

"It's an acknowledged and effective procedure, I'm told. After all, it's all in the cause of bigger and better vermiform appendect—" The undisguised anger on his face brought her to an abrupt halt.

"If you're trying to punish me for bringing us down here—" he began.

"I shouldn't have said that. I'm sorry, Alex."

"I'm the one who should apologize," he said wretchedly. "I knew he was here and should have told you. I tried to but—"

"Were you afraid I'd say no?"

"I guess so."

"I might not have been delighted at the prospect, but I wouldn't have. Anyway, I'm glad you told me. I feel much better than if you'd tried to pretend."

"I'm embarrassed at the whole business."

"You needn't be. If you want it, you want it. It's as simple as that."

She was changing from the slipover to a white blouse. She looked so lovely that he wished he hadn't urged her down to the beach. He wished they hadn't stirred out of the room.

Dressed, he put on his buff-colored sports jacket, standing behind her while she looked into the mirror to put on her lipstick. When she was finished, she leaned back against him, prim and fresh in her ruffled white blouse. Both had healthy tans, and he couldn't help noticing that they still made a damn good-looking couple.

"Know what I feel like now?" said Peggy. "Some of that tequila."

He opened the bottle and poured her a drink.

"What about you?" she said.

"I'd better save it till we get to the *cantina.* I'll have to take a drink or two there."

"It's a holiday, Alex. Let go a little."

Suddenly he wanted to. He was angry at himself for having provoked a situation which showed him in such a sorry light. He wanted to forget, forget the Amster baby, forget everything.

IV

THE CAR, moving cautiously, dipped and rose in the dirt ruts which passed for a road. Rounding into the Square, an arid mud-flat marked by the rusted skeleton of a car or an abandoned hulk of a fishing boat, they caught sight of the *cantina*, so designated by the lettering on its mud-pink façade. From within, as they approached, came the astonishing sounds of a Dixieland rendition of "When You Wore a Tulip."

The orchestra, a five-piece outfit, was led by a saxophonist in a long, draped Pachuca jacket and pegged trousers. His florid runs were lost in the wheezing complexities of sound issuing from a piano accordian manipulated by a smiling young man with a goatish red beard who also doubled as vocalist. Piercing through the windy harmonies was the clarinet, a stolid-faced man in a candy-striped shirt with pink arm bands. The rhythm section consisted of a guitarist, a fierce mustachioed character in a flowered sports shirt, and the bass fiddler, a vivacious little man in Levis and a straw hat, rising up and down on the balls of his bare feet as he plucked out the chords.

Quite a few of the fishermen at the bar were barefooted. It came as a shock, perhaps, because the lack of shoes seemed incompatible with the rough sweaters and mackinaws; perhaps because it denoted a poverty which made them uncomfortable.

The bar was like any other bar—with one exception. It had no brass rail. In its stead, running along its base at a rise of six inches, was a concrete trough. It was at once a foot rest, spittoon and receptacle for lemon halves, which the natives sucked after touching their tongues to salt cupped on the back of their hands and washed down by tequila. (One suspected but did not mention the other uses which a staggering drunk might find for such a conveniently placed trough.)

Stationed at the cash register behind the bar was the neatly dressed proprietor, a tight-lipped man with ice-blue eyes, alert to the drunken vagaries of villagers and *turistas,* to the undercurrents and moods (jocose to morose) which might unpredictably erupt into combative violence. In two strides he'd suddenly reach the other end of the bar where the village sot, but a moment ago deep in snoring slumber, had without warning lifted his head from the mahogany surface and vented a heart-chilling howl of animal anguish, epithets, and execrations shrilling from his throat. A matter of seconds to arrest the outburst; quick fingers applying pressure to the soft vulnerable area under the armpit, to nerves which responded with such urgency as to start the legs moving with the automaton jerks of a mechanical toy—and the unkempt, staring creature was gone, propelled through the back exit, flung face forward into the night's darkness to sob himself into a stupor on the parched earth.

Order as quickly restored as it was interrupted. The proprietor back at the register. Pablo, the bartender, all of sixteen, mixing drinks and serving them, hopping from bar to tables and back again.

Covering the left wall was a mural of San Vicente Bay, the foreground dominated by a richly appointed yacht, the central figure a raven-haired, voluptuous *señorita* who seemed to look down upon the crowded *cantina* with that supreme serenity that comes from long knowledge of man's waywardness, of his thirsts, lusts, and indulgences, which can in an unguarded moment, suddenly and without shame, betray a shabby truth, a blighted hope, a secret dream. For in a fishing village like San Vicente the men far outnumber the women and find a *cantina* preferable to a church as a confessional.

From a table at the far end of the mural, Frank beckoned to Peggy and Alex. They waved and headed in his direction, detoured first by a drunk zigzagging toward a door marked *Hombres,* then by a pair of husky Californians who suddenly backed away from the bar to illustrate a tricky lateral from T-formation, using a beer bottle for the football and spiralling it beautifully across the *cantina*, with the receiver, alas, fumbling and ball-bottle popping out of frantic fingers and arcing toward the concrete floor only to be snatched out of the air a few inches from disaster by a hand which seemed to spear miraculously out of nowhere. It was Alex's hand, and his body went with it, stumbling forward at a precarious fifteen degree angle before it recovered balance and straightened up. Frank and Bert applauded vigorously; there were several shouts of "olé" from awe-struck villagers; and the Californians started a chant of "We want a touchdown! We want a touchdown!" which was taken up by other *turistas*. Alex grinned, joined his hands above his head in boxer's acknowledgment.

"Beauty," said Frank, as they reached the table.

"Another inch and I'd have had the skin off my face."

"You can be on my team any time you want to," said Bert.

"A very talented man, your husband," said Ike Press. Then, turning to Alex, "As a matter of fact. I've been learning quite a lot about you this last week, doctor. You've been the subject of considerable discussion." His eyes took on a mischievous glitter. "You can't guess why, of course?"

"I *thought* my ears were burning," said Alex, with an abashed smile.

"Lot of things in your background I had no idea of. Did you know for instance, Bert, that the doctor, while he was still in his twenties, made some significant contributions in the field of parasitology with what I am told were brilliant papers on amoebiasis, fungus parasites, and a most unusual study of fishworms?"

"I'm duly impressed," said Bert.

"Oh, I was an eager beaver in my twenties."

"I can't see that you've slowed down any," said Frank.

"You'd say that again," remarked Peggy, "if you were in the car with him today."

"Is speeding another of your accomplishments, doctor?" asked Ike Press. "Because you have too lovely a wife—"

"Thank you," said Peggy.

"And you're altogether too valuable a man yourself. Anyone who could come up with as significant a paper as the one you turned out with Dick Lerner merits my complete respect."

"It wasn't considered significant then. No one paid the slightest attention."

"That's because it was ten years ahead of its time." He turned to Peggy. "Everyone's interested in the virus these days. You have every reason to be proud of this boy, my dear."

"I am," said Peg, putting her arm through Alex's.

Press caught sight of Pablo, the barkeeper. He motioned him over, ordered a round of drinks, rose abruptly. "Excuse me," he said, "I'll be right back," and made his way across the *cantina* to the door marked *Hombres*.

"You seem to have made an impression on the old boy," said Frank.

"Why? Did he say anything?"

"About our next surgeon-in-chief? No. But after his eulogy on your achievements—"

"Where there's a eulogy there's a corpse," said Alex. His attention turned to the bar where Ted stood between two Mexicans, one a bearded young man in a Navy pea jacket with a stocking-hat on his head. "Is that Carlos?" he asked.

"The same," said Bert.

The Mexicans draped their arms around Ted's shoulders, singing in a drunken off-key interspersed with wild animal yips. At the start of each verse Carlos exchanged headgear with Ted, putting his stocking-hat on Ted's head and transferring Ted's yachting cap to his. Obviously uncomfortable, Ted seized on a greeting from Peggy as an excuse to get away.

"Marines to the rescue," he said in relief.

"Getting kind of rough?" asked Frank, patting his mustache.

"They wanted me to walk down to the beach—to have a look at the boat."

"You look real cute in that," said Peggy, indicating the stocking-hat. "I just love the pink pom-pom."

Self-consciously, Ted lifted his hand to his head to remove it, stopped. "Now I'll have to wear the thing," he said. "They're looking, and I don't want to offend them."

"You can take off your hat, for Chrissakes," said Bert. "It's probably crawling."

"The boys are probably more meticulous about themselves than you and I."

"Besides," said Peggy, "it isn't a very friendly remark."

"Now don't start telling me I'm a chauvinist. I, too, am a member of a minority group."

"Mexicans happen to be in the majority in Mexico."

"All right. My remark had to do with the correlation between hygiene and slum conditions. Nits are nits in any language."

"There's always Quell," said Alex. "Quell quells 'em."

"Now what the hell is *he* talking about?" demanded Bert.

"God's answer to *pediculus capitis*. It used to be kerosene. Now it's Quell. Ever have your head doused in kerosene? I did. My third grade schoolteacher, a very considerate soul called Miss Angela Fisherdick, announced to the class one day that I had nits and sent me home not to return until they'd been drowned in the stuff. I never wanted to return, but I did—with the reek in my nostrils for months. I wonder if they've found any new ways to destroy the young. . . ."

"Do you think those boys are for real," said Bert, "or do they use this queer act to roll a guy interested in some extracurricular activity? Maybe you'd better park your wallet."

Carlos and Roberto were approaching with uncertain side glances at Peggy.

"Roberto," said Carlos, indicating him with his head, "he is wish to return the hat of the doctor," indicating Ted.

"*Sí*," nodded Robert.

"*Gracias*," said Ted, exchanging the stocking-cap for his own.

"Why don't you pull up a couple of chairs and join us, Carlos," suggested Frank.

"I think the doctor, he is wish to see the boat," said Carlos.

"It's getting pretty late, Carlos," said Ted. "And I think the *señora*—"

"*La señora es su esposa?*"

"*Sí,*" answered Ted, his eyes leveling with Peggy's. "*La señora es mi esposa.*"

"Ah-h," said Carlos and Roberto in sudden comprehension, a chagrined look passing between them.

Pablo returned with the drinks and Frank promptly ordered another round, including Carlos and Robert.

"I hope you don't mind my pre-empting your wife," Ted said to Alex, as Carlos and Roberto turned to the next table for chairs. "But it seemed like the easiest out."

"It's Peggy's party," said Alex. "If she doesn't mind having two husbands—"

"I rather like it."

"It protects Ted," said Frank. "But something tells me Alex is going to have his hands full."

"I'm not their type."

"Bet?" asked Frank, with a sly smile.

No sooner was Carlos seated when he asked if Alex planned to go fishing.

"For shark," said Alex.

"*Cómo?*"

"Shark. Rays. No *comprendes?*"

"Ai-i . . . Sharks! Ray! *Comprendo.* But you makin' joke, no?"

"No."

"What's the rib, Alex?" asked Bert.

"No rib. I mean it. I once did some work with Gulf of Mexico shark parasites. I wanted to see what Gulf of California specimens are like."

Bert turned to Peggy. "Is he on the level?"

"Probably."

Carlos, who had in the interval communicated this odd bit of intelligence to an incredulous Roberto, remarked, "Is plenty better fish. Plenty sea bass, *corbina, totuava.*"

"No shark?"

Carlos shrugged, an expansive grin on his face. "*Sí!* Plenty sharks! If somebody want."

"Where?"

"At the Point. You want boat? I got."

"I thought you were taking *us* out in your boat, Carlos," said Frank.

"*Sí.*"

"What d'you mean, *sí?*" demanded Bert.

"Is other boat. Is Roberto, is mine. You want me, Roberto, I don't care. *Pero*, the doctor, he ask me about sharks, I don't think Roberto, he's *simpático* sharks."

"*No simpático!*" Roberto signified, with vehement headshaking.

"I can take it out myself, for that matter."

"No, I take," insisted Carlos. "Maybe the doctor, he wish to see boat."

"In the morning," said Alex.

"Is only two minute to beach. The fresh air, he's nice."

"Do I win my bet or don't I?" asked Frank, fixing Alex with a superior smile.

"You bastard," said Alex.

"What's a matter you!" demanded Carlos, starting to rise, his eyes kindling with anger. "What's a matter you call me name!"

"Not you," said Alex, putting his hand on his arm. "Him," indicating Frank.

Carlos looked uncertainly from Alex to Frank. "*Es verdad?*"

"*Sí,*" said Frank.

"Ai-i . . . Is joke, huh?" he said, with an uneasy laugh.

"Big joke," chuckled Frank.

"You've got a warped sense of humor," said Alex.

"I think he organized this expedition to test our virility," said Bert.

"Think you're invulnerable?" Frank asked maliciously.

Bert was about to answer when Pablo came up with the second tray of drinks.

"I seem to be just in time for our nightcap," said Ike Press, who had returned. "I was talking to that charming young man in the chartreuse sports shirt."

"Luiz," said Carlos, with cutting condescension.

They all turned to look at Luiz, who, as if waiting for a spotlight, rose from his chair, draped a royal blue cardigan over his shoulders, ran a comb through his marcelled hair, inserted a cigarette in a long holder, lit it, and walked toward the bar with the cool aplomb of a Conover model, motionless from the waist up, the rounded buttocks, sheathed in tight jeans, swivelling with slow sassiness.

Bert couldn't resist a subdued wolf whistle which was, fortunately, lost in the orchestra's climbing chorus of "Tiger Rag."

"He thought we might be interested in hiring his boat, which he wanted to take me down to the beach to see."

"*Pero,* is my boat you hire!"

"Of course, I told him that."

"*Bueno,*" said Carlos. Then shaking his head in righteous disapproval, "That Luiz! Is big mistake go down beach with him."

Peggy choked. "Sorry," she gasped, reaching for a glass.

Ike Press lifted his glass, inclined his head toward Peggy. "To your very good health, my dear." He sipped his drink, then, noting that Alex hadn't taken a glass, said, "Aren't you drinking, my boy?"

"I've already had my quota. However—" Alex picked up the glass. "*Salud,*" he said.

"Talking about your friend Dick Lerner," said Ike Press, "didn't I hear he was in the hospital?"

"For a few days. Ulcers acting up. I'm worried about Dick. Working too damn hard. Practice and research." He shook his head. "Too much. Much too much."

"Who was it who was telling me about his research? At CalTech, is it?"

Alex nodded. "Molecular approach to mental disease. Phenylketonuria. Fascinating."

"I'm sure," said Ike Press.

The drinks were beginning to tell on Alex. High and giddy, he suddenly found himself talking with great authority and expansiveness about the concept of molecular disease. Addressing himself to Ike Press, who kept nodding very solemnly, Alex plunged on, talking about sickle-cell anemia and Pauling's theory of the lock and key mechanism. His excitement grew, and though the words slurred over a thick tongue and echoed in the alcohol-fuzzed chamber of his brain, he spoke with a heightened lucidity, his thoughts darting through the molecular maze, touching on the secret of life in the nucleic acids, on RNA and DNA, the master molecule, which, when abnormal, triggered the multiplication of abnormal cells to cause cancer. Oh, the day would come when they'd lick that killer, vaunted Alex. "Find the molecular basis of cancer, and you'll be getting at the answers."

"Well, what about it? What's stopping you, man?" asked Bert.

"Don't give him any ideas," said Frank. "Memorial's short of good surgeons as it is."

"I'm not the only one who thought of it. There's a man at Berkeley who's working on it."

There was a wistful note in Alex's voice. The moment's lull was quickly pre-empted by the orchestra's version of "I Wish I Could Shimmy Like My Sister Kate." An American couple whirled into the center of the floor. The man was about fifty, florid-faced and heavy of paunch; the woman had an orange dye job and wore a cutey-pie Lanz number which only accented the fact that her ingénue days were as far gone as her figure. The momentum kept them turning after the band had stopped, but the silence was filled in by the cries which echoed from all sides of the *cantina* as the men vented their approval in wild hyena yips and *olés*. . . .

There is a stage in drinking when anything and everything seems to tickle a group's funny bone. The six days of Creation and all that followed therefrom seem to have been especially shaped to a mirthful response. Little bubbles of laughter well up inside, bounce on the diaphragm in jigs of delight, take off like gas-filled balloons to crowd the throat's passage, exploding in shouts, seizures, and paroxysms. A good drinker, having reached this peak of euphoria, seeks to sustain it, for he is all too aware of the depressive drops ahead when the bloom turns to gloom.

For the moment everything that happened seemed wonderful and gay. The *cantina* seemed peopled with the most convivial companions, the holiday spirit, though this was only the eve of New Year's Eve, already evident. Fishermen from late-returning shrimp boats were hailed by stanzas of "Shrimp Boats are Comin'," lustily rendered by the football Californians and the half dozen Americans of their party who considered it a most witty conceit. Wit flowed as freely as the good Tecate beer. Though a detached observer might question its quality.

How else explain the hilarity with which they greeted the Coca-Cola calendar spotted by Bert. He took it off the wall and passed it around the table for all to appreciate. The drawing featured a sultry *señorita* in a red bathing suit which accented the curved fleshly demesnes of hips, belly, and breasts; and parallel to it, and not quite as enticing, in spite of its curves, a bottle of Coke. Underneath, the legend in Spanish read: "The same quality but in different containers." They howled when Bert first read it—and howled louder as each repeated it. "Long live the difference!" said Frank, and they exploded all over again.

It was at this point that the orchestra, whether distracted by the laughter or by the sight of a pair of stray dogs who seemed to feel that the center of the *cantina* was an ideal place for coupling, suddenly went sour on "Alice Blue Gown." The florid-faced dancer, annoyed by this unmusical lapse, stationed himself in front of the orchestra and proceded to conduct with the theatrical flourish of head and arms, the hip jiggle and beat of a Paul Ash leading his Paramount band of the twenties. The boys finished in harmonious accord. The florid-faced man disappeared as suddenly as he'd turned up. A moment later he was back with a trumpet case from which he produced a battered instrument. After a brief huddle with the Pachuca-jacketed saxophonist, he beat out the rhythm with his foot and off they went into "Limehouse Blues," the trumpet tones as light and limpid as a Bix recording.

Later they were to learn that, during the late twenties and thirties, he'd led a Dixieland oufit called "Bob White and His Red-Hot Blue-Blowers," and the tune was, of course, right up Nostalgia Alley, and Peggy said she felt like dancing. Alex was questioning Carlos about the outboard motor on his skiff and didn't seem to notice. So Ted said, "May I?" and took her hand as she rose from the table. Alex turned as if to say something but was interrupted by a grizzly-looking man of about seventy who hopped up spryly, if unsteadily, from the next table and, turning up the volume on his hearing aid, shouted, "Did I hear someone talking motors?" He lurched forward, throwing his arms around Bert to keep from falling.

"What's on your mind, Pop?" said Bert.

"Motors! Anybody talkin' motors, 's where I belong. Zachary Finch is the name. Mormon's my religion; money's my vocation; and motors're my avocation. The three M's that's me. Church elder, vice-president of the Orange Home and Loan, and president of the Motor Boat Club of Orange County, Cal. Nothin' about motors I don't know. Now what kinda motor you say you got, boy?"

"Martin," said Carlos.

"A good enough job," said Alex, "but not what I'd pick as a service engine for a fishing skiff."

"Now as president of the Motor Boat Club, I make it a policy never to recommend one make over another—"

"He may not," interrupted Mrs. Finch, a gray-haired lady in slacks, "but I will."

"Now wait a minute, Nellie."

"The Mercury," she said. "The Mercury first, last and always, and you can spit on the rest!"

"Whoa!" shouted Zachary Finch. "Now butt out o' this, Nellie. I'm talkin' motors and I feel good and by the holy, jumpin'—Boy!" He snapped his fingers at Pablo. "Boy! Drinks here! On me. Everybody on me! I'm talkin' motors now."

His exhilaration carried him through a verbose and highly

technical analysis of the Mercury, the Evinrude, and Martin. The drink only stepped up his garrulity, which was finally stemmed by Frank's rather pointed suggestion that Alex might like to show him his Ferrari, which was also "something of a motor."

"Lead me to it!" shouted the old man. He held out his hand, said, "Get me outa this chair, Nellie."

She took his hand and tugged. "Whee!" he shouted as he got to his feet. "Blow that thing, boy!" he called out to Bob White. He put his arm around his wife's waist and sailed out on the floor, made a sudden turn, lost his balance, teetered perilously for a moment until Nellie succeeded in righting him.

Alex rose, a bit unsteady on his feet.

"Hi," said Peggy, waving as she danced past him with Ted.

Alex stopped to watch, his eyes somber as they pivoted with them across the floor. Peg's body molded with Ted's, her head resting on his shoulder, her eyes closed.

Disturbed, Alex was debating whether to cut in when someone brushed by him. He felt the touch of soft cashmere on his hand; the odor of men's tweed cologne teased his nostrils. He looked up to see the boy in the chartreuse shirt and royal blue cardigan.

"Sorry," said the boy in a soft voice. His cocoa-brown eyes, emboldened by drink, explored Alex's. "Match?" he asked, putting the cigarette holder between his lips.

Alex flicked on the Dunhill. As the boy's face neared the flame, he noticed that he wasn't a boy, at all. He had one of those deceptively juvenile faces. He was probably in his thirties.

He inhaled and his eyes lifted to meet Alex's again. Without moving, he let the smoke out of his nostrils, then turned and walked slowly toward the entrance door, pausing before he exited to look back over his shoulder.

Alex, who had been watching him, turned self-consciously away. Discretion told him he'd better wait a while before going out to join Bert and the Finches or the boy in chartreuse—Luiz, wasn't that the name Carlos used?—would think he was following him.

Compulsively he cut in on Peg, taking her away from Ted and

holding her in a tight grip as he whirled her around in fast, almost reckless, turns. The last chorus built to a rocking finish. They were turning so fast it was hard to stop.

"You are but swacked, darling," said Peg.

He grinned. "You are but irresistible." He kissed her.

"Hey, Frazier!" yelled Bert from the entrance.

"Damn," he said. "I promised to show 'em the car." He grasped her hand and started toward the door, but the band was playing "Stardust," and Ted cut in and took over again. He watched them glide away, more upset than he cared to admit.

Outside he passed Luiz, who stood near the entrance.

The hood of the Ferrari was up, a sizeable crowd clustered around, as Zachary Finch, displaying a connoisseur's knowledge, expatiated on each feature.

"Hey!" he shouted as he caught sight of Alex. "That's what I call a motor! Peaches and cream, boy! Peaches and cream!"

"Want to hear what she sounds like?"

"Open her up! Want to hear that big cat purr!"

He could hardly contain himself when the low throb started. "Listen to that! Whee! I hear you talkin', boy!" Then as Alex stepped on the pedal, "Yessir! I'm gonna get me one o' those, Nellie! You hear me, Nellie!"

"I hear you, daddy," she shouted.

He grabbed hold of her, and they were whooping it up like a couple of Comanches when Alex and Bert returned to the *cantina*.

Luiz was no longer waiting, he was relieved to see. "Stardust" was reaching its last phrase. The number came to and end; the dancing stopped; the drummer announced the end of a set. Peg remained motionless in the middle of the floor for a moment, her head resting against Ted's shoulder. Ted put his arm around her waist, and they walked moodily to the table, as if back in another time.

Alex stood in the doorway, looking uneasily after them. Abruptly, he walked to the bar and ordered a double tequila.

V

WHEN Alex returned to the table, he found Luiz seated next to Ike Press, who introduced him as Mr. Rivera.

Frank, who was quite drunk by now, said, "No in'raductions necess'ry. Luiz and Alex ol' frien's." He crossed his fingers. "Like that." He giggled. "Who's on top?"

His laughter dribbled off into a frozen silence.

"How do you do?" said Luiz, with quiet dignity.

"I asked Mr. Rivera to join us in a drink," said Ike Press, as Pablo approached with another round.

"Go on with your story," said Peggy. "Luiz is a fellow Californian," she explained.

It developed from Luiz's story that he was born in Oxnard, in the twenties. During the depression, when the government shipped many thousands of Mexican nationals back across the border, his family was among them. As soon as he was old enough Luiz tried to get back but couldn't prove his American citizenship. He'd been delivered by a midwife who had neglected to register his birth. He did cross the border illegally, lived in Los Angeles for two years, returned when he got word of his father's death. He couldn't take his mother and three younger sisters back with him. So he stayed on, earning "fifty cents Mexican, fifty *centavos* a day, and that's no money in any language." They subsisted on fish and the milk one of his sisters got from herding goats.

He hated the place after L.A., where he'd earned fair money as an artist's model and movie extra and roomed with a sculptor who encouraged an interest in the plastic arts. One evening while he was having dinner at the Café Gala with his sculptor friend, an old-time movie director who'd directed a couple of Ramon Novarro pictures approached him and said that he had the same kind of magnetism and wanted to arrange a screen test. The studio people, he later reported, were crazy for him, and called him Zee Zee because of the way he liked to spell his first name. Unfortunately, his sculptor friend got into a drunken fight with the director and hit him over the head with a whisky bottle because, he claimed, he was trying to break up their friendship.

A few days later he got word of his father's death, so he gave up all dreams of becoming another Novarro, and life was very sad in San Vicente, very empty, until the new road was built from Mexicali a few years ago and the word got around about what a fishing paradise it was and fishermen and tourists started coming down from California and he had a chance to make a few bucks and buy himself a radio and listen to good programs, educational stuff, music—there was a real cool platter program that played records by Theopholis Monk, Shorty Rogers, Mulligan, and other real cool musicians—and, best of all, he could meet a lot of Americans, who made him feel like home, and even though he wasn't educated, treated him real democratic, and you could just bet your life it was a real pleasure to sit over a drink and shoot the breeze because everybody was *muy simpàtico*, why just last week, a very important TV producer had offered to do something about establishing his American citizenship. . . .

"I'd be very glad to have my lawyer look into it," said Ike Press.

Which called for another round of drinks and toasts to the prodigal's return. The milk of human kindness seemed to increase in direct proportion to the alcoholic intake. The sticky nostalgics of "White Christmas" added their touch. All was concord and cheer and good fellowship—except for the American boy with the doll bisque face.

He had come into the *cantina* shortly after Luiz began his story. And his cheeks did have the pink bisque look of a fine Dresden doll, his eyes the hard glister of glass, the lashes silken, the lips berry-red and bow-shaped. He was about seventeen, well over six feet, his height emphasized by the long black coat which was buttoned high around his neck and fell like a Navy cape in loose folds from his shoulders to his calves. The waxen face looked incongruously small and girlish above it. Walking stiffly and with drunken jerks, he came to a stop in the center of the floor. His glazed eyes found Luiz's face. They widened in pleasurable recognition, then narrowed in displeasure as they took in the rest of the table. His bow-lips pouted. He raised his hand and, with crooked finger, beckoned to Luiz. Luiz shook his head imperceptibly, remained impassive, as the finger, which sported a large moonstone ring, continued to wag at him.

The doll-faced boy finally retired to a table at the opposite side of the room, his agate eyes never for a moment leaving Luiz's face. Another boy, obviously his brother, sat down beside him. He had a scar on his left cheek, which turned upward from the side of his lip and gave the appearance of a perpetual grin. His white turtle-neck sweater and flannels and golden blondness were in shocking contrast to the brooding black dress and mood of the other.

The blond boy, after some talk with his brother, approached the table, apologized for intruding, turned to Luiz, said, "Arnold wishes to go."

"He may go," said Luiz.

"He wishes you to go also."

"When I am ready," said Luiz.

The same conversation was repeated five minutes later when the blond boy approached a second time. There was one addendum: "Arnold is angry." To which Luiz replied: "Tell me something I don't know."

"Perhaps you'd like to ask them to join us," suggested Peggy, as the blond boy walked away.

"Arnold isn't very good company when he's angry. He's a very sad boy, very spoiled. Always he gets angry when I talk to another American. I tell him I like Americans. He sits in the corner and sulks. Or he gets mad and shouts I am not his friend."

"Jealous," remarked Frank.

"What right has he got to be jealous? He's not my boss. Nobody's the boss of Luiz Rivera. I'm his friend, okay. But if I want to make friends with you—"

"Jealous," repeated Frank.

"I feel sorry for those two boys. Poor kids, they lost their father when they were children, and this year their mother is killed in an air crash. She leaves them plenty of money, but there are no relatives, no friends. When the father died, they loved the mother too much. Now the mother is gone, there is nobody. Nothing. Money, yes. Too much for their good. They are unhappy in school, they run away to Mexico. They love Mexico. The Mexican people, they say, are *muy simpático*. They like me. I like them. But they don't like the Americans. The American tourists, they say, spoil San Vicente. Make San Vicente commercial."

"It's true, isn't it?" said Peggy.

"Lady, what do you mean, spoil? Have you seen San Vicente? Do you know how the people live in San Vicente?"

"No," she said quietly, feeling his reproof.

"How can you spoil a place where people live in shacks made out of cardboard and paper and scraps of tin? How can you spoil a place where there's not enough to eat or wear? And not enough sanitation for the health? And children keep coming, oh, it's a shame before God how many, with almost as many to die as remain to live. How can you spoil San Vicente, beautiful San Vicente, where there's nothing to do and nothing to see, nothing for the mind and nothing for the soul, nothing but the water and sky and the dry, worn-out earth that grows nothing but rocks? So the tourists come and San Vicente is commercial. Not commercial enough, if you ask me. Oh, there's a little more work and a little more money but not enough to burn down those cardboard shacks and make the children grow healthy! Got to be more commercial, like Ensenada, I tell Arnold. Build a hotel, motels, curio shops; boxing, jai alai, bullfights. But Arnold says if you make it more commercial, the Mexicans will lose their dignity, they will be interested only in money. But what is dignity? Does a man have dignity when he cannot provide for his own?"

Luiz's eyes ranged around the table, fixing on each person in turn, as if seeking confirmation.

"Oh, the Mexican has learned how to suffer," he continued. "For centuries he has known every misery and learned how to seal the lips and carry high the head and show the proud patience of the poor. And the *gringo*—you will forgive me, I am drunk and talk too much—"

"Go on," said Alex.

"The *gringo* does not know what is in the heart. He sees the outside, the brown face and the white teeth, and it is charming, picturesque, and the *gringo* rushes with the camera to take pictures of *niños* with white teeth and brown skin—and I will tell you something funny, at least it is funny to me—I think the *gringo* is envious of our brown skin, or else why does he seek the sun when he is down here, and not only here but at home in the summer when the sun is hot, he runs to the beaches, why, why but to get brown? And yet it is funny—not funny ha-ha, but funny sad—that when a Mexican with this same brown skin, which he so admires, moves next door to the *gringo*, he is called unpleasant names and told that if he does not move away he will know the taste of lead or the feel of rope."

Again he looked around. No one stirred; no one said a word.

"I am drunk, I know. I talk of dignity and have none. But perhaps the *cantina* is not a place for dignity; it is a place to lose it, I think. So do not judge the Mexican by the *cantina*, nor by the *mal hombres* like Loco Charlie and Pepi el Borracho and me. Forgive me, my tongue wags, and I no longer know what it is saying. . . ."

"You had much to say, and it was well said," remarked Ike Press.

"You are kind," said Luiz, inclining his head.

"Jealous," said Frank, who had all the while been watching Arnold, who had not for a moment stopped staring at Luiz.

"You're a bit swizzled ol' boy," said Ted.

"Swacked," said Bert.

"Oh well, *toujours gai,*" said Peggy.

"My God," said Ted. "That dates us. Remember Archie the Cockroach?"

"And Mehitabel?"

"Remember Barney Google with googley, googley eyes?" said Bert.

"Remember Jetta Goudal and Nita Naldi?" said Alex.

"Drink to Nita Naldi," said Ted.

"*Salud,*" said Luiz.

"To San Vicente," said Alex, rising to his feet.

"To a bigger and better San Vicente," said Bert.

"Need an air service for that," said Alex. "Hop in a plane, two hours from L.A., couple more from Frisco. Bring 'em down in droves."

"Cinch," said Frank. "Ike call T.W.A., 'range it. Ike 'range anything. Can'tcha, Ike ol' kid?"

"If a tourist setup, such as Luiz suggested, were developed, I think the airlines might be interested." Drunk or sober, Ike's speech had the same deliberation.

"See. Cinch!"

"Who's gonna develop it?" asked Bert.

"What?"

"How sh'd I know? What the man said. Bullfights, jai 'lai, all that stuff'n stuff."

"Corporation," said Alex. "San Vicente Ennerprises, Inc."

"Cinch!" said Frank.

"Li'l matter o' money, you know," said Peggy.

"Money!" said Alex, snapping his fingers contemptuously.

"Cinch!" said Frank.

"Stocks," said Alex. "Bonds. Float issue."

"Ike 'range it. Great floater, Ike. Winner worl's floating shampeenship."

"I'll start 'er off," said Alex. " 's a sure thing. Gilt-edged. Put me down for fifty G's."

"Double it," said Frank.

"What the hell," said Bert, "cut me in too."

"I pass," said Peggy, with a giggle.

Luiz emptied his pockets, put the contents on the table. "Twelve pesos, sixty-six centavos," he said with a grin. "Big deal, huh?"

"Very big deal, 's matter fact," said Alex. "Agains' law for foreigners own property, 'm I correck?"

"Correck."

"But *you* can own it?"

"*Sí*. Me. My mother."

"Gennelmen, lady, wanna introduce our partner, pal, pres'dent San Vicente Ennerprises, Inc. Pearl of the Pacific!"

"Speech!" said Ted.

"Hear! Hear!" cried Peggy, clapping her hands.

"It's beginning to sound like an attractive proposition," said Ike Press.

"Drink to attractive prop'sition," said Alex.

They clinked glasses with slapdash recklessness. Bert's drink sloshed over the rim like a breaking wave, leaving a dark stain on Alex's cashmere sports jacket. Alex dipped his handkerchief in a chaser of water and dabbed it over the stained area. Then he removed the jacket and hung it neatly over the back of a chair.

"Such a beautiful shirt," said Luiz.

"Thanks," said Alex.

"The colors." Luiz sighed, his eyes fixed in fascination on the plaid. "Such beautiful colors."

" 's a pretty striking color you got here yourself," said Alex, indicating the chartreuse.

"You like it?"

" 's striking."

"If you like it, i's yours."

"Wouldn't think of it," protested Alex.

"I insist," persisted Luiz, unfastening the buttons and pulling out the tails.

"Thanks for generosity, but wouldn't dream—"

" 's an insult if you don't," said Luiz, drawing up his well-developed chest.

"In that case, I accept—on condition you accept mine."

"No, 's my gift; 's my pleasure."

"I's my pleasure give you mine," said Alex, furiously unbuttoning his shirt.

"Your pleasure is my pleasure," said Luiz. "I accept."

They made the exchange with drunken formality, their tanned torsos inclining toward each other in top-heavy bows which threatened to topple them forward on their faces.

"Touching," said Frank. "Very touching."

"Good neighbor pol'cy," said Bert.

"You look divine in chartreuse, darling," said Peggy.

"Fetching," said Ted, and Alex glared poisonously from one to the other.

"Such beautiful colors, such fine material," said Luiz, quite oblivious to anything but the luxuriant touch of the Viyella fabric. "I'm crazy for it!"

"Jealous," said Frank for the fourth time, as Arnold rose from his seat of watch and headed toward them like a black-sailed boat in a heavy gale.

"Take it off," he said thickly, as he reached Luiz.

Luiz, who hadn't seen him approach, jumped with guilt. A wash of red covered his face from neck to hairline. "You scared me, Arnold," he gasped in rattled reproach. Then, marshalling his poise, "Arnold, I want you to meet my friends—"

"Don't wanna meet 'em. An' they're not your frien's. I got eyes." His voice rose to a querulous, high pitch. "All they wanna do is take you away from me! You!" he cried, turning to Alex. "You give 'im back his shirt! What right you got to take the shirt I gave 'im? What right? What goddamn right?"

Alex stared at him in speechless dismay.

"Goof off, you li'l queer," said Bert. "Beat it!"

"You better go, Arnold," said Luiz. "You're drunk."

"I'm not goin' till you take off that filthy shirt. Take it off, you hear me, Luiz!"

"You're not the boss of me," said Luiz, buttoning it defiantly.

"You take it off, or I'll tear it off!" he screamed, grabbing hold of a tail and yanking violently. A button popped off; the shirt slid off one shoulder and down his arm.

"Let go, you bastard!" shrilled Luiz. "You're ripping it!"

"I'll tear it to bits! I'll rip it to pieces! Take it off, you bitch! You two-bit bitch, you're willing to sell yourself for a lousy shirt. You're nothing but a whore! A lousy, good-for-nothing whore!"

"Don't you call me that!" said Luiz, his face dark with anger.

"Whore!" repeated Arnold. "Just a dirty li'l two-bit—"

The slap of Luiz's hand on Arnold's face was as crisp and sudden as the crack of a rifle. It came in the silence which followed the last note of "Mexicali Rose" and was as startling to the occupants of the table as it was to Arnold, whose rosebud lips lost their color. They quivered for a moment. Then the silence was broken by the moan which came shuddering out of his body, followed by an uncontrollable spasm of sobbing. He turned and stumbled toward the door.

"Arnold!" Luiz called after him, in anguished contrition. "Arnold!" He hurried after him, caught up, put his arm around his shoulder. "Don't cry, Arnold. Please, Arnold. Please, don't. Please, forgive me, Arnold."

Together, they made their way out of the *cantina*, both sobbing.

Arnold's brother, who had started toward the table while they were struggling over the shirt, now confronted Alex. "I hope you're satisfied!" he said with a righteous tremor, and stalked off.

"What the hell did *I* do?" Alex said plaintively, after a dazed pause.

"Not a thing, darling," said Peggy.

"I didn't ask for his shirt. I tol' him I didn't want the damn thing. I couldn't insult the guy, could I?"

"Of course not."

"I must say I'm rather shocked," said Ike Press. "I've never seen anything like that before."

"Just a bunch o' faggots actin' faggoty," said Bert.

"Such an attractive boy, I'm really surprised."

"Queers 're queer," said Bert, sententiously.

The orchestra, marracas shaking, was playing a conga. A group of tourists, led by the footballers started a conga line. "Fall in!" they shouted as they snake-hipped past the table. "Whee!" shouted Zachary Finch. "Come on in, folks!" "Madame La Zonga danced the conga in Cucamonga!" screeched Mrs. Finch, reaching her hand toward Peggy, who rose impulsively to attach herself to the line. Ted followed. The line grew as it snaked around, Carlos and Roberto joining along with several of the bolder Mexicans, hyena yelps punctuating the less inhibited pelvic gyrations. The bulk of the men in the *cantina* who'd come in off the shrimp-boats for a beer, watched with gentle smiles.

"I suppose it's fun to let go like that," said Ike Press. "I'm afraid I'm pretty conservative."

"Sensitive," said Frank. "Full in'ibitions."

"As a young man I was very shy. To this day I don't know what it is to dance. I never kissed a girl until I married and I was thirty-three at the time. Fanny said I was overdeveloped mentally and retarded emotionally. I was known as 'the mathematical wizard'—I can still add eighteen columns of figures as fast as a machine—but I was sluggish in matters of the heart. Fanny was quite exasperated at first. She'd say I was so used to recording debits I had red ink in my veins instead of blood. Not true, as she found out in due time, but my wife has a wasp's tongue. Your analysis was more accurate."

"Sensitive," repeated Frank. "Full in'ibitions."

The conga line suddenly doubled back on itself and headed toward the table, undulating by with freewheeling hips and unrestrained bumps which accented the rhythm. Mrs. Finch's theme song had now been taken up by others. "Madame La Zonga danced the conga in Cucamonga," they chanted. Peggy and Ted waved. Bert directed a bump at them.

"Abs'lutely un'ibited," said Frank.

Alex kept his eyes fixed on Peggy and Ted.

"Doctor," said Ike, turning to Alex. "May I ask you a question?"

"Fire away."

"You were so good at research, why did you leave it?"

"The army seemed to think I was a surgeon. I guess they convinced *me*."

"You certainly made your place as one. I'm curious. If you had to do it over again, Doctor—"

Alex closed his eyes to stop the slow spiraling sensation which seemed to be creeping up on him. "When you're young," he said, "you have roman'ic ideas. I had a dream. Big dream. Alex Frazier, knight errant on big white horse. Had a quest, grail. Know what? Immortality. The great secret o' life without end. Pick up lance and charge! Do battle with enemy. Black knight on black horse. Joust after joust. Never won. Know why? Death won't die." He paused, passed his hand over his forehead. "If I had it do over again, Mr. Press? I don' know. What'm I doin' now? Still doin' battle with man witha scythe. Each time I cut out contaminated flesh, tissue, I put him off, shove him back. Sure, it's research man who'll give him final quietus. Salk, Dick Lerner. But I do my part."

"But you're still interested in research? You like it?"

His mind went back to the days when the boys called him Arrowsmith, to the project in Vera Cruz, to his work with Dick Lerner.

"Sure. Research my firs' love." He looked up. "Why?" he asked with sudden wariness.

"I was interested," said Ike.

It was at this point that Alex realized Frank was shaking his head at him. He couldn't ask why, and there was no chance to pursue the conversation because the khaki-clad police had just entered to signal the Saturday night curfew by blacking out the *cantina* lights. There were screams from the conga line. The lights came on again. The orchestra stopped playing. The police began waving the customers out, giving a forcible assist to the stupefied *borrachos* who refused to budge out of their sodden slumbers.

For a moment the *cantina* was confusion confounded. It was as if a boy had poked his finger into an ant hill. The conga line, like a stream of ants, was suddenly converted from an orderly unit into a directionless scramble. *Turistas* and natives scurried fanwise and crosswise, colliding and passing. Unfinished bottles of beer and tequila were carried outside. Less than ninety seconds after the warning blackout the place was empty; sober, tipsy, and blotto, the night's cargo of customers found itself outside the darkened *cantina.*

There, under the light of an unshielded bulb, the evening continued. The police, having enforced the strict letter of the *cantina* curfew, showed no disposition to extend it. The *cantina* was the *cantina,* it was housed in a building; this was in front of the building; the law made no provision; if bottles were passed from hand to hand, there was also no provision. In the meanwhile, there was this beautiful car, which had been transported across the ocean from Italy and which, it was rumored, was more powerful than the cars made by the *yanquis*; indeed, if Carlos could be believed, its owner was a champion of racers and had in this very car set a world record of meters per hour.

Alex, watching the crowd swarming around the Ferrari, decided that they'd better go. But Peggy, who stood arm in arm with Ted, wanted to remain.

The accordion player was singing "Guadalajara." Some of the Americans were playing leapfrog. This inspired the Californians to illustrate the "Statue of Liberty" play, which in turn brought back the chant of "We wanna touchdown! We wanna touchdown!" and, with no logic whatsoever, since he was a Princeton man, started Ted off on the Yale frog-chorus cheer. "Brek-ek, co-ex, co-ex, co-ex," he declaimed. "Brek-ek, co-ex, co-ex, co-ex, Oowah! Oowah! Parabalou! Yale! Yale! Yale!" "Olé! Olé!" shouted some of the Mexicans, with grins of amusement. Which, for no good reason, prompted Bert to do a series of fast cart wheels.

"More fun than a three-ring circus," said Peggy, clapping her hands.

"You blow a mean horn, Bob White and his Red-Hot Blue-Blowers," said Ted to the trumpet man.

"Jus' beginning to get my lip back," said Bob White.

"You wouldn't guess he hadn't played for fifteen years, now would you?" said his wife.

"No!" said Peggy.

"Jus' getting lip back. Selling real estate for fifteen years. Pulled out some old Brunswicks few weeks ago. Got a yen. Been blowin' a little every night since."

"Sound as good as Bunny Berigan," said Ted.

"Bunny . . . Broke my heart, that boy." He put his trumpet to his lips and reproduced the famous Berigan chorus of "I Can't Get Started."

"Doesn't he sound jus' like him?" said his wife. "Name any horn and Bob can give him right back to you. Bix, Muggsy, Louis, Wild Bill. Can't you, Cutie?"

"Le's dig the radio. Maybe there's a hot program out of Calexico or Dego. I feel like jammin'."

He led them to his Nash, switched on the light. The back seat, converted into a sleeper, revealed three kids, ages ranging from about six to twelve, stretched out under a blanket. The oldest stirred, blinked open his eyes, shaded them with his hand. "Light," he mumbled.

"Sorry, Butch," said Bob and turned it off. "Family," he explained, "whole shebang, bring 'em right along." He busied himself with the radio dial, caught a couple of pop programs, finally hit on something called "Discs from Dixie," which was at the moment featuring Wingy Manone's "Tin Roof Blues."

"Won't it wake the children?" asked Peggy.

"Bob can blow that trumpet in their ears, and they wouldn't know it," said his wife.

Bob was doing something very close to it. Sitting sidewise on the car seat, his legs thrust out the open door, he pointed his trumpet at the starry sky and blew open, brass-throated notes of sound at the moon, jamming in counterpoint to Wingy's horn. His wife, her eyes closed, body swaying, hummed in throaty accompaniment.

The crowd around the Ferrari was now gravitating toward the

Nash, engaged by the sight of a transported Bob White, his cheeks bulging, his eyes screwed up in fatty puffs as he blasted away at the midnight sky, pushing out full, rounded blue notes, sharpening them into strident jabs of ecstatic pain, easing off with a sobbing vibrato. The last note hung tremulous on the air, then faded into a silence broken by awed applause.

The voice of the announcer cut in with an old Red Nichols recording of "Sweet Georgia Brown," the music coming out clean and crisp above the driving beat of the Krupa drums, Goodman, Nichols, and Glen Miller romping off with the melody. And Bob White weaving in and out and noodling around, tonguing arpeggios, giving out with breathless, orgasmic gasps of sound which made the headlong tempo seem even more frenzied and started several couples hopping around with a manic abandon which was of another time and place, bringing the stomping frenetics of the Savoy Ballroom of the thirties to the dirt floor of San Vicente, feet moving faster than the eye, legs flicking and flailing, bodies separating, improvising solo, hips wiggling, torsos whirling, then coming together again in abandoned variations of the Lindy Hop and Big Apple, male grasping female and throwing her *wow!* over his shoulders and *whush!* between his legs and *wham!* up again and hoppety, hoppety on the quick-jogging toes and oh, shake that thing! shake it and break it, sister!

The Finches, in the middle of it all, going round and round in fast gyrations.

Mrs. White shagging away with one of the Californians.

Ted and Peggy bobbing their heads in the Big Apple. Alex watching.

A Californian cut in on Ted, and Peggy was flung *yow!* over his shoulder and *whush!* between his legs.

Alex lurched forward and grabbed hold of the Californian's arm. "Awright, that's enough, you! That's quite enough!"

The Californian glowered, said, "What'samatter you?"

Alex took Peggy's hand, holding it so tight his nails dug in. "Tha's quite enough!" he repeated. "Le's go now!"

"Now wait a minute!" said the Californian, swinging him round. "What's comin' off here?"

"Take your prehensile paws off before I knock 'em off."

"Listen, li'l man," said the football Californian, poking his forefinger at his chest.

"Le's go," repeated Alex.

"I don't wanna go," said Peggy.

"You heard the li'l lady," said the Californian.

"The li'l lady happens be my wife. Any objections?"

"In that case, I stan' corrected," he said, bowing low.

The trumpet reached for a high note held on to it for a moment after the record came to a stop. The dancers, who seemed in a state of imminent collapse, staggered toward their cars. The crowd disintegrated, dispersing singly and in small groups in all directions, on wavering legs. Motors came explosively to life. Cars plunged into reverse, careened around in reckless circles, then bumped over the lumpy corrugations of the rutted dirt roads as unsteadily as the walking *borrachos*. The radio announcer was, in the meanwhile, expatiating on the "buys" and "steals" in used cars offered by the "Smiling Armenian," who, if you listened carefully, was a philanthropist rather than a businessman, offering old Chevies, Plymouths, Buicks, and Pontiacs for a song ("If my wife let me, I'd give 'em away"). By the time the choice bargains had been itemized, the Nash was the only car left in front of the *cantina*, and Mrs. White was, in fact, pressing the starter button. Cuddled up on the other end of the seat, Bob White was blowing a soft harmonic accompaniment to "Melancholy Baby" as the car drove off leaving the square in front of the *cantina* quiet save for the dissonant snoring of two *borrachos* sleeping head to head alongside the wall.

Peggy and Alex drove back to the motel in silence.

"Sorry, Alex," she said after a while. "Had good intentions, but they didn't last. Made spectacle myself, didn't I? Didn't I, Alex?"

She looked up at him, her head falling slackly against his shoulder.

He didn't answer.

"Whyn't you tell me I let you down? One too many, tha's why. Two too many. Three. Four. Did I disgrace you in front o' Ike Press, Alex? I did, didn't I? Poor Alex."

He didn't say anything.

"Poor Alex," she repeated, and dozed off.

The car hit a sudden dip. The bottom clanked on the hard dirt and stone. Peggy, thrown forward, sat up, fully awake.

VI

THE FERRARI eased to a stop in front of the motel. A second later Frank's Cadillac, Bert driving, pulled up alongside.

Frank, looked up groggily and said, "Time f'r a nightcap."

"He say somethin'?" asked Bert.

"One f'r a road."

"Yeh, road's kinda dry. Shall we pour 'im out, Ted?"

"You implyin' I'm drunk?" said Frank.

"Stinkin'," said Bert.

Frank let out a cackle of laughter.

"Sh!" said Ike Press. "People are sleeping."

"Serves 'em right," said Frank, giving vent to another cackle.

"We better hit the sack ourselves if we're gettin' up at six," said Bert.

"Who's gettin' up six?" demanded Frank.

"You—if you're goin' fishin'. Otherwise, we're goin' without you."

"Did you make arrangements with Peggy and Alex?" asked Ike Press.

"No fishing for me, thanks," said Peggy.

"What about you, Frazier?" asked Bert. "You on the level about the shark?"

"Was," said Alex.

"Wanna change your mind an' come with us?"

"I'll sleep on it."

"Were you actually planning to fish for shark?" asked Ike Press.

"Done it before. Told the boys—I did a paper on shark parasites. Jus' curious about local variety."

"Busman's holiday."

"Not really. Part o' my past."

"Nobody as frustrated as ex-research man," said Ted.

"I wouldn't be surprised if Alex found a way to keep his hand in," said Ike Press.

"Well, if you wanna come," said Bert, "meet us here six-fifteen."

"Check," said Alex. "But don't wait for me."

He turned to go. Peggy, stepping out of the car, stumbled and caught hold of his arm. "Sorry," she said, as they started toward their room.

"Good night, my dear," said Ike Press. "And pleasant dreams."

"Thank you," she said, with drunken dignity.

"G'night," the others echoed.

"Look what I got," said Frank, producing the Coca-Cola calendar from under his shirt. He held it aloft, swaying, and raised his voice in a bloodcurdling approximation of the hyena yelp.

Ike Press shushed him again, but he kept at it until Bert clamped his hand over his mouth. He slipped out of his hold by sitting down abruptly, then rolling across the patio, yelping till someone bellowed, "Quiet!" out of a motel window. Bert got him under the shoulders and Ted by the legs, and between them they carried him into the room.

Peggy slumped wearily against the wall while Alex fumbled with the key. When the door was finally opened she made her way straight for the bed and dropped down on it with a sigh of relief. Alex, with as direct a purpose, headed for the dresser, opened the bottle of tequila which they'd bought in Mexicali, poured a slug into a glass.

Peggy looked at him in astonishment. "Alex," she said, "you're not going to—"

"Why not?" he said, taking a swallow.

"Aren't you way over your limit?"

"Three times—and sober." Surprisingly sober. His thoughts, even his speech seemed clear.

Another yelp from Frank sounded across the court.

"Funny about Frank," she said.

"Share a suite of offices with him for years and all of a sudden you find out he's ten other guys."

"I like your Mr. Press."

"He's cute."

"And he likes you. I think you're going to get it."

"Get what?"

"The appointment."

"Oh, that."

"What do you mean: 'Oh, that'?"

"Wrote it off hours ago," he said fliply. "And what's more, I don't give a damn."

"I wish."

"I don't." He poured another drink, then standing over her said, "You like him, don't you?"

"Mr. Press? I told you."

"I'm not talking about Mr. Press."

"Ted? I've always liked him. He's a very likeable guy."

"We're not being evasive, are we?"

"Not in the slightest."

"He's still in love with you, you know that?"

"Don't be silly. He never was. He married someone else. Remember?"

"And she's gone now."

"What does that mean?"

"Why do you think he moved out to L.A.?"

She looked at him quietly for a moment, said, "Darling, you *are* drunk."

"What's more," he said, narrowing his eyes, "you're still in love with him—and always were."

"I don't know about you," she said, after a pause, "but I'm going to bed." She got up and walked into the bathroom.

"Deny it!" he shouted.

She slammed shut the door.

Without turning, he hurled the glass against the wall. It shattered with the noise of a bomb.

The first thing Peggy noticed as she hurried back into the room was the wet stain on the wall. He didn't look at her, but sat huddled within himself, his big shoulders hunched in the posture of defeat.

In a rush of contrition, she dropped down beside him, took his hand in hers, kissed it, pressed her cheek against it. "Don't darling," she said. "I can't bear it when you look like that. It's my doing, I know. I knew how upset you were and, instead of helping, I aggravated things. I'm fond of Ted. But that's only because he was part of my childhood and adolescence. I did carry a torch for a while after he married Jean, but not after I met you. If you want me to say it's you I love and only you and that I couldn't feel the same way about anyone else, then I'll say it. But you know that, don't you?" He didn't answer, and looking up, she said, "Don't you believe me, Alex?"

As if returning from some distant place, his voice toneless, he said, "Yes, I believe you."

"Because it *is* true."

"I know."

"I'm sorry about tonight."

"It's forgotten."

"I hope I didn't prejudice Ike Press."

He shook his head. "Nothing to prejudice. Dan's getting the appointment."

She looked up sharply. "Is that what he told you?"

"Didn't need to."

He withdrew his hand, rose, walked to the window. His shoe hit a shard of the broken glass and sent it skittering across the floor. It came to a stop a few inches from her hand, and she reached over for it before she pulled herself up.

"All this stuff about research," he resumed, looking out into the darkness. "All this to-do about papers and contributions. What do you think he was laying that on for?"

"He *has* been looking into your record. He was probably impressed."

"Mr. Press is very scarce with his praise. It usually has a point.

Damn!" He smacked his fist against his hand. "And I fell right in with it! Frank made the connection. Tried to warn me. Not that it would've made a difference. Except that I fed him exactly what he wanted."

"What?"

"The fact that I never did lose interest in research."

"I'd say that was very commendable."

"So does he. Know what they're going to do? Hell, why didn't I see it! Arthur must have meant it as a hint when he mentioned it a couple of weeks ago. But I promptly forgot it. What did a whopping bequest of a million and a half to the Department of Microbiology mean to me? Even when he said it was earmarked for work on tropical diseases and that there'd been some talk of setting up a separate department. 'I wouldn't be surprised,' says Mr. Press, 'if Alex found a way to keep his hand in.' Why should Mr. Press be surprised when it'll be Mr. Press himself who'll probably propose a special research grant, or, who knows, even move the appointment of Dr. Alex Frazier as administrative head of research for a department of tropical diseases. Good way to solve the problem. Grease way for unanimous appointment of good ol' Dan Simon as chief surgeon."

"Where does this come from? Frank? Something Ike Press told you?"

"All I know is that I'm out and Dan's in. I know it and I *should* have known it, and why I'm getting in a lather about it, Christ knows! As if this were the goddamn be-all and end-all! Head surgeon, Sidney B. Lazarus Memorial Hospital. For two cents, I'd pull up and go east, get into a real setup: Johns Hopkins, Presbyterian, St. Luke's."

"If that's what you want, why not?"

"Because at my age you don't start all over. Especially with a baby to think of." He turned from the window, walked back to the chest. Again his shoe hit a splinter of glass. He stopped, looked down, said, "Another bubble burst."

"We'd better pick up the pieces or one of us is going to cut a foot."

"Better pick up the pieces," he echoed, and stood brooding until Peggy bent down. Then he said, "I'll do it. You get to bed. You must be dead."

"I should be," she said, straightening up and lifting her arms in a languid pose. "Physically I'm limp. But my mind's going like a five-alarm fire."

"A naïve character, your husband. A schnook, still believes in Horatio Alger," mumbled Alex, his fingers groping gingerly for the fragments of glass.

"Use one of these or you'll cut yourself," said Peggy, handing him a box of Kleenex.

He pulled out several sheets, rumpled them into a loose ball, brushed the floor for stray splinters.

"After all," he continued, "I'm an intruder, an upstart. What did I expect? An appointment on a platter?"

"Stop it, Alex. You're one of Arthur's pets. If anyone has an in—"

"Not where it counts. It's Dan who gets invited over to Ike Press's for a game of pinochle."

"You're not the pinochle type."

"And I don't have a repertoire of jokes with punch lines in Yiddish."

"You're not implying that Ike Press is anti-Gentile?"

He looked up sheepishly. "That *was* a stupid remark, wasn't it?"

"If your guess about research is right, would you honestly be unhappy about a chance to keep your hand in?"

"If it paid as well, no."

"Forget the money end of it. Is Dick Lerner unhappy?"

"Dick's Dick, and I'm me. I love, respect, and admire him. I may even envy him. But I'm no martyr. Why are you so contemptuous of money? Why do you resent the idea of my earning more?"

"I don't. It's just that it isn't important to me. Perhaps because I never had to worry about it. After all, I am an heiress."

"That's a moot question."

"Why?"

"Because the old man's never accepted me. And even if he did, I want no part of his dough. I'll make my own, thanks. Now. Not in some vague future. It may seem silly to you, but I want that appointment, want everything that goes with it."

"It's not silly, and I know what it means to you."

"Then don't talk about inheritances and the future. I have a particular fondness for the present. You can't be a surgeon and watch life running out under your hand and think there's any future in the future. You were talking about research—"

"Isn't that one of the answers? Get at the cause of a few more killers, and the lives won't run out so fast."

"They've got a better answer. Fission and fusion. Remove man and you remove his ills."

"No one wants universal suicide."

"There's a story called *Frankenstein*, a fable with a profound truth." He straightened up, the pieces of broken glass gathered into the folds of Kleenex held between his fingers. Standing over the tin waste basket, he let go. "Bam!" he said, as the bundle hit the bottom. There was a tinny reverberation. "Bam!" he repeated softly after a moment. "And an entire island disappeared into the Pacific . . . Research," he sniffed. "We're researching ourselves right out of existence! And who cares? Who gives a damn? Do you see any governments scrambling to solve the problem of malignancies? Do you see a billion dollars appropriated for heart disease?"

"For all your disinterest, you seem to be fighting mad on the subject."

He was silent.

Peg sighed. "Let's go to bed, Alex," she said softly. Slipping out of her robe, she snuggled under the covers.

He made no move.

"Alex," she repeated gently.

He walked abruptly to the chest, picked up the bottle of tequila, took a swig.

She shook her head. "Why you haven't been ill or passed out by now is beyond me."

"Delayed reaction," he said. "I'll probably topple over while I'm brushing my teeth. My temple will hit the sink and the corpus slump with a thud to the tile floor."

"That's not funny."

"Or at seven-ten in the morning, sodden and hung-over, I'll be jerked off my feet while trying to reel in a shark and pitch overboard for the shark to reel *me* in. At eight-fifty the mutilated corpus will be discovered washed-up on the beach. It will be described in the records as an unidentified body in a chartreuse shirt, sex undetermined."

"Alex!"

He grinned. "Gruesome?"

"Slightly—and I resent that last phrase."

"Oh, that's because of the sharks. The soft vitals are always the most delicious morsel—"

"Stop it, Alex."

"Besides, that's what Frank's been trying to prove all evening, hasn't he?"

"I can prove otherwise," she said, touching her abdomen.

He stood abstracted, said, "Question is: Shall I go fishing with the gang or stick to shark?"

"After that graphic note, the gang—please! You'll probably charm Ike into voting your way."

"I'm not an ass-licker," he said, in an unexpected burst of anger, and marched stiffly toward the bathroom, listing to one side for a moment before he grasped hold of the knob. He lurched in, banging the door shut behind him.

There was very little that Alex remembered after that. He couldn't remember getting to bed or getting up. He had gone fishing. He remembered a storm blowing up while he was out in the boat. But it was all pretty fuzzy. The twenty-four hours which followed remained as complete a blank as ever.

Book · II

I

PEGGY lay on the chaise in the morning sun, her eyes shut and her limbs draped in a counterfeit of repose. For all her sleeplessness, she could find no rest. The events of last night kept darting against the walls of her brain. She couldn't tell Alex what had happened, couldn't face it herself. She tried to forget, to veer away by thinking of other things, pleasant things in another time, another place. She thought of her childhood, of camp, of Paris, of the fun she'd had at Vassar. She thought of her youthful relationship with Ted and her meeting with Alex in Mexico City. She thought fondly of all the times they'd been back to Mexico and how happy they'd been. Each trip came back to her; she remembered every moment of every one of them. Her mind kept drifting back to their first meeting at the farewell party for Nacio Mendez, the young muralist disciple of Siqueiros, to the crowded apartment on Cinco de Mayo . . .

There were many farewell parties in that fall of thirty-six; many young men from many lands leaving for Madrid, which had suddenly become the crossroads of the world. There was hope in those days of making Madrid "the tomb of Fascism."

There was singing: a concert of voices giving due accent to the mocking stanzas of "Los Quatros Generales"; a lone girl's voice, warm and pliant, shaping a lament, surmounting it with the searing, wild notes of a flamenco, stabbing into the night like animal cries, fierce and ecstatic, carrying a supernal defiance, then fading into silence.

Listening, Peggy reached toward the coffee table for a cigarette. Anticipating her, a man's hand, holding out a package of *Delicados,* came into her field of vision. She looked up, her eyes caught and held by his. They were an intense blue and stared at her in unabashed appraisal, so frank and probing that she wanted to look away but couldn't, perhaps because she didn't care to show she was flustered, perhaps because she, too, was interested.

Without removing his eyes from hers, he flicked on a lighter. Inhaling, she leaned back against the couch, aware of her trim, tapered legs and the jut of her breasts against the jersey fabric. She wondered if he'd think her immodest, if her lipstick were too purple, if—

She was suddenly furious with herself. She was what she was, and damn what he thought! Angrily, she leaned forward to stub out her cigarette. Again he anticipated her, ash tray in hand. She stubbed at it so vehemently that it tilted and the ember end hopped up and hit his wrist, bringing forth an involuntary "Ow!" His arm jerked back, and the ash tray showered its mound of butts, matches, and ashes to the floor.

The singer's voice wavered. Every eye in the room found its target. Alex sat immobile, his face red, until the room's attention was redirected to the flamenco. And as the notes soared wild and free, he reached surreptitiously with his fingers, picking up butt by butt, match by match, until all that remained was a smattering of ashes.

"Are you angry with me?" he said.

"Why should I be? I don't know you."

"That's easily remedied. I'm Alex Frazier. May I get you a drink, Miss Strauss?"

"You work fast," she said. "How'd you find out my name?"

"Asked. I took one look at you when you came in, decided I wanted to know you, made inquiries, found out."

Before he returned with the drink she had time to check on the pull-thread in her hose, comb her hair, lipstick her lips, and wonder whether he was a foreign correspondent, actor, composer, or archaeologist.

She was rather taken aback when, as she was sipping the tequila, he announced he was a parasitologist.

The first two syllables sounded like Paris, which seemed odd.

So she said, "Oh," with an inflection which quite obviously betrayed her incomprehension, because he quickly added, "The study of parasites."

"Not the human variety?" she asked.

"No," he said, "but there are striking similarities. What I started to say was that I'm on a research grant and stuck in a God-forsaken tropical village near Vera Cruz and the only people I've been seeing are the poor, fungus-ridden natives I've been studying. So perhaps you'll forgive me for staring if I tell you that this is my first day back in a civilized community and yours is the first really refreshing face I've seen since—or a long time before, for that matter."

He seemed very earnest about it, so she said, "Thank you," then added that it was a very graceful speech.

He asked what kind of artist she was.

"Wishful," she said. "I study with the best. But I haven't a shred of talent. Tell you what I can do, though. Steal dress designs. My father manufactures them, and it's a great excuse for going to Paris. I have a photographic memory, so it's easy for me to sketch them. Also gives me an excuse for thinking I earn my way—which I don't. If you ever want to put a vertebrate parasite under your microscope, I'm it."

He shook his head, said, "I don't think you'd qualify."

"Why not?"

"A parasite is just content to feed on its host. You feel the need to compensate. So you copy designs."

"Also parasitic."

"In an ideal world. Not in the economic jungle we live in. Besides, you work too hard."

"I don't work. I dabble."

"And have a conscience—which a parasite doesn't."

She threw up her hands, chuckling. A band of *mariaches* was singing in the courtyard. Rising, she started toward the French windows, which opened on the balcony. He followed her out.

She was startled to find herself being turned toward him, his lips meeting hers. And for the moment, the song didn't exist.

He took her arm, guided her through the crowd and toward the closet which held their coats.

Outside the wind was kicking up. A newspaper skittered along the sidewalk, its pages taking off like so many kites. One of them wrapped itself around her legs.

They walked against the wind for a while, then dodged into a doorway for respite.

"I don't know whether that was such a good idea," she said with a shudder, as a flurry of leaves swept into the doorway. "Doesn't it bother you?" she asked, almost resentfully. "You look so damn robust and cheerful."

He grinned. "I love it. This is my kind of weather."

"Trouble with me is I've got thin blood." Futilely she made a muff of her sleeves.

"Let's see if we can't do something about it," he said, stepping closer. "Open your coat."

"What for? To make me colder?"

"Open it," he repeated, "and snuggle against me."

"What is this, Mexican bundling?"

"The most elementary law of thermodynamics. Body heat."

"Look, if you want to put your arms around me, just do it—and don't reach for fancy excuses."

"The object is to get you warm."

He put his arms around her waist, drew her to him. "Relax," he said, after a moment. She let her head lean on his shoulder, yielded the weight of her body against his.

"Comfortable?" he asked.

"As an iceberg."

"You'll thaw," he said. "Put your hands in my coat pockets."

Complying, she said, "You forgot to mail a letter," then added, "Is she pretty?"

"If you'd call U. S. Pharmaceuticals pretty."

She laughed, was silent a moment, then chuckled again. "We must look a sight."

"Couldn't think of anything more normal—or nice."

She nestled closer, the press of their bodies hermetic to the burrowing wind. He was kissing her hair, her ear, the back of her neck. She turned her face toward his. The touch of their lips was tentative, almost tremulous; then the searching sensations and soft savorings were lost in the crush and clamor of their importunity.

She pulled away, and in a breathless voice, said, "This is crazy."

He followed her into the street, caught hold of her hand. Leaning forward, they bucked head-on into the wind, running for a stretch, pausing to get their breaths, then plunging ahead again. Arm in arm, they rounded a corner like listing sailboats.

"*Libre!*" Peggy shouted, as she spotted a taxi.

Together they ran toward it. They scrambled in, slacked back against the springy upholstery, taking in huge gulps of air before the rasp went out of their breathing.

"Hotel Reforma," Alex said, in answer to the cabdriver's "*Donde?*"

She turned to him in surprise. "Is that where you're staying?"

He shook his head. "It's where you're staying."

"You don't miss a thing, do you?" she said, shaking her head.

In her room, they folded into the nearest chairs, limp and depleted.

"There's a bottle of tequila on that chest," she said, between breaths. "If you lean over a little, I think you can reach it."

"Just about," he said, stretching for it.

"Talk about thermodynamics," said Peggy, as her drink percolated down.

"Fine fuel, alcohol. Say when," he said, refilling her glass.

"When," she said, when he'd poured two fingers.

He was more sparing with his, and she remarked about it.

"You wouldn't want me to go drunk on you?" he said.

She took a swallow. "Depends on how close to it *I* am."

"I've got two ounces to go."

"Don't tell me you measure?"

"Scientific training. I can absorb about eighty-five milligrams per one hundred c.c.'s of blood over a span of three hours before I get polluted."

"Do you go about all your pleasures with the same scientific detachment?"

"I've never observed my pulse or blood pressure while making love, if that's what you mean."

"I wasn't thinking of anything specific, but I can see how it might interfere."

"Of course, I imagine it'd vary with the object."

She couldn't help thinking of herself as "the object."

Her breath quickened—out of excitation and fear.

She finished her drink sooner than she'd intended.

"More?" he asked, picking up the bottle.

"You're not by any chance trying to get *me* drunk so you can seduce me?"

"Hadn't thought of it, but sounds like a good idea," he said.

Abashed at her temerity, she watched in silence as he poured the drink.

They sat sipping and smoking, breathing in the aromatic scents of tobacco and tequila, their sensibilities cradled in an alcoholic fuzz.

"Getting warm," she said, stretching her arms in a languid yawn.

"Take your coat off."

"Too lazy."

He got up, said, "Come on," and, taking hold of her hands, pulled her up.

She let herself fall limply against him. They stood lapped in the warmth of each other, in the press and heat of their bodies, in the exhalations from their warm lips touching and molding together. She turned in his arms, wriggled out of her coat. It dropped to the floor. His hands moved with gentle urgency up the soft mound of her belly, circled the rise of her breasts, fondling the hardened tips, then closing over them until she gasped.

Abruptly she pulled away.

He caught her hand, whispered her name.

"Be back in a minute," she said softly.

Undressing, she tried to stem the impulse that was carrying her to him. The compulsion to obliterate a rejection—Ted's—in the act of love, in the tangible evidence of a man's desire. She too could feel desire, an overriding urge to be kissed, caressed, possessed, to be taken—out of time, place, self—by this handsome young man with his serious, scientific concerns and the brash charm which animated his boyish face and sensuous, full lips.

Standing before the mirror, she brushed out her hair, dabbed on some Mitsuko, and thought: I've known him for an hour and here I am rushing into bed with him. She should have been shocked at the thought but found herself intrigued with the image of daring which it evoked.

She slipped into her Honan silk robe. The fabric adapted itself to the curves and indentations of her body. Feeling for all the world like a scarlet woman, she walked to the door.

The bravado drained out of her with the touch of hand on knob. Apprehension twisted her stomach. Taking a deep breath, she turned the knob and walked in.

He was in bed, his clothes neatly folded over a chair. For some childish reason, that gave her reassurance.

Except for the lamp on the night table, the lights were out. She hesitated when she came near the bed, suddenly dismayed at the idea of disrobing in front of him. He seemed to sense her embarrassment, reached toward the lamp.

She was grateful to hear the click of the switch. Quickly she got out of her robe, draped it across the foot of the bed. The room was warm, but she was shivering.

She slipped under the cover, lying inert on her back, close to the edge. His hand reached for hers across the separating space.

"Hello, over there," he said.

"I'm so cold." Her voice was small.

"Again? You're probably in a draft. . . . It's much more comfortable over here." His fingers twined with hers, but she made no move. "I promise not to do a thing you don't want me to."

"Don't be so noble."

"I'm just trying to make it easier."

"Don't."

"All right, I won't," he said, urging her toward him.

She needed no prompting. Seeking the warmth of his chest and arms, she huddled against him. It was the shock of his caressing fingers which brought an occasional shiver now, the touch of his lips on nipples, navel, thigh. He was gently considerate and wildly unrestrained; and she was willess, lost, captive to his every humor and mood. Roused and responsive, companion and complement, she embraced him. . . .

The memory of that night and of the week-ends she spent with him in a hill hotel perched high over the blue waters of Vera Cruz was as real as the gentle lapping of the waves. The memory, too, of the Monday they stayed on to get married by a very garrulous judge who insisted on using the Spanish Margarita and Alejandro. And moving the next day to the very primitive village where Alex was doing his field research; and feeling very much like Helen Hayes playing Mrs. Arrowsmith as she learned to handle a syringe and give shots and make smears on slides. That was their honeymoon, harsh and devoid of luxuries, but bringing them as close as people can get when they are engaged in a common cause, working together in selfless idealism by day and spending the passion of a young love in the hot tropical nights.

Their trips to Mexico were more than nostalgic journeys. To Peggy they were a quest, an attempt to recapture not their youth but some of the spirit which had animated it: the zest for experience; the capacity for wonder and hope; the romantic hunger; the pristine idealism untouched as yet by the abrasives of time and success. The immediate change in Alex always amazed her. He seemed to find renewal, to breath once more the freer air of those days of dedication when research was means and end, torch and grail.

Not this trip.

From the start there had been undercurrents, moods, remarks. Even on the way down. And certainly after they'd arrived. In the *cantina*. And later in their room. If she'd given some thought to the things he said after they'd come back from the *cantina*, she might have realized that the seeds were there, might have had some premonition. But he'd been so drunk and, at that hour of the night, as tight as she was herself, they hadn't registered. And she'd said some pretty sharp things herself. That stupid crack about bigger and better veriform appendectomies. Waiting for him to come back from the bathroom, she'd realized how deeply she'd hurt him.

He took so long before he got to bed and, when he did, he avoided her. She reached toward him. He lay on the far edge, and the touch of his pajamas made her self-conscious about her nakedness. He didn't turn, and she could tell that he was huddled within himself. At home, when he got into a brooding mood, he usually slept in one of the guest rooms, so she wouldn't be "inflicted with his restlessness." Knowing him, there wasn't anything she could do but leave him alone like a hurt animal to lick its wounds, nothing but to turn to the wall, with a space cold between them, and choke down the hopeless feeling of inadequacy.

Lying beside him that night, she asked herself why he took it so hard. Dan was his friend; realism, protocol, and practical politics should have prepared him—in spite of the special circumstances and Arthur's personal pleading in his behalf. Was it strictly a matter of money—as he protested, with his ever-ready flow of blunt cynicism? Or wasn't it rather a striving for recognition?

Wasn't it all a matter of recognition; his whole life, every act, compulsive or calculated, aimed at acceptance? How could it be otherwise with his background? It wasn't only that his father had walked out on the family never to return. Even after his mother died and he was adopted by the Fraziers, who doted on him, he'd felt the need to prove himself worthy of an affection he couldn't really bring himself to believe. Love to the deprived kid who was Alex could only have been a reward—for exemplary conduct, for signal achievement.

Peg had learned soon enough that he never took her love for granted either. There was always the question, the doubt that had to be stayed by a thousand protestations. Love—even hers—

was still something he had to earn: by the title of surgeon-in-chief, by the best practice in town.

It seemed so unnecessary. He was an attractive, talented man; he had that rare capacity to communicate his enthusiasms, to reach people with his warmth, touch their imaginations. He'd proved himself a success a thousand times over. And yet he'd come back from the *cantina* wretched because he was convinced he'd lost out on that damn appointment. Just as she was wretched because it was the first of all the times they'd been in Mexico that they were lying on opposite sides of a bed with a chasm between them.

It was three-thirty that morning when she woke out of an uneasy slumber. Heartburn was one of the discomforts of pregnancy which she accepted philosophically enough when she knew there was a Gelusil tablet within reach on the night table. There was no table in the motel room, and she'd forgotten to take the tablets out of the kit. Blearily she sat up, reaching instinctively for her robe and slippers.

She felt her way around the bed and headed toward the bathroom without opening her eyes. Her hand reached toward the door, brushed along the chalky surface of the wall till it encountered the ridged wood of the jamb and then the knob. Her eyes blinked involuntarily as she opened the door on what seemed like a blinding glare. Alex had apparently forgotten to switch off the light. Opening her eyes only long enough to sight the kit, she found the tablets, popped one into her mouth, and headed back.

The distinct gurgle of liquid running out of an almost full bottle alerted her. Her eyes darted through the darkness to the moonlit window. Silhouetted against it in the slumped posture of weariness sat Alex.

The air which she'd sucked in with her first gasp of fright rustled out of her.

"Don't ever scare me like that again," she said. "What're you doing sitting in the dark?"

Without turning he said, "Couldn't sleep. Got up to take a drink."

He set the bottle down on the floor—a little too hard.

"It's cold," she said. "Better put on a robe."

He didn't answer. His raised glass glinted in the moonlight.

She snuggled under the cover. "Don't sit up too long." The words dribbled off. Her breathing was heavy with sleep.

She turned when the early morning sun slanted into the opened doorway. There was a mumble of voices, then the door closed. She was asleep again before the whir of a starter and the labor of a cold engine stuttered complainingly until it caught.

At eleven she was awake enough to open her eyes. Alex was gone. So was his fishing gear.

II

WHILE she showered and dressed she couldn't help wondering whether he'd gone out in a boat alone or with the others. The others, she hoped.

It was too late for breakfast and not quite time for lunch. Judging from the savory-fat odors which floated out of the motel kitchen, she wouldn't be up to the luncheon special when it was time. It seemed to be the only item on the menu, a combination plate consisting of *tacos, chiles rellenos, tamales,* and *frijoles,* and under normal conditions she'd order it without hesitation. At the moment, she wasn't up to anything more than coffee and toast.

The waiter obligingly brought it out to her on the patio, where she could sit at a table looking out over the calm, blue-green water of the bay. In the distance she could see dolphins leaping. There seemed to be plenty of fish, for the gulls were circling about, spotting the swimming schools before they plummeted down, glistening streaks of white with slate-colored mantles, plunging straight at their targets and coming up with the fish firmly clutched in their hooked mandibles. The beauty of their dives was marred by the greedy gulping of their prey. From the sands below, just out of sight, another colony of gulls rose suddenly into the air with a great whirring of wings, fanning out in a long straight line, hundreds of them, with the precision of an armada of planes and infinitely more graceful, and once more she was lost in their loveliness. And then they, too, were dropping in bomb-dives and scooping up the fish in their bills.

She wondered why nature was so harsh. A cruel and senseless design for one animal to live on another, to thrive on his flesh. And man was, in his "civilized" way, more cruel and wanton than the most savage of jungle beasts who killed simply for food and out of an instinct which gave him no choice. She could understand Alex's cynicism. It was hard to resist the prevailing temper of despair.

Still, Alex's forebodings meant less to her than the sight of a live fish going down a bird's gullet. Or a barbed hook caught in the mouth of a sea bass as it landed thrashing in the bottom of a fishing boat.

She couldn't avoid thinking of Alex's whimsey about the shark. God knows, if he had gone out alone and did manage to hook a shark in his condition, the whimsey might well come true. Though he'd fished shark before and knew how to handle himself—in spite of the tequila, the effects of which were probably gone.

She sneaked a look toward the Point. There *was* a boat. Which didn't mean that the one boat in the shark area was Alex's. It might be rounding the Point or heading for Guaymas. And, besides, there were now two boats. So you couldn't jump to conclusions, and she simply wasn't going to give it another thought. She'd take a nice, leisurely walk into the village and see what there was to see.

There was something of a main street. It boasted of a *lonchería*, an *abarrotería*, run by a Chinese, which sold everything from pinto beans to *huaraches* to fishing tackle, a *peluquería*, which consisted of a barber chair standing out in the open under four poles and a thin thatching of leaves and twigs, a fishing tackle store with an incongruously modern front (run by two ex-G.I.'s, one an American, who, she learned, was the silent partner, the other a Mexican who had lived in L.A. and who at the moment was sitting at a typewriter pecking out a poem called *La Corrida de Pancho Villa*). The icehouse, the one imposing structure in the village, loomed white and large on one side of the caked mud-flat of a *zocalo*, its generators making a fearful rumble; on the other, with the exception of the *cantina*, were the cultural establishments, the *escuela*, *biblioteca*, *farmacia*, and the shack which housed the *médico*.

Goats, dogs, and chickens shared the streets with the youngsters, predominantly boys, most of whom were playing the Mexican equivalent of "miggies." The girls, she soon discovered, were home helping their mamas with the infinitude of chores which devolve upon the females of huge families of no means and endless needs. She saw them, six-, seven-, and eight-year olds, lugging the infant brothers and sisters in their arms or slung around their shoulders, bundled in *rebozos*; saw them struggling with pails of water and helping with the cooking and wash. Their sober, responsible faces brightened into shy child smiles of wonder at the *gringo señora* who, "*Mira!*", looked so beautiful and greeted them with a cheerful "*buenos días*" and unlike other *turistas* ventured up the sloping, rugged pathways to the rows of shacks and huts which retreated out of sight of the village center as if to hide their squalor. They were pathetic pretenses at shelter. A flimsy patchwork of cartons, cardboard, manila cement bags, newspapers; a few branches for support; a weavework of twigs at best; slats of orange crates a luxurious exception; a hunk of tin as distinctive as marble. The level of poverty was unbelievable, worse than anything she'd seen in the Hoovervilles, those colonies of makeshift shanties which were the scabrous mark of the depression thirties. It made her shrivel to think of the huge families huddled within the windowless, dirt floor confines of these rickety, one-room structures, made her feel a personal guilt that she had so much when so many lived in deprivation. It made her for the moment impatient with Alex and his extravagant standards—until she realized that the slum warren in which he had been raised, the children sleeping six in a room, was but one remove from this, and having once escaped it, it was only natural that he aspire to the best.

Turning up the hill-path which led to *Campo Uno*, the first of the two trailer camps set up for fishing enthusiasts who seemed to ferret out every angler's paradise from the Rogue River to Guaymas and Mazatlan, she passed a young Indian woman balancing a basket on her head, her right hand carrying a large flounder by the tail. She was barefooted but walked with such dignity and repose that Peggy couldn't help feeling that these people displayed a spiritual health and inner resources which transcended their mean surroundings and, by contrast, made the tensions, pretensions, and perpetually restless strivings of her Beverly Hills friends seem petty and sick. But perhaps she was romanticizing. The lavender boys and *borrachos* in the *cantina* were another side of the coin. Her "*buenos días*" got a gentle-voiced response.

She was tired when she reached the camp clearing at the crest of the hill. There must have been a hundred and fifty trailers, small homemade contraptions fashioned of plywood to big bright aluminum affairs, all deserted now for the fishing boats clustered around the rocky promontory which plunged jagged and rust-colored into the green-blue of the bay.

Standing on the bluff overlooking the cove which served as the base for the fishing parties, she noticed that several of the boats were turning back. She waited, wondering whether Alex would be in one of them. A figure, unrecognizable at the distance, waved. There wasn't anyone else in sight at the moment, so she waved back, trying to count the number of people in the boat to see if it might be Frank's party. There were five. Could be. Except that that wouldn't account for Carlos if he were running the boat. Unless Frank was much too hung-over to have been able to go out. Or unless they'd decided they didn't need Carlos and Alex had taken over with the motor, which he usually preferred. The latter seemed the more likely, especially since the boat was now close enough for her to catch the unmistakable flash of chartreuse near the outboard. Alex had apparently reached in the dark for the shirt he'd worn last night without recalling it was the one he'd inherited in the trade with Luiz.

She was quite wrong. A moment later the boat chugged in close enough for her to identify its occupants: Ike Press and Bert, Ted and Frank—and Carlos, who apparently had a shirt which was the twin of Luiz's, which must have burned Luiz, or Carlos, depending on which got his first—or maybe they'd been that way about each other at the time of purchase and decided it was a cute notion.

She shrugged. The whole thing was just a trifle bewildering. All she knew at the moment was that Alex was not with the others; ergo, he was probably off at the other end of the bay by himself—and the shark!

He had, indeed, gone off on his own, Ike Press informed her.

"Roberto didn't go with him?" she asked, after a suitable interval, so they wouldn't realize she was anxious.

As a matter of fact, he hadn't gone out in Roberto's boat, Frank told her. His motor was on the blink—or so he said. Anyway, by the time they got there it had been arranged that Alex was to go out with Luiz. And Luiz had gone into a sulk when Alex insisted on taking the boat out alone—not, he was sure, because he didn't trust him to handle the motor.

Frank, she was quick to note, seemed disappointed himself. She could just see him leering if they *had* taken off for the rather deserted Point. He'd have made a very cozy thing of it indeed. She began to bristle with resentment but couldn't work up any real anger because he looked so wretched. He was clearly suffering from last night's debauch.

Except for Ike Press, who wore a wide-brimmed panama hat and whose face was coated with an ointment sun-filter, they were all quite burned—and considerably in a frazzle because they had caught no fish. It seemed that no one was catching any fish except for Zachary and Nellie Finch, who, unlike the others, were trolling and using a plug instead of live bait.

Hot, parched, and dispirited, Frank's party returned to the motel, where they quenched their thirst with bottles of cold Tecate and settled down to the luncheon plate special.

Her senses insulated and dulled by Tecate, Peggy found that by averting her eyes from the plates she could sit at the table with the others. She wondered how long Alex would stay out and whether he'd taken anything along for lunch.

"He can always slice himself a filet of raw shark," said Bert.

"Or the shark can slice himself a filet of Frazier," said Frank. "Rump of Frazier should be nice and *saftig*."

It wasn't the happiest of colloquies for Peggy. It dispelled the effects of the Tecate; her olfactories were alert again to the frying odors from the kitchen; she felt a rising nausea. She fought it, waited until the conversation took another turn, then quickly excused herself, walked out into the fresh air.

A look toward the Point assured her that the boat—if that *was* the boat—was still there. Of course a shark wouldn't be expected to chew up a boat and it was too far away for her to tell whether it was minus its navigator.

Ted joined her on the patio a moment later. "You look a little pale," he said. "You weren't upset by those stupid cracks about the shark?"

"Silly, isn't it?" she confessed. "But Alex did have too much to drink last night. And if he didn't have anything to eat—"

"We all had a whopping breakfast. I know *he* did, because he and I both ordered ham and eggs and the ham was half an inch thick. So he had enough protein energy to handle a school of shark. If there are any in this so-called fisherman's paradise. Personally, I think this place is a hoax. As far as I'm concerned I'd rather go swimming. How about you?"

She nodded. And after she'd changed into her suit, they walked down to the beach, where they were joined by Ike Press and Bert, who, indefatigably, had decided to try their luck with surf-casting.

At four, when the slanting sun had lost its fire, Ted decided to take a last dip. Though the water was much colder than she cared to admit, Peggy raised her hand for him to pull her up. Hand in hand they ran down the wet sand, high-stepped into the water without breaking their pace, dived into an incoming wave, and skimmed forward with a vigorous, relaxed crawl, product of their camp days. Curious how quickly one could telescope two and a half decades and return to the easy relationship of fifteen when they used to sneak out on moonlit nights, meet halfway between the boys' and girls' camps (situated on opposite sides of the lake), and swim side by side to the lake's center, Ted looking up every once in a while with a mischievous, pleasurable smile which she'd learned to anticipate either by rhythm or intuition. He was looking up the same way now, and neither had lost the rhythm or whatever it was, and both were childishly pleased. She always could sense when he'd turn over on his back to float, and now, as in those days, they involuntarily linked arms, their bodies touching, and looked languidly at the sky and at each other, only he didn't kiss her now as he used to then, their faces turning to each other till their lips met, their bodies inevitably turning, too, until they were clutching one another and treading water while they hung on trying to make that very wet kiss last as long as they could. They looked at each other now (a little tempted, a little self-conscious), then flipped over and started swimming in to shore, very much aware of Bert still surf-casting with his red and white spinner and hooking nothing but seaweed and of Ike sitting on the beach.

A scudding wind hit them. They ran shivering for their towels. She was glad she'd brought the terry robe, though the wind seemed to blow right through the porous fabric; it swept a salty spray into their faces, needled their skin with swirling sand. Clouds sitting fat and lazy in a serene sky, like flats of stage scenery activated by a stage manager's buzzer, rushed from all directions, converging in a dark mass, sinister against the sun.

The water was getting choppy. She looked up, worried. The boat was still anchored off the Point, rocking with the waves.

"I do wish he'd come in," she said.

"He will, and damn soon at the rate this is blowing up."

Ike Press was up on his feet, rod and tackle box in hand, ready to return to the motel.

"How about it, Bert?" he called.

"Be up in a few minutes. You start without me," shouted Bert, reeling in and casting again, his weight-lifter's torso a sculpturesque bronze in the wan rays of the sun which suddenly shafted through a rift in the clouds.

"Atlas," said Ted.

"Two of them," said Peggy.

"Two what?"

"Mad men. They'll ride out a storm rather than come in without a fish. Is there a road out to the Point?"

"Part way."

"I think I'd better take the car and go fetch him."

"I'll hop over. You'd better get out of that suit. Your teeth are chattering."

"I'm all right," she protested.

"I'm the doctor," he said. "I don't want you getting a chill."

When they got back to the motel, she went meekly to her room. All she seemed to be doing the last two days was taking showers. But a hot shower was just what she needed.

It was well over an hour before Ted returned. The road, he explained, had disappeared into soft sand sooner than he anticipated, and he'd had something of a trek in the face of a battering wind before he reached the Point.

"Alex," she interrupted. "Did you see him? Was he there? I still see a boat."

"I saw him; the boat's still there, and so is he. I told you there weren't any fish in the place. Doesn't daunt Alex. The man *is* mad. He's determined to get that shark."

"In that wind?"

"It died down while I was yelling to him. Just an occasional bluster. And Luiz chugged out while I was there. It's his boat. He'll keep an eye out."

"I'll bet."

"I tried, but I couldn't budge Alex."

"I should have gone."

"I don't think even you could. He sounded as hipped on that shark as the character in *Moby Dick* on the whale."

She sighed. "Stubborn man, my husband."

"Aren't we all?" He was silent a moment. "I feel I ought to explain why I didn't call."

"Forget it."

"No. I want to. Truth is, a couple of months ago I couldn't have faced you. I saw you parking your car near the hospital one night and started to call your name, then stopped because I wasn't sufficiently in control to just go through the amenities and not free enough to unburden myself. So I hid behind a tree like a kid afraid of papa spank."

He lit a cigarette, walked to the window, turned back. "I can talk about it now," he said, taking a puff and exhaling slowly. "You see, I usually drove when Jean and I went out, but I'd had a heavy day, and when I slid into the driver's seat, she said, 'You look pretty bushed, let me.' So I did, and dozed off. Next thing I knew I was lying in a field with a bunch of people over me. I'd apparently just sailed out the window when we crashed. Jean was caught by the wheel.

"I kept thinking all the things you think when something like that happens: that we needn't have gone at all; that I shouldn't have allowed myself to fall asleep. Well, you can dwell on these things and magnify them all out of proportion. And you can also be sensible and realize the same thing might have happened if you'd been driving: the other car skidded and was out of control. I can see all that now but couldn't for months because I really didn't want to; I wanted to flay myself and cry *mea culpa* because my relationship with Jean was based on guilt and I felt I had to go on paying penance." He paused, looked around. "I guess I'm not making much sense. I sound drunk and I'm not. Though I could use a drink."

"You sound clear enough to me. And there's a quart of tequila around."

"Not my drink, but it'll do."

"If I can find it."

It wasn't on the chest or on the either side of it, or in any of the drawers, or beside the bed, or in the bathroom.

"Now that's funny. It couldn't have walked off by itself. . . ."

"Maybe Alex took it."

"He never drinks during the day. Rarely does at night for that matter."

"Probably staring us in the face and we can't see it. Stop looking, Peg. I'd rather have gin anyway. Be right back."

Before she could turn around, he'd disappeared. The unlatched door was thrown wide open by a blast of wind which sailed in and swirled around like an ice dancer in bouffant skirt. It was getting dark outside. She could just make out the waves, wind-lashed into a white froth, the flat, swiping blows echoing over the water like a keening widow wild with grief.

The Point was lost in darkness. She told herself that Alex must surely have put in by now. She only hoped that in the darkness he hadn't run into a reef. The idea of being forced to swim through the shark-infested waters around the Point made her shudder. It summoned up an image of snapping jaws. I have a camera mind, she thought, and I'm behaving like a kid. She wished Ted hadn't mentioned *Moby Dick*. Shivering, she closed the door against the wind.

She was annoyed with herself. But the wind did sound eerie.

A loud knock sounded on the door. She jumped. It was Ted, and he'd hit the door with the toe of his shoe because he was carrying bottles in both hands.

"I didn't know what you liked so I brought the works. No tequila. How about some sherry?" He put the bottles down on the chest. "King's Ransom, Old Crow, Meyers's Rum and London Dry, my favorite food. What'll you have, Peg? In the old days, if I recall, you were rather partial to corn. No corn, either."

"The Old Crow'll do nicely. It's rather early, but I need one."

"Stop worrying about Alex. It's dark. He's on his way back."

"If he doesn't get lost."

"Not with Luiz around."

"That's a hazard in itself."

Ted laughed. "Don't worry, he won't assault him."

"He'll come back with a cracked jaw if he tried."

"No fear. Luiz is the subtle type. Besides, the weather's not conducive." He poured the drink into one of the two glasses which the maid had placed on a tin tray with a pitcher of bottled water. "Straight or water?" he asked.

"Straight."

He handed it to her, opened the bottle of gin, carefully measured two fingers. "Private recipe," he said, pausing. "Two fingers of gin and—" he resumed pouring from the bottle, letting it burble out till the tumbler was full—"gin."

"You're not going to drink that?"

"One before dinner. Another before retiring."

"You'll fall on your face."

"I had a good equilibrium to start with. It's developed in the last eight months."

"Do you do this every day?"

"Every day." He touched his glass to hers, said "*Salud.*"

"*Salud.*" She started to take a sip, then added, "Oh, and Happy New Year. It is New Year's Eve, you know."

He touched her glass again, but the jauntiness was gone. He seemed suddenly withdrawn. "It'll be the first one without her," he said, after a long moment. "That's one of the reasons I was glad to get away. I didn't want to sit alone in my apartment and I certainly couldn't take a party."

"I wasn't in the mood for one either."

"Not that you do get away," he continued. "I thought I was when I moved to L.A. I found out distance wasn't enough. There's a geography of the heart as well as of space." He took a swallow of the straight gin. "You don't mind my jabbering, or do you?"

She shook her head. "It's better to let it out."

"I have been—every morning from seven-thirty to eight-thirty —on my analyst's couch. But it isn't the same. You're you and you're all mixed up in it. You know that, don't you?"

"I'd be quite hurt if I hadn't made some impression along the way."

"You didn't have any doubts about it?"

"When you're abroad for six months and come back to find your fiancé married to your best friend, what do *you* think?"

"I know," he said quietly. "I was a bastard. It shouldn't have happened in the first place, and I should have had the guts to face you when it did." He paused. "That's a commodity I'm a little short on. It's why I went into pediatrics, I found out. Couldn't face adult situations. Can't face situations, period. . . ."

He was silent, took another swallow, then looked up. "You've been happy with Alex, I can tell."

"Yes," she said, meeting his eyes.

"Actually I was still in love with you. You don't know how often I cursed you for going off on that boat. Why the hell did you have to leave me and go to Europe?"

"Why'd you have to go to summer school? Of course, if I'd been more resourceful I, too, might have become a student-actress in a summer stock company which *just happened* to be a few miles away."

"You mustn't blame Jean. I'm sure she—"

"I'm not blaming anyone. As far as I'm concerned the book has long since been closed."

"No, I owe you an explanation." He lifted the tumbler. The drink was already at the halfway mark. "The reason Jean joined that stock company had nothing to do with me but with the leading man. As a matter of fact, she said I didn't appreciate you. Proof: Lucy Benedict had told her she and I had a roll in the hay the night of the Yale game."

"You did?"

"Sure. On a bet. Princeton lost, so I had to.

"And if Yale had lost."

"She'd have had to."

"I see, whoever lost, you both won. I'm shocked."

"What did you expect me to do, remain celibate till I married? It's bad enough to start out with a wife who's a virgin, but when the husband starts fumbling on the marriage night—"

"That isn't what you used to feel about virgin wives."

"Always. How many times did I try to deflower you?"

"One day when I was in your room there was an unfinished letter in your typewriter, and I couldn't help reading one sentence: 'I would no more think of marrying a girl who was not a virgin than I would of putting on someone else's jock strap.' "

"Did I write that? I *was* a sophomore! Do you mean to tell me if you hadn't seen it you—"

"I might have. I certainly had to apply a lot of will power."

He sighed. "Think of all the fun we missed." He looked up. "Is that the drink or are you blushing?"

"You'd better give me another, and we'll say it's the drink. What got us onto this anyway?"

"We were talking about Jean—and how it happened. We got drunk one night and lost our heads. I didn't see her after that—I had *some* conscience."

"There's no need to explain, Ted."

He got up, walked to the window again. Outside the wind was still blustering. A ball of tumbleweed came scudding by. He went on with the predictable and admittedly corny story of the pregnancy and Jean's fear of an abortion. She was shrewd enough to make no demands, and he was so indecisive, suggestible, and guilt-ridden that he let events steer him into a marriage he didn't want. Not that they didn't get along, but it wasn't what Jean expected and she sublimated all her love on brown-eyed Debby. It was a clutching, obsessive kind of love, so possessive that it was no surprise when Debby ran off and eloped at seventeen.

Peggy sat curled up on the bed, listening. He walked back from the window, sat down beside her, continuing the story. Truth was, the elopement upset him as much as Jean, and they were thrown back upon each other. She needed him and he her. It wasn't the healthiest kind of relationship. Jean was jealous, and there were quarrels. Gradually he felt so smothered, he began to resent her all over again. He went off on trips. Finally moved out. Jean called, made impossible scenes. "I finally came back—a week before it happened. Sometimes I feel it wasn't entirely an accident."

His voice was a gruff mumble, drowned in the gathering wail of the winds outside. Somewhere nearby a door banged shut.

He started to bend down for the glass which he'd set on the floor. The pressure of her fingers on his hand stayed him. He looked up.

"You can overdo that," she said quietly. "And it isn't the answer."

"It helps," he said.

"I'm sorry. I had no right to say that."

"No, you're perfectly right. That can be destructive, too." He sat, indecisive, his eyes on the glass.

Abruptly she leaned over, picked it up, handed it to him.

"One more sip," he said, "and I'll heed your sage advice."

He contemplated the clear liquid, a little self-conscious now.

"Truth is," he said, "I'm apprehensive about tonight. I'd like to get so stinkin' I'd pass out and sleep right through from six to six and skip tonight."

"I can understand that. The thought of New Year's Eve depresses me. Always has."

"Never did me—until tonight. I'm afraid, afraid I'll get maudlin. Too many associations, too many years. So, comes the midnight hour, stick with me, will you, Peg? Just take my hand and hold it, hold it tight. . . ."

She reached out again, gripping it with a reassuring pressure.

They were sitting together, silent, when the door opened.

"Nice'n cozy," said Alex, his head cocked to one side, his eyes focussed through narrowed slits on their hands.

"Thank God," said Peggy, extricating her hand and rising. "I thought you'd never get back."

"You hoped," he said, sardonically.

She walked toward him, said, "Alex, are you drunk?"

"Not enough," he said, and took a faltering step into the room, his hand clutching at the jamb for support.

"No wonder I couldn't find the bottle of tequila."

"Got another," he said, indicating the newspaper-wrapped object under his arm. "Stopped at *cantina,* fortified f'r big occasion." He looked up, puzzled. "What the hell's occasion?"

"New Year's Eve," said Ted.

"Whad'ya know!" he said with an inane grin. "Happy New Year!"

"Happy New Year," said Ted.

Alex giggled. "Have a drink to New Year," he said, pulling the wrapping off the new bottle.

"What did you do with the other bottle?" asked Peggy. "You didn't drink it all?"

Alex grinned.

"Alex, you didn't!"

"Alex, you didn't!" he mimicked. "Why didn't Alex didn't? 'Cause he did." He laughed intemperately.

"A whole quart? You couldn't have!"

His laughter continued for a moment. Then, with a mysterious grin, he put a finger to his lips and said, "Sh . . . Secret . . . I shared some witha sharks." He chuckled, pleased with his conceit. "Sure, pickled shark. Didn' you ever hear o' pickled shark?"

Ted shook his head.

"Unb'lievable! Here's man never heard o'—" He turned, shouted, "Hey Luiz! Where the hell are you?"

"Comin'," said Luiz, and appeared a moment later. "Here's the keys. Stuff's in the car."

"Tella man about the pickled shark."

Luiz grinned, "Honest to God, they go for that tequila like a bunch o' lushes. First they swim around like crazy, then all of a sudden they're stiff like a board."

"Pickled," said Alex. "Come to surface an' hiccup."

"Now, now, Alex," Peggy said indulgently. "Next you'll have them putting their fins around each other and singing 'Sweet Adeline.' "

"They don't believe us," said Alex, suddenly morose.

"Of course we believe you," said Ted. "I've eaten pickled herring. Why not pickled shark? Perfectly logical."

"In fact, I'm getting hungry," said Peggy. "How about some of that pickled shark?"

"Now you're making fun o' me," said Alex, in a hurt tone.

"Oh, my God, Alex!"

"*You* believe me, don't you, Luiz?"

"Swear to every word."

Alex put his arm around him. "You're a pal, *amigo, compadre.* You know he saved my life?"

Luiz smiled deprecatingly, shrugged.

" 's a fact! Storm comin' up. Hurricane howlin'. Black as hell. I start motor. Bam! Right into sonovabitch of a reef. Rock comin' through. Water pourin' in. Everythin' black, black. Can't tell north from south, east from west. If I dive in, I don't know if I'm swimmin' out to sea or in. All of a sudden, I hear a motor."

At this point Ted interposed a bravura phrase from the *Dragnet* theme.

"Who was it?" countered Alex. "*Mi compadre, mi compañero,* Luiz with the cat-eyes!"

"Drink to Luiz with the cat-eyes," said Ted.

"Drink," echoed Alex.

"Not for me," said Luiz. "I promised I'd be back at five."

"A short one," said Alex. "C'mon Luiz."

"No, please. Another time. Tonight at the *cantina.*"

Alex shrugged. "You disappont me, *compadre.* Where's your innapendence? Where's the ol'—?"

He stopped as Luiz, with a graceful bow and a soft "*Hasta luego,*" backed out, closing the door behind him.

" 's a crime an' a shame, tha's what. That li'l doll-face sonovabitch Arnold, got him completely 'ntimidated. 's evil, 's monstrous. Who's he think he is, Svengali?" He stopped, shrugged. "Drink," he said.

Walking to the chest, he placed the tequila bottle alongside the others, took a flat leather case out of his pocket, opened it. "Observe closely, doctor," he said, turned as if to a nurse, "Scalpel, please," picked one out of the case and holding it delicately between forefinger and thumb, he flicked it swiftly around the cellophane band, the cap flying off in the same spin of circular movement. "Note incision, doctor," he said, holding out the bottle.

"Very neat, doctor," said Ted.

Taking the tequila bottle in one hand and the sherry in another, Alex held them over his glass, said, "Observe closely, doctor," and poured from both spouts.

"Observing," said Ted.

Alex put down the two bottles, picked up the bourbon and rum, poured again. When the glass was two-thirds full, he switched once more, filling the rest of the glass with the mixed splash of Scotch and tequila.

"Contents, quantities noted, doctor?" he asked.

"With astonishment, doctor."

Alex picked up the scalpel and, using it as a swizzle stick, stirred the brew. The dark, syrupy Meyers's Rum and sherry whirled in rich streaks through the lighter liquids.

"Pretty," he said, holding it up to the light.

"It won't look pretty in your stomach," said Peggy.

"Look lovely inna stomach. Sprout plants, bear beau'ful blossoms."

"Poppies, no doubt. Poetic when we're drunk, aren't we?"

"Sure. 'The world is too much with us.' 'Out, damned spot!' 'Lay on, Macduff; and damn'd be him that first cries, "Hold, enough!"' "

"You know the rest of that?"

"What?"

" 'The world is too much with us.' "

"Cer'nly. Wordsworth. Got total recall on it. Remember Prof. Chauncey Brewster Tinker closing eyes and reciting it to hushed class o' future bankers, brokers, and brassière manufacturers. Churlish soul who'd forget it.

The world is too much with us; late and soon,
Getting and spending, we lay waste our powers:
Little we see in Nature that is ours . . .

I not on'y remember. I get the point. You're tellin' me I'm no better than a brassière manufacturer. I'm sober enough understan' that. Too damn sober." He lifted the glass, said, "To Wordsworth."

She put out her hand as if to stop him. "Alex, you're not—"

"I cer'nly am."

"I advise against it, doctor," said Ted.

"Go to hell, doctor."

He took a sip, said, "D'lishus," then drank half the glass in one gulp. It took him a long moment to catch his breath. He shuddered, then sat down as if to await developments.

Peggy and Ted eyed him with curiosity, awe, expectancy.

Nothing happened. He took another swallow, said, "Cut the fish-eyes. What am I—an exhibit? A specimen?"

"Just pickled," said Ted.

He giggled. "Me an' shark."

"By the way," asked Peggy "Did you catch any shark?"

"Ask me 'nother time."

"What's the matter with now?"

"Nothing's a matter now. You say now, I'm willing oblige. Your wish 's my wish. Hadda goddamn shark onna hook an' whatcha think happened?"

"He got away," Peggy said.

"The line snapped," volunteered Ted.

"Who's tellin' story? The leader snapped! Sonovabitchova Bev'ly Hills Sports Shop sells me a leader o' rotten gut and the shark amskrays, phht!—like that! Big joke, huh?"

"What?" said Ted.

"Joke! Big joke on Mr. Press!"

"What the hell's Press gotta do with it?" demanded Ted, his words beginning to slur. "If it's a joke, itsa joke on you—an' who says it's a joke? It's sad, 'ats what it is. Dem'nstrates futil'ty man's quest. 's a tragedy, 'ats what, a goddamn tragedy."

"You said a mouthful, doctor. Y'know wha' happened to man's quest? Y' know what's wrong with man's asp'rations?"

"What?"

"Man."

"Sad but true."

"Snapped—like the goddamn leader. Piece o' rotten gut someplace—snapped, d'fective. Man's a fraud, an' you know why?

'Cause he was created in God's image an' there ain't no God. A bunch o' friggin' nomads draggin' their rears over the dirty desert searchin' for food to keep from droppin', a bunch o' puny bastards so scared to death o' death all they could do was huddle around their campfires an' drag on dream pipes fulla dung and hashish and come up with all this lit'rary crap about a God an' Messiah who was gonna save 'em, an' when that wasn't enough, why, hell, they sell 'emselves onna *Big Deal:* there is no death; the soul lives on—big real-estate operation called Heaven, drop their friggin' pennies inna poor box: immortality insurance, down payment on enchanted acre in 'lysian fields. Man's a phony, a walkin' parasite who'da been better off if he was still paddin' aroun' on four paws insteada tryin' to navigate on two an' a brain."

"You, by any chance, leading a movement back to primordial ooze, doctor?" asked Ted.

"Happen soon enough, doctor."

"We're really in a jolly mood, aren't we?" said Peggy. "Whether you like it or not, Alex Frazier"—she picked up a bottle and glass—"I'm pouring myself a drink and offering a toast to the New Year—a happy one, if you please—because if I keep listening to you, I'll be mesmerized into believing there won't be one."

"Oh, it won't happen that soon. Gotta tease us a few years. Make your goddamn toast! That's just a prayer, too. Li'l ritual; say the magic words an' it'll happen. . . . Go on, drink it."

"You sure have one on today," said Peggy.

"You mean he's not always like this?" asked Ted.

"Do I look like a masochist? On the contrary. He loves life, don't you darling?"

"Life stinks. 's putrescent. Smells o' mortality." He swallowed the rest of the liquid, gasped for breath again. "Gone," he said morosely, "gone witha shark. . . ."

"What?" asked Ted.

"Alla pretty parasites. Joke. Big joke on Ike Press. Wanted me to go back to parasites. But they're gone. You hear me,

Peg, they're gone." He started to blubber, "The pretties', cutes', beau'fules' bunch o' lovable li'l par'sites. Makes me sad, Peg."

"Thought you said it was a joke."

"Jokes make me sad."

"You're crazy, darling."

"That'sa sanes' thing's been said since I came in 'ere."

He pulled himself to his feet, took an unsteady step to the chest. Once more he started pouring from two bottles at a time.

Peggy reached out her hand, said, "No, Alex."

A knock sounded on the door.

"Come!" shouted Alex.

Bert opened the door, said excitedly, "Did you see anyone hanging around our room? Some bastard sneaked in while we were taking a nap and stole all our—"

He stopped at the sight of the liquor bottles.

"There's the guilty party!" he declaimed, pointing his finger as Frank and Ike Press entered behind him.

"Sh'll I mix you one o' these?" Alex asked blandly, as he switched bottles and continued pouring.

"Is he putting on an act or is he swacked?" asked Bert.

"Jus' havin' frien'ly drink toasta New Year," said Ted.

"Well . . . You boys seem to be off to an early start," said Frank.

"If someone'll volunteer to get some glasses—" suggested Peggy, glancing apprehensively at Ike Press.

"Coming up!" said Bert, and dashed out of the room.

"Won't you have a seat, Mr. Press?" asked Peggy.

"Thank you, my dear," he said. "Well, I trust you had some luck with your shark, doctor."

"You trus' in vain," said Alex.

"Too bad. Then you didn't get your parasites?"

"Wha' makes you so innerested in par'sites, 'f I may ask?" demanded Alex, with a touch of belligerence.

"Mr. Press was merely being polite, dear," Peggy interposed. "You were so determined to get those parasite specimens—"

"Tha's not what I'm talkin' about!" he shouted, gesticulating with the glass. "What I wanna know is, why all this beatin' arounda bush, why all this hocus-pocus 'bout par—"

"Alex, do watch that drink!" said Peggy, trying to steady the tilted glass. "You're spilling it, darling!"

"Awright, awright, dona hatch," he said, gulping a good third of the drink.

The same hush, compounded of awe, apprehension, and expectancy, filled the room.

"I wonder if there's a Pulmotor in town," mused Frank.

"As I was sayin' when I was so rudely innerupted," resumed Alex. Then looking up with a frown, "What in hell was I sayin'?"

"Toast," said Ted. "Toasta New Year."

"Hold it!" said Bert, returning with three glasses and making his way to the bottles on the chest. "Name your poison, folks! Sherry, Ike? Or shall we make it something stronger?"

"I'll venture the tequila," said Ike, after a pause.

"Now you're talkin'," said Alex, throwing his arm around his shoulders. "Make a night of it. Here." He thrust his own glass at him. "Try mine. 's delishous!"

"That venturesome I'm not, thank you."

"I insist."

"Alex," said Peggy. "Mr. Press doesn't want it."

"Awright, if 'at's a way he feels, 's awright with me, if he wants be unfrien'ly, 's his business!"

"I have the friendliest feelings in the world toward you, my boy."

"Not your boy, an' frig frien'lies' feelin's."

"I'm afraid he's not quite himself, Mr. Press," apologized Peggy.

"Frig alla you," said Alex. "Whole goddamn bunch!"

"What you said!" exclaimed Ted.

"Naughty, naughty," said Frank.

Alex stood swaying in the center of the room, wavering between bad-boy truculence and bad-boy good humor. The latter asserted itself in a sudden giggle. The others seized on it, joined in uneasy chuckles which grew into a forced cacophony of shrill and overhearty laughter.

"Toast!" shouted Bert, who had by now poured drinks for Ike, Frank, and himself.

"Toast!" shouted Ted and Peggy.

The shouts of laughter came to a sudden stop. With one accord they looked expectantly toward Ike Press.

Lifting his glass, he said, "To a happy, peaceful, and recessionless New Year."

They clinked glasses, drank, pausing, one by one, to watch Alex slowly drain the still considerable contents of his without pausing for a breath, breaking into uneasy chatter as he looked up, aware of their scrutiny.

"I hope you're all getting set for dinner," said Peggy, with a glance of appeal at Ted and Frank. "Personally, I'm famished!"

"Could eata horse," said Ted.

"I'll settle for a steak," said Frank.

"What'sa rush? What'sa hurry?" asked Alex. "Takea time. Have coupla drinks."

"I could go for a plate of *chiles rellenos*," said Bert. "How about you, Ike?"

"Go 'head, suits me," said Alex. "I'm stayin' here till I havea coupla drinks. Go 'head. Walk out on me!"

He turned truculently to the chest and once again went through the pouring routine.

They glanced at each other, shrugged.

No one made a move to go.

III

IT WAS eight before they got to the restaurant. The preceding interval had been a game of distracting Alex's attention so that Peggy, or whoever happened to be nearest, could make off with his glass whenever he set it down and pour most of the drink into the sink. Another tactic was to keep shifting the glass from place to place so that he was in constant and befuddled search of it. At that, his intake was little short of prodigious.

And dinner seemed no solution. Peggy's hope of getting enough food and coffee into him to check the spiral of his aroused alcoholic yen wasn't working at all. He did eat a shrimp cocktail, then excused himself to go to the room marked *Hombres*, which, unfortunately, was located at the rear of the bar. After he'd been gone for ten minutes, Bert was delegated to reconnoiter. He found him at the far end of the bar with five shots of tequila lined up in front of him. Three made their way down his gullet in rhythmic succession. His hand had just deposited the third shot glass and was reaching for the fourth when Bert anticipated him.

"Did you go to the little boys' room?" Bert demanded.

Alex shook his head.

Bert took his arm and steered him into the cubicle.

"Hun'red proof," said Alex, directing a wobbly yellow stream into the bowl.

On the way back, he tried to persuade Bert to stop at the bar for a "quickie." When Bert was adamant, he reached out his hand and plucked a newly opened beer bottle off in passing.

A thick charcoaled filet surrounded by French fried onions and potatoes sat before him as he dropped into his chair. He disregarded it, hoisted the beer bottle, and let the amber liquid burble down his throat. As soon as he put it down, Peggy preempted it, passed it on to Frank. It never did get back to Alex, who had in the meanwhile decided to give the steak a try. He sliced it with surgical precision into neat cubes and bolted them down; he cleaned up the French fries and *frijoles*, swallowed the steaming chicory coffee, allowed the waitress—on Peggy's prompting—to give him a refill, drank that, smoked a *Delicado*, slumped, sated and drowsy, his lids closing over his eyes. And just when they had all relaxed to the pleasing prospect of getting him to bed and enjoying a peaceful evening, he came to with a start.

"Le's go to *cantina*," he said.

"Let's not," said Peg. "I'm awfully tired, darling."

"We're all tired," said Ike Press. "After last night, I think we could all do with a good sleep."

"I know I'm hitting the sack early," said Ted.

"What'samatter," he asked, "you 'fraid I'll get drunk?"

"Perish the thought," said Frank.

"Please, darling. I'm practically out on my feet. You don't mind, do you?"

"Your wish 's my command," he said cavalierly.

A moment later he rose, said, " 'scuse me," and, listing perilously to one side, lurched through the archway into the bar. Warily, Bert rose to follow him.

Looking up with a drunkard's cunning, a drink in his hand—he didn't wait to order, merely appropriated the first within reach—Alex tossed it down. And before Bert could get to him, he'd seized a second and made his way to *Hombres*.

"What the hell's comin' off here?" muttered the startled Californian who had cut in on Peggy the night before.

His companion whirled around, "You the sonovabitch stole my drink?" he demanded.

"Sorry, bud," said Bert. "My friend made a mistake and picked up the wrong glass."

"Two wrong glasses!" said the football Californian.

"I stand corrected," said Bert. "I apologize. My friend apologizes." He ordered fresh drinks for the Californians, one for himself.

Ten minutes later Peggy, Ted, Frank, and Ike Press came in from the dining room.

"Where's Alex?" asked Peggy.

Bert indicated the *Hombres* sign.

"You don't think he's ill, do you?"

"Either that or he passed out," said Frank.

"I'll go see," said Bert.

He returned a moment later with the announcement that Alex wasn't there. He'd either climbed out the window—which was open—or slipped out the back exit, though Bert had kept a rather careful eye on the *Hombres* door.

"He's probably halfway to the *cantina,*" suggested Frank.

"That's all we need!" Peggy said in despair.

"We'll soon find out," said Bert, leading the way to the front door.

The headlights of Frank's car picked him out on the road, halfway to the *cantina.* He swung around, startled by the sound of Frank's horn, then started to run. Frank kept pace with him.

"Alex," Peggy called.

If he heard, he gave no indication.

"It's us, Alex."

He stopped suddenly, said, "Who in hell ast you to follow me? If I wanna go to *cantina,* I'll go to *cantina.*"

"Get in, Alex," said Peggy.

"An' have you take me back to motel? Oh, no! Nobody's tellin' me what to do!"

"No one's telling you to do anything, my boy," said Ike Press. "If you want to go to the *cantina,* we'll take you to the *cantina.*"

"Tha's what you say."

"Please, Alex. We'll all go."

He hesitated. " 's a trick."

"My word of honor," said Peggy. "Please, darling. There's no point in stumbling around in the dark."

"Come on, Alex," said Ted, getting out of the car. "We'll all have a drink to the New Year."

"Happy New Year," mumbled Alex, lapsing from his belligerent mood.

He let Ted guide him into the car, slumped back against the seat, his eyes closed. By the time they reached the edge of town, he seemed asleep, and Frank swung the car around toward the motel. Immediately Alex's hand was on the handle. Before anyone could stop him, the door was open and he was out, carried headlong by the momentum, trying hard to keep his footing, then falling and rolling in the sand.

Frank braked the car, and they hopped out, hurrying to him. He scrambled up, confronting them in frenzied defiance, the right side of his face bruised, little trickles of blood seeping through the raw skin.

"Keep away from me!" he shouted. "You're not takin' me back to any goddamn motel!"

"All right, calm down," said Frank. "There's no need to get excited, Alex." He took a step toward him, touched his arm.

Alex threw off his hand, backed away. "Don't you touch me!" he shouted. "Don't you lay a finger on me or I'll knock your teeth in!"

He turned and ran, stumbled, fell, picked himself up, lurched on, a frenetic figure, with arms and legs shooting out in all directions, like a giant puppet.

Peggy started to call, took a step as if to run after him. The touch of Ted's hand restrained her.

"Let him go," he said quietly. "Give him a chance to get there, and then we'll follow.

The place was jumping.

Guaymas Joe, barefooted, mackinawed, and drunk, was trying to do a hat dance. His partner, a toothless, randy-looking old man in his seventies, had a sweater tied around his waist to serve as a skirt. Hands on each others' shoulders, they stamped on and around the edges of a huge *sombrero*, the old man wiggling his rear and stopping occasionally to scratch his scrotum. An appreciative group sounded off with wolf whistles and hyena yips.

Lining the walls were the gentle-faced fishermen and laborers of the village who rarely came into the *cantina* save for a holiday occasion like tonight. They looked on in quiet amusement.

Many-colored streamers looped from the ceiling. All around was bedlam.

In a corner a barbershop chorus of Americans, led by Zachary Finch, was soulfully absorbed in a maudlin-drunk rendition of "Let Me Call You Sweetheart." This in utter disregard of the band, augmented for the occasion by a tuba, drums, and Bob White's horn. And in seeming oblivion of both, a quartet of wives, led by Mrs. Bob White, was giving lusty voice to the round: "Row, Row, Row, Your Boat."

In the meanwhile, a gnomish-looking Mexican, with pointed ears and a satanic leer, was standing on a table and shouting, "*Miren! Miren!*" as he performed feats of magic, including sword-swallowing and fire-eating routines, the usual appearance, disappearance, and reappearance of scarves, coins, and bouquets of flowers. He hopped down, presented the paper bouquets to the ladies, and passed a hat, screaming with rage when a drunk who hadn't observed his performance—as most had not—poured beer into it.

Alex, who hadn't seen the act and wouldn't have had the vaguest idea of what was happening if he had, was at the moment in so euphoric and generous a mood that he dropped in a five dollar bill. Then, his attention caught by the hat dance, he wove toward it, reaching the dancers as the *jarabe* reached its climax. With great élan and more enthusiasm than control, he threw his arms around the old man and Guaymas Joe, his feet tangling with theirs, and bringing them all to the floor in a bewildered heap, much to the detriment of the *sombrero*.

It was at this moment that some playful soul threw a lighted string of Chinese crackers into the center of the floor. The tiny firecrackers popped and hopped in machine gun bursts of sound.

"Ai!" howled the old man, rolling over and over to get away from the exploding demons.

The quartet of wives terminated their round and ran shrieking to their husbands.

The drummer did a roll on the snare, pedaled the bass, and hit the cymbals.

And just as suddenly as it had started, the bedlam ceased. In the lull, Alex stood swaying in the cleared center of the *cantina*, his fists clenched. "Dare the sonabitch did that show his rat-face! Come out, why doncha? Yella belly sonabitch! C'mon out!"

Bert, who was the only one of their party whom Alex had allowed near him in the hour since they'd converged on the *cantina*, came toward him. In a placating voice, he said, "Just a joke, Alex. Some kid threw 'em in the doorway."

Alex disregarded him. "C'mon out, yuh yella-liver' sonabitch!" he roared. "No guts! 'at's what. I'll killa bastard!"

Peggy, who had made a previous attempt to coax Alex out of a bellicose mood, started to get up from the table to try once more.

"Better leave it to Bert," advised Ted.

She hesitated. Bert's efforts at persuasion seemed to be getting nowhere. If anything, he seemed to be feeding Alex's wrath.

The sudden appearance of Luiz, proffering a drink from a bottle of tequila, brought immediate results. Alex embraced him like a long lost brother, took a long pull on the bottle, handed it back, insisted that Luiz take one too. Docilely, he let Luiz guide him to the table at which Arnold (in the same capelike, black coat) and his brother (in the same white, turtle-neck sweater) sat. Their long necks lolled over like drooping flower stems as they listened in drunken solemnity to an anecdote about André Gide, told by a fleshy-faced man of about sixty. He wore a cream-colored coat and maroon muffler and leaned forward on a cane, his iron-gray hair hooding his massive head in stiff ringlets. When he opened his eyes, he looked for all the world like Gertrude Stein. Glancing up at Alex, he gestured to a seat, without interrupting the flow of his punctilious sentences. Arnold, either because he was lulled by the narrative or too sodden to recall last night's set-to, showed no reaction to Alex's presence. Indeed, after the anecdote was finished and the man had passed a bottle of absinthe around the table, he leaned forward to listen with great intentness to something Alex was saying.

The colloquy that followed, especially if observed from a distance, was as deferential, formal, and dead-sober a performance as only drunks can put on. It had the gravity of doctors consulting around a deathbed, a seriousness that could be expressed in hushed tones only, with heads leaning toward each other and ears straining to hear, as if each word were fateful. Nor did it seem a break with the solemnity or portentousness of their discourse when they got down on hands and knees to watch the man who looked like Gertrude Stein drawing with chalk on the concrete floor.

They were soon ringed by a crowd curious to see the design of the drawing, which was taking on the aspect of a rather grandiose architectural plan. It was, in fact, a ground plan for a Greater San Vicente, a projection of the tourist mecca which Luiz had suggested the night before, elaborated now by Alex, who was at the moment carried away by the idea that he must forthwith sell his house and practice and convert every tangible to cash in order to put the plan into being.

They'd come here to live, have Neutra design the goddamnest modern house ever dreamed up. Hell, this was a cinch, a setup. All you had to do was use a little imagination. They'd clean up, make a lousy fortune. Christ, he had ideas, millions of 'em! Not just to lure the fishermen and sun-lovers and the usual run of vacationers and *turistas* . . .

They'd build a hospital *and* research lab, make a goddamn Mayo Clinic of the place and better, have 'em flying in from the four corners because, hell, with the kind of staff he could pick and the quality of research (they'd crack every humpin' disease there was), they'd be one up on any health operation that ever was. Everybody and his brother'd be coming down in droves because, hell, this was gonna be *it,* the model medical institution in the world. . . .

That was one idea. But there were all sorts of 'em. Millions! Take Armando Lopez, the Stein-looking character. Luiz claimed he was the hottest crafts' designer in Mexico. Have him put some of the villagers to work, hire a hundred, two hundred boy apprentices from Guadalajara, turn out the goddamnest lines, export to every novelty, gift shoppe, and department store from Dallas to Madison Avenue, from Miami to the Golden Gate.

And then, the simplest thing. The mammoth shrimp, the fantastic prawns the boats brought in and sold wholesale for fifteen cents a pound down here (got anywhere from a buck fifty a pound and up in L.A.). Any reason why they couldn't be cleaned, cooked, packaged, and quick frozen down here fresh out of the sea? Hell, they could prepare 'em in a dozen ways: French fried, Chinese style, à la Newburg, in bisques, Louisiana style, etc. Sell the best for less.

Another pull on that tequila, Luiz, ol' pal, ol' pal, ol' pal. Thanks. And now we'll sample a swig o' your absinthe, Armando, ol' boy. C'mon, perk up, Arnold. We're drinkin' to San Vicente. To the first million! . . .

They threw their arms around each others' shoulders and drank.

The band was playing a conga. A long line snaked around the *cantina* chanting last night's refrain: "Madame La Zonga danced the Conga in Cucamonga." The magician stood in the center and kept an arc of vari-colored balls juggling in the air.

The number ended. The conga line disintegrated. The magician shouted, "*Miren! Miren!*" and started juggling Indian Clubs.

Before the band started its next number the football Californians entered the *cantina* and proceeded in a phalanx to the bar. One of them spotted Alex, who had just risen, glass in hand, to toast the Greater San Vicente.

"There's the sonabitch stole my drink!" he roared.

"I don't think we been in'roduced," said Alex, giving him a blank stare.

"I demand apology!"

"Frig apology," said Alex.

"Why you sonabitch," said the Californian, taking a wild swing at him.

Alex side-stepped with the easy reflex of a trained boxer. The Californian stumbled forward. He was stopped by a left to the midriff. Alex's right connected with his nose.

Peggy saw the spurt of blood, then the dark stream flowing bright and viscous down the Californian's chin and shirt. She stood watching in sick fascination as he grabbed hold of Arnold's brother, then slid to the floor. His white turtle-neck sweater smeared with blood, Arnold's brother let out a hoarse, mangled shout.

By this time the Californians had belatedly come to the rescue. Two of them stepped in from either side and clamped hold of his arms. He struggled futilely, kicking at their shins. But they clung to him, letting the third and biggest of the lot work over his face. He went at it methodically, with hacking lefts and rights and stiff jolting jabs which quickly bloodied Alex's nose.

Bert, Ted, and Frank were trying to get to them, but a crowd had closed in, and they could make little headway.

Ike Press took Peggy's arm and said, "I think it would be best if you went to the car, my dear."

"No," she said, and started after the others.

She saw Alex's knee come up and catch the big man in the groin. He doubled over in pain. The second man moved in, unloosing a wild uppercut which sent Alex back on his rear.

Luiz bent over to help him up. Alex disregarded his extended hand, reached, instead, for the bottle in the other. Before anyone could stop him, he heaved it at the second man. It sailed over his head and across the room barely missing the Finches, who Charlestoned! Charlestoned! to the tune of "When the Red, Red Robin Comes Bob-Bob-Bobbin' Along, Along," which Bob White led off hastily to distract from the fracas. The bottle terminated the number by crashing into the bass drum and toppling it over with cymbals, blocks, gongs, and the works. The racket startled the *cantina* into an astonished silence. It gave Bert, Ted, Frank and the proprietor a chance to interpose themselves between the phalanx and Alex. The phalanx stuck out its prognathous jaws. Alex, Luiz, Armando, Arnold, and his brother glared back. The situation seemed stalemated, the belligerence confined for the moment to fierce facial attitudinizing.

Bob White tactfully led off with the sweet, soothing notes of "Let Me Call You Sweetheart." Peggy, as if on cue, walked up to Alex, held out her arms, and said, "May I have the pleasure, darling?"

Completely bewildered and as if obeying some inner dictate which he couldn't comprehend, Alex put his left hand on her waist, took her hand, and moved with her—let her guide him, to be more accurate—out on the floor. The phalanx, yielding to the imperative of respect for American womanhood, parted to let them through.

A moment later, as if realizing that Peggy had diverted him from answering a challenge to his manhood, Alex suddenly stopped, left her in the middle of the floor and staggered back. The phalanx stiffened in anticipation. Bert, Ted, and Frank hastened to head Alex off. Luiz grabbed hold of a chair, ready to use it if need be.

At this juncture, with all the elements of a free-for-all about to mesh, the police entered the *cantina*, moving casually through the battle-posed groupings. "*Vamos, vámonos*," they said, in gentle but firm tones.

"Break it up boys. Break it up," pleaded the proprietor.

The phalanx glowered, hesitated, eyed the prominently displayed Police Positives, and drifted to the bar, muttering something about "no justice, anybody come along an' break your pal's nose and yuh can't even beat the crap out of 'im."

Alex, looking after them in complete befuddlement, suddenly found himself being directed toward the exit, Frank and Bert flanking him, their hands on his elbows. He pulled up, said, "What'sa big idea?"

"Time to go home," said Bert.

Alex wrenched loose with a violence that sent Frank staggering against the wall. In a moment Alex was back to the sanctuary of Arnold's table, content to listen to a solemn discourse between Armando and Luiz.

"Those boys seem to have a very soothing touch," said Frank. "You and I don't rate anymore, Bert."

"As long as they keep him quiet . . ." growled Bert.

Ted, who was as surfeited as Peggy with Frank's cracks, turned to her and asked if she'd like to dance. She rose with alacrity.

The band, sticking to nostalgic and tranquil selections, was playing "Zwei Herzen in Dreivierteltakt." The gay waltz, which carried an overtone of sadness, took them back to the flush time of their relationship. Jean, she remembered, had seen the movie with them. . . .

The number was interrupted by a sudden roll on the drums. Bob White was holding up his arms and shouting, "Happy New Year, folks! Happy New Year, *amigos!*"

The proprietor stood in the doorway and shot off a forty-five. Salutes and Chinese crackers exploded outside. Toy horns, rattles, and shouts joined with car horns in a bedlam chorus.

Ted stood lost in the center of the confusion. He turned from Peggy, struggling to keep hold of himself. She gripped his hand. The band started to play "Auld Lang Syne." A strangled sound broke through his lips. Impulsively, he sought the solace of Peggy's shoulder. She held him to her, her hands soothing his back.

"Damn," he said. "I knew this'd happen. I just knew it."

"I'm not exactly composed myself."

"It's that damn music." His voice was still tremulous. "Just hang on a minute."

She held him tighter.

He took a deep breath, said, "I'm all right now."

Just as he broke from the embrace, a fist smashed at his jaw. He staggered back, hit a chair. His fingers grappled for support. The chair went down, and he went with it.

When he looked up, Bert and Ike Press were holding Alex,

who was struggling to pull loose and screaming at him: "You sonabitch! Sonabitch bastard! Nobody do that to me an' get away with it! I'll killa bastard!"

Peggy stepped in front of him, gripped his arms, said "Stop it, Alex! Do you hear me, stop it!"

He looked at her with glazed eyes, his head cocked to one side, his lips twisted. "You whore," he said.

Bert yanked back his arms and pulled him away.

"Whore!" he shouted again.

"Now look here!" interposed Mr. Finch. "That's no way to talk to—"

His words were silenced by the straight-arm thrust of Alex's palm against his mouth. Finch staggered against the wall.

"Whore! Bitch! Whore!" Alex continued to shout as Bert propelled him to the exit in a fierce, driving anger that practically lifted him off his feet.

The Mexicans lining the wall looked on in gentle-faced wonder.

It took the combined efforts of Bert, Frank, Ted, and Ike Press to get him into the car. He screamed and thrashed about as if his life were threatened.

"Luiz!" he screamed. "Luiz!"

But Luiz didn't deem it wise to intervene.

They sat him between Bert and Ted in the back seat so he couldn't get at the door and jump out as he had before.

Once the car was under way, his resistance wilted. His head drooped forward on his chest and he began to snore.

Peggy, who had been holding her breath, said, "Thank God. . . ."

IV

HE DIDN'T wake when the car stopped in front of the motel. Aside from a moan and an inarticulate dribble of words, he showed no awareness of being carried into the room, had no more reaction than a bag of cement when they dropped him on the bed. He lay sprawled out in a sodden stupor while they pulled off his trousers, shoes, and the chartreuse shirt (which still carried the odor of Luiz's toilet water).

Looking at him, his long body toned and trim, the overhead light catching the glint of reddish-gold hairs on healthy tan, one side of his face bruised by the fall from the car, a line of caked blood from nose to lip, one would take him for a football player stretched out in exhausted sleep after a hard game. Clad only in beige silk shorts, he looked so boyish and clean-cut and all-American that it seemed inconceivable that he was in any way connected with the drunken, bellicose bluster which preceded.

A mumble of phrases slurred over his lips. He turned over on his side, then on his stomach, restive, muttering. He turned again, very close to the edge of the bed. Peggy started forward. Before she could stay him, he had moved once more, his dead weight sliding off the edge and thudding to the floor. He moaned, still asleep.

Taking hold of his arms and legs, they lifted him back on the bed. His breathing was heavy.

"He's good till noon," said Bert.

"If there's any Scotch left," said Peggy, "I could do with a drink before we clear the bottles out of here."

"I think we could all do with one," growled Bert.

"I've been so busy watching Alex's intake," said Frank, "I'm disgustingly sober. This is one of the driest New Years' Eves I remember spending."

A moan from Alex shunted their attention to the bed again. He lay on his side, his hands groping vaguely, then rolled over on his back again. His breathing was as heavy as before.

"Scotch," said Bert, turning to the chest and picking out the bottle.

Alex started to mumble again—a mushmouth miscellany of expletives which maundered off into silence. He lay relaxed for a moment, then started, as if in sudden fright. Every muscle was instantly taut. Slowly, blinking against the light of the overhead lamp, his eyes opened. They stared glassily from their sockets, straining to make identification out of the blur of faces which ringed him from above. Warily he looked from one to the other, puzzlement mingled with fear. For a while he lay inert.

Without warning, in an unbroken sweep of movement, displaying an agility completely at odds with his condition, he rolled to the edge of the bed, swung over and up on his feet, and threw a wild punch at Bert, who had just poured a drink and was bringing it to Peggy. The liquor sloshed out of the glass as Bert tried to duck the blow. It caught him on the shoulder. He stepped aside as Alex hooked with a left. The force of it carried Alex forward and over on his face. He made no effort to get up. In a moment he was snoring.

They put him back on the bed again, as sure as they were last time that he was safely tucked away for the night. The quiet lasted for a moment only. As unexpectedly as before, he was on his feet, wild-eyed, embattled, his fists flailing wildly, one of them clouting Ted on the side of his head, one catching Ike Press on the arm and turning him around.

"Alex!" Peggy said sharply.

"Easy, my boy. Easy," said Ike.

Alex continued to swing. A blow glanced off Frank's shoulder. Another just missed Bert, who grabbed hold of his wrist and swung him around.

"All right," commanded Bert. "Cut it! You hear me, cut it! We've had just about enough of your shenanigans. You've had your fun. Now you're going to bed and you're going to stay there if I have to sit on your chest. Now why don't you simmer down and behave?"

"You sonabitch!" Alex swung at him with his free fist.

Bert caught hold of it, yanked him toward the bed.

Alex pulled back, shouting, "Leggo, you bastard! Help! Lemme go!" He sat down on the floor, resisting Bert's efforts to drag him along.

"Let go of him, Bert," said Peggy. "There's no point in getting him all worked up again."

"I think Alex will listen to reason," said Ike Press. "Won't you, my boy?"

"I'm not letting go till he promises to get to bed and stay there."

"Now that's not at all unreasonable, Alex. As a matter of fact, I think we'd all promise to get to sleep if you would. It's late. We had very little sleep last night. We've all had a big day and a big night. And I know I, for one, can hardly keep my eyes open. And your good wife has to get her beauty rest, you know. Also, there's the little one to think of. So be a good boy and promise us you'll go to sleep."

Alex sat looking at him, his head resting on one shoulder, his lips screwed up, eyes glazed. "Leggo," he said in a low voice.

"You promise you'll cut the brannigan and get some shut-eye?" asked Bert.

"Promise," he mumbled, after a pause.

Bert released his hold.

Alex scrambled to his feet, confronted them, his face contorted, the muscles on his neck corded. "You sonabitch Jew bastards!" he said. "Lemme out o' here!"

"Alex!" Peggy said incredulously. "For the love of God, what's wrong, Alex?" She took a step toward him.

"Keep away f'm me. Get outa my way, alla you!" he said with growing hysteria. "Anybody take a step to me an' I'll kill 'im,

I'll tear 'im apart!" His voice rose to a shout, "Lemme outa here! Get outa my way!"

No one moved.

"You friggin' Jew bastards, lemme out o' here!" he screamed.

There was a dead silence. Then Ike Press said, "Now what's the point of talking that way, my boy? We're your friends. This is your wife who loves you and your very good friends. Believe me, boy."

"All agains' me," he said in a half cry, half sob which carried a mingling of fear, hysteria, and defiance. "Gangin' up on me, alla you. Wanna get rid o' me, tha's what!"

"Look, bub," said Bert, with contained anger, "if Peg here weren't around, I'd smack you down so fast . . ."

"Lay off, Bert," said Ted.

"I'm not taking any anti-Semitic crap from anybody."

"He doesn't know what he's saying, Bert," said Peggy. Her mind refused to accept what he was saying. She was hearing words, but the words had no meaning, couldn't possibly have the meaning they might seem to have, because they didn't go with the person.

"What makes you think we're against you?" asked Ted, stepping casually before Alex. "If you want to go, I'm sure no one has any objection."

Alex eyed him suspiciously, hesitated, made no move.

"You've got us all wrong, Alex," said Frank. "We're your friends, pals. You haven't forgotten your old colleague? This is Frank. We've got our name plates on the same door: Franklyn R. Meyers, M.D., Alexander Frazier, M.D. Now you wouldn't call me unfriendly, would you? What in the world would I have against you? I wouldn't refer my patients to you if I did, now, would I? Of course not. I have only the greatest respect and admiration for you." He took a tentative move toward him. "Of course, you've had a few drinks and I know how things get distorted but—"

"You take another step," Alex said threateningly, "an' I'll pulverize you."

Frank hesitated for a fraction of a second, then continued toward him with seeming calm. "If it helps you to hit me, then hit me," he said, stopping in front of him, his hands at his sides, his head tilted in a martyred pose. "Go ahead, hit me. I don't mind. Hit me and get it out of your system."

If Alex was somewhat befuddled by this unconventional request, he recovered quickly. "Stupid shite," he muttered and waded into him.

"Stop him, somebody," Peggy pleaded. "Alex!" she shouted, "Alex!"

"All right," said Bert. "Let's call it a day, Alex."

Frank gasped and doubled over as a wild blow caught him in the stomach.

"Did you hear me? Cut it!" said Bert, stepping in.

Alex took a poke at him. "Jew bastard," he said.

Grabbing his wrist in a judo hold, Bert sent him flying across the room. Alex landed on his back, his head hitting the wall. He turned over, clawed at the wall, then, unable to get up, scrabbled on hands and knees, sobbing, and uttering little animal cries, until he reached the door. Clutching hold of the knob, he pulled himself up. Then, flinging open the door, he ran in a blind frenzy, stumbling, lurching, falling, picking himself up, and running again, naked except for the silk beige shorts which blended into the color of his tanned body and made him look wholly unclad but strangely devoid of organs or hair.

He ran into the road, stopped short as a car turned round the curve of the approach and impaled him on the brights of its headlights. He darted off at a right angle and zigzagged down the sand, heading toward the water.

"Alex!" shouted Peggy, running after him with Ted and Frank. "Stop him! Please! Alex!"

"Let him go," Bert had said with a touch of contempt. But she was afraid. All she knew was that he was ill and desperately frightened and capable of violent hurt to himself, and if they didn't stop him, he'd run right into the bay and probably fall under the first wave, and who knew whether they'd be able to find him and pull him out, in all that darkness.

"Alex!" yelled Frank.

Their cries only seemed to spur him on to wilder flight. "Help!" he screamed. "Help!", as if someone were murdering him.

The occupants of the car, two men, took after them, convinced that they were out to do him bodily hurt. "Let him alone!" they shouted.

Alex plunged on. His toe caught in a tangle of scrub and he pitched forward on his face. The interval until he got to his feet brought Ted quite close. His shrieks of "Help! Help!" became more desperate and agonized.

Once more he fell, and this time Ted was able to catch up and get a hold on him. Frank puffed up a moment later and between them they got him started back to the motel, though he pulled back and continued to howl for help.

The men from the car were running up from one direction, Bert and Ike Press converging from another.

"What's coming off here?" demanded one of the men from the car. "What're you doin' to the guy?"

"Grab him under the shoulders," said Bert, disregarding him. "I'll take his legs."

"Wait a minute," said the man. "I want to know what the hell's comin' off. He runs out in the road stark naked, yellin' for help and now you're luggin' him off and how do we know what you're—"

"If you're concerned about the young man's safety," said Ike Press, "you can rest assured. This good lady is his wife, and we're friends. He's in the very best of hands."

"Hey, is he the character been havin' himself a time in the bar and *cantina* all evening?"

"The same," said Bert.

"He'll simmer down," said the first man.

"He'd better," said Bert.

Alex was, as a matter of fact, snoring. They carried him back to the motel. He continued to snore until they got him back on the bed. Then it started all over again. It was almost ludicrous. A sit-up, stand-up, on-a-spring automaton, he lay about as before, catching Frank, who was no longer yelling "Hit me," with a stiff right to the eye, missing Bert, who ducked, and falling flat on his face again, then scrabbling toward the door like a pursued animal, but anticipated this time by Ted, who stood before it.

Alex's eyes caught sight of the legs, traveled up to Ted's face. He threw himself at the legs, caught them just below the knees in a perfect football tackle. Ted, who was completely unprepared, went over, his head hitting the floor with a whacking thud.

Alex was reaching for the knob when Bert stepped in, grabbed hold of his wrist and twisted his arm back.

Alex slumped to the floor sobbing. "You hurt me. It hurts. What'd I do, you tryin' to crucify me?"

"Who's trying to crucify whom?"

Peggy leaned over, gripped his arm. "Alex, listen to me," she started to say. But he reared back in panic as though her hand held a knife or gun. Then he recognized her and said: "Help me, Peg. Help me. They're hurting me. They're tryin' to kill me. . . ."

"Get that one out of your head, Alex. The only one who's trying to hurt you is yourself."

"You're my wife, an' you're agains' me, too. Help me, for the love o' Christ, or they'll murder me! Get 'em outa here! Oh, sweet Jesus, smite them down before they do me in! Oh, blessed Mary, mother of God, help me!"

He threw his arms around Peggy's knees, buried his face against them, sobbing over and over: "Help me, Peg. Save me. Oh, sweet Jesus, save me."

"There's nothing to save you from. Pull yourself together, Alex." Her fingers gripped his shoulders. "Alex! Get hold of yourself!" She cupped his chin in her hand, raised his face, said, "Look at me. Do you think I'd want to harm you or let anyone else harm you?"

He was suddenly on his feet. "It's a plot," he said. "A Jew plot to get rid o' me so you can marry him. You knew he was down here, tha's why you were so ready to go. Tha's what you were cookin' up while I was gone, wasn't it? How to get me outa the way so you an' your friggin' boy frien' could get married, keep it inna faith!"

She was so blindly angry that she didn't realize she had slapped him till she felt the sting in her hand and saw the white mark of her fingers on his face. "Damn you," she heard herself saying, "I've had enough of this! You have no right to talk to me like that; I don't care whether you're drunk or not!"

He stared at her blankly for a moment, then said, "You have hazel eyes. Luiz has brown eyes."

A tremor went through her.

"Mac had brown eyes," he continued.

She stood rigid, her fists clenched at her sides.

"Go ahead, marry him," he said. "Why the hell should the famous Strauss fortune go to a goy when you can keep it inna family?"

She told herself she wouldn't listen. It was just too fantastic. But he was going on and on, the phrases pelting at her like hail-stones. She heard Frank say, "Now look, Alex," but he went right on. Then Bert said, "Shut up, Frazier," and she could sense the embarrassment in his voice, embarrassment for her.

Why didn't he stop! She put her hands over her ears to shut out the sound.

He was still railing, back to last night's dancing. "That's why you were jitterbuggin' all over the place, tryin' to abort the kid! An' you know why? 'Cause you're afraid to have it! Afraid ol' Joe might go soft an' forget his objections to me!"

"Alex!" she sobbed. "For the love of God, stop it, stop it."

"Alex!" he mocked. "Sure, you got it all figured out. You an' your boy frien'. Both o' you tryin' to crap me about last night bein' the first time you seen each other. Tha's what you say. How d' I know? How d' I know you haven' been sneakin' off an'—"

Ted swung him around, said, "All right, Frazier, we've had enough of that. Either you're going to shut that foul mouth or I'll shut it for you."

Swaying on his feet, Alex stared at him, his eyes narrowed, his lips tight. "Fuggin' bastard," he said, about to let go with a haymaker when his attention was diverted by the sight of Ike Press, who had gathered up the liquor bottles. Alex lurched toward him, his hand stabbing at a partially filled bottle of rum. "Gimme that!" he demanded.

The bottle slipped out of Ike's shaking grasp. He stood uncertain, his eyes fastened fearfully on Alex.

Ted put his foot on the bottle, but Alex was quick to snatch it out from under it.

"No!" moaned Ike.

Bert grasped hold of Alex's arm, whirled him around, said, "Give it to me."

"Screw you," said Alex. "I wanna drink."

"Give it to him, Alex," said Peggy.

Bert started to reach for it, but Alex jerked his arm back over his shoulder, his fingers laced around the bottle's neck. "Get back or I'll brain you."

Bert stood poised on the balls of his feet, debating whether to try to jump him or retreat.

"If all Alex wants is a drink," Frank said softly, "I don't see why he shouldn't have one. Do you, fellas?"

"I certainly have no objections," said Ted.

"None at all," said Ike Press.

"Let's have that bottle, old boy," said Frank, reaching up, "and I'll pour it for you."

Alex stepped back. "Oh, no. You're not puttin' anythin' over on me. I'm hangin' on to see you don't pull any funny stuff. You wanna make me a drink, make it outa other bottle."

"Okay." Frank picked the Courvoisier out of Ike's arms.

Ike was so shaky that a second bottle slipped and clattered to the floor, rolling around in a crazy arc before Ike recovered it with an apologetic "Sorry."

Frank poured two drinks, handed one to Alex. "*Salud*," he said.

Alex stared at him, suddenly cagey. With a look of drunken slyness he lifted the glass to his lips, took a sip. Immediately he spat the liquid out. His left hand went back, spattering the drink over walls and floor, then shot forward, the glass catapulting straight at the window, both shattering on impact.

"Bastards!" he screamed. "Tryin' to poison me! Dirty, sonabitch Jew bastards! I'll kill you! Killa whole goddamn bunch!"

Brandishing the bottle he advanced on Frank, who backed toward the bathroom, dodged, turned, darted in, slamming the door shut just as the bottle in Alex's hand smashed down, splintering the wooden panel instead of his skull. The bottle remained intact.

This is Alex, my husband, Peggy had to tell herself. The room quivered with impending violence. She stood petrified as Bert stole up behind Alex. Intuitively Alex whirled about to confront him, slashing at him with the bottle. Bert's foot went up as if he were getting off a fast punt in a football game. The toe of his shoe hit Alex's wrist. The bottle popped up out of his grasp and came down with a bounce. Alex lunged for it, but Bert anticipated him, seizing his hurt wrist in a judo hold that sent him skidding across the floor.

Alex grabbed hold of the chest, pulled himself up, howling. Again he whirled frantically as Bert came at him. He seized up a chair, but before he could bring it down on Bert's head, Bert had hold of his arms. They stood locked for a moment, the chair above them. Then the pressure of Bert's hold opened Alex's fingers, and the chair dropped, Bert jumping aside to avoid catching it on his back.

Automatically, as if she were trying to make order out of the phantasmagoria, Peggy bent down to pick it up. She was setting it on its legs when she was met with a completely unexpected and staggering right to her cheekbone. The blow straightened her up, sent her back a few steps.

She stared at Alex, incredulous, her hand on her face.

"Are you all right?" asked Ike Press.

He had to repeat it before she answered because Alex had

pulled loose of Bert and snatched up her overnight. With a grunt he hurled it at them. It hit the door above their heads, the bang! augmented by the snapping open of its two locks. A silk scarf which Peggy had left in it floated out and brushed her face as the case clattered to the floor. The unexpected soft touch frightened her, and she let out an involuntary cry.

"Look out!" yelled Bert.

She looked up, horrified. Alex had yanked the gas heater free of the tubing and now held it above his head, raising himself on his toes as he heaved it. They scattered. It caught Ted on the ankle and foot.

Before Bert could stop him, Alex veered toward the big chest, shoving it over with a maniacal cry. It landed on its side with a splintering crash, drawers shooting open, contents flying in all directions.

A judo grip tossed Alex on his face. Straddling his back, Bert pulled back his leg in a vicious toe hold.

"This is going to go on and on," he said to Peggy. "I'm going to have to clip him."

Peggy looked at him—helplessly.

"Unless," he added, "we call in the police and have him locked up."

"I couldn't," said Peggy.

"But you could see him doing violence to all of us, including yourself. What if that heater had connected with Ted's skull? Damn if I can work up any sympathy for a guy who's been sounding off the way he has."

"In all deference to our friend," said Ike Press, "I don't think he has the vaguest notion of what he's been saying."

"Natch," said Bert. "Or he wouldn't have. Not in this company, anyway."

"I've been married to him for twenty years, Bert. He's never showed the faintest sign of prejudice."

"*In vino veritas*," Frank said softly, and suddenly walked out.

There was an uncomfortable silence, then Bert said, "I'd like to know what he's been thinking those twenty years."

"Look, Bert," said Ted.

"I'm sorry," Bert hastened to say. "I shouldn't have said that. I'm just too goddamn blunt for my own good. Though there are some things . . ."

Peggy put a hand over her eyes. They were wet with tears. She didn't know what to say or think.

Frank reappeared as suddenly as he'd left, carrying his medical bag. Deftly he snapped it open, took out a hypodermic, tore open the cellophane wrapping, which encased a sterile needle.

"You mean you've had that out in the car all this time?" asked Ted.

"If I'd been using my head I'd have remembered I packed some sodium amytal on a call the other day. I really should have paraldehyde, but three grains might do it."

"What're we waiting for?" said Bert.

He started to pull down Alex's shorts to bare a buttock for the shot. Alex struggled and yelled like a vestal about to be raped. It took the combined aid of Ted, Ike Press, and Peggy to anchor him down. Bert got a firm grip on Alex's thigh to steady him for the shot.

Frank pinched the skin of his buttock between his forefinger and thumb and inserted the needle.

Alex let out an incredulous cry that was half gasp, half gurgle. His thrashing ceased for a moment. "Mother of God, what've they done to me?" he said, in a strained whisper that had the agony of death in it. "They've killed me. They've crucified me like sweet Jesus at Calvary."

Frank kneeled down before him, lifted his face so that he could see him. "Listen to me, Alex," he said.

Alex looked at him with a blank stare.

"I want you to listen to me," Frank repeated. "You're ill, and we're here to help you. Do you understand? No one's out to hurt you. We're here to help. We've just given you a shot of sodium amytal. Now if you won't fight it, it'll put you to sleep, and you'll get some rest and be all right in the morning."

"Sodium amytal," the words seemed to register; he seemed to be giving it some thought. "Sodium amytal . . . sleep," he said, almost wistfully. His eyes suddenly glinted with suspicion. "How do I know i's sodium amytal?" His voice rose hysterically. "Oh, blessed Mary, mother of God, save me! Oh, sweet Jesus, have pity, protect me, save me!"

Peggy couldn't keep from weeping. Ike Press sat down beside her and took her hand. "Now, now, child," he said.

Alex, convinced that he was at death's door, started saying the Act of Contrition. "Oh my God, I am heartily sorry for having offended Thee. I detest all my sins because of loss of heaven and pains of hell . . ."

He went on. His voice dwindled, then became silent. It seemed as if the shot were beginning to take effect. Then he started speaking again, in a much more subdued, almost placating tone. "Peg, please tell 'em to lemme up. I promise I'll behave."

"You promised before," she said.

"Word o' honor. Jus' lemme up, an' I'll go away. Honest. Won't bother a soul."

"Where would you go?" asked Ike Press, motioning to Bert to let him up.

"Home. L.A. City o' Angels."

"You're in no condition to drive. You know that."

"I'll walk."

"Do you know how many miles it is?" asked Frank.

"I don't care. I'll walk."

"It's the middle of the night. It's dark," said Ike Press.

"Alex," pleaded Peggy. "Will you just please let yourself go to sleep. We can leave in the morning if you still want to."

"What you got against me? Whyn't you let me go? I wanna go home. Now."

"In the morning," said Frank.

"Now, goddamnit, now! Why do you torture me? Why do you persecute me? You people should know what it is to be persecuted. I love the Jews. I love 'em for all they've suffered."

"Pardon me while I puke," said Bert.

"What've you got against me? I'm talkin' to you, Mister

Press. I'm askin' you a simple question. What've you got against me?"

"Not a thing."

"I was good enough for you when Trattner kicked off and Dan Simon was havin' himself a time in Europe. You tol' me you appreciated it. Whyn't you appreciate me now? What you got against me now?"

"I've appreciated you all along. You've done a tremendous job and you have a brilliant career ahead of you—if only you don't throw it away by this destructive behavior."

"Is it because Dan Simon is one o' the brethren?"

"Is what because of Dan Simon?"

"You know what. The appointment, that's what."

"That'll be decided by vote of the Board."

"By your vote. Who you kiddin'? It's your decision, and you made it before I got stinkin'. Awright, if that's the way you want it, go ahead—and the hell with what it does to good name o' hospital! Who the hell gives a damn if he's qualified or unqualified—"

"Now just a minute," said Bert, stepping toward him, "I'm not letting a drunk malign the reputation of a man like Dan Simon!"

"He's not in any condition to know what he's saying, Bert," Peggy intervened.

"You're a good buyer," said Alex. "Good judge o' merchandise. Lousy judge o' mental faculties. Know exac'ly what I'm sayin'."

"What exactly?" demanded Bert.

"I'm not in the slightest bit interested," said Ike. "I've spent the last two weeks studying the records of the men under consideration and Dan's happens to be unimpeachable."

"On paper. You watch him diagnose, op'rate? How you know half o' cases need surgery?"

"Look, Frazier," said Bert, grabbing hold of his arm and swinging him toward him, "what the hell're you trying to do, accuse Dan of malpractice?"

Alex's voice rose, high-pitched and out of control. "You don't give a damn! Nobody gives a damn! Awrigh', Press, go ahead! See if I care! Hand the hospital over to a knife-happy surgeon who's more innerested in fat fees and statis'ics than the life or death o' his patients! Who the hell cares long as a goddamn rabbi took a slice o' his pecker."

Bert put everything he had into a well-timed right to the jaw. This time it hit home. There wasn't any question or pretense about it.

Alex folded to the floor.

Bert stood over him, breathing hard. "Jesus Christ . . ." he said, looking down with a mingling of pity and contempt.

V

WHY? Peggy asked herself. Why in God's name did it have to happen? Twenty years, twenty good years—and, without warning, a world had collapsed. Without sense and without reason. Because what had happened last night had nothing to do with the man she'd married and lived with for all those years. Nothing to do with the life they'd made or the feelings shared. Last night was a lie, a fraud! It had to be!

Oh, how she'd like to believe that. Oh, how she'd like to black out on last night—as he had—and pick up from before.

But there was no point in crying over might-have-beens. They *had* come down. It *had* happened. The question was, what would be? She didn't know. Didn't begin to know. Couldn't formulate an attitude. Or even define what she felt. Because she was feeling many things: anger and despair, bewilderment and sorrow, bitterness and self-pity. She felt a compelling need to confront Alex with every single detail of his behavior and a contradictory desire to spare him. And wavering between the two, a fear of facing the consequences if she did tell him. So, unable to decide what she wanted to do or to focus her thinking on what might be wisest, she lay inert on the chaise, pretending sleep, because to do otherwise was to expose herself to his questioning and to the necessity of taking an attitude, whatever it might be.

She wished now that she'd had the courage to do what the others had urged upon her when they decided suddenly to return to L.A. at nine-thirty that morning before Alex had wakened. They'd wanted her to go with them—though Ike Press, realizing she might have compunctions about leaving him alone, had offered to stay on and handle the situation. She'd been tempted but hadn't let herself consider it. Whatever had happened, she was still his wife. She couldn't, no matter how strong the justification, walk out on Alex. Not until she knew he was all right.

Since she'd insisted on staying, Ike Press declared he'd stay with her. But the Ferrari was a two-seater, and there was the problem of how he'd get back. Ted had his Corvette along and decided he'd stay instead—just in case there were any difficulties when Alex got up.

The difficulties weren't with Alex, who remained blank on what had happened. They were all in her.

The rays of the sun were no longer slanted. They speared down in searing perpendiculars. Peggy turrned in discomfort, taking a sidelong glance toward the table where Alex had been sitting. He was no longer there. Like her, he lay on a chaise. His breathing had the regularity of sleep.

Sitting up, Peggy looked over at him. He seemed so tranquil and innocent that the bruises which were the marks of his violence seemed wholly out of place. It was the old business of appearance and reality. Both, in this case, showed their faces to the clinical light of the sun.

Quietly, she moved across the patio toward the motel room. Ted was coming to join her. A flight of gulls skimmed over the placid water of the bay.

"Everything's so calm," she said. "So still and peaceful . . . Hard to believe, isn't it?"

"The usual quiet after the storm," said Ted.

"That it happened at all, I mean."

"It didn't. That's the sanest attitude to take about it—for the time being at least."

"He's asked and he'll keep asking. Sooner or later I'll have to tell him."

"Better wait till you get back." He opened the door. "They've straightened up," he said. "Ike paid the manager to take care of the damage."

The room had been swept clear of the debris, the chest and heater restored to their original positions, a whole chair substituted for the broken one, the shattered window covered by the Venetian blind. Except for lath-exposed gaps in the plaster of the wall, the room looked pretty much as it had two days ago. If only, Peggy conjectured, it had been taken care of before Alex awoke. Perhaps he'd have had no questions and there'd be no dilemma about telling him. But that wouldn't have changed what had happened or altered in any way the impression it had left on Bert, Frank, Ike Press, and Ted. It wouldn't have answered her problem, the big problem of the future and of how and whether she'd be able to go on living with Alex now that it had happened.

She opened a drawer of the chest. Her clothes had been neatly folded and stacked. Below it, in the second drawer, lay Alex's.

"I might as well start packing," she said.

Ted opened the overnight, and she started putting the things into it.

"I'm glad you stayed," she said.

"Not that I did anything, but so am I."

"As soon as he wakes, we're off. And I can't get away fast enough . . ."

The last word dribbled off as her fingers encountered the sleazy rayon fabric of Luiz's chartreuse shirt. She stood staring at it, the agitation evident in her face.

"Why don't you throw the damn thing away?" said Ted.

She had a violent desire to tear it to shreds, but handling it gingerly, she took it out of the drawer and placed it carefully on the bed. "That's for him to decide," she said, and returned to the packing.

For a long moment neither said anything, then, as if from far off, Ted asked, "Who's Mac?"

"I haven't the faintest idea," she said in a strained voice. "Why do you ask?"

"No reason," he said quickly. "I was just wondering."

"What you were wondering is whether he was a homosexual like Luiz, is that it?"

"No. I was curious. His name sort of came out of left field, and I—"

"Why don't you be frank and say you're curious because it came up in context with Luiz's."

"Look, Peg. Let's drop it, for God's sake. I shouldn't have said anything and I'm sorry I did."

"If you think there's something odd about his interest in Luiz," said Peggy, her voice rising querulously, "you'd better forget it, because there isn't. He was drunk; he latched onto a pal. That's all there was to it."

"Of course," said Ted, a little too quickly.

"Alex likes Mexicans; he's lived among them, spent a lot of time with them. Luiz had a raw deal, and Alex has known enough poverty and bad breaks to identify. So he's his pal." The rush of words stopped. Peggy glanced over at Ted, said, "You're not saying anything. You're convinced he is, aren't you?"

"Stop it, Peg. You're beating a dead horse."

"Well, he's not. It's just laughable!" Her voice had an unnatural pitch.

Ted reached out his hand in compassion. She stumbled toward him, thinking how undignified it was to bare her doubts, because it was obvious the lady did protest too much. She was grateful it was Ted. She could let down her hair and be human with him because he was Ted and because he'd seen her in fallible moments before, when the circumstances were less extreme, her condition less vulnerable. That was back in the days when she still worshipped her father and was trying desperately to please him because he'd never got over the fact that she was a girl and not a boy who might have worked into the business with him. Strangely enough she'd turned into a damn good business woman. But that was after she'd met Alex, when the possibility of working with her father was nullified by his opposition to their marriage. Ironic to think that he might have been right . . .

"I think he's getting up," said Ted, looking out the open doorway. "I'd better clear out. I'm just about ready to take off, anyway."

He walked swiftly out the door, keeping his face straight ahead.

"Crisler," called Alex.

"Hi," said Ted, without pausing.

Alex looked after him with a frown. "That's the second big greeting I got from him this morning," he said, stepping into the room. "He wouldn't be trying to avoid me?"

"He's on his way back to town," said Peggy. "Stopped in to say good-by."

"I see you're packing too. What about the others? I haven't seen a sign of them."

"Left hours ago."

"Why?"

"Probably wanted to get back early."

"It wouldn't be because they were trying to avoid me, too?"

"We're not being subjective, are we?"

"When a man like Finch cuts me dead—"

Peggy turned her head in the direction of the bed. "What do you want to do about that shirt?"

He looked at it as if it were a curiosity, then, walking over to the bed, picked it up and flung it into the wastepaper basket, an oath on his lips. For what seemed like ages, he stood staring at it.

Impatiently, Peggy lowered the lid of the overnight, pushing it down to snap shut the latches. One of them kept springing open. "Well, don't just stand there!" she said sharply. "Help me."

He came to with a start, walked over and closed it without effort.

Five minutes later they left. The last thing Peggy noticed was the glint of the chartreuse shirt in the wastebasket. And outside the door, still standing, the row of empty liquor bottles. All she could do was hope that there, in symbol, among the discards, was the end of both.

The rayon sheen of the chartreuse remained in afterimage as they drove off. Perhaps, she suspected, because it represented a salve to her vanity. Then she realized that it was a sad reflection on her pride, ego, womanhood, self-respect if this small triumph over a Luiz was something she had to hug to herself. A rayon rag in a wastebasket. All right, he'd flung it there, with an expression of contempt and an epithet. But he'd worn it proudly. And he remembered the color of Mac's eyes.

Who, in the name of God, was Mac? And were there others like him, the color of whose eyes he also remembered? The notorious movie star he'd treated over a number of months, perhaps? The modern composer? The fashion stylist? All his patients. Oh, you could let yourself go, snatch at a coincidence, a name, a random phrase and come up with the wildest conclusions, make insane certitudes out of foundless nothings.

The landscape was spurting by, jagged thrusts of ancient rock, rising in rust and copper folds to either side, the car picking up reckless momentum, hitting high into the seventies and then into the eighties. And all she could think of was her bruised ego, her woman's pride, tortured by these senseless, sorry suspicions. Was she to take the maunderings of a drunk as meaningful? Take every alcoholic conceit as gospel?

What was she getting so worked up about?

Was there a Mac? Or was it just a name that had strayed into the ramblings of a moon-struck mind? Suppose there was such a person. Did he mean anything more than a Luiz? Had anything happened, really? Here she was ready to condemn Alex. On what proof? Everything about their life together proved the opposite. Everything that she knew about him before then, for that matter.

Alex had been frank about his sex life. At Meriden High there had been a couple of girls who weren't adverse to "putting out." And Yale had provided several very obliging girls from the Art and Drama schools and one nurse to whom he'd been faithful during his internship. She felt silly about having any doubts that he could be other than the normal specimen he certainly was, and as for his interest in Luiz, the drunk-pal theory wasn't just rationalizing, and most men did have a certain amount of the soft and feminine in them, and even the gruffest had buddies and were more sentimental about their male comradeships than a bunch of misty-eyed campfire girls.

Why was she upset? Because he kept wearing that Tweed-scented, chartreuse shirt of Luiz's? He'd been drunk since that silly exchange of shirts—which had been forced on him—and you didn't think about putting on a fresh shirt when you were drunk.

What, then?

The one thing, the remark which had come like an unexpected slap in the face. The remark about the eyes. Her eyes and Luiz's and Mac's. There had seemed to be a note of pique, of displeasure, in his voice. Because her eyes weren't the same color as theirs.

Why, she asked herself, had he even compared her with them?

There must be some way to explain it, to remove this dread tangle of questions, doubts, mistrusts. Nail them down and what did they come to? How much did they weigh against the years of love-making, against the interests and intimacies, the pleasures and sorrows which a devoted couple share every day of their married lives?

Or seem to . . .

She did. It was real for her.

Was it for him?

She couldn't discard all those years. Somehow he'd have given himself away. Or was last night the giveaway?

Oh, damn Alex! Why did he do it?

And why was he driving like a madman? The needle hovering near eighty-seven, then creeping up to eight, nine, and ninety, until she was ready to scream.

"Damn you! Goddamn you!" she shouted.

He turned to her, a startled look on his face.

"The speedometer," she said harshly.

Glancing at it, he eased the pressure on the pedal. "I'm sorry," he said. "I wasn't watching. And I swore I wouldn't pass sixty." He shook his head. "Don't let me do that again."

The speedometer dropped to fifty.

"I must have been a million miles away," he said.

Peggy remained silent.

"I can't get over last night," he continued. Then, "I'll have to know sooner or later. Let's have it, Peg."

She sat immobile, her teeth biting her lips, her eyes fixed on the desert vista, on the clumps of gray-green cactus which dotted the dunes.

"What's wrong, Peg?"

"Not a thing," she said tightly.

"When you're ready to tell me, I'm waiting to hear."

She decided not to answer and just as abruptly, her voice, edged with mockery, said, "You can't guess?"

"I can guess—lots of things. Too many things."

"No, I don't think you can." Voice controlled, the mockery still there.

"All right, I can't. But whatever it is, I think I'd better know. I've got to, Peg!"

When it came down to it she panicked. The words were there, ready to come out—and a fury, which urged her to get them out, to fling them like rocks, to bruise and lacerate him with their sharp edges. Something just as strong, whether fear or compassion or a mingling of both, held her back.

"I was just talking," she said. "I haven't got anything to say. Why I'm shooting off when I'm so dead tired that all I can think of is—"

"It's on your mind. There's no point in holding back. You're not helping me and you're not helping yourself."

Because she felt she had to tell him something, she decided on one thing. "Do you know why you gave me that poke under the eye?"

He shook his head.

"You implied it wasn't the first time I'd seen Ted."

"What made me say a thing like that?" he said, incredulous.

"You tell me."

"You can think up the damnedest things when you're drunk. Though I guess I can see why."

"Why?"

"Because I'm jealous of the guy. Always have been."

"Why? Because you married me and he didn't?"

"I know it sounds foolish. But you did marry me on the rebound—"

"What have we been doing, playing house all these years?"

"No. I'd say we were pretty happily married—until he came back and I saw you together."

"Which was less than forty-eight hours ago. But that wasn't what you thought. According to you I've been sleeping with him for six months."

His foot lifted from the pedal and he brought the car to a stop. His hand shuttered his eyes; he leaned forward against the wheel. "Oh, Christ, Peg! I didn't *say* that?"

"Yes."

"In front of everybody?"

"Yes."

He groaned. "How could I have? Oh, God, it must have been ghastly for you."

"Not that anyone believed it." She caught herself. No, she wasn't going to make it easier for him.

"I feel terrible," he said. "What else did I say?"

Plenty, she felt like telling him, but kept silent. When he looked up at her, she shook her head.

"I'm sorry, Peg," he said. Then, "I don't know how I'll be able to face him again. But I'll have to. And I'll have to apologize."

"Yes," she said, as if that would take care of it, as if the whole thing were that simple. *You don't know!* she wanted to shout. *You just don't know!* Instead she slumped against the back of the seat and tried to go to sleep, tried to shut it out entirely.

It wasn't any use. The shutting of her eyes only seemed to increase the activity of her mind. She sat up, seeking distraction in the scenery: in the crystalline white beds of a long-dry *laguna salida,* in the ferrous and copper outcroppings of rock, in the desert stretches, marked by scrub and vines bearing green gourds (on the sands the broken yellow husks of last year's crop). Occasionally a puffball of tumbleweed sailed over the rock-gray dunes. For miles a mirage of lakes, glimpsed through the ever-changing valley vistas, appeared and reappeared and finally was gone.

There *was no* distraction. And why, she asked herself, should she seek it? He was right. It *was* on her mind, and there was no reason for her to hold back. Why was she protecting him? Why shouldn't she let him know precisely what was in her mind, everything he'd done, everything that was bothering her? Why should she bear the complete burden and shield him? Who was he to escape untouched, this man who'd hurt them all, who'd destroyed an image, a life, a relationship? Why did he deserve it, this stranger, this calculating man who'd dissembled, brought her down under false pretenses, whose whole life with her was probably a deception?

Say it, Peg. Explode! Be done with it! Why do you keep silent and pretend nothing happened! Face it. This man lived with you, and for all those years he disguised what he was, kept hidden every vicious thought, nursing a venom which had to boil over as it finally did and reveal him. For the love of God, this is an anti-Semite you're protecting, Peg!

Yes, keep silent. Fold your hands. Look at the scenery. The nice cotton fields, the pickers dropping the fluff into long burlap bags. A tiny settlement. Indian children running with a yelping dog. Then the incongruous sight of a Richfield station and the realization that they were hitting the outskirts of Mexicali.

One part of her mind noted the bleakness of the run-down landscape, the other reflected her own despair. Oh, you could rationalize a good part of it away. You could say, as Ike Press had last night, that Alex wasn't responsible, that it was all as preposterous and untrue as the accusations he'd made against her and Ted, or the conviction that they were all out to murder him. The world of unreason had its own logic, and in his state it must have seemed real. Bert's judo wasn't exactly gentle. So he was convinced they were persecuting him, that it was a plot. He'd whipped himself into a madness, reaching back for prejudices he'd outgrown, for the anti-Semitic garbage that was no more a part of him than the Hail Marys he was spouting last night.

Or was it? Who was this man? Did she know anything about him anymore?

No, there were no excuses. There was no lessening or diminishing the enormity of the bigot phrases which had come pelting out of him. Just as there was no mitigating his assault on the character of Dan Simon.

Dan was his friend. More than anyone, he'd helped him achieve his present prominence. And he'd always acknowledged it. He liked Dan. How fantastic to think that he could turn on him. Oh he wanted the appointment, no doubt about that. But that he'd want it enough to be ready to villify a colleague, knife a friend?

Did it really mean that much to him?

How sad. How far from the person she'd met and fallen in love with.

What had happened to the dedicated, selfless Alex she knew? Why and when had he changed?

In a strange way she knew—though one could never pinpoint what was essentially the product of a lifetime of pressure and circumstance, of chance and will, of conflict and desire. But there were moments which stood out as markers.

One was the time when he'd discovered that she returned from her Friday night dinners with enough food from the Strauss pantries and refrigerator to last the week. Alex never went to these family functions. Perhaps because he sensed he wasn't welcome, perhaps because he resented the orthodox ritual—he had a hatred of all religious ritual, Catholic, Jewish, whatever. At any rate he always found a reason to be in the lab on those nights.

"What's the matter," her father had commented, "your shagitz doesn't like chicken soup?" Talk about bigotry!

On that particular night Alex had come home early enough to see her and the chauffeur enter with the carton of packages. She'd never seen him so angry. "I'm supporting this family. Not your father!" he shouted. "And if what I earn isn't enough to supply your tastes, then we'll do without. Or I'll go out and get myself a job that does!" He'd seized one of the packages, ripped it open and heaved it into the garbage pail. The others followed. "We're not eating leftovers from the Strauss table!"

There was that other time, soon after the war, when he was in conflict about returning to research (there was a modest grant at the Rockefeller Institute) or accepting Dan Simon's offer of going into his office. The folks had just come back from their first post-war trip to Europe and there were gifts: a half-dozen custom-made shirts for Alex, a couple of Diors, and, for no reason except that Dad had stumbled on a magnificent stone, a diamond ring for her. She'd known Alex wouldn't like it, and the minute they walked out he'd said: "What's that for, to underline the fact that I never could afford to buy you one? If you want diamonds, tell me. . . ." "I don't," she'd said, and taken it off never to wear it again. Alex was upset enough about her job at Blacks-Beverly, which he also took as a reflection on his ability to support her.

The next day Alex took Dan up on his offer to join his practice. Success as a surgeon came quickly. His apprenticeship in the army had been the best possible training. And he worked at it, drove himself, as if to make up for lost time. He had a confidence which communicated itself to his patients. He knew how to anticipate and allay their fears. He gave himself unstintingly, and they swore by him, spread his reputation. In two years he had his own office; in five he'd been approached by Frank. He was reaching the movie industry, the wealthy Beverly Hills' clientele. And all the things he'd denied himself he began to seek, all the tokens of affluence. As soon as he could he bought a house, then another, in the proper location.

It wasn't what she wanted. The big Beverly Hills house wasn't her idea of a home. She disliked the show, the constant emphasis on the material, on possessions, on money. Actually, she'd always disliked it. As a kid, when her father used to send her to school in the Pierce Arrow, she had an understanding with Andy, the chauffeur, to let her out a couple of blocks away. At camp she was glad for the anonymity of a middy and bloomers. And at college she underdressed, rode a bike when she owned a car, turned down a bid to a sorority because she was the only Jewish girl being rushed and couldn't help feeling it was because of her father's wealth. And as a mature woman she shunned the trappings of wealth and for the same reason: she wanted desperately to be accepted as a person, not as an heiress.

For some strange reason the question of whether she was desirable for her own sake or for her potential wealth had never entered into the area of her relationship with men. There'd always been Ted, whose family was wealthy. She'd met Alex almost immediately after, and it had been one of those instantaneously combustible things, so deeply and continuously gratifying that it hadn't ever occurred to her that it was anything but the purest kind of love on both their parts.

She was now forced to re-examine that assumption. Was it her he loved? Or the Strauss heiress? How else explain all the ranting and hysterics about "getting rid of him" and "wanting to marry Ted" and "keep the money in the faith."

Vanity told her that he had loved her, that it was genuine. Everything he did had seemed as natural and unrehearsed as thunder or rain.

But couldn't she just as readily look back on their first meeting and say the opposite? He'd singled her out at that farewell party for Nacio, made a definite play for her. You could say he was taken with her and that it was the most natural thing in the world to do. Yet he'd found out about her beforehand. He'd been thoroughly briefed. The information might have made her quite desirable.

Oh, you could make out a definite case. She'd wanted so desperately to feel loved that she would have willed it into being whether it was there or not. As it was, he'd professed his love, and she'd had no reason to doubt it. Until she began to think, as his statements of last night had turned her mind to thinking, in terms of the last will and testament of Joseph Gedaliah Strauss.

Professions are easy when measured against a cool couple of million.

God, you could compound this thing. Doubt breeds doubt.

Suspicion is a wild growth. The more she probed, the more muddled she got.

Had she been so head over heels in love that she'd lost mind, reason, senses?

There had been reservations. But because she'd married in defiance, she'd been determined to show her father that what he called an impossible marriage was not only a workable but an ideal one. In her zeal to make it so, she'd thrown a halo over it, romanticized and play-acted it into something too perfect to be real, leaning over backwards never to see the flaws, overlooking every imperfection and weakness in Alex and in their relationship. She hadn't seen because she didn't want to see.

Oh, she was face to face with a few realities now. And it wasn't only last night. Nor the two occasions when he'd so angrily expressed his resentment of the folks. But the many, many times when he'd left his feelings unvoiced and withdrawn into those agonized periods of brooding and hurt. Often enough she'd been the cause. Her tongue was too quick and sharp, his sensibilities too vulnerable. And too frequently she'd expressed a dissatisfaction, given barbed utterance to a disappointment, fretted over a vanity, indulgence, or profligacy, not because any one thing was so momentous but because each became a token of the surrender which had taken him, she felt, from the high asceticism of the lab to the posh practice in Beverly Hills. She'd never really accepted Alex's switch to surgery, never got over the feeling of disenchantment.

Perhaps she expected too much of him. She certainly wasn't any paragon herself. She couldn't blink the fact that she was pretty willful and spoiled, the indulged daughter of a rich and doting father, always wheedling her way. But she hadn't been able to wheedle Dad into accepting Alex. After her first defiance, she'd never made an issue of it. For all Dad's faults, she adored him, couldn't risk alienating him further. She knew Alex disapproved of their closeness. So she saw him alone and was quiet about it. But there were always those moments of deep resentment. How deep she didn't realize until last night.

The car was turning into a suburban section of Mexicali. Chimes sounded from the belfry of a mission church. Peggy's eye was caught by the lone figure of a young woman descending the long flight of stairs. She was in the last weeks of pregnancy and was carrying big and low. With complete lack of self-consciousness she reached the street and walked off, her bearing gracefully erect, the same look of serenity on her features that she'd remarked in the Indian girl with the flounder on her walk of yesterday. (It seemed months ago now!)

Peggy was surprised at the intensity of her feeling. Her throat was full, and tears welled in her eyes. She didn't know why. Perhaps because the girl was so dignified and beautiful. Perhaps because of the clear contentment with her coming motherhood—a contentment she'd never know now.

Peggy couldn't help feeling it might have been providential if she had lost the child. No, that wasn't true! She still wanted it. God, how she wanted it—especially now! To have something to cling to, someone to love. It was selfish of her, she supposed. Because it wouldn't be fair to bring up a child in a fatherless home.

Now, why was she jumping to that!

Because she had to be realistic about it. Because if she became convinced that he'd married her for her money, then that was that, child or no child.

Nor would she sit and pine. There were others.

Ted? Was that what was in the back of her mind? He was conveniently available. They still liked each other. She could see him as husband and father. Love? Love is need, and if she needed Ted . . .

She caught herself. It was awful to be thinking this way. But the mind had a way of protecting itself against an anticipated hurt or loss.

"I'm all out of cigarettes," she heard Alex say.

She opened her purse. There were a few *Delicados* left. She lit one, handed it to him, lit another for herself. The romantic association, she realized after a few puffs, was gone. All it summoned up now was the nightmare of San Vicente. She flicked it out into the road.

He noticed it, said, "Anything wrong?"

"I didn't really feel like one."

She found herself closing her nostrils against the sweet-smelling smoke from his cigarette. It was almost sickly sweet, and she fought down a rising nausea.

The wind seemed to be directing the smoke right at her.

"Don't," she said abruptly.

He looked up, startled. "Don't what?"

"The cigarette. Please."

He threw it out of the car. "You do look a little green. Want me to stop?"

She shook her head, but he slowed down anyway.

"You sure you're all right?"

She didn't answer.

"You should have told me sooner. I'm sorry, darling." He leaned over and kissed her.

Her skin seemed to shrivel; her whole being recoiled. It was as if she'd been violated, as if his touch contaminated. And suddenly she couldn't bear the thought of going home with him, of sharing the same bed. The idea of lying beside him, of shrinking from any physical contact, from the passing brush of his arm or the turn of his body was insupportable.

Why was he speeding again! For the love of God, she couldn't stand any more! And the indicator was creeping up, up, the car shooting out to pass a yellow blur and hurtling straight toward the sudden threat of an oncoming black Cadillac. The rush of wind stopped her breath. The cars zoomed toward collision, veered, scraped in passage. And she found herself screaming! screaming! then suddenly ill as the car came to a stop.

For once she didn't allow herself to be touched or moved by his contrition. No question that he meant it. She wanted to cry, to give way to the utter helplessness she felt, yet she knew she mustn't, because he'd only try to comfort her and that was the last thing she needed. So she made herself hard, insisting with desperate stubbornness that she wouldn't drive any farther. Let him argue, reason, cajole—she wasn't listening. She'd made up her mind. Yes, she *was* being emotional but maybe she had a right to be. He could drop her at Palm Springs if he wanted. She'd make connections with a train or plane there.

They drove in silence.

"I don't blame you for being angry," he said after a while. "And I know it isn't only about this. Or what you told me about last night. It's all the things you haven't told me and which I wish you would, because there's no point keeping them bottled up and brooding."

Perhaps not, but maybe she preferred to brood. If she wanted to huddle in her misery, it was damn well her privilege. How often had he done so? How often had he sought the refuge of a solitary bed in a solitary room, away from the sound of a solicitous, inquiring voice? It was she who needed sanctuary now. Respite from his questions, from his presence.

They stopped at the Desert Inn to see about a reservation. There wasn't anything leaving for a couple of hours. He wanted to wait with her, but she insisted he drive on.

Only when she saw the Ferrari taking off down the road did she feel she could breathe again. Without her restraining presence he'd be hitting a hundred, she was sure. For once, she didn't care.

For the two hours until plane time she took a room in the hotel, undressed, got under the covers. Wistfully she asked herself why she couldn't stay overnight and perhaps another. There was no reason why not except that she was due in the store in the morning when the January sales would be starting. It wouldn't be fair not to show—although she was sure they'd manage without her. But it wouldn't really solve anything. She could hide her head in the sand for two days but when she emerged she'd be face to face with the same problem, the same questions.

Unless she just never went back, never again set foot in the big Beverly Hills house. Unless she called it quits right now.

The boldness of the thought took her breath away. She played with it, beguiled by her daring, skimming on air like a paper plane riding a current before it takes a sudden drop.

No, it wasn't that simple.

First, there was the matter of deciding whether or not it was what she wanted. And if not, what it was that she did want now that the bottom had dropped out of everything.

How uncertain everything was! All this stress on security when the only secure thing was that life was insecure. Children brought up dependent on parents, then learning to be independent of them, marriage making for dependence on husbands, then a divorce or death and the necessity to become independent all over again. You had to be one of a lunacy of romantics to think there was any security on this benighted planet.

No, it wasn't at all simple.

Book · III

I

For the third time in as many minutes Alex looked at his watch. She should be home by now, he told himself with an anxiety totally unwarranted by the actual hour. True, the plane, if it were on time, should have arrived forty minutes ago. But it took at least that long to get from the airport, allowing for normal traffic. On New Year's night, with the influx of cars returning from the holiday week-end, it wasn't unreasonable to add ten, fifteen, or even twenty minutes. So there was no ostensible reason for his unease. Underlying it, he realized, was a vague apprehension that she might not return at all. Oh, she'd been explicit enough about the plane. But she'd been so adamant about his not meeting it that he couldn't help wondering. "I won't hear of it," she'd said. "And I don't want you waiting up for me, either. You need the sleep."

"So do you," he'd said. "More than I do. And it'll take you much longer to get home and into bed than if you came with me."

"I'm not setting foot in that car!" she said, trembling.

"Not that I blame you, but I swear I'd go no more than—"

"No!"

He offered to stay till the plane left. "I *can't* leave you alone," he pleaded, reaching out with his hand.

She'd turned away. Everything about her, the way she sent him on, the way she avoided his touch, gave him the sense that she was reading him out of her life. She'd been so forceful about it that he hadn't dared disregard her injunction about picking her up at the airport. He'd wanted to. He wished now that he had. Because if she wasn't planning to come back—

But it was a little late for that. The plane had long since arrived, and wherever she was bound, she was already on her way.

It wouldn't be long now. One way or the other he'd know. He tried to prepare himself against the possibility that she wouldn't return. But he couldn't accept it—any more than he could accept or prepare for death. The whole idea was strange and shattering.

No point in asking himself, as he had a hundred times during the day, what it was that he could have done that was worse than she'd told him. Nothing to do but wait now.

The house was quiet, the room so still that the perking of the electric coffee pot which Deeven had plugged in for him sounded like the rumble of a volcano. Though he'd had several cups, he poured himself another. He sipped slowly, bit into one of Deeven's oatmeal cookies, letting the black coffee soak into the sweetness of the crisp fragment and dissolve it on his tongue. He ate three cookies, measuring the sips so it would come out even. There was a sweet aftertaste which called for a pipeful of tobacco. He went through the business of separating stem from bowl and poking the fuzzy cleaners through both until the sticky residue of tars and nicotine disappeared and he could reassemble them, fill the bowl, light the fragrant mixture, and puff away, preoccupied all the while with the endless ritual of tamping and relighting to keep it going.

He sat back, his head against the down cushioning of the couch, his glance embracing the room's spaciousness, lingering over the exposed oak beams, on the floor to ceiling brick fireplace, on the Steinway, its bellied surface covered with standing Christmas cards and near it the tree, the reflections from its colored lights tinting the silvered balls. The muted gold expanse of drawn drapes. And on the walls the collection of paintings, auction prizes carried off by a sudden jump in bid (the blood pressure accelerating, the intake of breath held till the gavel banged and the sale was consummated, soul satisfaction for the aesthetic yen of Alex Frazier).

How many tens of thousands he had lavished on that wallful of pictures! On the lush snow scene by Vlaminck, the Fauvist colorburst by Matisse, the elongated Modigliani, the brooding Rouault, the Klee, Venard, and Buffet.

Strangely enough, it was an inexpensive water color by David Levine, who was relatively unknown, which pleased him most. It was a simple mood piece, a bleak, rain-swept street scene: a sagging shack of a house, a billboard, an old lamppost, an ancient car, two figures laboring uphill against the slanting rain, their reflections caught in the slick of wetness on the pavement. It was the wettest damn picture he'd ever seen. He wondered why he'd never sought out Levine, who used to live in town, to see what else he'd done. Was it snobbery, show that made him go for the money-pictures? Couldn't he at one tenth the sum have picked up as pleasing and tasteful a collection? What was it in him that made him drive for the accepted and expensive, the signature, the brand, the model?

He sighed, glanced at his watch, rose, walked to the window, parted the drapes to look out. The street was deserted. No sign of a cab.

Perhaps the plane had been delayed. Perhaps there'd been an accident. He called the airport. The plane had arrived on schedule.

She wasn't coming back, that's all there was to it. What to do? Call the Hilton? The Beverly Hills? He'd wait a few minutes.

Nervously, he emptied his pipe into the ash tray, then once more went through the ritual of cleaning and refilling it. Too disturbed to settle down, he walked back and forth across the room, stopping every time he heard a car drive by. His pacing took him into the hallway. On the table lay yesterday's unopened mail. There were four late Christmas cards, one datemarked Florence, Italy. The Italian card, from Herb MacDonald, was a photo of Michelangelo's *David*. "Berenson is dead," it read, "and Florence has lost its luster. But the paintings and sculpture remain. I return each day to refresh my senses with the beauty of *David*." It was signed: "Mac."

He was on his way to the piano to add the four cards to the others when he heard the car pull up. He turned, walked swiftly back to the entry hall, flung open the door. The sight of the yellow cab was a reprieve.

"I should have come to get you," he said, as she came up the walk.

"I didn't want you to," she said wearily.

"I was worried."

"There was an accident. A pile-up. On the Freeway."

"You must be exhausted."

"No more than you. I told you not to wait up for me. I expected to find you in bed. In fact, I was all set to sleep in the guest room so I wouldn't disturb you. And I still intend to," she went on, her voice strangely breathless, the words coming out with unnatural vehemence.

It struck him as an odd thing for her to say. She disliked sleeping alone, complained that it made her restless. Why didn't she come out with it, tell him what she felt about him instead of resorting to these obvious circumlocutions?

She was standing uncertainly in the archway to the living room, as if she couldn't make up her mind to enter. "Aren't you going to take off your coat?" he said, stepping forward to help her.

She moved away. "I'm cold."

"There's some coffee." He started toward the electric pot, then noticing the cards still clutched in his hand, turned and handed them to her. "Yesterday's mail," he said.

She sat down and glanced through the cards while Alex poured the coffee. "Who's Mac?" she asked in an odd voice.

"Herb MacDonald. You ask that every Christmas when his card comes."

"Do I? I didn't remember. Who's Herb MacDonald?"

"Classmate in med school. Lived across the hall from me."

"What's happened to him since?"

"He became an internist. In Baltimore."

"And he still sends you Christmas cards. Do you reciprocate?"

"No."

"You must have made quite an impression on him."

Alex let out an uneasy laugh. "You mean I never told you?"

She shook her head. "And I don't know that I want you to now."

He looked up. "Why? Has it got anything to do with last night?"

"What made you think that?"

He shrugged, was silent a moment, then said: "There was nothing between Mac and me."

"Fine," she said, starting to get up.

"No, I want to tell you."

She sank back into a chair, took a sip of the coffee.

Nervously Alex picked up a cigarette, lit it. "Mac, as you probably guessed, was a homosexual. Still is, judging from that card. Anyway, he sort of took a fancy to me. Why, I don't know."

He rose, walked toward the window.

"He was always inviting me out to dinner and shows. I was living on such a Spartan budget, and he was so filthy rich that as often as not I'd accept. He wasn't the aggressive type. In fact, he was rather shy. But there was something amiable about him, and he knew so much about the theater, books, and art that it was fun to talk to him. One day he found out it was my birthday—I must have let it slip, I suppose—and he invited me to have a drink in his room. He had several. And he gave me a present of a line drawing, that Cocteau I still have. Then we went out to a Greek restaurant. We'd been there before. He ordered a bottle of raki and got quite high. We were sitting in a booth, next to each other, and I was suddenly startled to feel his knee rubbing against mine. As unobtrusively as I could I moved away. A moment later he bent down to pick up his napkin—or that was his excuse—and his hand grabbed hold of my thigh to help him up. It remained there. I sort of froze. But when his fingers started to inch over, I suddenly jumped up and mumbled something about having to go to the john. Actually I headed for the kitchen and the back door. I practically ran all the way back to the dorm. He showed later and knocked on my door, but I pretended I wasn't there.

"For a couple of days I managed to avoid him. I'd climb in

through the window so I wouldn't bump into him in the hall. I used the upstairs john. I ducked and dodged. Each night there'd be a knock on the door, but I wouldn't answer. Until one night it became impossible. He was so drunk he wouldn't stop pounding. Then he went into a crying jag, said he knew I was there, begged me to let him in. It was when he began declaring his love out loud that I decided I'd better before someone came along.

"Damnedest thing. As soon as he stepped in he threw his arms around me. I tried to shove him off, but he hung on. Before I could break his grip we'd fallen to the floor and were wrestling all over the place. Which only excited him all the more. When I pinned him down, he wept, said he loved me, kept pleading with me. I felt sorry for him. The damn fool was so drunk he didn't know when to stop, and I wound up by letting him have it, right in the groin, with my knee. The poor bastard didn't know what hit him. But that was that.

"The next day there was a note under my door. He was miserable. Didn't know how to begin to apologize. He'd give anything to undo what had happened. It was something he'd been fighting since he was a kid, but there were times when it got the better of him. Usually when he was drinking—as it had in the Greek restaurant. Actually all he wanted to do was apologize. But when I kept avoiding him he felt so badly he went on a binge. And when I finally let him in, instead of apologizing, as he'd intended to do, he couldn't seem to help himself, became the victim of a compulsion he couldn't control. Could I understand that? Could I possibly forgive him? Forget it ever happened? Because it never would again. He wanted my friendship. Wanted to see me. Wanted things to go on as if it had never happened. Was that possible?

"Strangely enough it was. Not at first. Things were strained. We were reticent with each other. But by tacit agreement the subject never came up. And bit by bit we drifted back into the easygoing relationship we'd had before. It lasted through graduation. I never could really condemn the guy. Because, somehow or other, I did understand."

Alex had been so involved in what he was saying that he failed to notice Peggy's agitation. The blood seemed to have drained completely out of her face. Slowly she put the cup back on the table. In a self-consciously casual voice she asked: "Have you seen him since graduation?"

"Six years ago. At a medical convention."

"Was I with you?"

"No, that's the one you didn't go to. In New Orleans."

"Oh . . ." She sat transfixed for a moment. Suddenly she rose. Drawing in her breath, she said: "Did he have brown eyes?"

"Did he? I don't recall. Yes, come to think of it, he did. Why? How did you know?"

"I didn't. I just had a mental image of your friend and, for some crazy reason that I can't explain, it occurred to me his eyes must be brown. So I asked you. And curiously enough, you confirmed it. Now isn't that strange?" Her voice, high and strained, wavered, dribbled away. Abruptly she started walking out of the room. "I'm going to bed," she announced.

Her agitation seemed to increase with her stride. Without warning, as if she'd turned her ankle, she suddenly lurched to one side, saving herself from a fall by grabbing hold of the piano. Her arm hit some of the Christmas cards. They fell over, knocking others down with them.

Within a second Alex was at her side, his hand on her arm.

She jerked away. "Don't touch me," she said, hysteria strangling her voice. "Don't touch me!"

He stepped aside. "You really meant that didn't you? Are you afraid of me?"

She stood motionless a moment, then dashed past him into the hall, tripped on the first stair and lay sprawled. She heard his footsteps. Feverishly she tried to get up.

"I'm not going to touch you," he said quietly.

Gripping the rail of the banister, she pulled herself up.

"Are you all right?" he asked.

She nodded.

"You're sure?"

"I wasn't trying to abort myself, if that's what you mean."

"Whatever made you say that?"

"You accused me of it last night."

"I think it's about time we opened the book on last night. Obviously it's so bad it scares you to be alone with me. You're so frightened your teeth are chattering."

"It's just a chill," she mumbled. "I'm probably coming down with a cold."

"A shot of whisky wouldn't hurt you in either case." He turned to the liquor cabinet.

"No, I don't want any," she said hastily.

"If you're afraid I'll be tempted, forget it. After last night I doubt if I'll ever touch a drop again."

He filled a double shot glass, handed it to her. "Drink it," he ordered.

She gulped it down, shuddered. "I needed that," she said, leaning against the banister.

"I know it isn't very considerate of me," Alex said, in an apologetic voice. "I know I've been badgering and that you're beat and dying to get to sleep. But you probably won't be able to sleep—I certainly know I won't—until you tell me. Please Peg. Just come out and say it."

"There are some things that are better left unsaid."

"Not when I know they are. Not when I see what I see in your eyes. For the love of God, I'm your husband, Peg, the father of the child you're carrying. If I've done something so terrible, the least I deserve after all these years is the chance to make up for it. And I don't even know what! I can't fight ghosts! *I've got to know!* Because it wasn't only in front of you. Ike Press was there, the others. Men I see every day in my work. Men I'll be facing tomorrow in the hospital. I can't go on playing guessing games, Peg! I'll have to know what it is I see in *their* eyes!" His voice rose tortured and hoarse and then was suddenly silent.

"Suppose I do tell you," she said, after a pause. "Suppose it changes things."

"Then I'll have to face it."

"Because, although last night may be a blank for you, it isn't for me, or the others. There's no way of removing it or wishing it away. It happened. And, like Mac, you may wish it never had and want everything to go on as it was. But I'm warning you, you may not be as fortunate. You understood; you were compassionate. I *don't* understand! And I can't forget or excuse or be magnanimous—if that's what your story was supposed to achieve. I can't take your cue, cleverly calculated as it was."

"It wasn't calculated and it wasn't supposed to achieve a thing. You asked and I told you."

"And now you've asked, and I'm telling you." Her voice broke. "And I'm not going to soften it. You wanted to know, and I'm not going to spare a single, sordid detail!"

She started, her words tentative and groping. "Do you remember coming back from the boat with Luiz? You had a fresh bottle of tequila because you'd already done away with one. And you kept drinking, God, how you kept drinking, anything and everything, all mixed together, and no one could stop you. We tried to keep you from going to the *cantina* because we knew there'd be trouble. You climbed out a toilet window and you got there, and there was trouble. You were ready to take on anyone. 'Come on, you yellow belly sons o' bitches!' you shouted."

She plunged on, her words gathering momentum and sardonic coloration. Incredulously he listened to the blow-by-blow description of his encounter with the Californians, to the story of the broken nose, the beating, the free-for-all, his assault on Ted and her. It was as if she were talking about a third person, a creature alien to his attitudes, feelings. So strange to think of himself as a barroom brawler.

" 'Whore!' you called me, shouted it, screamed it at me."

"In the *cantina?*" he asked numbly.

"In the *cantina.* In front of all the natives and tourists, in front of Frank, Bert, Ted, Ike Press. And that was nothing. It was only a prelude. It wasn't till we got you back to the motel, and you were safely 'out' on the bed—or so we thought—that you really let go! You saw that gas heater. Do you know you tore it out of the wall and heaved it at us? That you aimed a bottle at Bert's skull? That you ripped up the place, went berserk, swinging, slugging, smashing at everyone of us?"

Her headlong recital piled detail on clinical detail, called up the scent and taste of blood and violence. Alex listened in shock and revulsion. It was unthinkable, beyond comprehension. And yet, the more fantastic and unreal it sounded, the more authentic it became. Willessly, repelled, he found himself drawn into the sick and frenzied atmosphere of the charged motel room, becoming one with the manic, possessed creature, uttering its slobbering animal cries as it flailed, thrashed, and bashed in mad fury.

Although it was fully in character with this tale of the idiot amok, the phrase: *Jew bastard!* hit him with the stunning impact of a rock hurled at his temple.

A hoarse denial rasped out of him, a mangled sound of horror and disbelief.

"Jew bastard! Son of a bitch Jew bastard! You kept repeating it over and over. It was a Jew plot. We were out to get you, poison you, do away with you. *I was! I!* Because I wanted to marry Ted and keep the Strauss fortune in the faith!"

No, he wanted to shout. I didn't. I couldn't. Yet something told him he had, and he crumpled to the sofa, a cry strangling in his throat. And Peg, as if afraid the slightest pause might bring her to a stop, hurried on, relentless, piling horror on grim horror, adumbrating the crude catalogue of anti-Semitic obscenities, of his warped accusations, of his charges against Dan, pouring out the whole paranoid parade of hate and filth.

Suddenly the rush of her words stopped. And the void which should have been silence was an echo chamber; the room resounded with the hollow babel of all she'd said, with the muffled mockery of her accusations, the words chasing each other in a mad mumble.

"You asked," she said in afterthought, "how I knew Mac's eyes were brown. Do you know how?"

He looked at her numbly, without moving, without a word.

"Not that it matters. No, it doesn't matter at all . . ." Her words trailed off, and again she lapsed into a silence which was no silence.

No, it didn't matter. Nothing mattered any more, Alex felt.

"Perhaps I shouldn't have told you. Perhaps I should have kept quiet," Peg said uncertainly.

He didn't answer. All he could do was sit like a stone and wish he were stone. It became intolerable.

"Should I have?" she asked, and there was fear in her voice again and fright in her eyes, as if she were expecting something to happen, something as terrible, perhaps, as the things she'd been telling him.

And still he couldn't say anything, couldn't reassure her, couldn't throw himself on her mercy, couldn't abase himself, couldn't communicate in any way the shame, the sorrow, and sadness that such as he could exist, sit in the same room, breathe the same air. And suddenly he couldn't. He had to get out and away.

He was on his feet. Stumbling toward the door and out.

"Alex," he heard her call after him.

He was running, heading up the driveway, throwing himself into the car.

"Alex!" cried Peg, stepping out on the porch.

He backed the car down the driveway with the roar and speed of a missile taking off. And she was running after him, running to the walk and shouting: "Alex! Wait, Alex! Alex, please!" There was terror in her voice now, because she was probably convinced that this was last night all over again. And it might be. Or that he'd kill himself by speeding. And that could be, too. The mood he was in could lead to the one or the other or both. Because he had to do something. Something to take him out of himself, to remove him from the awful prospect of having to confront and live with himself.

He shot up the street, scudded around the corner, turned another on two wheels. When he reached Benedict Canyon, he really let it out. The Ferrari zoomed down the clear stretches; it tore around the sharp turns; it darted out of lane to pass cars on hills and curves; rocketed toward oncoming traffic with a recklessness which invited collision and miraculously escaped it by split-second swerves. Time after time he'd squeeze out of an impossible situation only to head straight into another. It was as though he was creating hazardous situations to keep his mind concentrated on the immediate, to shut out what was and what would be.

There were moments when the reality of what he'd done would sneak up on him, stab into his mind, and he'd race furiously toward an oncoming car and say, now, now, let it happen! and veer away at the very last moment because it wasn't only his life but the life or lives of those in the other car, and the old training, the white knight versus black knight battle would reassert itself and Sir Galahad, having won another joust in his quest for an immortality he no longer craved, would tell himself he'd streak up that topmost curve with the sheer drop on the other side and plunge headlong through space to the bottom. But always a car would show up, and before he knew it he was over the canyon and in the Valley and hurtling, hell-bent down the Sepulveda Highway toward Calabasas.

Speed wasn't enough. The burden of last night rode with him as palpable as a passenger on the seat beside him. It went against everything he stood for, everything he believed in. The very concept was anathema to him. As a scientist and human being he couldn't countenance racism or intolerance in any form.

And yet he'd said these things! Somewhere, from some murky bin, from some festering convolution of his brain this filth had issued. And what he as a rational, conscious being thought and believed had nothing to do with the thought processes of this hidden being, this dark presence within. Oh to remove it as a deft surgeon removes a malignancy!

The scalpel, doctor.

Not so simple, is it?

A carcinoma, yes. Cut, snip, scrape. But a thought, doctor? An emotion? A hidden prejudice?

Can you put your hand on it? Find it? Cope with it? When you don't know. Don't know it exists even. Until one unguarded moment, on a devil's carnival of a night, you find yourself on a darkened stage, the curtain suddenly lifting, the glare from a hissing arc light hitting you in all your nakedness, revealing the Dark Presence within which has now taken over and become all of you and, in the white glare, like an exhibitionist in a peep show, you twist and squirm and writhe in a macabre dance full of bumps and grinds and every obscenity of posture and gesture, and from your throat, in ribald croak, come the rancid verses of a prurient song.

Know thyself, Alex! It comes not from nowhere. It is in you. Hidden it lies and suddenly it strikes. And what has been covered is revealed. You act, therefore you are!

The neon lights of a bar. Another. Slow the car. Stop. And go in and start all over? Why not? It was expected of him, wasn't it? That was his fate. Fate is character, he'd read somewhere. And if that's the kind of character he was, then why fight it? Besides, he wanted a drink, wanted a couple of good stiff ones. Because somewhere, somehow he had to get rid of the passenger on the seat beside him, duck his shadow. Though the Dark Presence was within.

He got out of the car, slammed shut the door, walked resolutely into the bar.

"Johnny Walker, Black Label. Double," he ordered.

II

A cool combo. Piano, sax, bass, and drums. Cerebral. Intricate. Atonal. Gershwin sired by Toch. Porter by Schönberg. Fancy arpeggios, tricky glissandos. Cool. Dispassionate. Head music. What's the matter boy, don't we show what we feel any more? The cool generation. We do not engage. Feelings on ice. If only some of it would rub off on him. That's just the way he'd like to play it now. Cool, man, cool.

The girl in slacks and apron put the Johnny Walker on the table. Alex sat contemplating the amber liquid. Now that he had it before him it was no longer a matter of urgency. He could take it or leave it. Once started, chances were it wouldn't bring the quick oblivion he sought. Which would lead to another and another until the chain reaction was in force, and God knows where it would end. He might even top last night. Now that he'd shown this unexpected talent, he might as well see how accomplished he really was. No telling what potential he had. Anything was possible. A little rape, mayhem, murder. Anything at all might happen. Of course, he might be slugged or shot in the process. Or hauled off to Camarillo in a strait jacket. And would the newspapers have themselves a ball! *Beverly Hills Surgeon Runs Amok! Mad Doctor Mutilates Murder Victim! Jekyll-Hyde Strikes Again!* Fine! Let them smear it for all to see. Peg, Press, Frank, Bert, and Ted. Wasn't that what they were expecting of him?

Nonsense! What was he trying to do? Put the onus on them? Take it out on others because he was unwilling to face himself? If he wanted the drink, there it was. Nobody was pushing him. Nobody had forced him to keep drinking at San Vicente.

He raised the glass, hesitated.

This wasn't the answer. Oh, it might numb things for a few hours. But when it wore off? Sooner or later—and it might as well be sooner—he'd have to face the portent and meaning, the sober and shabby truth of last night, the who and what of Alex Frazier.

The rasp of the saxophone was an abrasive. The thick swirl of smoke, the din of drunken voices, the shrill bursts of concupiscent laughter, the crash of a falling chair made the place unbearable. He put down the glass, walked quickly out.

He was no longer trying to break any speed records; he was hardly conscious of driving. For the first time his mind was deliberately turned to the problem he'd been fleeing. To the consequences. It was foolhardy to imagine that there wouldn't be consequences—as drastic perhaps as his transgression against the code of acceptable behavior. An egregious action begets its reactions. He'd already encountered them: in Finch's snub, in Ted's brush-off, in the abrupt and early departure of Frank, Bert, and Ike Press. But they couldn't go on avoiding him, nor he them. Nor could he expect them to remain passive.

God almighty, could you in one atavistic lapse become everything you abominated!

If he had reason to despise himself, what must Peg feel?

He knew. Had known since he woke in the shambles of that motel room to find her standing over him. Hung-over as he was, he'd sensed a strangeness in her. A coldness and a wariness that had nothing to do with any attitude she'd ever displayed toward him. She'd been repelled by him. Every twinge of revulsion had registered. Now that he knew why, how could he blame her?

Ever since he was grown he'd had a certain image of himself. He'd considered himself honest, prided himself on being a principled and decent human being. Now there was egg on that image. Dirt. Excrement.

How little we know ourselves. We look back to a moment of courage, an act of integrity and say: *Ecce homo!* Strange that one such moment should linger in his mind now.

It wasn't such a monumental thing. He'd merely stood by a

friend when he needed him. At any other time he wouldn't have given it a second thought. Coming as it did at the height of the hysteria of the early fifties, it had taken on an ominous coloration. Dick Lerner had been called before a congressional committee and refused to co-operate. As a result he'd been dropped from the staff of Olive, cut off from research. In outrage Alex had written a letter of protest, which Dan and he circulated around Memorial for signatures. A meeting called by a committee from several hospitals was scheduled, and he was asked to read it and appeal for more signatures. Arthur, who'd heard about the meeting, pleaded with him not to, warned against the consequences. Frightened as he was by Arthur's tone, he couldn't think of backing down. The threat of a possible subpoena hung over him for weeks. Luckily it had never materialized, and he'd never been hurt. But he could just as easily have been, and it gave him a certain satisfaction to know that in the time of the smear he'd refused to be intimidated.

But last night *he* had smeared! He'd taken a fine surgeon and made a quack of him, defiled his reputation, tried, by climbing over his back, to secure that damned appointment. And ended up by triggering off the abomination of last night. He was faced with it now, with all the sordid and brazen truths which had come tumbling out of him, all the blustering, bully demands of a swollen ego, of an ambition so twisted, a corruption so sick that he couldn't tolerate or live with himself.

Was he that warped, depraved? His image so defaced? Oh to smash it, smash it against that tree!

A row of giant eucalypti looming ahead. His foot pushing down on the pedal. The Ferrari spurting toward the huge trunk of the first tree.

The tree growing bigger now. The wind whining in his ears. Under him the throb and clamor of the motor. And inside the rush of blood sluicing through the ventricles of his heart as he raced toward crash-contact, closing his eyes, shutting it out, crying *mea culpa*, and begging forgiveness of Peg, Dan, God. Damn

God! Why wasn't there some way to undo, erase? There must be some way to blot out, make up for the horror which he'd perpetrated!

Frantically his hands yanked the wheel to the left. He heard the screech of tires, felt the helpless, suspended sensation of sitting in an uncontrolled vehicle skidding in a crazy, zigzag of directionless movement, then spinning suddenly as metal hit concrete and a fender came shearing off in one prolonged scream which left a grating echo in his ears. The car bumped to a stop in a shallow rutted culvert, and he sat stunned and dazed while headlights of approaching cars blinded him and sped by.

The whoosh-whoosh-whoosh of passing traffic suddenly ceased. Darkness came. He sat still, trembling, asking himself what he was doing here alive and whole when he should be insensible and dead at the base of that eucalyptus tree. Why at the moment of crash-contact had he yanked the wheel? Was it panic, fright, lack of guts? A whimsical stubbornness that wouldn't allow him to yield to his old enemy, the Black Knight? No, the need for surcease was stronger than any of these. He yearned for it now. But he wanted something else, too. Wanted to repudiate by some token or gesture what he'd done. How was another matter. Having spewed out the anti-Semitic poison, what could he say? That he didn't mean it? Who would believe him?

But he *could* say he'd lied about Dan. Admit that out of desperation and self-interest and envy he'd tried to ruin the reputation of the man who was getting the appointment he coveted for himself. He owed it to Dan. And to Ike Press. The least he could do was try to remove any questions his accusations might have raised in Ike's mind.

For a moment he sat becalmed. However small the gesture in the face of the vast wrong he had committed it came from a decent impulse.

He started the motor. The wheels spun without making traction. He got out to look for hunks of wood or boards to put under the tires. The stream of traffic roared past, headlights jabbing at him and sweeping on. He heard the squeal of a brake. An MG was pulling up. A friendly couple, in the fraternal tradition of sports car owners, stopped to ask if they could help. They scoured around for a few moments, unable to find anything but twigs.

"Wait a minute," said the young man, and opening the trunk of his car, pulled out some tire chains. "Just came from the snow," he explained.

He spread the chains in an S shape at the back wheels.

The tires bit into the chains; the car started up out of the rut. Before it could slide back, the young man wedged a rock behind the back wheel. It held. Again he spread out the chains. This time Alex was able to get the car up and out.

"Shame about the fender," said the young man. "That's a beaut of a car."

"As long as you didn't get hurt," said the girl. "You're lucky."

"Yes, I guess I am." For the moment, in some odd way, Alex felt he was. Perhaps because someone was humanly concerned. "Thanks for the hand," he said gruffly.

"Any time," said the young man, throwing the chains back into the trunk.

If you could start over with people you didn't know, Alex reflected as he eased into the line of traffic. If you could start fresh with nobody knowing.

The car made its way back over Ventura and into the Canyon. Without any conscious planning he found himself turning into Foothill and passing Ike Press's house. It was after eleven, but the lights were lit. He drove on, wondering whether he dared stop by. He wanted to, wanted to get it off his chest—and knew he didn't have the guts. Besides, Ike was probably about to go to sleep and it wasn't fair to barge in on him. God knows, he'd given him a sleepless night last night. Yet in fairness to Dan, late or no, it was precisely what he should do. Because if Ike was sufficiently upset by his charges against Dan, he might relay them to Arthur or other Board members. He might get to them first thing in the morning. He couldn't in good conscience allow it.

The lights were still on when he circled the block. The urgency to unburden himself grew as he continued to drive on, circling a second and third time. He pulled up to the curb, torn between conscience and shame. If the lights weren't out within five minutes, he told himself, he'd go up and ring the doorbell.

III

THE LIGHTS remained. Within seconds after his ring Ike Press opened the door. Although he was trained to mask his feelings there was a tell-tale jump in his eyes.

"Oh, it's you," he said in a controlled voice.

"I hope you'll forgive me. It's hardly an hour to go calling, I know."

"I was, as a matter of fact, about to go to bed."

"I'm terribly sorry," Alex mumbled. "I really had no right to—"

"You're here," Ike Press said coldly. "Now what is it that's on your—?"

"Who is it, dear?" asked a feminine voice, and a moment later Mrs. Press, a matronly woman in a velvet pegnoir of faded blue, appeared in the hallway. She'd just come from the kitchen and was carrying a small tray with two cups.

Motioning Alex to step in, Ike Press said, "I don't know whether you've ever met Dr. Frazier. Doctor, Mrs. Press."

Mrs. Press's eyes widened. Severity set into her countenance. "Oh, so *you're* Dr. Frazier," she said glacially. She turned to her husband. "Here's your Ovaltine, dear." Then sardonically, "Would *you* like some Ovaltine, doctor?"

Alex shook his head. The rebuke was so obvious that his face reddened. Ike had of course told her.

"You'll excuse me," Mrs. Press said bluntly, "but I'm going to bed. And if you don't mind my saying so, darling, I don't think you'd better stay up either."

"I'll be up presently."

Mrs. Press swept majestically up the stairs, the blue pegnoir ballooning behind her.

"What's on your mind, Frazier?" asked Ike Press. He remained standing, clearly determined to make the conversation a short one.

Alex hesitated. "It's about last night."

"Last night's a pretty big subject and, frankly, I don't know but that I haven't had quite enough of it."

"I can understand that," said Alex in a crushed voice. "I'd like to apologize, though I know there isn't any apologizing for what I did, or any explaining or undoing. But one thing I'd like to set straight. About Dan Simon—"

"You made yourself quite clear on that score," Ike Press said grimly. "If you've come to influence me further—"

"I came to tell you that what I said was untrue. Dan's my friend, and I don't want anything I said—"

"Do you have any idea of *what* you said?"

"Peg told me," he said in an abashed voice.

"You realize you made a very serious charge against him."

"I don't know whether it was a drunken conceit or—"

"You accused him of malpractice. You know that?"

"It's simply not true. That's why I came, late as it is, because I felt you ought to know that it was out of the whole cloth. The last person in the world to be accused of malpractice is Dan. You could just as soon say it about me. Sooner. Dan's the soul of caution about surgery. I'm the radical. And as for fees, Dan's as fair and honest as they come. It's no secret I wanted the appointment. That I should stoop so low as to malign Dan, who's been such a friend—"

"Unfortunately, you did."

"There's absolutely no foundation for what I said about him. I wish you'd take my word for it."

"It's easy to make charges, Frazier. Not so easy to undo them. I'll have to look into it now."

"There's really no need. You won't find a thing."

"That's for me to decide," Ike said sharply.

"I feel sick about it." Alex's voice faded. "I hate to embarrass Dan. He really deserves the appointment."

"That will be voted on on Wednesday."

Alex glanced up, puzzled. Was he implying that his name was still under consideration?

"I'm withdrawing my name, of course," he said quickly.

Ike Press didn't say a word. A self-conscious silence encompassed them.

"If anyone ever merited that appointment," Alex repeated awkwardly, "it's Dan."

"The Board is quite capable of deciding who merits appointments without your recommendation," Ike said brusquely. Then, after a pause, "Now if you don't mind, I would like to get to bed."

"Of course." Alex turned to the door, opened it, stopped. "Thank you," he mumbled, "for listening."

Ike Press didn't say anything.

"And will you please ask Mrs. Press to forgive me for disturbing you at this hour. I know I had no right—" His voice trailed off. He took a step out, stopped again. "I'm sorry. Sorry about last night . . ."

"So am I," Ike Press said sternly.

"Good night," said Alex, and stumbled to the car.

For a moment he sat immobilized at the wheel, wishing somehow that he could disappear, dissolve into nothingness. The idea of going to the hospital tomorrow, the thought of having to face Bert, Ted, Frank, or anyone else who might have heard about San Vicente filled him with terror. He couldn't even countenance the idea of facing Peg. It wasn't merely disapproval or censure which he dreaded. It was a sense of shame so deep that it felt unseemly and indecent to show his face.

Right now, at this very moment, as the car turned into Bedford and nosed toward home, he knew he couldn't stay there. He simply didn't have the courage—or gall—to come back as if nothing had happened. How could he look at Peg? How talk to her? He could no more face her than she seemed able to face him. And it was he who was the offender, he who had desecrated and profaned twenty years of a relationship based on love, respect, trust. . . .

He needed time, as she did, to assimilate what had happened. They needed the distance to judge its significance, to weigh just what it meant in terms of a future relationship—if any were now possible. They needed respite, a period of lull in which the raw hurts might abate, the heat of emotions wane, the self-consciousness subside. Then they could talk and see whether there was any going on or if it wasn't already over.

He knew what he had to do now. He'd stop at the house, pick up what he needed, and then register at the Beverly Hills Hotel.

As he approached the house he was dismayed to see the lights in their bedroom and in the spare room. He should have known, of course, that Peg would be upset about his wordless and wild departure. He'd torn out of the place as if he were hell-bent to destroy himself. And she'd probably waited in fearful anticipation of an emergency call from the police. If he'd had any consideration, he'd have called from the bar to tell her not to worry. She was probably sitting up in bed trying to find distraction in a book. Well, there wasn't much choice about it. He'd better go up and tell her he was all right and what he planned to do. Perhaps, if luck were with him, she might out of sheer exhaustion have fallen asleep with the light on. Then he could leave a note, gather his things softly, and tiptoe out.

For twenty minutes he sat in the cold of the open Ferarri willing it to happen, if it hadn't already, hoping that the light would go out and after a suitable interval he'd be able to steal up the stairs. Nothing happened. It was after midnight when he let himself in and tiptoed carefully up the carpeted stairs, stopping with each squeak.

The bedroom door was open. The cover was turned down, but she wasn't there. Propped up against the lamp on the night table was a note. "Am sleeping in spare room," it read. "Am tired and didn't want to be wakened when you got in." It was a polite way of saying: keep away, I don't want any part of you. But, for the moment, he was relieved.

Taking out a bag, he started to gather enough changes to last a week. He moved quietly, but a floor board creaked under his foot and he heard Peg call: "Alex, is that you?"

Everything in him cramped. His heart hopped. "Yes," he said.

"Are you all right? I was about ready to call the police."

"I should have phoned. Yes, I'm all right."

She didn't say anything, and he made no move toward the connecting room.

"I saw Mr. Press," he added. "To get the record straight on Dan."

Silence as if she were weighing what to say. When she did speak it was off the subject. "There was a call from the hospital about five minutes after you left. From Steve Fried. In relation to Dick Lerner, who'd just been admitted. They were getting him ready for surgery, and he asked for you."

"Surgery!"

"He had a perforated ulcer."

He picked up the phone, dialed, asked for the extension. "Steve? Alex," he said. "Sorry as hell I wasn't in. What's with Dick?"

"He gave us a few anxious moments, but everything seems to be under control. He's in the recovery room. Did you know he had a cardiac history?"

"No. He never said a word."

"I called Greenstadt as soon as I found out. I don't know whether we'd have got through it without him."

"Oh, Christ! As if he hadn't had his share. I'll hop right over."

"No point. You couldn't talk to him, anyway. And Greenie isn't budging till he knows it's okay."

"It's got to be."

"Will be—if Greenie has anything to say about it."

It was a relief to know Dick was in Greenie's capable hands. There wasn't a better cardiac man on the coast.

Poor Dick. If he didn't pull through then there was no *yoisher*, as Peg would put it. Funny that he should be falling back on a Yiddishism now. *Yoisher* would have chosen him, not Dick. And how much more sense it would have made. Because Dick, after having been dropped from the research project at Olive and having grants withdrawn in St. Louis and Boston—he'd had to start all over in private practice—had finally landed the job at Cal Tech. He was functioning with his customary zeal and brilliance, in research, where he belonged. But he was still carrying his private practice as a kidney consultant and giving odd hours to his nephritis studies. Alex had pleaded with him just two weeks ago that he drop his practice. "You keep on working eighteen hours a day, and something's going to give," he'd warned. "I can't," Dick had protested. "I've had three grants shot out from under me, and it can happen again. The practice is the one thing I'm sure of." What avail to argue there was nothing anyone could be sure of except that some day the man with the scythe would come along and no predicting when? Dick might still hold him off. He had to. Because it was too appalling to think that after all the stupid waste, after being at last restored to the useful functioning of his talent, it would come to such an absurd and senseless end. Even knowing that there was no *yoisher*, that life was not governed by reason, sense, justice, or worth, Alex still couldn't give up the hope that in this case a more rational design would prevail.

Peg was asking about Dick. He told her. And for a moment they were united in anxiety for the fate of a man they both revered. Then the reality of his own situation returned, and Alex told her of his plan to go to the Beverly Hills. Peg started to say it wasn't necessary, but there was no conviction in her words; it was almost as if she were asking him to insist on it.

"I think it is," he said.

She was silent a moment, then said, "I won't pretend that I'm not confused or that I don't need time to think this through."

"We both do."

He closed the lid of the bag, fastened it, and started out.

"If anything comes up, or if you need me, call me at the Beverly Hills," he said.

Walking down the stairs, he couldn't help wondering if she would and if he'd ever come back.

He was about to switch off the light when his eye fell on the Levine water color in the living room. Odd how that picture affected him. This time more than ever before. Because he suddenly felt as desolate as the two figures plodding uphill against the rain which sieved down on the bleak walks of the street.

IV

THE SECONAL didn't help. In the sleepless nights of the past when a problem, like a pesky mosquito, droned endlessly in his mind, there usually came a point when the drug took effect. Not tonight. Try as he might to shut out thought, his mind was as active as a battery recharging.

When he wasn't pursued by the nightmare reminders of San Vicente, he'd find himself thinking about Dick, or Dan. He'd have to face Dan, tell him, because inevitably it would get back to him. Devastating as it might be, he'd rather suffer the agony of such a confession than have it come from someone else. That he'd lose him as a friend went without saying.

These were the two men whose friendship had meaning for him. Their lives had touched and twined ever since their freshman days at Yale. Tonight he knew that he'd destroyed his relationship with one, and the other lay in a recovery room with his life in question.

And Peg, whom he loved, lay alone in the big house, he alone here. He saw no answer. His world seemed to be blowing up on him.

There was no lying still, no rest. Sitting up, he swung his legs over the side of the bed. Immobile, he stared out into the darkness as if hoping to summon up some reason for what had happened, to grasp a bit of sense out of the madness. It made no sense—unless you believed in demons. Try as he might he couldn't identify himself with the monster of last night, with the pathetic paranoid creature spewing venom and shrilling accusations of conspiracies to do him in, to "deprive him," to keep the stupid money "in the faith." This, after he'd boasted to Peg that he wanted no part of Joe Strauss's money, that he preferred his own. He'd believed it then, did now.

Oh, he'd resented Joe Strauss, resented the fact that Peg's brother was rewarded with huge hunks of Strauss real estate because his marriage was a Jewish marriage and Peg denied because she'd married a goy. It wasn't the money, it was the idea—or so he'd thought. Maybe it was a money-hunger, a greed that went down deep. Conscious or unconscious, it had to be in you to come out of you.

No, it didn't come from nowhere. All the bigot phrases and gutter shibboleths of his childhood which were part of the air he breathed, all the pap about the Jews killing Christ, all the epithets which studded the language like four letter words: kike, Hebe, sheeny, Jew bagel . . . Izzy Katz coming down the street from Hebrew school, the gang lying in wait and pounce! when he rounded the corner. "Kiss the cross, Jew bagel." "Show us where the rabbi took a slice of it." And down with his pants and someone smearing dog-do on his circumcized member.

So many years since he'd thought of these things. He hadn't liked them then and had buried them deep, long, long ago. But he hadn't exorcised them and, remembering now, he felt unclean and wanted to cut and run, as fast and far away as he could go. . . .

But that wasn't getting to sleep; it wasn't getting the rest he'd need to command the response of an alert mind and quick reflexes when he went into Surgery the next morning. He couldn't take a second Seconal, couldn't risk waking with his senses dulled.

The faint sounds of a dance orchestra, probably from the restaurant below, wafted in through the open window. He decided that a half hour's distraction wouldn't hurt. Perhaps he'd try the Press recipe, order a cup of warm Ovaltine.

The orchestra was playing an old Ellington mood piece when he got down. It was a number called "Solitude," and he'd first heard it on a jukebox after Peg and he had returned from Mexico. They were driving up to the Cape for a holiday and had stopped at an eating place on the New Bedford Bridge. He remembered it so vividly because it was perched high above the water, and a sudden downpour of rain, beating on the tin roof, added a melancholy accent which always crept in whenever they heard the piece afterwards. It was there now, and he missed Peg as he never had.

He couldn't help wondering if he hadn't made a mistake in coming to the hotel. If Peg had any idea of wanting a separation, this was making it very easy for her. He'd acted precipitously and, though she'd said it was unnecessary, she hadn't really tried to dissuade him. Wistfully, he wished she had. Not, he realized, that he had any right to expect her to.

Sitting disconsolate, caught in the song's last somber phrase, he was startled to see a menu thrust in front of him. He hadn't noticed the approach of the waiter. As if by reflex his hand went to his pocket for his reading glasses. If he were going to order Ovaltine, he might as well have something to go with it. Sandwich, cake, pie, he mused, his eye moving down the card.

Out of nowhere, a voice, bemused and mildly reproachful, said: "You shouldn't be wearing glasses. No one with eyes like yours should be wearing glasses."

Alex looked up to meet the solemn, quizzical gaze of a young woman of twenty-eight. She was standing near the table, a drink in one hand, the other groping toward a chair. The hand took hold and with it seemed to restore an uncertain balance. Her cheeks were flushed, her mien drunkenly earnest. Her red hair swept up and was piled loosely on her head in the style of an old-fashioned Gibson girl. "Do you mind if I sit down?" she asked.

He shook his head.

Her hand still gripping the chair, she took a step forward, turned sideways, lowered herself stiffly and cautiously to the seat, then turned forward. Her gaze, intent as before, fastened on his eyes.

"You have such blue eyes," she said. "It's a shame to wear glasses when you have such blue eyes."

"I only wear them when I'm reading."

"You're not reading."

Alex took them off.

"Sad," she said. "You look sad. Doesn't she love you?"

"Not tonight," said Alex.

"He doesn't love me, either. Not tonight, never. Sad. Isn't it sad?"

"Very."

"Said he was going to New York. He didn't go to New York. Went to her. Always going to her. Thinks I sit home and cry. Am I crying?"

He shook his head.

"I can go out, too. You think I need him? I don't need him." She paused. "Don't wear glasses, Blue Eyes. Never wear glasses. Promise?"

"Promise."

The orchestra was playing "Laura."

"Dance?" she said.

"I'd rather not."

"Please," she coaxed.

"Later," he said.

But she was rising, reaching for his hand. "Please."

He got up, helped her to her feet. She clung to him, managed somehow to follow his step. The heat of her body, the yielding weight of her breasts, the mingled scent of perfume, alcohol, and perspiration combined to stir his senses. She stumbled suddenly, stopped, her face burrowed in the hollow of his shoulder, and he caught the muffled sound of her weeping.

"Suppose we get back to the table," he said, when she'd had a moment to get control of herself.

"I'm all right," she said. "Be fine after I powder my nose. Excuse me." She straightened up. "You won't go away now?"

He shook his head.

"Promise?"

"Promise."

She squeezed his hand. "Good. Because I don't want you running out on me." She looked up at him. "You have such blue eyes. . . ."

He stood looking after her as she wove her way toward the Ladies' Room, the scent of her still in his nostrils. If he didn't go he had the feeling he'd end up in bed with her and, for a moment, he was tempted. What better way to shed everything that had happened, to lose himself, find surcease? He needed human solace just as she did. He needed the release, the exhaustion, the good sleep of fleshly giving. Why shouldn't he give in to the spin of desire which had so palpably taken hold of him?

As if he needed an answer. Never in the twenty years had he ever cheated on Peg, never felt the urge or given it a serious thought.

Now?

He still couldn't. Even in this tenuous moment of their relationship when finis may already have been written on the twenty years.

He turned, walked quickly across the floor and out into the lobby, continuing on to the elevator without a break in stride.

In his room he undressed, then started to draw the drapes. For a moment he stood looking out on the moonlit lawn, his forehead touching the dark windowpane, as lost and forlorn as in the days when he'd first come to live with the Fraziers. He'd get up in the middle of the night and stand looking out the window, as he was now, feeling adrift in an infinity of space and skies and darkness, an outsider, not rooted, not belonging, wondering what he was doing there.

He felt as abandoned now and wished he could wish himself out of this situation which he'd so stupidly precipitated, wished somehow that he could remove the week-end as you could pages out of a calendar and that Peg, the Peg of three days ago, were lying in the bed ready to turn to him, alert even in her sleep to his step. If he ever needed her, he needed her now.

But that was fantasy. Reality was a cold, empty bed in a cheerless hotel room. Reality was Mrs. Ruth Levitt, scheduled for surgery at seven-thirty A.M., Operating Room Two, Memorial Hospital. Reality was facing the accusing or avoiding eyes of Bert, Frank, Ted in some corridor or lounge at the hospital, at some unexpected moment—if face them he could, if he had the guts to go there in the first place.

Well, he wasn't thinking about it now. He wasn't thinking about a thing but going to bed and getting enough sleep to perform an always touchy operation on the heart.

At five, forty-five A.M. the hotel operator's buzz woke him. For a long, befogged moment he resisted opening his eyes. And after he did, he was bewildered by the room's unfamiliarity. With recognition came remembrance of the whole sordid situation, which sleep had so blessedly veiled. He sat up, reached for a cigarette. His head felt heavy and dull, but he was aware of the tremor in his hand as he struck the match and brought it shakily to the cigarette. It bothered him more than he cared to admit. He took a few puffs, hoping somehow that the jump of his nerves would subside. Slowly he lifted his arm, holding it straight in front of him. No matter what strain he'd been under his hand had always been steady. It wasn't now. But he'd better not get panicky about it because it would only get worse.

A hot, steaming shower, though enervating, relaxed him. He let it beat down, let the steam wisp into his nostrils. Shoulders drooped and arms dangling, he felt a nice lethargic limpness overcome him. Then he turned abruptly to the cold, turned it up full till it felt like pellets of hail storming down on him. He toweled himself briskly into dryness and felt renewed.

It was while he was dressing that he recalled his phone conversation with Steve Fried. Steve would probably go off duty at six. Hastily he dialed the hospital to see if he could reach him.

"Steve?" he said.

"Yes," Steve answered wearily.

"I was afraid I wouldn't catch you."

"I'm sorry you did—for what I have to tell you."

Alex's breathing stopped. He waited.

"It's all over. It was too much for his heart, and we couldn't do anything about it. God knows, we tried. The works. Greenie had a whole crew working on him. No go. All the king's horses and all the king's men—" His voice dwindled away, futile-sounding and sad.

Grief blocked Alex's throat. "God," he managed to whisper.

"He meant a lot to you, I guess," said Steve.

"A great deal."

"I heard you speak out for him when they dropped him from Olive. I admired your courage."

"Thanks," said Alex. He hung up slowly. A sob wrenched out of him. "Why couldn't it have been me?" he asked aloud. "Why couldn't it have been me?"

He sat humped over on the edge of the bed as if stricken. He should have gone, he told himself. Not that it would have been any different. Not that it would have helped or changed a thing. But that's where his place was. Yet he felt less guilty about that than about the fact that he, who was so unworthy, had been spared and Dick, who had everything to live for, had not. Fate, if it had a mind, used it perversely.

Poor Madge and the three boys. Dick was the center of their universe. As busy as he was, he always made time for an outing, an occasion, for the thoughtful word or act that animated their family life.

Dick wasn't religious in the ritualist sense of the term, so there would probably be no formal period of *sitting shiva*. But he should go to see them. Except that word of San Vicente might very well reach Madge, and then it would be ghastly. What might be even worse was her not knowing and naming him as pallbearer. Then he'd really be in a spot. He couldn't possibly accept and he couldn't very well refuse. It would be especially flagrant if they had a rabbi officiating. Chances were it would be a Unitarian service, which was more in keeping with Dick's beliefs. But that wouldn't really alter things. The whole prospect was so shattering that he sat trembling, incapable of deciding what to do or how to act, knowing only that he felt totally inadequate as a human being and as a friend who should be present and functioning in a time of crisis rather than feeling that he had to hide. He'd probably wind up by writing a long letter, which was a cowardly but diplomatic way of handling an untenable situation.

It all seemed so wrong. But, then, what could be wronger than an untimely death, than a life and talent so unjustly curtailed. It had no purpose, no meaning. Except to proclaim to the world that life was without meaning, except to mock man and his puny pretensions to reason and rationality.

Alex's mind went back to an evening in New Haven when Dorothy Horstman, Yale's famous virologist, had invited Dick and him to her birthday party. She'd had big ambitions for them, confided they had the temperament and mentality for research. What dreams they'd shared! Alex's had long since been dissipated. Dick had remained true to his—in spite of everything.

Alex wept now for his unfulfilled dreams—and for Dick's, which had been so abortively terminated.

With fumbling fingers, he pulled out a cigarette. The tremor in his hand was as pronounced as before. A feeling of helplessness overcame him. He couldn't possibly go through with the operation now. It was getting late, and he'd better do something about it, postpone it, or see if he could get Chris Sullivan to take over. But something held him back. Ben Levitt, perhaps. He felt he had to call him and explain. Which was strange, because this wasn't a private patient. Ruth Levitt was a clinic case. But in the fifteen minutes in which he'd talked to Ben Levitt, the man had communicated a feeling of such gratitude that it was he rather than anyone else who was going to do the surgery that he felt he'd be letting him down. Perhaps he'd been touched because he'd never seen a man so thoroughly devoted to and in love with his wife, nor anyone as frightened at the prospect of anything happening to her.

Alex called him now.

"What's the matter, Doc?" Ben Levitt asked in alarm. "Is something wrong with Ruth? She didn't start clotting again?"

"No. It's not that. It's just that something's come up, and I thought I ought to let you know. I'm transferring all my surgery cases to other doctors."

"No, Doc. You can't."

"I'll try to arrange for Dr. Sullivan or Dr. Simon."

"Look, Doc. Ruth's in the clinic, and I know we ain't got nothing to say about doctors, but if you don't do it, the way Ruth feels about it, there ain't going to be no surgery."

"Now that's very foolish, Mr. Levitt. The two surgeons I mentioned are every bit as good as I am."

"Like I say, Doc, we're in no position to tell you who or what. It ain't as if we were paying patients. But if it's a matter of money—"

"Money has nothing to do with this, Mr. Levitt."

"I filled out the forms. I wasn't lyin', Doc. We're broke. But maybe I can get Ruth's brother to take another mortgage on his house—"

"It isn't money. It's just that something has come up and—"

"Look, you can't do it, maybe you can persuade her to take someone else. I don't think so. We've been through it. You got to understand: Ruth's never been under a knife. She's scared. After all it ain't appendicitis. It's her heart. All right, so you say the operation's necessary. Dr. Greenstadt says it's necessary. But Ruth's scared to death. Till we persuaded her to consider it even! The only thing that convinced her is she's got absolute faith in you. It's like you're someone holy. The Lord God Jehovah or something. That's the way she feels about you. But someone else? She wouldn't hear of it. She wouldn't go through with it. I'm not making this up, Doc. All right so something's come up now—" His voice broke. "So what're you going to do, walk out on her, give her a death sentence? Because if it's not you, she's going to take her chances without surgery. . . ."

"You make it very hard, Mr. Levitt."

"I'm just telling you facts. Look, Doc. It's now six-thirty. The operation's scheduled for seven-thirty. One hour, Doc. Another and it's done. What's so hard? It's a life, Doc. Two. Because if anything happens to her—"

"That's no way to talk, Levitt," Alex said rather sharply.

"I suppose. It's unfair, I know. Why should I put it on you? After all, it's not your obligation."

Alex bit his lip. Strictly speaking, it wasn't. Chris or Dan would do the job. Or Dave Gordon, the chief surgical resident. With any one of them she'd be in good hands. Yet he did feel a sense of obligation. One, because Ruth Levitt would resist; two, because her fright might make the difference between success or failure in the operation. Weighing as much as these was the complete faith which the Levitts had in him, the utter and helpless dependence.

"You still there?" Ben Levitt was saying.

"I'm here."

"I know I put you on the spot, Doc."

"You did—and I'll be there," he said, and knew suddenly that he couldn't have done otherwise.

He could no more walk out on Ruth Levitt, when it came down to it, than he could let himself crash into that eucalyptus tree without first setting straight the matter of Dan Simon.

You are what is expected of you, he realized.

Knowing this didn't in any way diminish the ordeal of facing the hospital.

V

BERT'S car was heading into the hospital parking lot as Alex turned the corner. Rather than follow him into the lot and risk an encounter, he drove twice around the block. When he finally parked no one was in sight.

He walked quickly in through the doctors' entrance. Without looking at the attendant, he signed in. It was as if he feared that the story had already made its way around the hospital and that he'd find its reflection in the eye of any doctor, intern, nurse, orderly, or attendant.

He noted Bert's name on the tape. Dan Simon had signed in just before him and after Frank. They were probably having breakfast in the dining room. Usually he'd have his breakfast there also. But this morning, because he wanted to avoid people, he'd stopped at a Drive-In. He couldn't however restrain the impulse to glance in as he passed. They were sitting near the door. Frank was talking, Dan listening. Bert, who was facing the door, stared at him and through him, his eyes cold with contempt.

Alex turned and walked shakenly away. It's beginning, he told himself. Not that he could blame Bert. He wasn't even angry at Frank for telling Dan. It was simply that he would have preferred to tell him on his own. Of course he wasn't sure that Frank *was* telling him. He might just be talking about the fishing in San Vicente, or about other aspects of the trip, which were colorful enough without his particular contribution to the holiday hilarity.

Except for a couple of nurses and Miss Ribak, the operating room supervisor, Surgery was pretty deserted. Relieved, he proceeded to the dressing room, changed into a green scrub suit and the comfortable old glove-leather shoes with ridged rubber soles in which he usually operated. He was closing his locker when Chris Sullivan, towering big and burly, walked in.

"Hi!" he said affably. "How's the New Year treating you, Alex, old boy?"

Alex shrugged.

"A little subdued, are we?" He cocked his head. "You do look a little green around the gills. A little bit too much holiday dissipation, eh?"

"A little."

"I tied one on, myself. No better way to greet a new year. Happy, happy, man."

"Thanks," said Alex, anxious to get away from the Sullivan heartiness. "You too."

He walked out into the corridor. The sound of Bert's approaching voice made him turn to the first door and duck into an operating room.

"You never can tell about people," he heard Dan say as they passed.

He felt weak, as though he'd been hit in the solar plexus and all the wind knocked out of him. Well, Dan knew now. And others would, too. He wanted to cry aloud in his anguish. How could San Vicente have happened? How could he possibly have done and said the things he had? He sucked in his breath; it rustled out with a sob. There was no answer. And to dwell on it now was to invite madness. He fought for reason, calm. However much he might like to run, he had an obligation which he couldn't flee.

A few more minutes and he'd be set to go on Ruth Levitt and that *mitral stenosis*. He'd widen the constricted valve, sew her up, and be free of the feeling of obligation which the Levitts called up in him. Funny that he didn't feel the same way about his private patients. Perhaps because they were financially privileged and could command pretty much anything they wanted.

Alex stepped out into the corridor and turned to the bulletin board to find out in which of the rooms the operation was scheduled. Room two had been designated, but he was startled to find a line drawn through it. The room had apparently been preempted by an emergency case. Ruth Levitt's operation was rescheduled for nine-thirty.

He stood, staring at the chart, bewildered, unable to adjust to the unexpectedness of the change. Perhaps because he'd geared himself to this moment, screwed up all his resources—and suddenly found himself suspended, incapable of facing a simple two-hour wait. It was as if he'd been stricken helpless, not knowing where to turn, what to do or think.

Why, he asked himself, had they scratched his case rather than anyone else's. Not because it was less important. Goodman, for instance, had a hernia case. But then Goodman's was a private patient. Clinic cases could wait.

Miss Ribak was calling to him, explaining that she'd left a message with his exchange—apparently after he left. She was sorry. It was one of those things. There'd been a car crash, the driver was in critical condition, and there was no waiting.

Logical enough. But why his case rather than Blum's, which was also a clinic case? If it was a question of rank, he rated higher than Blum. Was something else involved?

It occurred to him that something was. That word of San Vicente had probably reached the front office. That Ike Press may have decided he owed it to the hospital to let Arthur know. He didn't blame Ike. His behavior of two nights ago couldn't be described as anything but psychotic. Wasn't it a responsible Board Member's duty to raise the question? There had probably been no accident or emergency case. They simply needed the time to talk it out, come to a considered decision. Question was, would they want him in the hospital at all now?

Why he was so upset, he didn't know. Just an hour ago he'd decided he wanted out. Nothing would have suited him better than the thought of never having to enter the place again. Now, perversely, because it was an actual possibility, he wanted to hang on. It seemed desperately important that he be allowed to continue at the hospital. Because if they eased him out here, question was whether he'd be welcome elsewhere. Rumor traveled; bad news had wings. If he ever needed the preoccupation of work it was now.

Chris Sullivan's voice, then Bert's. They were coming toward him. He pivoted, strode out the doors, and headed for the elevator.

"Happy New Year, Doctor."

He turned as Miss Roth, in her Beth Israel nurse's cap, came up. "Happy New Year," he said.

The light of the descending elevator passed his eyes. The door opened. Automatically he followed Miss Roth into the crowded cubicle. His eyes met Ted's. Ted looked away. Alex dropped his eyes. He was dirt. Let them ease him out. He didn't care.

He got out at the clinic. Ruth Levitt greeted him with pleased surprise. No one had let her know about the postponement.

"I'm glad you told me," she said. "I'd have bust a gut if I had to wait for two hours without knowing. I wonder if Ben knows."

"Probably not. I'll find him and tell him."

"He's probably on the front steps. When his brother had his stomach operation we sat on the front steps. That was five years ago, and it was cancer. And today he's as good as new. I hope I have that luck."

"You will."

"My old job's waiting for me if I'm okay. Ben talked to the boss yesterday. He says customers keep asking for me. Don't want anyone else doing their hair."

"I see you did a job on your own," said Alex.

"I wanted to look right—in case anything happened."

"Now that's showing great confidence in me. I've a good mind to muss it up."

A blush colored her face. It was as if she'd betrayed him by even thinking of such an eventuality.

"I deserved that," she said, and, with a sheepish smile, passed her fingers through her hair.

She was one of those rare women who looked as attractive with her hair rumpled as in place. If anything the disarray added a piquant note to the symmetry of her features. She'd been a show girl and model in her day and a very stunning one, he'd guess.

Because it was more comfortable and distracting, he stayed to chat a while. For the moment this was sanctuary. He refused to speculate over what was happening in Arthur's office. It was much more pleasant to talk about the old shows she'd been in. She was a *Vanities* girl and she'd graced the line in *Harry Delmar's Revels* and in *Oh, Please!*, the Beatrice Lillie revue. He'd seen the last two in their New Haven tryouts. Dick had, as a matter of fact, been with him at the opening night of *Oh, Please!* Because he wanted to please her, he pretended to remember more about the shows than he actually did.

But he couldn't sit talking all morning. He had his patients to check on. And, it suddenly occurred to him, he had some reading to do. In all the turmoil he'd completely forgotten that he was scheduled to lead a Clinical Pathological Conference at noon. The thought of standing up before the staff and presenting an analysis of an unusual case, then guiding the discussion—usually a challenge he enjoyed—filled him with dread. But he wasn't going to dwell on it. He had his rounds to make.

He avoided the elevator this time, walked up the stairs instead. He was strictly business now. Things were pretty much under control. The charts showed no crises for the days he was gone. He changed dressings on his lobectomy and sympathectomy patients. New chest X rays were ordered for a patient who complained of pain. Diets were altered, medications readjusted. He walked from room to room, brisk, efficient.

After he'd checked with the exchange, he recalled that he'd forgotten to tell Ben Levitt about the change in time. As Ruth predicted, he was sitting on the front steps, his face drawn and white.

He jumped up when he saw Alex, as grim as a prisoner facing a judge for sentence. Alex was quick to tell him.

"Crud," said Ben. "You mean to say I've got to go through that all over again? I feel as though I've been holding my breath underwater for an hour."

"Surface and exhale," said Alex. "I could use some air myself. Let's take a walk."

It was a clear day. In the distance he could see the Hollywood hills, brown and purple and burgeoning green. They walked around the block, and, as they returned, a Lincoln Continental, sleek and white, glided up to the curb. A chauffeur jumped out and hurried around to open the door. Coming down the stairs was Ike Press. He made straight for the car and entered it without noticing Alex. But Alex had noticed him and knew that the session with Arthur was over. What he didn't know was what they'd decided.

Whatever the decision, there was no indication on the bulletin board. The schedule remained as before. He was standing before it when Dan Simon came out of the first operating room.

"You know about Dick?" Dan said.

Alex nodded without turning from the bulletin board. He wondered why Dan was talking to him.

"The wrong people die," Dan said, after a pause.

The words hit him with the shocking suddenness of a knife thrust. He stood numb, cold, inert. Then as Dan continued to speak he realized that he'd probably misunderstood, that Dan hadn't meant what he, out of his own sense of guilt, had jumped to. At least not directly, because Dan was talking about someone else, a notorious film producer he'd just operated on, a man known for his ruthless manipulation of talent, business dealings, and a predatory and sadistic sex life, which had driven two wives to suicide.

"The bastard goes on that operating table with two strikes against him and a very dubious chance of getting off alive, and I do an endoartectomy that's so clean and smooth I know he's in. So Dick goes, and this *shtunk*, who'll probably cause a couple of more suicides, remains." Dan sighed. "It's a lousy crap game, and the dice are loaded in favor of the wrongos." His voice sounded bitter and weary. He looked up at Alex, who hadn't moved or taken his eyes off the board. "You're pretty subdued. Is it Dick or the two-day bender?"

"Both," he mumbled.

Dan moved down the corridor toward the lounge. "I could use a cup of coffee. How about you?"

"Just had some."

"Join me anyway. I want to talk."

Reluctantly, Alex followed him into the lounge. He didn't know whether he was up to the showdown that Dan was heading for. Not now. Not a half hour before surgery. He wanted to say: Look, Dan, let's talk about it later. Instead he found himself saying: "I'm sorry you had to hear it from the boys."

"Why? It sounds as though you had yourself a blast."

"It would have come better from me. I mean I don't want you to get the idea I was ducking. Because I did intend to tell you. I owed that to you. As well as an apology, which doesn't, of course, begin to make up for—"

"For what?"

"For the things I said."

"What did you say, precisely?"

"Didn't they tell you?"

"They told me you got yourself swacked and started throwing punches and breaking noses and ripping up the joint. Nothing that would call for an apology to me. As a matter of fact, it was probably very salutary. As good a way as any of getting things out of your system. The Roman Saturnalia had a function. A hell of a lot cheaper and probably more effective than a year on the couch."

Alex watched him fill a cup from the electric coffee pot. "I've changed my mind," he said, "I'll have one too."

It seemed inconceivable to him that Frank and Bert had told Dan so much and yet had told him nothing. He felt ashamed at having jumped to the conclusion that they'd give him away. They were obviously being very decent about it. It occurred to him that he didn't really have to tell Dan. Though he'd said enough to raise questions in his mind. Besides, he wouldn't really feel comfortable until he got it off his chest.

"The boys were very considerate," he said, "but they didn't tell you the whole story."

Dan took a sip of the coffee, pulled out a cigarette, and lit it. "I'm listening," he said.

Alex told him.

"Oh, for Chrissake!" Dan exploded in disbelief as Alex was talking. And when he finished, the incredulity was still there. "I wish the hell you hadn't told me," he finally said. "The boys didn't find it necessary to, and I don't know why the hell you did. Who asked you? What's the point? And what the hell am I supposed to do about it?"

"I don't know. I felt I owed it to you."

"What you owed me after indulging in that drunken bilge was the decency of silence. There are some things which you just let lie. And if you had any sense you wouldn't have embarrassed me with it. I like you, damn it. We've had a damn good relationship, and I don't want it disturbed. But I'm human. What shall I say, that I'm not sore, that I'm not affected? I am!"

He was suddenly silent. And Alex didn't know what to say or do.

"If you're so hungry for the goddamn appointment," Dan continued, "you can have it! If it's going to do this to us, who wants it!"

"I thought I did. But I don't now."

"Of course the reason I'm getting so riled up about it is that I'm as sore at myself as I am at you. Because I feel every bit as guilty and vulnerable. How did I behave? You, at least, had the grace to call me, and I, good Joe that I was, said, what the hell, I didn't care whether I got it or not—and five minutes later I was packing my bag and rushing back to do some infighting. For what? A prize that isn't a prize? Ambition? Vanity? Why can't we be content to do our jobs, big jobs at that? Why do we grasp for more?"

Alex sat huddled in his wretchedness.

"Don't look so crushed," continued Dan. "So you got stoned and fabricated this drunken drivel which you didn't mean and which no one took seriously in the first place. You didn't have to tell me but you told me. And as far as I'm concerned, I didn't hear it. It has nothing to do with you. I know you better. We go all the way back to New Haven, and I'm writing it off. It never happened. You hear?"

Alex nodded, turned, and walked quickly into the bathroom. Dan's generosity was too much for him. And this was the man he'd maligned! Dan was friend enough to overlook his hostile and malicious assault as a lapse, as something which had nothing to do with the Alex Frazier he knew. "I know you better," he'd said. But did he?

Who was Alex Frazier, really? The Alex that Ted saw and couldn't look in the eye wasn't the person that Dan saw. Certainly not the Alex that Chris, who knew nothing of San Vicente, saw. Each had his own image. Just as Alex had his.

But had he ever faced himself, really? Ever questioned that image compounded of daydreams and fancies, of the pretty fictions and fibs we tell ourselves, of the longings we project and desires we fondle?

Who was Alex Frazier? The son of a drunk of a father? Of the genteel Fraziers? Of his Ivy League alma mater? The dedicated being who'd given himself so selflessly to research? The confident Beverly Hills surgeon—art collector—sports car enthusiast—gourmet—bon vivant? How much of each? And what really weighed in the scale of truth? What was essential, what acquired? What real? What pretense?

Who are you, Frazier? The image you created? The appearance you parade? The visible presence—or the dark one which lurks within? (Is the submerged part of the iceberg not there because it isn't visible?)

The crack had opened, and the one showed behind the other, and he no longer knew what was true, what false. The one contradicted the other. And what was he to think? Believe? How was he to judge?

He'd had certain convictions about himself. Were they moonshine and dust? Could he even say he was the fine surgeon he thought he was? After the death of the Amster baby, he wondered.

His mind returned to the circumstances of the case, to the conflict and anguish involved in his misguided decision. And all the doubts were back, all the self-questioning and shakiness which he could ill-afford now that the hour of the Levitt operation was at hand.

He turned on a cold faucet, let the water run over his wrists, patted some on his forehead and the back of his neck. The window which looked out on the sunlit hills was open. He walked over and let the brisk air play over the wetness. It felt cool and renewing. Taking a deep breath, he exhaled slowly, straightened his shoulders, and walked out.

Jack Singer was the resident who usually assisted Alex. It wasn't until he got into the operating room that he learned Jack had been shifted to another emergency case. Dave Gordon, the chief surgical resident, was already in the room ready to take his place. Alex didn't think too much about it until he'd scrubbed and Nurse Farber was helping him on with gown and gloves. Dave Gordon, he noticed, was standing at the side of the operating table and watching him. There was no reason why he shouldn't. But Alex suddenly got the notion that there had been one "emergency" too many this morning and that Dave Gordon had been assigned not only to assist Dr. Frazier but to observe and take over in the event that Dr. Frazier wasn't quite up to it. A little far-fetched perhaps. But Ike Press *had been* visiting with Arthur, and Arthur was just the one to take such precautions. In the course of the morning Dave would, he was sure, be summoned into Arthur's office and skillfully drawn out on the subject of Dr. Frazier.

The thought did nothing to add to Alex's calm. Fortunately, Dr. Greenstadt was entering to stand by. Though he'd been up most of the night, he'd apparently caught a few hours of sleep and decided to be on hand rather than send in a resident cardiologist. He nodded to Alex, a grave look on his face.

Otto Lederer, the anesthetist was signaling that the patient was ready. Nurses Farber and Klein stepped in to drape the patient and paint the operative area. Then they moved aside, and Alex stepped in. A nerve throbbed in his forehead. His stomach braced against a sudden queasiness. For a moment he had an image of Ben Levitt sitting on the stairs, depending on him, and he couldn't help wondering whether he might let him down just as he'd let Ted down. He tried not to think about it, turned instead to the instrument table. His eyes checked the gleaming implements, the wicked-looking but merciful operating tools which would in a moment become ruthless and powerful extensions of his hand. There was a neatness about this array of steel weapons. Each item was cunningly devised for its specific function. Each was an impersonal and reliable agent of the surgeon's will. He depended on them. On the sharp scalpels, the clamps, the periosteal elevators, the costotome, the rib retractor. He wished that, like them, he were a mindless mechanism free of the emotions, the hesitations, doubts, and fears which plagued him now.

A glance at the suspended flask of blood, at the tubes inserted into the arm. His eyes taking in the team: Otto, Dave, Jim Diamond, the intern. Nurses Farber and Klein. Greenstadt standing by, his eyes somber. Drawn and tense, like a *torero* facing the moment of truth, Alex nodded toward the instrument tray.

The scalpel smacked into his palm. He sucked in his breath. Again the image of Ben Levitt intruded into his mind. Ben's eyes, trusting and helpless, seemed to hover above him, to supplicate. Shaken, Alex looked down at the painted area. The blade knifed through the carmined skin. His hand was at work, knowing without thought what it had to do.

The image of that lonely figure on that long flight of stairs persisted. Ben had pleaded with Alex, held out for him when Alex had wanted so desperately to withdraw. And now he was stuck with him, his wife's life completely dependent on a skill which had lost assurance, an authority which had turned to doubt, a daring dissipated in fear. How much smarter he'd have been to settle for Dan, for Dave. Well, it might still be Dave, because if he felt he were losing command, if his doubts spread to his hands, if his mind began to freeze, then he'd step out and tell Dave to take over.

The big vein in his temple throbbed and jumped, his heart beat accelerated. He could hear it, hear the quickening of his breath. But all the while the dissection proceeded; the scalpel cut through the chest tissues with smooth strokes. Another knife waited. He grasped it, made a long incision in the periosteum. Nurse Klein had the periosteal elevator ready for him before he asked for it. He got the blade under the fourth rib and with a quick movement stripped the tough membrane away.

The mechanics were proceeding in the rhythm of habit; one reflex of movement seemed to cue the next. It was a performance by rote and Alex was relieved to see each step following almost automatically upon the last. It would get more difficult as he reached the constricted valve. For the moment he was a mechanic reaching for his tools and methodically clearing the way to the seat of the trouble.

The costotome now. The blade biting into the rib. One end, then the other. The length of bone free so that he could lift it out.

Now the rib retractor. The opening spreading as he applied pressure. The heart exposed.

The needle ready. Alex reached for it, sewed a purse-string suture into the heart. Through the loop of the purse-string he cut a hole into the wall of the heart.

Carefully, his finger probed at the constricted valve. It was even narrower than he'd anticipated. He stepped aside to let Dave check on it.

Dave shook his head. "Bad stenosis," he said.

Alex took over again. There were no instruments to rely on now. His finger, which could feel its way, as a piece of inert steel could not, began the work of widening the valve. It was a delicate business of knowing just how much pressure to apply.

Carefully, ever so carefully, he bore down, felt the opening give, give, grow wider but not wide enough, and he knew he had to push, force it, more than he cared to, but damn, it wasn't good enough, it had to be better, and he bore down a little, then just a little bit more until suddenly he felt the wall rip and the blood spurt and spout like a gusher breaking loose. He froze.

"Suction," he heard himself say.

He felt the tube in his hand, inserted it. The image of Ben Levitt on the stairs steadied him now. He was applying pressure on the rip with another finger, pressing, pressing against the surge of blood.

"All right, pull it," he said to Dave, and Dave pulled tight the purse-string.

The suture held. The suction pump cleared the area.

Alex turned to Jim Diamond, who had anticipated his order to pump blood into the veins. "Push it," said Alex. "Keep pushing it."

He was himself again. The suture was holding, the blood-rush stemmed. And now he could put in other sutures, neat and firm. Greenstadt, he noticed, was checking on the blood pressure and respiration. Alex looked up inquiringly.

"Pressure rising. Everything under control," said Greenstadt.

With Dave's help, Alex closed the incision.

Yanking off the gloves, he said, "That was a little close for comfort."

"I've seen you pull out of worse," said Dave.

The casualness of the comment reassured Alex. He had the sudden sense that he could go on, that nothing would happen. Bert and Frank had been good enough to keep quiet; Dan had been amazingly understanding; he'd proved to himself that he could function at his work. He asked no more. He'd go on, take each step in its turn. It wouldn't be easy. If only Arthur didn't pull the rug out from under him, he'd face everything he had to:

the accusation in Ted's, Frank's, and Bert's eyes, the guilt which he had to live with. At noon there'd be the Clinical Pathological Conference. He'd better get at that paper of Brice's if he hoped to be set for it.

Then he knew he didn't need any paper, didn't need any preparation. Because, he suddenly decided, it wasn't the scheduled case he wanted to discuss. He had a need to talk about the case of the Amster baby. He could, of course, make it impersonal, use the usual cover of anonymity, present the symptoms of infant X, and throw the floor open to clinical diagnosis. But he had no desire to. He wanted to be open and honest about it, make a first person report, describe it as his case, his failure.

VI

An hour and a half later the C.P.C. was in session, and he was glad he'd made the decision he had, because, by discarding his own anonymity, he could give credit to Ted for his original and correct diagnosis, borne out later by the autopsy. With confessional zeal he felt compelled to take on the burden of the blame. It was, he was aware, a form of penance. But this was no sheltered cubicle. This wasn't an unseen Father he was confronting. He was face to face with his colleagues. And he felt an unspoken guilt that went much deeper than his failure in this particular case. For he'd vilified and traduced most of the men on the preponderantly Jewish staff of Memorial. And though he was confessing error, he felt that he was concealing, felt, while he was talking in aseptic clinical language, that he wanted to open up and tell about San Vicente. He wanted somehow to abase himself, to demonstrate his unworthiness, to ask their forgiveness. And all the time he saw the slight, knowing smile on Bert's lips, saw the cynical challenge in Frank's face, the closed look in Ted's.

What he was talking about was the case of the ten-day-old infant who, from birth, showed symptoms of gagging and cyanosis while feeding. And later the characteristic triad of paroxysms of coughing, abnormal distention of the abdomen, and persistent pneumonitis. Dr. Crisler had diagnosed a probable tracheoesophageal fistula. But X rays and tests showed no supporting evidence. Yet all clinical symptoms certainly pointed to a fistula. Alex had concurred with Dr. Crisler's diagnosis. And when gauge feedings failed to help and the infant continued to decline, an exploratory was definitely in order. Alex had undertaken an exploratory thoracotomy but, though the exposure was excellent, he had found no evidence of a fistula. He was inclined to believe that there might be a neuromuscular difficulty, though the seemingly normal mentality of the infant made Dr. Crisler rule it out as unlikely. The symptoms persisted, and Dr. Crisler and Dr. Simon, the consultant, argued that clinical deduction called for the presence of a fistula if not in the thoracic area explored, perhaps higher up. Though Alex conceded the logic of their position, he wasn't convinced enough to risk the danger of another exploratory so soon after the first. He pleaded for delay. The next evening the infant began having periods of apnea and died. An autopsy was ordered. The pathologist's report revealed the presence of a fistula in the cervical area. Though the second exploratory would have been a risk, Alex was quick to confess, it might very well, by removing the fistula, have eased the pneumonitis condition which was directly responsible for the death. It proved once again that, in the absence of corroborating X rays and tests, the clinical diagnosis based on classical symptoms had its own logic and imperatives. Where there was conviction the risk was warranted. It would have been warranted in this case, Alex concluded.

During the discussion which followed, a folded slip of paper was handed up to Alex. He opened it. It was signed with Bert's name and read: "It may interest you to know that a 'Jew bastard' called Phil Gross performed an identical exploratory at Olive two months ago. Logic, as you term it, called for a cervical approach when the thoracic failed. This 'Jew bastard' followed logic and removed the fistula. The infant survived."

Alex could feel the blood pumping into his face. A mortifying sweat made his shirt cling to his back. He glanced toward Bert. The thin smile still marked his lips. Frank, too, was smiling, and he wondered whether Bert had showed him the note.

Rising, Alex said, "I'm informed that Dr. Philip Gross had a similar case at Olive two months ago and that cervical surgery was successful in locating the fistula. I'm sorry I didn't have the benefit of his experience."

Someone was asking Ted whether the question of a neuromuscular dysfunction could so easily be discounted.

"No," said Ted. "Dr. Frazier was quite proper in raising it as a possibility, especially since mental normalcy is difficult to determine in so young an infant. However, the conjunction of symptoms, the 'characteristic triad,' as Dr. Frazier put it, was much more persuasive."

Grateful as he was for Ted's considerate and objective response, he couldn't forget Bert's note, which in two words brought back the whole madness of San Vicente. What a simpleton he'd been to think, as he'd wishfully allowed himself to, that things would work out, that he could go on as before.

The session was adjourned; the men broke into groups. He managed to slip out, but Chris Sullivan caught up with him just outside the exit. Together they walked to the parking lot.

"Good talk," said Chris, "but why in hell did you have to present it in that form? You'd have been a lot smarter to present the symptoms and lead an objective discussion. What was the point of pinpointing it as your case?"

"That's the way I felt."

Chris shrugged. "In your position, you can afford it, I suppose. But it's not so good for the rest of us."

Alex looked up. "What's it got to do with anyone else?"

"Not anyone. Us. We're a minority. A handful out of the whole staff. So you get up and admit an error in judgment. You know what they're probably saying? I can just hear them. 'What do you expect from a *goyische kopf*?' Because that's the way they think of us."

"Oh, Christ!" said Alex.

"I know."

"You're being overly sensitive and overly subjective."

"Think about it," said Chris.

All the way to the office he kept thinking about it, and it annoyed him that he should. Because it wasn't typical. They were doctors, damn it, good doctors, bad or indifferent. Not Jews or gentiles. Doctors!

He kept thinking about Bert's note and all that it implied. It wasn't merely a question of the two words. For it raised his own question of the imperative of logic, an imperative which Gross had followed and he had not.

It bothered him, raised further questions. Why, for instance, hadn't he known what Bert knew? Was it that he'd been so overworked the past months? Or was it that he kept himself so aloof from the rest of the staff? He was aware of the fact that he stuck pretty much to business in the hospital. Was it because he didn't really want to mix, that he felt alien? One of a handful, as Chris put it? And wasn't that an indication of an anti-Semitism he simply wouldn't have believed until Peg had spelled it out for him yesterday? And now that the seam was opened and his awareness roused, was he reaching, turning possibles into probables, conjectures into facts? Because there was a wide gap between aloofness and bigotry.

So many questions and so few answers.

The office, for instance. For eight years he'd shared the suite with Frank amicably, smoothly. To the advantage of both.

Now? How could he?

He had to pull out. At least offer Frank the chance to get someone else. Whomever it was, he'd have a sinecure. Because Frank remained the most popular internist in Beverly Hills. He didn't like the idea but, in all decency, he had to consider Frank's feelings, defer to what he wanted.

There were other questions. The question of whether it was any longer tenable for him to stay on at Memorial. Of what alternative, if not. And basic to all these: the question of his relations with Peg. How could he make any plans or decisions until that was resolved, until he had some sense of where he stood, of whether they could go on or not? He might as well put everything on ice till then. There wasn't any point in being precipitate. If anything came up he'd have to play it by ear.

When he got to the office Frank was already there. On any normal day there'd be a dozen occasions for one to seek out the other, usually to consult about a patient, to check on X rays, to take a coffee break. Not so today. They might just as well have been in separate buildings. Frank did send over some X rays via his nurse. On a neatly typed note, which was pinned to the envelope, were the comments and questions which he always presented verbally. And instead of calling Frank back or walking into his office to discuss his conclusions, Alex dictated a memo, which his nurse typed and delivered to Frank's nurse.

It was perhaps a more businesslike procedure. But it wasn't comfortable. Nor as satisfactory as the give and take of a discussion, in which the articulated opinion of one touched off a new line of thought in the other and often led to a modified or more developed conclusion.

It was the longest afternoon he remembered and the most uncomfortable. By four his head was larger than the building. Codeine didn't help. Nor did the thought of another afternoon like this, or of several. He couldn't live like this. Precipitate or not, it was better to raise the subject now, get it off his chest, and clear the air.

Picking up the phone, he asked the receptionist to connect him with Frank's office.

"Yes?" said Frank. "What's on your mind?"

"I'd like to talk to you. Whenever you can squeeze in a few minutes."

"My appointments are running behind schedule, but I'll call you back."

Alex was through with his last patient at five-ten. If Frank was really behind schedule, he preferred not to be on his tail, so he decided he'd wait a while.

Several times he started to pick up the phone, changed his mind. Mrs. Quigley, the nurse, stepped in to ask if he needed anything before she left. He found himself asking about her husband, who did bit parts in TV, and about her son, who had a reading block and was taking remedial classes with a man who used slides, a tape recorder, and other mechanical gadgets to induce interest. He knew she was anxious to get home but he was so desperate for the distraction of talk that he kept her engaged longer than he intended, then in sudden guilt let her go. He paced around the room, glanced at the last issue of the Medical Journal, sharpened some pencils, cleaned his pipe, pulled out a pack of cards and played solitaire. And still the phone didn't ring.

At five-forty he called the receptionist, who told him that Dr. Meyers had left on the dot of five. Yes, she was sure he'd gone for the day. If he'd promised to call him back, he must have forgotten, because he seemed in a hurry to leave.

Frank hadn't forgotten; he hadn't been behind schedule if he'd left at five. Well, it would have to wait till tomorrow. At least, he could get out of the office, go to the Athletic Club, work off some of the tension.

The club was a refuge. For once he didn't mind the acrid smell of the locker room. The sour aroma of sweaty gym clothes, of woolen socks and jock straps, seemed to cut through the loginess. For an hour and a half he drove himself, pounding over the handball court, trotting around the track, taking turns at the rowing machine, the bike exerciser, the sandbag, weights, and barbells. By the time he got into the steam room he was too exhausted to think. It was nice to sit on the wet bench, to feel the heat caressing his body, the steam wisping into his nostrils, the sweat taking over. Through half-closed eyes he contemplated the paunches and bulges of fat on some of the men. His own body remained tapered and trim. Even now he had a stupid narcissistic satisfaction in that.

He showered, took a swim, gave himself to the luxury of the massaging table, to the pummeling and kneading, to the fingers which worked their relaxing magic on forehead and neck and spine. He breathed deeply of the penetrating odors of unguents and liniments and thought of nothing but the drowsy, aching sense of self. I'm a disgustingly, self-indulgent physical creature, he told himself.

Driving back to the hotel, he was glad that he wouldn't have to see or talk to anyone. He'd have Room Service send up dinner, get into bed with a book, and probably doze off in the middle of the second page.

The clerk handed him a message with his key. It was from Peg. "Call me as soon as you get this," it read. "Important."

The last thing he wanted to do right now was talk to Peg. It would be much better for both of them if they didn't communicate. He didn't want to open up the raw wound which the last couple of hours had covered over. It could wait awhile, he told himself. Then he remembered the word 'important' and wondered if there'd been a call from the hospital. Perhaps something had gone wrong with Ruth Levitt.

He reproached himself for not calling the hospital while he was at the club. Turning, he headed quickly for the phone booths.

"Doctor!" called a familiar-sounding voice, which he couldn't place. Recognition loomed with the approaching figures of Peg's parents, Joe and Dora Strauss.

VII

ALEX couldn't imagine what the Strausses were doing here when they should be in New York. Peg hadn't mentioned anything about their coming. He wondered if she'd called them. Of all the people he didn't want to see at this moment they headed the list. He wondered if Peg had told them he was staying at the hotel, wondered if they knew what had happened. If so, they were behaving oddly, because they were both beaming, their faces warm with welcome. It was so out of character that it threw him. Not that they couldn't be genial and warm. But this had nothing to do with their attitude toward him, which was usually dour to grim.

"Talk about the devil!" said Joe Strauss. "Who would expect to see you here!"

"I promised to drop in on someone," he improvised. "What brings *you* here?"

"Peggy wrote us the good news," said Dora Strauss, "and we dropped everything and flew out."

"*Mazeltov!*" Joe Strauss extended his hand, a big grin on his face. "Congratulations!"

"For what?"

"For what? Don't be so unconcerned and blasé. We were so excited we had to fly out to celebrate. It isn't every day you find out you're going to be grandparents."

"When did Peg write you?"

"It was datemarked four days ago. We got it this morning. On a New Year's card. A casual afterthought. The both of you. You act as if it was an everyday occurrence."

"Isn't it?"

"After twenty years, no."

"Anyway we're old-fashioned enough to think it's very special," said Dora Strauss. She took his hand in both of hers. "Congratulations, Alex."

"Thanks," he mumbled.

"And now that we found you, we'd better call Peggy," said Joe Strauss. "She's been calling you all over. You're having dinner with us. At the hotel."

"I was just going to call *her*."

"So make the call. We'll be in the dining room."

Alex entered the booth, completely bewildered at the Strauss's attitude. That they should welcome the idea of a half-gentile grandson was unfathomable to him.

"It's me," he said when he heard Peg's voice.

"Are you at the hotel?" she asked. "Because I wanted to warn you—"

"I could have used a warning."

"Don't tell me you bumped into them? How did you explain your being there? They don't suspect you're registered, I hope."

"I doubt it."

"Because they're so high about the prospect of a grandchild it'd be a shame if they got the idea anything was wrong."

"Why *are* they so high about it? It just doesn't jibe."

"I know. I was simply flabbergasted. I expected exactly the opposite. I put off writing about it for months. And then I only mentioned it because I thought they might as well get used to the idea."

"They fell all over me as if I were the prodigal returned. Anyone'd think I'd suddenly turned kosher."

There was silence from Peg's end of the phone.

"I suppose I shouldn't have said that. I suppose you'll take it as another evidence of anti-Semitism." Was it? Why had he said it? For the hundredth time he asked himself how the whole thing could have happened.

"Don't, Alex," she said. "On the basis of their past conduct it was perfectly justified."

"I wouldn't even have thought about it before. Now I'm suddenly self-conscious." He sighed. "It seems they're expecting us for dinner."

"I had to say yes. Do you mind?"

"What am I supposed to say: I don't? But I'll keep up my end. You don't need to worry about it. Only come fast, because this sudden display of parental affection is pretty cloying."

Peg was dressed and promised to be over in a few minutes. He rang the hospital and talked to the ward nurse, who read him the notations on Ruth Levitt's chart. Dr. Greenstadt had just seen her, and she seemed to be in good shape.

One more call: to the exchange. He half-hoped there'd be some emergency which would take him away from a situation he might once have appreciated but which galled him now. He didn't know whether he could go through this farce of a celebration. How could he pretend to be happy about something which had suddenly taken on the aspects of a tragic mistake?

The exchange gave him two unimportant messages. With a heavy sigh, he headed for the dining room.

They were waiting for him, Dora Strauss looking so much like a faded version of Peggy and Joe Strauss with his shock of white hair and his quick eyes darting about in his still handsome face.

"She's on her way," said Alex as he sat down at the table.

"Good," said Joe Strauss. "Funny, running into you like this. To tell you the truth, I'm glad we've got a few minutes with you before she comes." He picked up the menu. "How about a drink?"

"No, thanks."

"Peggy, a mother," sighed Dora Strauss. "It's so hard to believe."

"You know what that foolish girl told us?" said Joe Strauss. "She plans to go back to work after she has the child."

"I know."

"And you approve?"

"No," said Alex, aware that they were both looking at him. "I never liked the idea of her working in the first place."

"So put your foot down," said Joe Strauss. "January sales or no January sales, she shouldn't be working now. I don't like how she looks. Peaked. Pale. Her face drawn. Rings under her eyes."

Intended or not, the words were a reproach. "She hasn't been sleeping the last few nights," Alex said defensively.

"She's too wound up, too tense, too overworked."

"She should have long naps," said Dora Strauss. "Plenty of rest."

"You know Peg," said Alex. "She seems to think she has an obligation to—"

"She has an obligation to herself, to the baby!" said Joe Strauss. "After all, she's no spring chicken. A woman over forty carrying her first child! Is this a way to behave? Does this make sense? I ask you!"

"I'm not disagreeing with you," Alex said quietly.

"You're getting too excited, Joe."

"It's just that I don't want anything to go wrong."

"It won't," said Dora Strauss. "Alex said he agreed. He'll talk to her, and she'll listen. After all, he's a doctor."

"You'll see," Joe Strauss said to Alex "you'll be a father; you'll see some day why I get excited." He sighed. "I have a confession to make. It wasn't so long ago that if someone had told me Peggy was having a baby I would have been excited another way. I wouldn't have liked it."

"That doesn't surprise me," said Alex.

"It's no secret that I opposed your marriage. I gave you a rough time and I know it."

"It's nothing to brag about," said Dora Strauss.

"The truth is the truth. I didn't approve of mixed marriages. I still don't. So for all these years I was glad there was no child. Now, not only am I not upset by the news, I'm tickled to death. Don't ask me why."

"It's no great mystery," said Dora. "A grandchild is a grandchild, and at our age—"

"I'm getting mellow in my old age."

"It's a crime?"

"All these years I had a stubborn wish the marriage should fail. A foolish thing, I suddenly realize. Why should I wish unhappiness on my own flesh and blood? Peggy wanted it. She went ahead in spite of us. It was done. So common sense would say: all right, hope for the best. Why then did I wish for the opposite? Where do I come off telling my daughter what will make her happy or unhappy? I can't live her life. And she's proved me wrong. All of which is to say that I owe you an apology. It took me a long time to get around to it, but what better occasion could I pick? With a full heart I say to you: I was wrong. I admit it. It was a good marriage. You've been happy and with God's will may you continue to be."

"Amen," said Dora Strauss.

Alex sat, embarrassed and bewildered by the extravagance of the speech. The strange thing about it was that he probably meant it. It seemed such a mockery that the hostility which he'd resented in Joe Strauss should have taken this turn.

"I look at it now," continued Joe Strauss, "and I can say what I couldn't before: we have a lot to be proud of. We have a son-in-law, a gifted surgeon, respected by his colleagues and by the community, a talent with golden hands which has saved the lives of hundreds of people. . . ."

Resentment rose with each phrase. Alex had had enough. Thanks for the testimonial, he wanted to say, but you can keep it. All the years when he didn't exist, when he was anathema, mud. And now, now of all times!

Joe had broken off and was rising to his feet. Alex looked up to see Peggy approaching. She had obviously taken pains with her make-up and dress to forestall any further comments about her appearance. Joe Strauss was advancing toward her. "Isn't she beautiful!" he said, and kissed her full on the lips. "Beautiful . . ." he repeated as he stood off to inspect her, a possessive and proud glint in his eyes. "Only one thing." His finger wagged. "The circles under the eyes."

"Naps in the afternoon," said Dora. "Plenty of rest. That's what she needs. Ask Alex. Ask the doctor."

"You haven't been wasting any time, I see," remarked Peg.

"What's the matter," said Joe Strauss, "it's a crime for a father and mother to talk to their son-in-law about their daughter?"

"I don't want you ganging up on me. I'm not a child and I don't care to be told what to do."

"To me I don't expect you to listen. You've *never* listened to me!" he said bitterly. "But to Alex? Tell her, Alex, what you feel about her job."

So ironic to have Joe Strauss turning to him as an ally. "Peg knows what I feel," Alex said tightly.

"You're the husband, the father," said Dora Strauss. "You think it's right for her to let a stranger bring up your child?"

"I think that's up to Peg," he said.

"You have no feelings about it?" demanded Joe Strauss. "No rights? No say?"

"Stop bullying him," said Peg.

"Who's bullying? I'm asking him what he feels."

"I know what he feels and I know what you feel. And I'll be damned if I'm going to be pushed around. If you brought me here to quarrel with me—"

"All right. All right," said Joe Strauss, lifting finger to mouth. "Sh! Not a word, not a whisper. After all, this is a happy occasion. A celebration."

As if on cue, a waiter appeared with a bottle of champagne in a bucket of ice.

"You see," said Joe Strauss.

The waiter grasped the bottle in his toweled hand. The wire and golden foil came off, with a flourish. His thumb pressured the cork tentatively, then forcefully, and it popped with a proper ceremonial report. The glasses were filled. Joe Strauss raised his. "To you, my darling." He nodded to Peg, then to Alex. "And to you, my son. And to the coming child. May it bring you much happiness."

Joe and Dora Strauss took a sip. And after a moment, Peg and Alex took theirs.

"The miracle of life," Joe said sententiously. "A grandchild is coming, so you'd think I'd feel older. On the contrary, I feel younger. Maybe it's because our other grandchildren are already grown, and I feel like we're starting all over again." He sighed. "Why is it that a new life gives you new eyes? I was telling Alex, all these years I looked at your marriage one way, now all of a sudden I've got an entirely different point of view."

Peggy sat taciturn, her face grim. Alex could tell that she was probably thinking, as he was, that the change was a little late.

"To tell the truth," Joe continued, "I feel ashamed that I could be so narrow-minded and prejudiced. I look back and ask myself: what right did I have to favor one child over the other? To provide for your brother and not for you? I protected him with cash gifts to cut down on inheritance taxes, with real estate which I transferred to his name, with trust funds for his children. Oh, my will makes some provision for you. But not the same. Not as much. I've got to change that will. A lot of things I've got to change."

He went on to elaborate, and Alex wished he hadn't opened the subject, because money, this kind of money, which might have had some meaning in the past, loomed now as a roadblock to the possibility of restoring his relationship with Peg. He didn't know whether there was any such possibility, only that this might complicate what already seemed complicated beyond repair.

The talk seemed to be just as disturbing to Peg. "How did we get into all this?" she asked. "Can't we think of something less morbid to talk about?"

"Money is morbid?"

"It embarrasses me."

"I should be so embarrassed. With such an attitude maybe I *should* forget about it. And you know what you'd have? *Bubkes.*"

"Are you threatening me? Because I really don't care. Oh, before I forget it," she added, trying to divert him again, "Ike Press wanted to be remembered to you. We saw him over the week-end. He said something about arranging a pinochle game the next time you were in town."

"I'll be glad to oblige him. Wonderful man, Ike. I got a letter from him the other day about my annual contribution to the hospital. It seems they'd like to build a new wing. What would you say, Dora, if I offered to donate the whole thing?"

"I'd say you were crazy. Do you have any idea how much it would mean?"

"I could afford to donate a garment factory for Israel, so why not a quarter or half a million for a hospital in which my grandson will be born?"

"If you ask me, it's an expensive delivery."

"I'm not saying I'm doing it, but it's an idea. After all. Alex works there. Maybe I made smaller contributions in the past because he did. Tonight I feel different. I'm in a generous mood."

Alex wondered if he'd be in such a generous mood if he knew about San Vicente. He was tempted to blurt out the whole story. If he were half a man he would. "I think it's fine for you to be generous," he said uneasily, "but not on my account."

"Naturally not just on your account. On my account. Because it gives me pleasure. Because it satisfies my ego—and I've got a big one, I admit it. Besides, I'm a civic-minded citizen, and now that we're thinking of buying a place and becoming permanent residents—"

"When did this happen?" asked Peggy.

"Yesterday. When we got your card. What's the sense of having a grandchild if you're not around to enjoy him? You don't like the idea?"

"I think it's a very good idea," said Peggy, and Alex couldn't tell whether she meant it or was just being polite.

"Then if you still want to go back to the store" Joe said slyly, "your mother will take care of the baby."

"Let's not get into *that* again!" flared Peggy.

"Okay, okay," he said with a crafty smile. "But to get back to Ike Press. The more I think of it, the better I like it. Why shouldn't there be a Joesph G. Strauss wing of the hospital? And if something should brush off on Alex, is there any objection?"

Was he referring to the appointment? Had someone told him he was up for it? If so, it was before Alex had told Ike Press he was withdrawing his name, before Ike had relayed the word to Arthur. Though a half million gift from Joe Strauss might suddenly reverse things. All Joe had to do was mention it to anyone on the Board, and it would follow automatically. If he didn't speak up, Joe might do just that. He found himself hesitating. Why was he silent? Why were the words so hard?

"You're not drinking your champagne," said Joe.

"I don't really care for the stuff."

"Then drink something else. What do you like, Scotch?"

"Nothing, thanks."

Joe shrugged. "I can just imagine the look on Ike's face," he said, "if I should suddenly put the check in front of his eyes." He chuckled.

Alex glanced uncomfortably at Peg, half expecting she'd say something. She was as silent as he, her face inscrutable.

"Maybe I'll give him a ring," said Joe. "See if we can get together later in the evening."

"Don't," Alex heard himself say.

Joe looked up. "Why not? You don't think Memorial needs a new wing?"

"It needs it."

"So?"

Again the hesitation.

"It needs it, but you don't want me to call." Joe looked at him quizzically.

"Not until after Wednesday," he said.

"You don't think that would be too late?" Joe asked with meaningful emphasis.

Alex looked up. "I might have guessed you'd know about it."

"Ike Press is no fool. Such information he wouldn't withhold when he writes to ask for a contribution. And why shouldn't I bring a little influence to bear?"

"I'd rather you didn't."

"I'm making the contribution. So it's a day later or a day earlier, what's the difference?"

"I'd prefer to have it later if you don't mind."

"In other words, you're telling me to keep out? You won't take my help?"

"That's right," he said grimly.

Joe Strauss regarded him through his heavy lashes, his jaw jutting out at an angle, his wide nostrils flared. "You know something?" he said after a pause. "I wouldn't blame you." A chuckle rumbled out of him. "You know something else? I think you're *meshugeh* but I respect you for it."

Alex realized that he'd been holding his breath. Slowly he let it out.

When they'd finished with coffee and smoked their cigarettes, Peggy pushed back her chair and said to Alex, "Well, if we're going to see Madge, we'd better get going. I told Mother and Dad about Dick Lerner, so they'll forgive us if we run."

"Certainly," said Joe Strauss.

"A tragic thing," sighed his wife.

As if he were in on it from the beginning, Alex managed to cover his surprise. Rising, he pulled back Peggy's chair.

After they'd left the folks in the lobby, Peggy said, "Sorry to spring that on you, but I knew you wouldn't want to spend the evening with them and I don't know about you, but I do feel I want to see Madge."

He'd decided against going, but he suddenly knew that he would. Whatever objections he'd had no longer weighed against the simple human consideration of being with a friend when his friendship was called upon.

"I feel I should go," he said. "The only thing that's holding me back is the thought that word of the San Vicente episode might have got around."

Peg shook her head. "I'm sure it hasn't. Ike Press made it pretty clear that it was to be confined to those present. Madge'd be upset if you didn't show."

They took both cars, but on Alex's suggestion they drove to the house so Peg could leave hers. He was sorry the moment he saw her park her own car and walk toward the Ferrari. The constraint which had marked their trip back from San Vicente seemed to take over again. The same mood stifled any ease of communion. For a few blocks they drove in silence.

"Funny about the folks," Peg finally said. "I never expected that the mere mention of pregnancy would cause all that commotion. I certainly didn't expect the change in attitude."

"Unfortunately, it's a little late."

Peg didn't comment. He regretted making the remark. If he'd expected any disclaimers or reassurances, they weren't forthcoming.

"Why didn't you tell them?" he asked.

"What?"

"About me."

"What would have been the point?"

"What's the point of pretending something when you no longer feel it?"

"I don't *know* what I feel. I'm too numb and confused to begin to sort out what I feel. All I know is, it's the first time they've felt good about me since we got married. Even if I were clear about things, this wasn't the time to raise questions."

"They might as well know now as later."

"Know *what!* I told you *I* don't know. Do you? How can I tell them?"

"You know what happened."

"I *saw* what happened. I *heard* it. But I don't know what it was. I don't know why. I don't begin to understand its meaning or significance. If this were the Middle Ages and I believed in dibbuks and demons maybe it'd be simple. Maybe it *is* simple. A simple matter of too much alcohol blowing the lid off a Pandora's box. Though where it came from and what it has to do with the person I lived with and thought I knew so well—"

"Apparently you didn't," said Alex.

"Did you?"

"Not too well, it seems. But I've got to accept what happened.

And when I sit with your folks and hear them sounding off about my newly discovered virtues and say nothing, it makes me feel like a crawling hypocrite. If you didn't tell them, I should have."

"Why? To prove he was right all along?"

"Wasn't he?"

Peg didn't answer.

"Is that the conclusion you've come to?" he asked.

"I've come to no conclusion. I don't know, I told you, and until I do, I don't intend to talk about it, much less run to Dad. It wasn't his business in the first place; it isn't now. And all this to-do about money, withholding it to get his way or offering it when it suits him—"

"I'm not taking," said Alex.

"It simply infuriates me. I'm glad you made it clear you don't want him bandying around that half million until after Wednesday."

He probably wouldn't after Wednesday, when he'd find out it was Dan Simon who'd been appointed. Well, that was his affair. "Do you think they meant it about moving out here?" he asked.

"Probably."

"What do you feel about it?"

"I think I'd like having them close."

It was a rhetorical question, he realized. Of course she would. She'd liked it in New York. Liked the Friday nights. Liked the attention and fuss and adoration. For all her bluster about Joe Strauss, she worshipped him. And he doted on her. Was as possessive and jealous as a lover. Marriage or no, there was an emotional tie between Peg and her father which had persisted through everything. It had cast a blight on their relationship. And now that it was in question, naturally she'd want him close. Because if things didn't work out she could fall back into the cozy and comforting pattern of her childhood. It disturbed him. He didn't want to think about it. Didn't want to admit the possibility.

"I wonder about Madge's money situation," Peg was saying.

"After all the lean years, I don't imagine Dick could have left much. I wonder if he was able to keep up his insurance."

"I'd better talk to her," said Alex.

He recognized Dan's car as they pulled up. His fingers tightened on the wheel. Dan would be perfectly civil, he knew, but Alex couldn't stand the thought of walking in with Peg. He'd be self-conscious, and so would she. He wondered if Dan had told Kay. Because if he had, she wouldn't be as generous as he about it. Kay had an abrasive tongue. But maybe she'd keep quiet under the circumstances.

He debated telling Peg he'd changed his mind and would be back for her later, then decided he couldn't. Madge would ask where he was, and he couldn't let her down. There was really no choice. We are what is expected of us, he realized once again.

There were about a dozen people in the living room. Madge was sitting on a couch beside Dick's mother, who'd probably flown in from New York the moment she was notified. Alex had seen her through the years when she came out to visit Dick, but his memories of her went back to med school and a Christmas vacation when Dick had invited him to stay at their house. She'd been so gracious and outgoing and full of fun. She sat with dignity now, a stunned look in her eyes. But she rose with Madge when she recognized them. Peg was embracing Madge. Alex approached Dick's mother. She threw her arms around him, and a sob broke in her throat; her tears touched his face, "Alex, Alex," she said. "You're the oldest friend he has out here. You stood by him when he needed you. He never forgot it and neither shall I."

He mumbled something inarticulate about being sorry. "It shouldn't have happened," he said. "It was one of those unpredictable and unpreventable things."

"Why to him?" she cried. "He had so much to do, so much to contribute."

"More than anybody I can think of," he said.

Then Madge was turning to him. He kissed her cheek. She

seemed to crumple and slumped against him, yielding to her tears. He cradled her in his arms and wept with her. And all that he'd been holding back came out, all that he'd been feeling found release. It was not only grief for the loss of his friend and the dream they'd shared but for the loss of self.

"I'm glad you came," Madge was saying. "You were the first one he asked for when it started. He wanted you to be there when he went into the hospital."

"And I failed him."

Madge's sobbing subsided. She eased out of his arms and sat down. Ron, her oldest son, looking manly and grave and younger than his seventeen years, approached with a bridge chair, which he placed beside the couch for Alex.

Alex reached out his hand. Ron gripped it in silence, his eyes somber and tearless. "Thanks for coming," he finally said.

Next to Alex, sat Dan and Kay. They nodded to him. Dan reached over to shake his hand. And Kay seemed to be extending hers, so he got up and shook it. Obviously Dan hadn't told her. And for the second time that day Alex was grateful for his decency.

Jim Stevens, of the staff of Children's, who'd worked with Dan and Alex on the Medical Committee in defense of Dick, sat opposite them, along with Israel Meltzer, the liberal plastics manufacturer who'd raised money for the Committee.

"I think this is the first time the four of us have been in a room together since the Olive business," commented Meltzer.

"I wish it could have been a happier occasion," said Dan.

"The happier occasions *we* have to make—and for those we don't seem to have time," said Meltzer. "The others are made for us."

"Since we *are* here, I don't think it'd be a bad idea to reconstitute that Committee," said Dan. "I'd like to see some sort of fund or award or grant set up in Dick's name."

"We're in business," said Meltzer.

"Oughtn't it to be something in relation to civil liberties?" suggested Stevens.

"Either that or a research fellowship, which I think is probably more in character," said Alex. "What do you think, Madge?"

"I think Dick would have liked that. He didn't like being a crusader, but with his sense of justice, he couldn't avoid it. Research was his gospel. It was truth. And he pursued it with all his being."

"Alex knows that more than anyone," said Dick's mother. "They started off together under Dr. Horstman at Yale. You don't know how often Dick spoke about her hopes for you two, Alex."

"They were warranted in Dick's case."

"And in yours, according to Dick. I can't tell you how disappointed he was when you changed to surgery."

"Speaking for surgery, we were very pleased," said Dan.

"Mother's right, though," said Madge. "Dick really regretted your choice."

"Looking back on it," said Alex, "I'm not sure but that I don't myself." He caught the look of surprise on Peg's face and quickly turned back to the subject of the fellowship fund.

They were discussing how they'd proceed to get contributions to such a fund and how it should be administered when Bert walked in.

He made his way to Madge and offered his condolences. Then he turned to the others, shaking each hand in turn, but deliberately bypassing Alex. Just as deliberately, he turned his chair so that he sat with his back toward him.

Peg, Alex could see, was as upset as he was. And Dan, too, was aware of the slight, because he made a point of addressing Alex directly to draw him into the conversation. Before Alex could say anything—though he was too paralyzed to talk—Bert cut in to continue the conversation as if Dan hadn't asked the question.

It wasn't anger which made Alex tremble. He felt it as a punishment which he'd merited. But that didn't make it any easier to take. Much as he wanted to leave, he forced himself to stay rather than risk offending Madge and Dick's mother by the shortness of his stay.

Madge was leaning toward him and telling him about funeral

arrangements. As he'd anticipated, she'd chosen him as one of the pallbearers. He knew what Bert and the others would think, but there wasn't a thing he could say. Somehow he'd go through with it. For her he was still the same person, Dick's friend and defender. She saw him through Dick's eyes, and he couldn't bring himself to destroy the image for her. Not under these circumstances. Rather, he found himself strengthening it by offering to lend any money she might need. Dick's insurance, she told him, would take care of things for awhile. In time, she'd find a job. He asked about Ron and college. Ron was applying for a scholarship to Stanford. "I want to help out with that," Alex said, and insisted that they talk further about it in May when Ron would be more definite about his situation.

Other people were coming into the room. He found it a good excuse to say they'd better run and make room. Peg apparently had the same thought because she came over to kiss Madge again.

Stevens, Meltzer, and Dan said good night as they walked by. Conspicuously, Bert looked up at the ceiling.

VIII

"WHAT did you do? Have a run-in with Bert?" Peg asked as they got into the car.

"Didn't have to. Wasn't the other night enough?"

"I knew he was angrier than the others and I know he's blunt about what he feels, but, after all, there's a time and a place."

"I don't think Madge or Dick's mother noticed—and that's all that really counts."

"No, they weren't in any condition to, poor things. I feel so badly for them." She sighed. "But I'm glad they could break down and let out their feelings. It's so much better than trying to be stoic."

"It helps," said Alex.

"You talked to Madge . . ."

"Yes. There is insurance, and they'll be all right for awhile. I offered to help with Ron's college."

"I'm glad you did. . . . He's the one who'll take it hard. He was trying to be so manful about it."

"He is. A lot of dignity in that kid."

They drove on, lost in the mood of mourning which they'd carried from the room. And before Alex knew it, he was turning down Bedford and pulling up in front of the house. They sat silent, preoccupied.

"I still can't get over the way Bert behaved," she said.

"Bert's hardly the man to pretend. He hates my guts, and I can't really blame him."

"I know. But under the circumstances!"

"He feels pretty intensely about it. I don't think the circumstances cut much ice." He took out Bert's note and handed it to her, waiting till she read it.

"Good God," she said. "What brought that on? And when did he send it to you?"

"During a C.P.C. session I was conducting." He went on to explain the circumstances."

"Whatever he feels," said Peggy, "I don't think it's excusable. It certainly isn't my idea of professional behavior."

"I *was* at fault, in the case of the infant and at San Vicente. And after ripping Dan and maligning everyone else, I can't expect Bert to pull any punches."

"For that matter, neither did I when I spilled over last night."

"It wouldn't have been any kindness if you had. I had to know." He paused, took a deep breath. "I don't know but that I won't pull out altogether."

"I think we're all a little too close to what happened, but I don't think that's the answer. It needs time. I know I do. So do you. After all, it was one incident, one night in a lifetime. I don't know what it adds up to."

"Maybe it *is* the lifetime. The sum and substance of Alex Frazier."

"Nonsense."

"*In vino veritas.* Wasn't that what Frank said even before it happened, that first night in the *cantina*?"

"I've been thinking about that. And like most glib aphorisms, it doesn't stand up. I've heard some awful whoppers come out of the drunken mind. So I'm not jumping to conclusions."

"Not everyone's that patient, I'm afraid. I'm not. Truth's a hard thing to arrive at. And no one ought to know that better than a research man."

"Did you mean what you said about research?"

"In some ways. I don't think this would have happened if I'd stuck to research. I don't think my values would have got so mangled. I don't think I'd have been so dazzled and distorted by money."

"No, you were another person in research. Was that what was in your mind when you talked about pulling out?"

"I don't know. At this moment I don't know what I want. I could go back to Mexico. I could go to Hawaii or Africa, for that matter."

"Be honest. Would that really solve anything?"

"I guess not. I was just being wishful."

"What about us? Where would I fit in?"

"I was thinking that if you wanted out—"

"Is that what's on your mind?"

"No. But I thought it might make it easier for you if that's what you—"

"Don't put things in my mouth. I don't know. And all this talk about taking off for the veld or the land of the lotus doesn't help."

"I was just talking. It's all sort of meaningless alongside the problem of you and me. I know what *I* want. I want things to be the same as they were."

She was silent. "What do you think I want!"

"I suppose," he said sadly, "it can never be. That's why I said if you wanted out—"

"You keep saying it. Why?"

"I don't know. Because I don't see how I'd go on if you did. I probably wouldn't. You're the only one who's ever meant anything to me. You know that?"

"Even though I don't have brown eyes?"

He looked up puzzled. "What?"

" 'You have hazel eyes. Luiz has brown eyes. Mac had brown eyes.' That's the one thing I didn't tell you about San Vicente."

"I said that?" he asked in horror.

"And I think it hurt worse than anything else."

"Why! What prompted it!" he cried.

She was silent.

"Do you, for one moment, believe I'm a homosexual?" he asked.

"Until you said that, I had no reason to. And even when

Frank tried to make something of the Luiz business, I didn't give it a thought."

"That's why you asked about Mac. And I told you. Don't you think I'd have withheld it if I were?"

"You never told me before."

"It was a shabby episode. I wasn't very proud of it. But when you asked me, I told you. And there wasn't anything more to it than what I told you."

"You made the remark. It was pretty shattering."

"I made plenty of remarks. They were all shattering. I'm so goddamn shattered, I don't know whether I'll ever be able to pick up the pieces!"

"I didn't mention it last night. I don't know what prompted me to bring it up now."

"I do. All that damnfool talk about making it easier for you if you wanted out. Which seemed like confirmation and which I didn't really mean and which would just destroy me if you ever took me up on it. Actually, I was trying to be fair. If I were completely honest, I'd have been making a pitch for you to stick with me and see this thing through. But I don't think it's right to pressure you and I'm not going to. You know what I feel."

She didn't say anything.

"I'd better get back to the hotel," he said after a moment.

"I'd rather you didn't. There's always the chance of bumping into the folks again."

"My stuff's in the room."

"It can wait. They're leaving for Palm Springs in the morning. You can sleep in the guest room."

"Whatever you say."

"I'd prefer it." She opened the car door and stepped out.

"I'll park it," he said.

When he returned from the garage, Peggy was already in the house. The phone was ringing, and he could hear her voice as she answered it.

"For you," she said, when he entered. "It's Ike Press."

"I've been trying to reach you," said Ike.

"We've been with Madge Lerner."

"Of course. I should have realized. When I was told about Dick's passing I couldn't help but recall our conversation of two days ago when you spoke with such high hope and enthusiasm of his new project. A shocking loss. To you personally, I know. And to the world."

"It is."

"I don't know Mrs. Lerner or the family situation, but if there's any way in which I can be helpful, please call on me."

"Very generous of you. Fortunately Dick kept up his insurance. But there will be a fund for a research fellowship in his name."

"I'll be happy to contribute." There was a slight pause, then a change in tone. "I called really to apologize. I'm afraid I was quite abrupt with you last night."

"If there's any apology it should come from me."

"Considering the burden you were under I should have been more understanding. I confess I was completely impatient with you."

"Understandably, after keeping you up the night before."

"I realized later the desperate need you must have felt to talk about what had happened. Actually, I wouldn't have been in a very sympathetic mood. I'm much more objective about it now that I've had a chance to think about it, and I'd like to talk with you."

For some reason, perhaps because he knew he'd seen Arthur, Alex felt himself drawing back. "There's really no need. I wouldn't want to take your—"

"Nonsense. Suppose we have lunch tomorrow. Unless you're tied up."

"No. But aside from telling you how ashamed I am—"

"I have some very definite thoughts on the episode and I suppose *I* now feel the need to talk about it. Shall we make it for lunch then?"

"Fine," said Alex with a sense of apprehension.

"At my house, I suggest. Mrs. Press will be out, and we'll be quite alone to talk in quiet. Twelve, shall we say?"

"Twelve," said Alex. Then, impulsively, "I guess Arthur must have been shocked."

"Arthur? Oh, about Dick Lerner. Everyone was."

"About me."

"What about you?"

"I know you saw him this morning."

"Of course I saw him. I see him the beginning of every month —to talk budget with him." There was an uneasy pause. As if in afterthought, he added, "Till tomorrow, then," and hung up.

Was it just budget? He hadn't really said. Though the pause had. He wondered how much he'd told Arthur about San Vicente and whether they'd come to any conclusion about his remaining on the staff.

Strange, Alex realized how he'd been feeding on his anxieties, magnifying them, casting up phantoms. Not only the nightmare delusions when he was out of control. But the conviction before then that Ike Press had dreamed up the idea of a post or research grant in the department of tropical diseases to euchre him out of the appointment. Maybe he'd like such a research grant now. But it would undoubtedly go to a young man recommended, as he had been, so long, long ago, by Dorothy Horstman of Yale. He was so many light-years away from research. So mad to think that anyone would want him!

A sudden weariness caught him. Peg had already gone up to bed. For a moment his eyes lingered on the lonely figures plodding up the desolate, rain-swept street of the water color. He sighed, walked slowly up the stairs.

In the guest room he suddenly realized he was without pajamas or toothbrush. Making his way back into the hallway, he paused before Peg's door, knocked tentatively.

"Just a minute!" said Peggy, a start of panic in her voice. A second later, she called: "All right."

She faced him, self-conscious in the robe which she'd hurriedly clutched about her. He found himself as uneasy as she was.

"Sorry," he said, cutting through the unnatural constraint. "I just wanted to get a toothbrush and pajamas."

He walked into the bathroom to pick up the toilet articles he needed, then returned into the room to take some pajamas out of a drawer. He passed her to get a robe from the closet. She hadn't moved since he'd come in; her hand still clutched the neck of her robe.

Is she afraid I'm going to see something? he asked himself. Does she think I'm going to force myself on her? This wasn't Peg; it wasn't he. It was all so wrong.

At the door he paused to say good night. She answered inaudibly. He saw her standing in the same stiff pose, a look of complete wretchedness in her eyes. When he closed the door he knew she'd break down and cry. He was close to it himself.

His mind was too restless for sleep, and he couldn't get himself to go back for Seconal. The phrase about Mac's eyes came back to plague him. It *was* an odd thing to have said, and he couldn't help questioning whether it implied something deeper than he was willing to accept. Maybe there was something latent in him, something which Frank may have discerned when he made the bet that Carlos would go for him that first night in the *cantina*. And Carlos *had* made a play for him. So had Luiz.

Was there something in him that attracted homosexuals? Of course, boys like Carlos made a profit out of it. So it didn't mean much—except that they were angling after likely customers. Mac had been real enough. And, although he couldn't respond to Mac, Mac had been attracted by something in him. Looking back, he could recall a couple of occasions when he'd been alone at a bar and men had come up to drink beside him and made tentative conversation that had the overtones of a pickup. But hadn't that happened to lots of men he knew? And what was he getting in such a stew about? One passing remark when he quite obviously wasn't himself, and here he was building it into something deep-seated in his character.

It was absurd. He couldn't go on accusing himself of everything under the sun. He had to have some sense of proportion about what had happened. If he worried every drunken remark into an essential truth about himself, he might as well slit his throat.

He couldn't, of course, dismiss the episode as meaningless. It had raised too many questions which he had to face and weigh and try to understand. But it didn't cancel out the good things. It wasn't that simple. And he mustn't, out of guilt and shame, tear down what he was and had been.

Peg wasn't condemning out of hand. She hadn't, as she might so easily have, fallen for the over-simplification of the *in vino veritas* platitude. There was a perception and a will to understand in what she'd said about it. He loved her for it.

He let himself think about her lying in the big bed on the other side of the wall. The wretchedness in her eyes stayed with him, and he wished he could be with her to kiss it away. An ache went through his body, and a longing.

The importunity to be with her dissipated the questionings of a moment ago, and he gave himself to the pleasurable reverie of the fulfillment they'd always had together. Recalling the fearful figure clutching the neck of her robe, he wondered, with growing uncertainty, whether they ever would again.

IX

DRIVING by the front of the hospital the next morning, Alex was startled to see Ben Levitt sitting on the stairs where he'd found him the day before. He braked the car to a stop, honked and called his name, wondering what on earth he was doing here at seven in the morning. For a moment he had the awful feeling that something had gone wrong with Ruth Levitt, but when he asked Ben, Ben said no, nothing that he knew of.

"Then what in the name of God are you doing here?" demanded Alex.

"Sitting," he said casually.

"At this hour?"

"I couldn't sleep. I got up at five and was too restless to stay in the house. So I came here. At least I'm close to her."

"And visiting hours aren't till two. Have you had any breakfast?"

"Orange juice. It's all I wanted."

"You'd better come with me and have some."

Ben protested but went along.

Alex was signing in at the desk when an envelope was handed to him.

"Oh, that's from me," said Ben. "Ruth asked me to bring it. It's nothing really. Just a memento."

The memento was a glossy theatrical photo of Ruth Levitt in a chorine costume from *Oh, Please*. She was every bit as beautiful as Alex had imagined. Her hair was cut in the Dutch boy style affected by Louise Brooks, one of his movie favorites of the period. In her eyes was all the intensity, the eagerness, and wonder of youth. He was curiously moved.

"She said she'd autograph it for you," said Ben. "She was a knockout in those days. Could have had anybody. Millionaire playboys begging her to marry 'em. Why she glommed onto me I don't know."

"She knew you'd be around on the front stairs at seven in the morning."

It wasn't until he opened the door to the dining room that he regretted the impulse which had made him ask Ben to breakfast. Fortunately Bert and Frank were seated at the far end of the counter. After the first glance he avoided looking in their direction. But he could sense them looking up, feel the resentment which seemed to bristle in the air. There were a couple of empty chairs near the door. He would have preferred a table which was removed from the line of exit, but they were all taken.

Nervously he lit a cigarette, busied himself with the menu. He was grateful for the coffee which Eunice, the waitress, placed before him, as she always did without prompting. In his disturbed state the burden of making conversation with a relative stranger was too much for him. Luckily the photo had thrown Ben into a reminiscent mood, and he was soon launched on a nostalgic monologue of his meeting and courtship of Ruth.

Without looking, Alex knew when Bert and Frank rose from their seats. He could feel himself tightening with the sound of each footfall. They had to pass him, but his back was turned, so there'd be no encounter. Yet his heart was pounding, his skin hot, hands moist. He tried to concentrate on Ben's story and, though he heard the words, they didn't register.

Bert's did. They weren't loud. He didn't stop to direct them at him. They were uttered in a conversational tone, in passing, but they might as well have been shouted into an amplifier.

"Nice to have a Jew bastard of a father-in-law who can buy a hospital for you."

He couldn't believe that he'd heard or credit the fact that they'd been uttered.

"Easy, Bert," Frank was saying.

"It takes all kinds," Bert said, a little more loudly as he stepped up to the cashier. "Yessir, it takes all kinds."

Alex sat rigid, his mind grasping at the implications of that first remark, then rejecting them. Yet he knew it wasn't a random remark. Bert had been quite deliberate about it.

The cashier counted out the change from a twenty-dollar bill. A puff of air from the closing door brushed Alex's neck. He sat irresolute a moment, the flow of Ben's story rolling over him. Abruptly, he rose. "Excuse me," he said. "Be back in a minute."

As if they'd been expecting him, Bert and Frank were standing about ten feet from the door.

Alex walked up and, addressing Bert, said, "Just what did you mean by that remark?"

Bert didn't say a word, merely looked at him for a long moment with a slight smile of disdain, then turned on his heel and walked off down the corridor. Alex wanted to run after him, to grab hold of his arm and whirl him around. Instead he turned to Frank.

"What was that crack supposed to mean?" he repeated.

"Self-evident, isn't it?"

"Not quite. I get the drift. But it doesn't make sense."

"Doesn't it? I'll pinpoint it for you. Bert was at the club playing gin last night. So was Ike Press. In the course of the evening Joe Strauss came in and sat down at Ike's table. It wasn't long before word got around, the way word does, that Memorial was going to be honored with a new Joseph G. Strauss maternity wing."

"Son of a bitch," Alex said half-aloud. "He promised he wouldn't say a word until after Wednesday."

"It wouldn't do you much good after Wednesday."

"I'm not asking for any good. I'm not asking for a thing."

"Rather quixotic on your part, isn't it?" There was skepticism in his tone and look.

"You don't believe me, do you?"

"Frankly, no. . . . Not that it matters. You wanted it and you're getting it."

"Not any more, I don't. And not this way."

"You made yourself pretty clear on the subject the other night, and the way didn't seem to matter."

"I know," Alex said in a low voice. "And I don't blame you for thinking what you do. I told Dan. I tried to apologize—if you ever can. I owe an apology to everyone who was there. . . ."

Frank didn't say anything.

"That's why I called you yesterday," Alex said after a pause.

"That's right, I was supposed to call you back, wasn't I?"

"I can understand why you didn't. That's one of the things I wanted to say. If you feel uncomfortable about having me around, perhaps you'd prefer to have someone else in the suite."

"The thought occurred to me. I didn't call because I hadn't made up my mind. I still haven't."

"If there's any question, it's very simple. I'll move out."

"It's not that simple. Whatever I may feel—I'm not much of a Jew, but still, as the man said, 'prick me and I bleed.' I bled a little. . . ."

"I'm sorry," Alex said wretchedly. It was a stupid and inadequate thing to say, yet he repeated it. "Terribly sorry . . ."

"I haven't made up my mind, because it isn't simply a matter of feelings. We've had a pretty profitable partnership. Business-wise, I don't know whether I care to disrupt it. . . . As you can see, I'm a man of principle and conviction," he added sardonically.

"Actually," said Alex, "there are a dozen surgeons who could do as well for you."

"One. Exactly one. Dan Simon. And then only if he got the appointment. But he isn't going to. Not now."

"You may be surprised about that."

"Are you kidding? What's Dan got to offer that stands up against a maternity wing? Yesterday, yes. But today? He shook his head. "No, I'm not letting any surgeon-in-chief walk out of my office. So forget it. It's still yours—unless word of San Vicente gets around. It's one thing for me to know about it, but if it gets to the patients—"

"Then it's not."

"That's right. I told you, I'm a man of principle." The sardonic note again. "Incidentally, I didn't care for your C.P.C. performance yesterday."

"I wouldn't worry about it," said Alex. "Because I think you'll find Dan's your man after all. You don't want me."

"You'll do. I'm not saying I love you. But money-wise, I'm satisfied. Isn't that the proper attitude for a Jew bastard to take?" The words had a caustic thrust which seemed directed at himself as well as at Alex.

Alex stood motionless for a long moment after Frank had walked away. Then he turned and proceeded resolutely toward Arthur's office. He was almost at the door when he realized Arthur wouldn't be in for another hour. He'd have to come back later, after the endoartectomy he was scheduled to perform. Not that Ike Press hadn't told Arthur about the withdrawal of his name. But now that Joe Strauss had pulled his little surprise, he'd better make sure that he had it absolutely straight. His father-in-law wasn't "buying" any hospital for him. . . .

Damn Joe Strauss's interfering hide! He stopped at a phone booth, dialed the Beverly Hills Hotel. He'd tell him off in spades! But there was no answer from the room, or from the restaurant or lobby where he had Joe Strauss paged. Then he recalled Peg's telling him they were leaving for Palm Springs first thing in the morning. They were undoubtedly on their way.

He called Peggy, told her what had happened.

"I can't believe it," she said. "Not after you asked him not to. He agreed, said he respected you for it."

"And the minute I left picked up the phone and called Ike Press."

"Not that I should be so surprised. Damn, why do I insist on being so naïve about him? Why should I expect him to keep his word?"

"Not when he can swing his weight around, show what a big shot he is, bribe the Board, put me in his debt—he thinks!"

"I'm furious. The more I think about it the more furious I

get! I'm putting in a call to the Desert Inn. They're driving, so they won't be there for a couple of hours, but I'll leave a message for him to call me. I don't think he'll like what I have to say."

When he hung up, Alex suddenly remembered leaving Ben Levitt in the dining room. He hurried back. Ben was smoking an after breakfast cigarette.

"Sorry I had to run off like that," Alex said.

"Perfectly all right. With a doctor I can see that it would be happening all the time. Nothing serious, I hope."

Alex shook his head. It was time that he start getting into his scrub suit, but he wanted to sit a moment. Gratefully he watched Eunice, who was immediately on deck with a refill for his coffee. He took a cigarette from the pack Ben was holding out for him, let Ben light it. Fortunately Ben was content to sit and enjoy his cigarette in silence.

No, it was nothing serious, Alex reflected wryly. Merely a cataclysm. He was suddenly overcome with the utter pointlessness of all that had happened. Anxiety about the appointment had taken him down to San Vicente; it had precipitated the catastrophic violence of the week-end. And after all the damage was done, when he'd ruined any chance he might have had, papa Strauss had blown in out of left field and handed it to him on a platter. And now that it was all sewed up, Alex was going to walk into Arthur's office and tell him he didn't want it!

Sense? Not a shred. It was completely insane from beginning to end. Yet it couldn't be any different. He had no questions, no qualms.

Until, nearing the finish of the endoartectomy, he suddenly realized the finality of his decision and a delayed reaction sent him into a sweat of doubt and confusion. Could something he'd wanted so desperately become so meaningless? Or did he, down deep, still want it? He didn't know, couldn't think, couldn't tell whether he was being pressured by what people would think, or acting out of a conviction of what was right. Why, damn it, was he so unclear, unsure?

It wasn't until after he closed the incision with precise sutures that he noticed his scrub suit was clinging wet. Wearily he moved toward the locker room and shower. Why, he wondered, had he allowed himself to doubt when there was no doubt? So foolish to dig up the corpse of an old ambition when he knew better. There was only one right and decent thing to do, and he was going to do it. Whatever uncertainties might have remained were gone with the shower.

As he dressed he prepared himself for Arthur's objections. Count on Arthur to blow his top and make it damned uncomfortable for him. It was perhaps providential that he was tied up in a meeting when Alex asked to see him. So he wrote a letter instead.

"Dear Arthur," it read. "This is to confirm in writing what Mr. Press told you yesterday: I wish my name withdrawn from any consideration for the chief-surgeon appointment.

I appreciate the fact that you thought well enough of me to propose me. But after considered reflection I have come to the firm conclusion that it is neither in my personal interest nor that of the hospital. I regret that I didn't reach this decision immediately. Many thanks for everything.

Yours,
Alex Frazier."

He placed it in an envelope, scribbled Arthur's name on it, and handed it to the secretary.

It was done. And how good it felt.

He was coming out of the ward after a cheerful visit with Ruth Levitt when he saw Dan coming down the corridor toward him. He should have guessed, should have anticipated from the sudden pallor in his face, but he was totally unprepared for the heavy sarcasm of Dan's greeting.

"Well, I suppose congratulations are in order," he was saying.

"You son of a bitch, if you couldn't get it one way, you got it another, didn't you? You weren't content with—"

"Look, Dan," Alex interrupted, "before you go any farther and say something you'll regret—"

"The only thing I regret is that I didn't tell you off in the first place. But no, I had to be a good Joe, understanding. And you knew just how to disarm me, didn't you? You didn't wait for anyone else to tell me what you did at San Vicente. You came on the run and confessed all. And you were so frank and earnest and ingenuous that I thought what the hell, we're all human, it was a drunken aberration of the moment which you couldn't in your right mind mean or intend because, Jesus, we were friends, we went way back, you were the guy I roomed with, you shared my practice and it simply wasn't in you, you couldn't. But now I see you could. And when Arthur put your name up against mine, what did you do then? Pulled the same disarming trick. Called me in Rome. Told me in all frankness and honesty and horrified concern. You didn't want it, you said. You'd told Arthur. So what was I going to do, be a slob when you were being so decent? Forget it, I said. Let it be. I didn't give a damn one way or the other. But apparently I did. Because on second thought, I asked myself why in hell, if you were such a good friend, you were calling me at all? Why hadn't you just categorically refused to have your name put up?"

"I should have."

Dan went on as though he hadn't heard. "Because what you were doing, really, was asking me to say it was okay. You caught me off-base, and I was schmoe enough to fall for it. Nice technique, Frazier. All right, I'm the dope, and the best man won. If not the best, the smartest—or richest. And what the hell, it's all in the interest of good old Memorial. Bigger and better babies will yowl, richer milk spurt from more contented breasts in the Joseph G. Strauss Maternity Wing. Congratulations."

"You're the one to be congratulated," said Alex.

"For what? Being so naïve?"

"For the appointment. It's yours."

"I'm not in the mood for—"

"I just handed in a letter withdrawing my name."

"I'll believe it when I hear it from Arthur."

"Go ask him."

Dan stared at him. "If that's true, it's a hell of a thing to pull on me after what I've been saying."

"What you said was quite valid. I thought I was being honest and aboveboard. I wasn't aware of trying to disarm you. But subconsciously, I suppose I was."

Dan was silent. "I feel like crud," he finally said.

"Why?" said Alex. "For saying something that makes sense?"

"Crud," Dan echoed. "You kid yourself into thinking what a great guy you are, then you find that all the shoving and grasping you've resented in someone else are in you."

"I'm the crud for allowing it to happen in the first place. You were right. I should have refused. Not only because I was your friend but because you had every reason to expect that apointment: record, seniority, ability, character. You deserve it."

"I'm beginning to wonder."

"Don't," said Alex. "You do and you know it."

Dan stood silent, his eyes troubled. "The test is," he finally said, "that when it came down to it, you could say no. I doubt if I could."

"Why should you? There's no reason. You were in line for it. Not me. And you certainly don't have a father-in-law calmly trying to buy your way. Maybe I ought to be grateful to him for stirring up a little vestige of self-respect."

His words drifted off. An awkward constraint seemed to settle over them. Abruptly, Alex walked away, his steps echoing down the corridor.

When he'd finished the rounds of his patients it was already noon and he realized he'd be late for his lunch date with Ike Press. That too would take on another dimension now that his decision was made. He was emerging from the elevator when he heard his name over the speaker. "Dr. Frazier, will you please report to Mr. Portugal's office. Dr. Frazier, you are wanted in Mr. Portugal's office."

He decided to disregard Arthur's summons. He was in no mood for a long hassle. When he got back he'd say he'd already left for lunch. Quickly he hurried to the exit. As he passed the desk, the attendant handed him an envelope. He shoved it into his the attendant handed him an envelope. He shoved it into his pocket and rushed out to the parking lot.

X

As if to make amends for his coldness of the other evening, Ike Press greeted him with an outstretched hand and a warm "How are you, my boy?"

"Sorry I'm late," mumbled Alex, his eyes turning uncomfortably from Ike's direct gaze. The sense of shame, submerged the other night in the urgency to repudiate his false accusations against Dan, seemed stronger now.

"One doesn't expect a banker's punctuality from a doctor. And, fortunately, I cleared the decks so that we'd have time to talk."

Ike led the way through the vast living room into his study. It was a pleasant pine-paneled room. A Filipino houseboy was setting a log into place in the fireplace. He turned on the gas jet. Immediately the kindling caught and blazed into flame.

"There's been a bit of a chill in the air, and I seize on any excuse for a wood fire. Nothing like the smell of burning eucalyptus." Ike waved to the leather armchairs which flanked the big copper-topped coffee table in front of the fireplace. The table was set with a spread of cold cuts, a tray of breads, potato salad, and an aspic.

Nervously Alex lit a cigarette and sat down.

"Would you like coffee now or later?" asked Ike.

"Now, if you don't mind."

Ike started to pick up the electric coffeepot, but the houseboy anticipated him and poured out a cup for Alex and a cup for Ike.

"Thank you, Robert. Now if you'll turn off the gas under those logs, we'll be all set."

Robert waited a moment to be sure the logs had caught, then shut off the valve. "Anything else, sir?" he asked.

"Not a thing."

Robert nodded, turned, and walked quickly out of the room. His footsteps sounded on the tiled flooring of the study, then were lost in the deep pile of the living room rug.

"You're probably famished," said Ike. He gestured toward the table. "Help yourself."

"I'll get to it," said Alex, taking a sip of coffee. "Don't wait for me. Go right ahead."

Ike Press proceeded to fill his plate. He seemed to deliberate over each choice, and Alex got the sense that he was probably as apprehensive about their "talk" as he was.

His plate filled, Ike sat back as if he no longer had any interest in it. The tips of his fingers came together tent-wise. "As I told you," he began, "I feel very badly about the other night."

"You needn't," said Alex. "You were annoyed, and I understand why."

"I wonder if you do. You see, I pride myself on being a very rational and disciplined person. I rarely act out of impulse or emotion. A banker can't afford to. You say I was annoyed. It went much deeper. Deeper than anger. If I can describe it at all, I'd say it was a blind, almost primitive hostility. I felt it in the motel room in San Vicente. I felt it when I opened the door the other night and thought: 'How dare you! How dare you, after all that happened, come shamelessly to press your case?' You hadn't, of course. But I was in too hostile a mood to be civil. So I was brusque, abrupt."

Ike paused, leaned forward. "Why do I tell you this?" he asked. "Because my reaction, my blind and unthinking hostility was in its way a counterpart of what happened to you. For the moment we were in the grip of old bigotries discarded with our childhood. I was suckled on ghetto prejudices. When I was a boy I was taught to spit when I passed a church. I hated the *goyim*, passionately, fiercely. Until I was old enough to have a mind of my own, until I discovered the brotherhood of man. Then I could put aside such feelings, bury the senseless hatreds and grow up to be a decent, enlightened human being. Just as you could and did."

"Or thought I did."

"Did—from what I know of you, personally and from others. You must remember I've been giving rather close study to your records and character this past week."

"Didn't prepare you for what happened, I'm afraid."

"No, it didn't."

"I thought I knew myself fairly well until that little episode."

"It would be wrong to give it more significance than it has. I talked to your wife this morning. She tells me there's been no past history. In fact, it's the one time she's really known you to get drunk."

Alex stubbed out his cigarette. "The one seems to have made up for all the times I never did."

"In a way I feel responsible, because I did urge a drink on you after you protested you'd had your quota."

"I'm a free agent. I knew better. Why I let go, I don't know."

"You have been under a strain since you took over from Trattner."

"That doesn't excuse the anti-Semitic slime that came out of me."

"You were too far gone to even know what you were saying."

"You mean if I happened to close my eyes I wouldn't be responsible for driving into a telephone pole? No, consciously I'd never think in those terms. But fact is, it had to be in me to come out of me."

"It's in all of us to some degree. That's what I was trying to tell you. We all carry around our secret little sacks of evil. The good doctor from Vienna taught us that. We're not all so unlucky as to have them revealed."

The phone rang. Ike Press reached over to pick it up from the side table.

"Hello," he said. "No great mystery, Arthur. I often have lunch at home. What's on your mind?"

He listened. Alex lit a second cigarette. He could tell from the excited rasp of the phone and from Ike's quick look at him that Arthur was telling him about his letter of withdrawal.

"When was it dated?" asked Ike. "I see . . ." The electric crackle of words again. "No, I haven't the faintest idea. I'm not in the habit of repeating confidences, Arthur. Though you and I know that a confidence at the Club is a contradiction in terms. . . . As a matter of fact, Alex happens to be right here with me. Would you like to talk to him?"

Ike picked up the cradle of the phone, handed it to Alex. "Arthur Portugal," he said.

Alex placed the cradle on the end table beside his chair, took the phone from Ike. "Hello, Arthur," he said.

"I got your letter. You're not serious, of course."

"Just as serious as when I told Mr. Press."

"What's your thinking, Alex?"

"I told you. It's not in the interests of the hospital or myself."

"There isn't a surgeon in the city who wouldn't consider such an appointment to his advantage. And as to the interest of the hospital, you don't think I'd have proposed you if I had the slightest doubt that it wouldn't be? What's your real reason?"

"I no longer want it."

"This is a fine time to come to that! Why?"

"For several reasons. One, because I'm not taking anything my father-in-law bribed the Board to get."

"That's not much of a compliment to the integrity of the Board or Joe Strauss. There were no strings attached to that donation."

"You mean he didn't say flatly that he'd give it *if*—"

"There were no ifs. He probably anticipated you'd misunderstand, because he asked us not to announce it for a couple of weeks. And if it hadn't been for some blabbermouth, you wouldn't even have known."

"But I do know and I understand—all too well."

"You can understand what you will. I don't accept your implications and I don't accept your withdrawal. After all, you have an obligation to the hospital—and to me. I've worked damned hard in your behalf—long before there was any question of a maternity wing."

"I appreciate that."

"So let's forget this foolishness. As far as I'm concerned you never wrote the letter. In fact, I'm tearing it up right now."

"That won't make me take the appointment."

"Do you want to continue to work in this hospital, Frazier?"

"Are you threatening me, Arthur?"

Ike Press, who had risen from his chair and was standing above him, reached down, eased the phone out of his hand. "Excuse me," he said. And into the phone, "Arthur? Ike. I doubt if any good purpose will be served by pursuing this conversation. Alex is here. We're having lunch. If he's so disposed, we can perhaps explore it in a more leisurely fashion."

The angry sputter of Arthur's reply was quite intelligible to Alex. "I'll be goddamned if I let him screw up that donation!" he heard him say. "All we need is to have Joe Strauss get sore and yank it."

"Let me handle it, Arthur," Ike said quietly.

There was a grunt of acquiescence from the phone.

"I'll talk to you later," said Ike, and replaced the phone on the cradle.

"You mustn't blame Arthur for his disappointment. He's been most diligent in trying to persuade the various Board members you were the ideal man for the post. He promised many innovations in Surgery if you were appointed."

"That was before San Vicente."

"I don't see why San Vicente should change it."

"You did on Monday night."

"I don't think either of us were accountable for what we felt on Monday night. We were much too close to the incident."

"Would you be trying to persuade me now if the wing weren't involved?"

"I'd be trying to persuade you not to make the incident more important than it is."

"And the wing's not a consideration."

"It's a factor. Of course."

"A damn big one."

"The question, if you don't mind my saying so, is not whether it is, or how the appointment is decided, but whether it's the best appointment, whether you're the man for it."

"How is very much the question—to me. But putting that aside for the moment, *am* I the man?"

"Do you doubt it? You certainly went to great lengths to convince me if you did."

"That was then. Now I don't know."

Ike Press picked up his fork, placed a slice of turkey between two pieces of rye bread. "Do you, by any stretch of the imagination, believe that one night, one lapse could have altered your ability as a surgeon or administrator?"

"Doesn't character come into consideration?"

"Of course."

"Would you consider a character who behaved as I did responsible?"

"My dear boy, I don't condone what happened. I deplore it. I told you my initial reaction—I reverted, I wanted to spit—which was irrational and which I also deplore. I've thought about this. I'm not willing to measure a man by a single incident. Do you in all honesty believe that you're a different person today than you were a week ago? You may be a little chastened perhaps; you may know a little more about yourself—"

"Less."

"Less, perhaps. But essentially you're the same person. I think you have to distinguish between the man and this outlandish thing which has happened to him, between a moment of insanity and a lifetime. Is a man's character, his life, to be weighed against a single display of the Mr. Hyde in him?"

"You acknowledge there is a Hyde."

"In all of us. To the degree that we master it we're whole and decent. When we let it master us—"

"No question of who mastered whom on New Year's Eve," Alex said sardonically.

"I refuse to accept the protrait of New Year's Eve. It isn't you; it isn't the man. It's a wild beast spouting memories of ancient barbarisms long suppressed and civilized."

"And suddenly very much alive," said Alex.

"Once. When you weren't yourself. When the controls were down. I have every confidence it won't happen again."

"I'd like to know what you base it on," said Alex. "Reason or wishful thinking? Why the concern about my not wanting the appointment? I'll tell you. Because you think it'll rock the boat and jeopardize that donation."

Ike Press started to say something, changed his mind.

"What you're arguing for is that maternity wing and you know it!"

"My dear boy," said Ike Press, "when was it I called to ask you to lunch?"

"Last night."

"It's true I already knew about your father-in-law's generous offer. But I'd called before, and you weren't in. And the reason I called was that I was concerned about you. I still am."

"With that added reason."

"All right!" There was an impatient edge in Ike's voice. "If you've ever tried to raise money, as I have year after year, you'd know what an unexpected gift of a half million means. Naturally I don't want to rock the boat. Do you blame me?"

"No."

"So in a sense I *am* arguing for a maternity wing. But that doesn't invalidate what I'm saying. I would have said it anyway. Before the offer. Before your letter of withdrawal. Because it's important. To me as well as you—quite apart from the wing. I know what you feel about San Vicente. I know what I felt. But let's not magnify its meaning. What was it that actually happened? Do you know?"

"Too well."

"I took the liberty of talking to Sandy Berniger, who's dealt with these things professionally. I didn't mention names, of course. An excessive intake of alcohol, he tells me, can, in susceptible individuals, bring on an acute toxic reaction. Which is undoubtedly what happened. And since there's no previous history, chances are, says Sandy, it'll never happen again. Hence my confidence."

Alex was silent.

"The fact that the chemistry of the moment precipitated a psychotic reaction doesn't mean you're a psychotic personality. It wasn't you speaking. It was your unconscious or subconscious. And how responsible are you for that?"

No more then he was for his dreams, Alex reflected.

Out of the corner of his eye he caught the abrupt glance which Ike directed at him. It had a quizzical, ruminative glint, as though he'd decided to take a fresh look at him, as if he'd suddenly asked himself whether there wasn't more to it than he was trying so hard to make out. Beneath all his arguments and reassurances there must have been a lingering question.

Ike turned his attention to the coffee. There was a slight tremor in his hand as he poured. He took a sip, set down the cup. "What a dread contradiction the human being is," he said with a sigh. "There's a Persian fable about a man who was such a model of virtue, a devout man who gave himself so completely to the worship of God that God revealed himself to him one day and said: 'You have been so good that I have decided to grant any and every wish you may have.' The man thanked Him. But he soon began to notice that people he knew and people he met were falling dead one after the other, in the streets, everywhere. And so he called out: 'Please, God, do not grant me any more of my wishes!' "

"Now that's a sweet little homily," said Alex. "Why don't we all cut our throats and be done with it?"

"That's not the conclusion I draw from it."

"I know. You're getting back to the proposition that 'we all carry around our little sacks of evil' and therefore I'm no worse than anyone else, San Vicente or no."

"Let me ask you a question," said Ike Press. "Suppose you'd

gone down to San Vicente alone. Without Peggy. Without any of us. And suppose you'd blacked out as you did. Would you think of yourself as any different than when you'd gone down there?"

Good question. He wouldn't have known what had happened. He'd have seen the evidences of violence. But would he have guessed it had been anything more than a drunken brawl? Probably not. He'd probably have come back and picked up from before without any sense that he was anything but what he'd always been.

"I guess I wouldn't," he acknowledged.

"Of course you wouldn't. And there's no reason why you should now."

"Except that you *were* there and I *do* know."

"The logic still holds. The person is still the same."

"Who is the person, Mr. Press?"

"We have a Hebrew saying: 'What we are is God's gift to us. What we make of ourselves is our gift to God.' What God makes we have no choice about. But what we make of ourselves—ah, there, I believe, is the measure of the man! We are what we shape ourselves to be, what we attain by will, effort, and purpose. You are a doctor. You have chosen a calling in the service of your fellows. And into it has gone long years of learning, of endless application and discipline. You have devoted your talents to research, to the perfection of surgical techniques, to the saving of human life. And I can't help thinking: this is the person, this what you have made, this your gift to God."

"Very noble. But not very accurate. And if it's designed to persuade me to withdraw my withdrawal—"

"What's this terrible thing I'm trying to persuade you to do? Be fair to yourself? You wanted that appointment."

"It's true I wanted it. A little too much, I'm afraid. San Vicente changed that. It's no longer important. Especially under the circumstances. I asked Joe Strauss to postpone his donation. He chose not to. He can't buy me that little gift, because I won't accept it."

"That's up to you. Pride can be an expensive luxury."

"I don't think I could afford anything better in my life," said Alex. "I'm sorry if it jeopardizes your maternity wing. If it does."

"It may not. He made the offer. It's on the record. But whether it does or doesn't, I'd like to make a confession. Though I've been arguing to the contrary, for your sake, I'm glad you made the decision you did."

"Thanks," said Alex.

"Now, suppose you have something to eat."

"Now, I think I can." He speared a slice of roast beef, transferred it to his plate. "While we're leveling—" he began, and left his thought suspended.

"Yes?" said Ike.

"I'm being very moral and righteous about this, but I'm avoiding the morality of telling Joe Strauss about San Vicente. Do you think I should tell him?"

"It's not for me to say," Ike said after a pause.

"I'd really like to know. What would *you* do if you were in my place?"

"Fortunately I'm not. It's a problem. You have your relationship with your wife to consider. I can't tell you. Only you can decide."

"But you have an opinion?"

"Perhaps."

"I know. And I know what it is. But you're not saying, because if I followed your advice—and I don't know whether I'd have the guts—Joe Strauss would probably blow so high he'd wash his hands of me and anything having to do with me, the hospital, the maternity wing, everything. But forgetting that for the moment, confidentially, would you urge me to?"

"You do raise dilemmas."

"The practical man would say: 'let sleeping dogs lie.' I want to know what you, Ike Press, would say."

"I'm that curious anomaly, a practical man with ideals," Ike said slowly.

"I don't know why I'm pushing you. Unless it's because I want to be pushed."

"Then I'd better stop playing," said Ike Press. "The hospital needs that wing."

There was no point in pursuing it, Alex told himself. It *was* his decision, and he'd do what he felt like doing when he got to it. For the time being Joe Strauss was in Palm Springs.

It was getting late. Like Ike, he made himself a sandwich. He was hungry enough to enjoy the rare beef and the corn rye bread.

Both munched in silence for a while. "The older I get," Ike said reflectively, "the more I realize what imperfect creatures we are. When I was young I was intolerant of human weakness. But one grows to understand. A person like Bert would call me soft. Perhaps I am. Perhaps I lack principle. But I'm too aware of my own shortcomings. Like you, I chided myself for my own lapse at San Vicente. The comforting thing is that man can be guilty of all that's base and reprehensible and yet—" He looked up at Alex. "Have you ever read Rousseau? I leafed through his *Confessions* after you left me the other night. The amazing thing is not that he could sink so low but that he could rise so high, that he could, along with Voltaire, forge the concepts of the Age of Enlightenment. He could dream of man's perfectibility. We despair too easily, I'm afraid. How much of that concept can we afford to give up these days?"

"We're interested in another kind of perfectibility," said Alex. "This is the hardware age."

"Yes, we'll reach the moon and leave our souls behind."

It was getting late. Dick's funeral was scheduled for two o'clock. He asked Ike Press if he could use the phone.

The exchange had a message from Peg. She wanted him to pick her up on the way to the cemetery.

As he hung up he was again aware of that speculative look in Ike's eyes.

XI

IT WAS when he got back to his car and was bending down to slide into the seat that he became aware of the bulk of the envelope in his jacket pocket. He pulled it out. Bert's name, he noticed, was typed in the upper left hand corner. A flutter of apprehension warned him to put it back without opening it. He couldn't. Compulsively he tore it open.

Although Bert had made his attitude unmistakably clear, the letter was as shocking as it was unexpected. Bert had become a man with a mission, and, if indirection wouldn't accomplish it, he wasn't a person to shrink from a frontal attack.

"After what has happened," read the letter, "I had hoped that conscience and common decency would persuade you to resign immediately from the staff of Memorial. Instead, through the brazen manipulation of your father-in-law's wealth, you have appropriated for yourself a position which by every right belongs to someone else.

"You knew full well when you joined the staff that Memorial was a Jewish hospital. It was organized as such because of Jew-hating gentiles like you who set quotas to exclude us from so-called 'Christian' hospitals. It happens to be the best hospital on the West Coast. It gave you prestige to be associated with it. So, even though you hated our guts, you piously hid what you felt and, through the sponsorship of a man who has been your friend and whose character you didn't hesitate to assassinate, you effected that association.

"On New Year's Eve you revealed yourself for the anti-Semite you are. Yet you still had the unmitigated gall to show up at the hospital as if nothing had happened. You had the crust to talk to the very man whose character and career you tried so viciously to destroy. You had the effrontery to pay a condolence call on the widow of one of the despised race. I'm told you wept unctuous tears. I am also told you will act as a pallbearer at his burial. The very thought makes me ill.

"There must have been some human consideration in you once. Otherwise, you would not have chosen this calling. To whatever remnant there is—if any there be—I address myself. Harboring the feelings you do, you don't belong here. Have the good grace to resign. I find your presence in these chambers and corridors an affront.

"Furthermore, I seriously question your responsibility as a surgeon. Your behavior of New Year's Eve cannot be described as anything but psychotic. It is my considered judgment that you're not stable enough to be entrusted with a scalpel.

"I don't know whether all who were witness to what happened are of my opinion. To them I have addressed copies of this letter. I leave it to each individual conscience to act as it will."

It wasn't that the letter said anything new. Every question it presented he'd raised and considered on his own. But where he'd equivocated, Bert was ruthless. And to see it on paper, the categorical judgment of a colleague, now being read by other colleagues, shook him. There it was, blunt and inescapable. And there was no disregarding it, no pretending it didn't exist.

One thing was clear: to accept Bert's premise about him was to accept his conclusion. If he were the person Bert described and if he had the merest shred of self-respect, he had no choice but to resign.

Two nights ago, when Peg had told him what had happened, in the first flood of guilt and self-recrimination, he'd been ready to take his actions at face value. Blindly, because he wanted to punish himself, he'd accepted everything he'd said and done as a true revelation of his inner and therefore essential self. He'd belabored and beat himself with it. In a sense, it was protective, a form of self-pity. And because he was so smothered in it, he'd been unable to think with any clarity or objectivity. It had taken

Peg's observation about the *in vino veritas* remark to jog his thinking into a more realistic frame. He was grateful now for the further perspective which Ike Press had given him.

Not that it was as simple and unqualified as Ike put it. San Vicente may not have changed him; perhaps he was the same person. But he was beginning to catch overtones, glimpse disturbing vistas which he hadn't sensed before.

How responsible are we for our unconscious? Ike had asked. For one moment San Vicente had thrown a light on that dark terrain, on the nightmare landscape of violence and terror. But how reliable was it, what did it tell about a person, this random glimpse into a black bin, into the tombed storehouse of lost memories, blind emotions, and the malefic unknown? What did it have to do with the conscious man, with the mind in control of thought and action, gifted with the power of choice, responsibility, reason?

For all the anti-Semitic filth which had spewed out of him that night, he knew in the full consciousness of his being that he wasn't an anti-Semite. As a thinking adult, the one thing he couldn't tolerate was intolerance—especially as he sensed remnants in himself. In the rare moments when blind anger or a black, frustrate emotion had unthinkingly called up a racist epithet, he'd never articulated it because the conscious part of his brain refused to allow him to express something he'd be so utterly ashamed of. It wasn't merely principle; it was the way he thought and felt.

The tragedy of San Vicente was that the specters of the past had in those mindless hours swarmed out of the grave. It might not have been the conscious person speaking, it might be the disinterred echo of another time, but once expressed, it became tangible, alive, forever associated in the minds of those who had witnessed and heard with his person, his feelings. And however he might think and however forget, it would always be there, reflected in their eyes, an eternal reminder, calling up the horror, shame, and revulsion. Could he ever escape it? Having once, in the senselessness of blackout, given voice to these rejected ideas of the past, was he condemned forever to live with them? Try as he might to exorcise them, there'd always be the accusation in Bert's eyes.

To face Bert before he'd written this letter was devastating enough.

Now?

He couldn't continue in the hospital, couldn't tolerate the thought that every turn in a corridor, every opening of a door might bring him face to face with Bert, Frank, or Ted, and, mirrored in their eyes, the monster of San Vicente.

He'd faced it yesterday; somehow he'd survived. It seemed worse now. Because there was no leavening of what they might be thinking. Here it was in black and white: indictment, verdict, sentence. It had been presented to him with the suddenness of an unexpected blow, a kick in the groin. The breath and spirit were out of him. Nothing was left but pain.

Yet the more he thought about it, the more Alex resented it. Not that he questioned Bert's right to feel as he did. But he did rebel at his self-appointed role as public prosecutor and judge. He resented the intimidation. Because this was a private decision. He had raised the question in his own mind without Bert's assistance. He didn't care to have a spotlight on him while he worked out in his own good time what he thought was right and best to do.

He had, thank God, followed through on the withdrawal. He was glad for that, glad he'd done it before he got Bert's letter.

But for all his brave talk about pulling out altogether, he didn't care to be pushed. Underneath, he wasn't quite as ready as he indicated. Little tentacles of fear reached out, brushed against the walls of his stomach, warning him against being triggered into a move he'd regret. It wasn't simply a matter of career. He could find a way to function, wherever he was. But that wouldn't help his situation with Peg. It needed time. He didn't want any premature move which might upset things still further. Better to feel his way, to sit it out and follow time's good counsel.

Very nice, with Bert's letter ticking like a time bomb in his pocket.

Peg was waiting at the curb. "What makes Bert think he's God?" she said, as she got into the car. "Who gave him the right to sit in judgment?"

"He's a man of strong convictions."

"I hope you're not going to let yourself give in to that kind of pressure."

"It's hard to disregard."

"It's beneath consideration."

"I'm not a block of concrete. I have certain sensibilities and sensitivities. Bert didn't invent San Vicente. It did happen."

"What happened has nothing to do with your ability as a surgeon or your usefulness to the hospital."

"I'd like to think that. Ike Press does. Bert doesn't. And I can't blame him. We're all human. He is. I am. You can't sieve out the emotions. They're there."

"And so highly charged he's making no sense. I'm trying to, but I'm as vulnerable as anyone else. More so, probably. Maybe I'm taking it out on Bert because I'm so confused. But not about this hospital business. I wish I were as clear about other things."

They drove along in silence for a while. "Thanks," Alex finally said, "for asking me to pick you up. It'd be awfully tough showing up alone."

"For me as well. Besides, there's no point in giving anybody ideas. About the hospital, I want you to promise me you won't do anything for a couple of days."

"I already have. Not in response to Bert's letter. Because I acted before I knew there was one. I bowed out of the appointment race, you'll be glad to know."

"I am. Though I know someone who won't be. You didn't say anything about leaving the hospital?"

"No."

"Because I don't think you ought to. I don't think you can run out on a situation like this. Especially under intimidation. And of this particular kind. Bert can be so all-fired righteous. But what is his letter except chauvinism in reverse?"

"That doesn't make it any less uncomfortable."

"No, it doesn't." She conceded and fell silent. "Dad called me back this morning," she resumed. "At first he tried to deny he'd said anything about the donation. I convinced him I knew he did. In fact, I let him have it. Both barrels. He didn't know what hit him. I've *never* talked to him like that! Sort of felt sorry for him afterwards. Even though he's still convinced he was justified. He'll probably blow his top when he hears about the appointment. He's going to call at six. Wants to explain to you. So I guess you'd better come for dinner. Unless you want me to say you're out on an emergency."

"No. I've got a few things to say to him."

"Don't *you blow*."

"No guarantee what I'll do. I might just tell him the whole business."

"What business?"

"San Vicente."

"Don't you dare! It's bad enough as it is."

"If I feel like it, why not?"

"Because it's unnecessary and I don't think he could take it."

"Are you protecting him or me—or yourself?"

She didn't answer, and he sensed her hurt. He wanted to say: "Forget it; I didn't mean it." But he hesitated, and then it was too late because he was caught in the jam of traffic turning into the cemetery entrance, and his thoughts turned from preoccupation with problems and self to Dick.

The crowd was unpredictably large. Because the chapel was inadequate, seats had been set up on the huge sweep of lawn, a platform improvised against the ivy-covered chapel wall. Organ music issued in muted solemnity from within. People were converging from the several driveways which led into the cemetery and past the rows of tombstones.

Dan and Kay Simon, who were standing with Jim Stevens and Israel Meltzer and his wife, nodded to Alex and Peg as they came up.

"They didn't turn out like this at our meetings when they could have done something for him," said Meltzer, looking at the huge crowd. "Now they're here."

"And I hope there's someone from the Board of Olive to see them," said Dan.

"If there is, I personally guarantee to knock his teeth in."

"They'll hear about it," said Jim Stevens. "And I think they're going to have very guilty consciences."

"The seven plagues aren't good enough for them."

"You're certainly in a bloodthirsty mood," said Mrs. Meltzer.

"My best friend's going into the ground. What do you want me to do, throw kisses at his enemies?"

Someone was signalling them to take their seats. Dan, Alex, Jim, and Meltzer walked down to the first row, which was reserved for the pallbearers. Peg sat with Kay and Mrs. Meltzer.

The last swell of organ music faded away. The buzz of talk stopped. On the platform a figure stepped forward. He paused for a moment as the sound of an approaching plane sputtered in the sky. When it was gone, he began to speak, quietly at first, then with growing fervor.

"Even when a life has run its course into old age, we are never adequately prepared to face our mortality," he said. "When it strikes abortively, terminating a young life, stilling forever a mind so brilliantly engaged in an endeavor to extend the understanding of man's life and its maladies, our sensibilities are stunned, reason outraged. For we insist on a design to human life; we demand order, progression, flowering, and completion. Death is no respecter of patterns; it follows no discernible design. It is the great mystery which confounds all of us, implacable and inscrutable.

"Richard Lerner would not have admitted its inscrutability.

For he was a student of death. He contemplated it under his microscope. Every day, in his laboratory, he grappled with it, tracked down one and then another of its secret weapons, learned how to turn them on themselves, to deflect them from their intended victims. In countless numbers they walk the earth today, alive and laughing. Some of them sit among us now to honor what he was and did and to wonder why he, who had saved them, couldn't save himself.

"Death has many allies. And those who hounded Richard Lerner and withheld his hand and brain from its labors have much to answer for. There can be no doubt that the ailments which precipitated his death were exacerbated by the trials and torments which they visited on him. They have not only to answer for him but for the numberless many who face the mortal dangers of the diseases he understood so well. The community, indeed mankind, has been deprived of the benefit of that understanding.

"It is hard to believe that he is no longer with us. If he were standing in my place today and speaking of a friend who had suffered his untimely and unjust end, he would have said that there was no justifying it except as an example of how far the world is from perfection. And he would have urged us, with the indomitability of spirit that was his, to work toward that vision of perfection which was his goal."

Listening as the speaker went on to detail the considerable strides which Dick had made toward his goal, Alex felt there was glory in what he'd achieved. In his seventy papers written in a five-year period before he was thirty, in his discoveries in the field of kidney diseases, in his textbooks on the subject, in his revolutionary attack on nephritis, and finally, in his work on the molecular approach to mental disease.

How much he might have contributed if he'd been allowed to work for another twenty-five years! As he should have been. As millions, less endowed and less selfless, were. The world, which had been so harsh to him, was the loser. All the insight he might have brought to bear on man's ills gone, dissipated; the scores of disciples who might have been trained in his techniques, schooled in his thinking, inspired by his vision, deprived, denied.

"It's so hard to write third acts," a playwright friend had once said. If the theatre had its share of faulty ones, life had more. The whole plan was wrong, Alex told himself. Growth, flower, decay —or sudden blight. It was a botch, a perversion, a cheat. And because it was and man rebelled at his fleeting moment in time, in gallant and desperate defiance, he strove to extend it, to mark his name by some immortal work or deed. The same mechanism was operating in Alex now. He wanted suddenly to take over from Dick, to take up where he had left off. But he knew he couldn't. He was too many years away from research. A war and two decades had intervened.

The eulogy was over, the organ music sounding in solemn sonorities from within. Falling into step with Dan, he walked into the chapel and up the aisle to the open bier. The lines and harassment were gone from Dick's face. He looked so poignantly young. On the second finger of his left hand was one of the matching silver and turquoise rings which Alex had brought back for Dick and Madge when he'd first returned from Mexico.

Standing with the other pallbearers, as the long line of mourners passed, all he could think of was that he wanted to live up to the image Dick had once had of him, wanted once more to find the meaning in his life which Dick had never lost in his.

The line came to an end. Madge, Dick's mother, and the boys stepped forward to take their last look. Madge's face was stoic; a proud defiance gleamed in her eyes. Dick's mother wept soundlessly. Trying manfully not to show their emotions, the boys stood stiff as rods—until Tommy, the youngest, suddenly broke and burst into heartbreaking sobs. Alex felt like running forward to gather him in his arms.

The lid of the coffin was finally closed. The pallbearers moved in place, Alex between Dan and Meltzer. They bent down, lifted the coffin and bore it to the hearse. Then, as the hearse rolled slowly forward, they walked with it toward the burial site.

Again, they took hold and carried the coffin to the black opening of the grave. In the despair at death it was always shocking to Alex to find himself so aware of the tokens of life: in the smell of the freshly mown grass, in the birds wheeling above, in the sun slanting down and white clouds drifting by, in the hum of traffic from behind the cemetery walls. Beside him, Dan was mumbling something in an undertone. The words were foreign, but he'd heard them before. They were the words of the Hebrew Kaddish, the prayer for the dead: "Yisgadol v'yiskadash sh'meh raboh—" Something in Dan had called forth the traditional and familiar. It wasn't meant for anyone to hear; it was Dan's farewell to Dick, and it was strangely touching and fitting.

The coffin was being lowered, the spade of earth thrown upon it. Then it was over, the crowd dispersing. He found Peg standing beside him, her eyes red. Together they walked across the cemetery toward the car.

He had just closed the door on Peg's side and was rounding the front to the other when he suddenly came face to face with Bert, who was cutting across to his car. Neither said a word. Bert moved past him, and Alex opened the door and slid in beside Peg. He sat trembling for a moment, then turned the key.

Peggy, who hadn't seen Bert, seemed lost in a revery which carried over until they were back in traffic. "I'm glad it was the kind of eulogy it was," she said. "It made me angry all over again about the Olive Board and what they did to Dick. The amazing thing is that, in spite of those lost years, he accomplished so much." She paused. "Apropos of what you said about research last night, I couldn't help thinking how wonderful it would be if you were able to work your way back on Dick's project."

"They wouldn't want me, and I wouldn't be able to handle it," said Alex. "I think we'd better forget my remark about research. It was wishful to say the least. I wasn't very serious about it."

"I think you were. And it's still possible. If you stayed on at the hospital and volunteered two or three days a week in the lab, you'd probably be able to feel your way into it again. It's where you belong! What you should have done long ago!"

He didn't say anything. Why was Peg always so damn righteous about research! He felt annoyed with her—and with himself for ever having made the remark. Not that he knew *what* he wanted any more. With Bert's letter in his pocket, he didn't know what he'd do.

The question stayed with him after he'd dropped Peg and returned to the office. He wondered what Frank, but a wall away, was thinking about Bert's letter.

Whatever Frank felt, he wasn't expressing himself. It was yesterday all over again. Alex decided that he'd make it easy for him. He wrote a note saying that as soon as he could he'd make arrangements to move out of the office.

The phone rang just as he was about to leave. It was Chris Sullivan. "I meant to call you earlier," he said. "If I had, I'd have said 'congratulations.' Unfortunately, they're no longer in order. Too bad. It would have been nice to have a Christian in a Memorial administrative job. Good for the rest of us. Status-wise. And what the hell, it might have opened the door for a few more. Men like Judd O'Brien and Cal Young and Doug Banner. For a while there, when I heard the news about your father-in-law's gift, I thought it was cinched. Sonofagun, I thought, you really pulled it off. Shrewd move, getting the old man to kick in, really Jewing your way in."

"Damn you!" Alex said sharply. "What the hell does that mean?"

"No offense. Hell, I thought it was smart. You wouldn't have had a chance any other way. You know that. The Tribes of Israel take care of their own. Little matter of a foreskin."

"Oh, for Chrissakes!" Alex exploded.

"Look, don't get so huffy! It's one thing for me to be a little frank with you. But when you go shouting off in public— Yes, I know about San Vicente."

Alex winced. "Who told you and what?" he asked wearily.

"Somebody who was goddamn sore. I don't need to mention names, but it wasn't second hand. If he didn't tell me all the gory details, he told me enough. As a matter of fact, that's why I called. I'm kind of disturbed about it. Hell, I'm all for a good tear once in a while, but if you're the kind who babbles in his cups, then, for Chrissakes, either lay off or pick the proper companions. Sure it's a free country and you've got a perfect right to your opinions, but if you're going to sound off, be sure it's in front of your own kind, man."

"Thanks for your advice, but I'm afraid it's a little late."

"I'm afraid it is. It's already generated a lot of heat. What I'd like to do is contain it."

"How?"

"Well, you brought this on yourself, you know. The fire's on you. It's kind of presumptuous of me to say: 'bow out and let it dissipate itself.' But damn it, you're not the only gentile in Memorial. You hang around, and, sure as hell, it's going to spread to the rest of us."

"If whoever told you is going around and stoking the fire by telling people—"

"He isn't. This was in the strictest confidence. He said everyone in the party was pledged to keep it absolutely under wraps. He made an exception of me because he felt that as a fellow gentile I could talk turkey to you."

"About 'bowing out'?"

"Well, yes. He sort of suggested it as a way of avoiding any further feeling."

"If there's a pledge to keep it quiet and you're the only one else to know, then isn't it sort of contained now?"

"Maybe. It's playing it safe, I guess." He hesitated and when he resumed there was a troubled coloration in his voice. "Look, I suppose it is sort of presumptuous of me to suggest it. The only excuse I have is that you might feel uncomfortable enough about the whole business to want a change of scene. I mean, with your reputation, you certainly wouldn't have any trouble getting on another staff. Although, now that I've said it, it's not as casual-sounding as I thought. Look, it's none of my business. The whole thing'll probably blow over anyway. Forget I mentioned it."

"You've raised a point. I want to think about it."

"I was a little carried away. Don't let yourself be stampeded by it."

"I won't. This is my headache, and I'm—"

"Sorry I had to add to it." He sounded fussed. "As I said, it'll probably blow over. See you in the morning."

"See you." Alex hung up slowly.

If the story did get around the hospital, it *would* make it uncomfortable for the others. Chris wouldn't let it get beyond him out of sheer self-interest, Alex knew. But Bert had told him. Would he "in strictest confidence" tell someone else?

It was getting much too complicated. He didn't want to be stampeded. But, inexorably, he seemed to be pushed into a corner. Chris might, in sudden realization, try to mitigate what he'd said. Bert, it was apparent, was playing for keeps.

XII

HE RECOGNIZED Ted's voice the minute he stepped into the hallway, and his first impulse was to turn back. But Peg was saying, "Is that you, Alex?"

"Hi," he said without looking directly at Ted, and Ted answered without looking up at him.

"Ted called," said Peg, "and I asked him to drop by because I thought you'd like to hear what he felt about Bert's letter."

"Actually," Ted said uncomfortably, "it was Ike Press who suggested I call. He wanted to know about my reaction to the letter. I told him I thought it was a pretty unfortunate document. I think you ought to know that it doesn't speak for anyone but Bert."

"I'm grateful for that," said Alex.

"Bert may have been offended by what happened. I was, and with greater reason. But that doesn't give anyone the license to carry on the way he is. I don't feel too happy about the way I've been behaving for that matter. I've been avoiding you because the whole business sort of embarrasses me. I'm pretty weak about these things, probably wouldn't have called if Ike hadn't suggested it."

"I'm the one to be embarrassed," said Alex.

"To be truthful, I was pretty sore—until I realized that only a crazed mind could accuse me of sleeping with Peg and plotting to get rid of you. You couldn't in any rational state think or say any of the things you did. Not the person who could agonize so over a decision about the Amster baby, nor the person who could stand up before his colleagues and assume responsibility for error, nor the person who'd give up the appointment when you had it sewed up. I respect that."

"It's generous of you to say so."

There was an uneasy pause. Peg lit a cigarette, said, "I was talking to Ted about the question of telling the folks about San Vicente."

Alex looked up. So that was why she'd asked Ted to drop by. He was aware of a sharp resentment. This was between Peg and himself. Why should he be talking it over with Ted?

"He thinks it's unnecessary," Peg continued.

"Not that it's any of my business," Ted said uneasily.

"I'd like to hear what you feel, now that Peg's brought it up."

"I think it's an honest impulse. But from what Peg says, the relationship with her folks hasn't been very happy. Why vitiate it more? They don't know. They don't have to know. Why tell them?"

"Because I'm hiding something and feel like a hypocrite."

Ted shrugged. "It'd probably relieve you to get it off your chest. I wonder if it's worth it."

"Knowing Dad," said Peg, "it's the better part of valor to forget it."

"I hate to see anything come between you two when it's all so unnecessary. I'm one to talk, of course. I've always ducked, never been able to face things. The only reason I'm talking now is that I think it's a shame to complicate things all over again. You owe it to Peg—and to yourself—not to. I'm concerned, for both your sakes."

He was protesting just a little too much, trying just a little too hard to show how adult and magnanimous he was, to convince Alex of his concern. Although, to be fair, he'd probably convinced himself. Alex wished that Peg hadn't brought him into it. It clouded rather than clarified.

The doorbell was ringing. Peg rose and walked into the hallway. "I wonder who that can be," she said.

"I'd better be getting along," said Ted, and got up from his chair.

"What on earth—?" began Peg as she opened the door on Joe and Dora Strauss. "Is something wrong? What are you doing here?"

"A good question," said Joe Strauss. "We go away for a few days of sun and rest, and my daughter doesn't even give us a chance to get there; she's already on the phone calling me names."

"You deserved them and you know it."

"You see. She's still ready with an argument."

"You'll forgive me," said Ted, "but I've got to be on my way."

"Of course," said Peg. "You remember Ted Crisler. . . . Mother, Dad."

"Ted Crisler!" said Dora Strauss. "Naturally. It must be a good twenty years."

"That Ted Crisler?" said Joe. "The one who married your best friend Jean?"

"The same," Ted said nervously. "It's good to see you again. Sorry I've got to run like this. But I do have a call to make. Forgive me."

He made a hasty and agitated exit.

"Forgive him!" snorted Joe Strauss. "The nights that he made you cry. Such crying it broke my heart to listen. And I should forgive him yet!"

"It was twenty years ago," said Dora.

"I don't forget. I never forget."

"That's his trouble," said Dora Strauss.

"What made you come back?" asked Peg. "You were there. You needed the rest. Why didn't you stay in the sun?"

"And think of how you called me a double-crosser? Yes, she called me that!" he said, addressing Alex. "I'm dishonest! Two-faced! I go behind the backs of my children! 'Double-crosser!' Beautiful like a flower—and she can say such things. And in her condition. When she should be having pleasant thoughts. Who'd have believed it? *Never* have I heard such talk from her."

"Perhaps it's time you did. You and your money."

"People have respect for my money."

"Not I."

"Obviously not you. You want me to sit in the sun and be happy about all the fine things you said to me. So I sat and I burned. Not from the sun, believe me. I couldn't nap and I couldn't eat. And rest like that I needed like a hole in the head. So we came back."

"I'm sorry."

"*Now* you're sorry. Why weren't you sorry *before* you opened your mouth?"

"All right," said Dora. "She said she's sorry. Kiss and make up before it starts all over again. I'm the one who has to live with him."

"Why don't you come in and sit down?" said Alex.

"Thank you," said Joe with mock elaborateness. "At least somebody in the family has some manners. Tell me, Alex, do you also think I double-crossed you?"

"Please, Joe," said Dora. "Enough already."

"I want to know."

"I asked you to put off the donation until after Wednesday," said Alex. "You didn't."

"Did I say I would?" demanded Joe.

"Of course you did," said Peg.

"I'm asking Alex."

"That was my understanding. You knew why I asked you to. You said you respected me for it."

"Correct. That's exactly what I said. But you're not answering my question. Did I say I *would* wait until after Wednesday? Did I give you my word as my daughter insists I did?"

"If not explicitly, you certainly did implicitly."

"I'll recall the conversation. I said: 'I'm making the donation anyway. What's the difference if I give it before or after Wednesday?' "

"And I said I'd prefer it after. To which you answered: 'In other words, you're telling me to keep out? You won't take my help?' Which was exactly what I was telling you."

"And I said: 'I think you're *meshugeh* but I respect you for it.' Where was the promise, Peggy? Find the words and I'll eat them!"

"When you say you respect a person for what he wishes then obviously you respect his wishes."

"You went to college and studied logic but you think with your feelings, not your mind," he said bitingly. "I can respect my doctor when he tells me to stop smoking because it may shorten my life, but does that mean I'll do it or even intend to? 'I respect' does not mean 'I promise.' "

"Nonetheless," said Alex, "that was the implication you meant to leave."

"According to your interpretation."

"No, according to the objective evidence."

"You've invented an objective instrument that can read my mind?"

"No, merely your words. When you made that donation last night you made it in confidence. You asked that no announcement be made for two weeks. Why? Precisely because you wanted me to feel that you had respected my wish!"

A flush of red colored Joe Strauss's neck. "Where did you get this information?" he demanded.

"What difference does it make? Are you denying it?"

Joe stared at him, a hostile glitter in his eyes. "Why should I? I have nothing to hide. And if I did, am I responsible to you? When Joe Strauss gives a donation of a half million, he'll say when and how! He'll decide whether it's after Wednesday or before Wednesday. You want it after—fine. But you also want the appointment. And it so happens that I'd like you to have it. So what should I do? Wait and say nothing? And if they vote against you, *then* I'll give my half million? Oh, no. I'm not in kindergarten. I make my money work for me."

"The Board meets tomorrow," said Alex. "There's one candidate. Dan Simon."

"You mean one candidate, Alex Frazier."

"No. Alex Frazier withdrew his name."

Joe looked from Alex to Peggy. "Is he joking?"

"No," said Peg.

The color washed out of Joe's face. He turned on his heel and strode into the den. In a moment he could be heard dialing a number on the phone. "Arthur?" he said. "Joe Strauss. What's this I hear about my son-in-law? . . . That's what he tells me, only I didn't believe him. . . . *Who* told him? *How* did he hear? . . . What do you mean it's all around the hospital? Who talked? I know you didn't. Ike Press didn't. So it had to be Rukeyser. Well, tell him from me that he's going to be sorry. Tell him no one who's honored with a confidence from Joe Strauss repeats it without being sorry. . . . Naturally you're upset. Nobody's blaming you if I got a *schlemiel* for a son-in-law. . . . He let me down too. But something tells me he'll change his mind. He changed it one way, he can change it back again. . . ."

"You're wrong," said Alex when Joe Strauss returned. "I've made my decision. This isn't a dozen custom shirts you bought me in Paris. Which I didn't wear, by the way."

"Are you trying to make me angry? I refuse to oblige you." Joe took out a cigar, bit off the end, and planting himself directly in front of Alex, said: "One question I'd like to ask: What do you think you gain from this?"

"My self. My soul."

"Big words. What meaning do they have?" Joe asked contemptuously.

"To a businessman, very little."

"You think you crush me with such a remark, you with the degrees and the doctor in front of your name?" Joe's eyes fixed fiercely on Alex's. "Cut me open with your scalpel, doctor, cut anyone open and find a soul, a self. Not in a businessman and not in a poet. Who can find his self, his soul these days? Where? In the air? In the wind? They're floating around somewhere, perhaps. They existed once. But today? You'll look in vain, doctor." He paused. "Stop fighting me, Alex. Take the appointment."

"I don't want it."

"You'd spite yourself because *I* tried to help?" said Joe, staring at him incredulously.

"I asked you not to."

"Does that mean you have to punish yourself? You want to

punish me, all right. Maybe I deserve it. But not for this!" he said with an intensity which bordered on anger. "I carried a grudge for twenty years. That's something else. It was foolish, and, better late than never, I realized and wanted to make up for it. So be big enough to accept. Forgive a little. Don't begrudge an old man. It's in your interest. It's for you."

"It's no longer important to me."

"You lie. It is, and you know it. Because, fundamentally, you're like me. You want success, recognition, money, comfort. You like your fast Italian cars and your high-priced French paintings. And you want to run the show just as I would. You want to be looked up to and respected as the top man, the chief, the best surgeon in the city—and charge the best prices."

"What if I told you," said Alex, "that I'm thinking of getting out of the hospital altogether?"

"To do what?"

"He's not, of course," Peg said hastily.

"I may."

"Why, Alex?" asked Dora Strauss, her voice reflecting her bewilderment.

"What did you do, line up a chief of staff appointment at another hospital?" asked Joe, fixing Alex with challenging eyes.

"No."

"Just like that you'd pick up and quit?"

"He's not quitting," Peg insisted.

"If I want to, why not?"

Joe shrugged. "No reason. It's his privilege. A man has a right to want a change." His tone was carefully casual. "I wouldn't mind if you came back to New York. A good surgeon is always in demand. I'm on the board of Beth Israel. And I've done favors for enough internists so referrals are nothing to worry about."

"Thanks. But that's not what I had in mind."

"What Alex is thinking of," said Peg, "is going back to research."

Joe Strauss looked at her in surprise. "Alex has a short memory.

He's forgotten when you lived in a fourth floor walk-up on 18th and Eighth Avenue. He's forgotten how you came every Friday night and stocked up so you'd have decent food for the week. Where will you park your Ferrari, Alex?" he said sarcastically. "In the street for the Puerto Ricans to make junk out of? Where will you hang your paintings? You're a surgeon. You make a fine living. You have a good name. You can be chief of staff. Why should you start fiddling around with research again?"

"Because that's where he belongs," said Peggy. "He started out in research, and he never should have left it. And if you were as quick to hand out half million dollar gifts for research as you are for maternity wings and textile factories for Israel, maybe Alex wouldn't have to worry about going back to it."

"I have no intention of going back," Alex said impatiently.

"You said you'd like to. We talked about your staying on and working into it."

"*You* talked about it. You've always talked about it."

"Because you said last night you were happiest in research."

"Forget research! I wish you'd stop crowding me, Peg. Everyone trying to tell me what to do. Arthur, Ike Press, Bert, my father-in-law, you. I wish the hell you'd all quit being so zealous in my behalf."

"Gladly," said Joe. "Nobody owns you. You've got something in mind, tell us, and we'll shut up."

"I don't. For all I know, I may ship out on a freighter. I told Peg. I might go back to Mexico or take off for Hawaii."

"To do what? Bum on the beach?"

"That, too, is possible."

"Have you lost your senses?" demanded Dora Strauss. "How can you give everything up and run off with a baby coming?"

"He's got a rich father-in-law," said Joe. "Why should *he* worry? Joe Strauss will provide! You want to go, go! Go sit on your behind under the banana trees and make eyes at the hula-hula girls!"

"Stop talking nonsense," said Dora. "What's happened, Peggy? There's something wrong between you two?"

"Nothing's happened and nothing's wrong. Alex has been under a strain. He's been doing the work of three men and he's tired. I can understand his wanting a change."

"So take a month off, the both of you, and go to Palm Springs."

"I can't," said Peggy. "Not now."

"You think the store will close up if you stop work? You can't, but Alex can? He can say no to the appointment, leave the hospital, give up his practice, and go traipsing off to God knows where?"

"Let him," said Joe. "If he wants to quit and run out, let him."

"What do you mean, let him? What kind of foolishness is this? He's not a schoolboy. He's a man with responsibilities." She turned to Alex. "My daughter has a way of trying to hide things. But *I* know when something is wrong. Tell me. What happened, Alex?"

It was a direct question, and all he had to do was give a direct answer. He'd been telling himself he would. The moment was there, the words rehearsed, but somehow he couldn't articulate them. And while he chided himself and tried to rally his courage, Peg was again repeating her denial that anything was wrong—and the moment was gone.

"Then what?" demanded Dora Strauss. "What's all the *tzimmes* about a change? What's this talk about a freighter? If Alex is tired, let him take a rest. If he doesn't like what he's doing, let him do something else. Maybe he'd like to go into the business."

"The surgeon with the degrees?" Joe said derisively. "What's he going to do, cut piece goods with his scalpel?"

"I'm serious! Arthur said he was a good administrator. If he can handle the doctors and problems of a hospital, he can handle the workers and problems of your factory."

Joe turned to Alex. "She's already got you running the place," he said tartly. "Is that what you had in the back of your mind? A place in the business? A cushy job with maybe fifty thousand a year salary? You want to be vice-president of Strauss Casuals?"

"I can just see myself," said Alex.

"And I'm sucker enough to go for the idea. Or maybe I'm not such a sucker. Come to think of it, it's a pretty good idea. I'm getting older. I'm beginning to slow down. In a few years I'll be thinking of retiring. Sidney's in the business, but, between us, my son Sidney'll never be anything but a first-class superintendent. Initiative, ideas, imagination, which he hasn't got, I have a hunch you, with proper training, could supply. You'll work with me and you'll pick up the fine points. The Strauss touch. Why not?"

"I never heard anything so insane," said Peggy.

"What's insane? It's a good business. Look in Dun and Bradstreet, and you'll find out. It's big money. But I forget, my daughter isn't interested in money."

"This isn't a joke."

"Who's joking?"

"You know Alex isn't a businessman!"

"*How* do I know? Did you know your abilities as a businesswoman until you tried? Why shouldn't Alex give it a try? He's up in the air, looking for his self, his soul! Who knows, maybe he'll find it in business. Stranger things have happened." He turned to Alex. "You're quiet."

"I haven't anything to say."

"You're above it? You're a snob like my daughter? You, too, think money is contaminated?"

"No, but I think the idea's kind of far-fetched."

"Let it percolate a little. Don't dismiss it so easy. There's a small fortune involved. Why should I call in a stranger? Why shouldn't we keep it in the family?"

The words carried an awful echo of his own, of the words he'd used in San Vicente about the Strauss fortune and "keeping it in the faith." And here he was confronted by this absurd turn which would make him the acceptable one, him the recipient of the Strauss largesse. Guilt and anger and sadness stirred a bitter ferment in him and when Joe Strauss persisted and asked: "What about it? You want to give it a try? You want me to take you in as a partner in Strauss Casuals?" he heard himself say: "Your goy son-in-law?"

With a visible effort at control, Joe Strauss said: "After twenty years maybe a little kosher has rubbed off."

"If you only knew."

"Alex," Peggy said in warning.

Alex disregarded her. He turned to Dora Strauss: "You asked if anything had happened . . ."

"Please, Alex!" Peggy pleaded. "Mother and Dad have driven to and from Palm Springs. They've had a rough day, and so have I. I think we'd better let them get washed and relaxed and have Mrs. Deevan set two more places for—"

"Alex was going to tell us something," Dora Strauss said quietly.

"Something did happen," Alex began.

"We had a silly difference, a quarrel," Peggy cut in breathlessly. "I've long since forgotten it and I don't see any point in burdening Mother and Dad with it."

"Go on, Alex," said Dora Strauss.

"I wish it were a quarrel. Unfortunately—"

"Unfortunately, Alex got drunk and made a few indiscreet remarks about Ted and me."

"If you're going to tell it, tell it all!" Alex said angrily. "Because if you don't, I damn well will!" He pulled Bert's letter out of his pocket, said to Joe Strauss, "I think you'd better read this."

Before Joe could take it from him, Peggy snatched it out of Alex's hand. "This is between the two of us," she said fiercely. "I'm not going to have you dragging my father and mother into it!"

"I'd like them to see it."

"No!"

"Let's have it, Peg."

"This is utterly ridiculous! Why do you insist on making something out of nothing?"

"Are you going to give it to me or aren't you?"

She crumpled the letter into a ball, turned toward the hallway, said, "I'm going to tell Mrs. Deevan to—"

"Peggy!"

The sharpness of his tone stopped her.

"You'd better give it to me," he said.

She turned, stared at him defiantly. His hand seized her wrist.

"Alex!" she cried.

Silently he tried to force loose her hold. She fought him, tried desperately to pull free, then, as he began to pry the wadded ball from her grasp, wilted suddenly and broke into hysterical weeping.

Joe and Dora stared at her in astonishment. Then Dora led her to the sofa, saying, "Now, now. It can't be as bad as that."

Joe shook his head in hapless bewilderment. "What's going on here?" he mumbled.

Unrumpling the letter, Alex handed it to him.

Joe glanced at the imprinted letterhead. "Bert Krantz. I saw him at the Club last night."

"That's right," said Alex.

Joe began reading. "He, too, with the 'father-in-law's wealth,'" he remarked. "What position? You're not taking the position."

"Read the rest of it."

Joe read on in a silence which was only accented by the sound of Peggy's sobs. When he finished, he handed it to Dora, who read halfway down the page, then compulsively crumpled it as Peggy had. "I can't read any more," she said.

"'A few indiscreet remarks,'" Joe said sardonically. "I know these indiscreet remarks." He sighed. "All right you wanted to tell us, tell . . ."

"I don't want to hear!" said Dora. "If he wants to make a confession, let him go to a priest!"

Alex felt a sudden weariness. The need, the great desire to bring it out into the open was gone now. He was sorry he'd started.

"I don't particularly want to go into it. It's easier for me not to," he said.

"You'll tell us and you, Dora, will listen," said Joe. "I'm not satisfied to leave it at that. *I want* to hear. Go on, Mr. Frazier, my Christian son-in-law. Tell us. Every detail. Your 'indiscreet remarks' won't kill us. We've been in training for such remarks all our lives. We thrive on them. They give us strength."

There wasn't much alternative. Alex had really known that from the beginning. He plunged in, talking out of shame and sorrow, adumbrating the wretched catalogue of violence and bigotries, leaving nothing out, neither the accusations of trying to do him out of the Strauss fortune, nor the attack on Dan. It *was* a confession, his voice fraught with the desperate fervor of repentance. And when it was over, he stood spent and limp yet aware of the charge emotions which had gathered so thickly in the room.

"You're proud of your performance!" Joe Strauss said with contained wrath. "It's something to brag about!"

"No. But I had to be honest."

"Why? She tried to stop you. Why were you rushing? To boast?"

"Out of guilt, I suppose."

"Guilt," Joe said bitterly. "Go rub your nose in your guilt! You think this is a surprise? You think I'm shocked? How many times have I heard it in my mind? How many years have I waited for it to come out? I knew. I've always known."

"You don't know and you never did!" said Peggy.

"Like a book! Every one of them. Like a book."

"Why did you have to tell him!" she cried to Alex. "Why did you feed him what he believes about all gentiles?"

"You're still protecting him!" Joe said, incredulous. "For twenty years you've lived with an anti-Semite and you still won't admit it!"

"Because it isn't true!"

"What came out of his mouth, what you and I just heard with our own ears isn't true? He didn't say it? It didn't happen?"

"It happened. When he was so drunk he was out of his mind, when he wasn't himself, when he didn't even know until the next day when I told him. In all the twenty years I never heard a word."

"You only need to be caught to be a crook."

"Alex is *not* an anti-Semite!"

"I don't hear him denying it."

"I think I would deny it," said Alex. "I was brought up with anti-Semitism but I grew out of it and hated it and except for that one lapse when I wasn't myself—"

"Contradiction. When you *were* yourself! The 'self' you were looking for, that you'd lost somewhere. You think people change? They don't change!"

"You'd like to believe that. 'A goy is a goy.' Oh, I've heard you say it! You hate the goyim. You hate my guts. You always have."

"Yes!" Joe shouted.

"And yet you yourself are capable of change. That wasn't how you felt last night when you admitted you'd been wrong, when you were ready to do anything for me, to give a half million to make me surgeon-in-chief."

"I'm glad I gave it! I'll give more! Everything I have! Every cent I set aside for my daughter! So you won't have it, so you won't get a smell. Yes, last night I felt different. My daughter told me I was going to be a grandfather, and I let myself dream, I let myself juggle pretty balls in the air, everything so beautiful and lovely, we'd live in peace and harmony and happiness, what plans I made! And then you opened your mouth and I came crashing back to earth. Thank you, my Christian son-in-law, for showing me what a damn fool I was! A grandson—and I get soft in the head. Thank you for reminding me what I should never have forgotten, yes, that a goy *is* a goy!"

"And you're one to talk about anti-Semitism!" cried Peg.

"Who then, you? What do you know about it, you with your gentile husband and your respectable gentile name? What does it mean to you? Yes, I'm prejudiced against the goyim. I don't deny it. I don't hide it. I carry it in my heart and on my tongue. Because I, too, was brought up with anti-Semitism. Not part of it, like you, my Christian son-in-law, but the object, the victim. They had a game in Berislav Gubernia when I was a boy. Every Yom Kippur, on that high holy day when we fasted and prayed, the *skutzim* would descend on us as we came from temple. They would pounce on us and throw us to the ground and force raw pork down our throats. I can still taste it and the vomit that came up with it. Every year until I was fourteen, when we organized a defense group and met them with rocks and clubs. They ran, and we never tasted pork again. But one day the Cossacks came to town and with them, in the middle of the night, they struck. Their torches fell on the roofs, and the flames burned down a street of Jewish houses. Jewish skulls were cracked, Jewish blood ran. They raped and pillaged. I saw my married sister taken on the floor with two Cossacks holding her down while another pumped his seed into her. And when her husband flung himself at them, a rifle cracked and he was still, and their child, a boy of three months, lying in his cradle, was lifted on a bayonet like a piece of meat on a spit. So don't talk to me about anti-Semitism, my daughter, who is no daughter! My daughter, who has no pride or shame, who refuses to see or hear because, if she did, it might not be so easy to go to bed with her prize, her jewel, her anti-Semitic lover!"

"Enough, Joe," said Dora. "What are you saying!"

"I'm saying that she's either the daughter of Joe Strauss or the whore of Alex Frazier. Let her choose."

"He's her husband. A child is coming. What do you want from her?"

"I want her to open her eyes. I want her to stop lying to herself!"

"Joe, he was drunk. He didn't know what he was doing."

"You're defending him, too?"

"What is she to do? She's our child, Joe!"

He was silent, his face suddenly tired and old, his shoulders slumped in defeat. "I know," he said heavily. "And I weep for her." He looked toward Peggy, said quietly, "Come to your senses, my daughter. You can't keep hiding. In the end he'll leave you because there won't be any Strauss fortune. Come back to your own. Come back to the big house with the empty rooms which have been waiting for you. Come back where you can raise your child to know who he is."

"The goy as well as the Jew?" asked Peggy.

"My grandson will be a Jew!" Joe said fervently. "And he'll be proud of it. Not like his mother!"

Peggy started to say something, then burst into tears.

"Cry, cry!" said Joe. "You have good reasons. Someday you'll realize. Someday you'll tell me . . ."

Her sobbing increased.

"Peggy," Dora said softly. "Don't Peggy."

"It's time to go Dora," said Joe, and started toward the door.

Dora remained seated, her hand stroking Peggy's arm.

"Are you coming, Dora?" Joe called from the hallway.

Dora hesitated. "Wait, Joe," she said.

"I'm through waiting. I waited twenty years for my daughter to come to her senses. Are you coming or are you, too, bewitched by the blond anti-Semite with the blue eyes?"

"Don't, Dad!" cried Peggy.

Joe Strauss didn't answer. He strode out the door. The echo of his step rose from the concrete walk. "Dora!" he shouted.

Dora hesitated. "He didn't mean it," she said in a pleading voice. "He didn't know what he was saying. Later he'll realize. And he'll lie awake all night crying. I know him." She sat silent a moment, then kissed Peg hastily on the cheek, rose and walked out after him.

XIII

ALEX heard the sound of the door closing, then the whimper of Peg's weeping, and was suddenly overwhelmed by the sorrow he'd caused and which need not have been. He felt sad for all that had happened, for Joe Strauss, whose attitude he couldn't bring himself to condemn or condone, for Dora Strauss, whose ambivalence he understood, for Peg, whose grief he couldn't endure or assuage. He asked himself why, on top of everything, he'd felt so compelled to precipitate the scene with Joe Strauss and heard Peg asking: "Why! Why did you insist on telling?"

"I don't know," he said. "I felt I had to. To clear the air perhaps."

"You certainly succeeded," she said bitterly. "Are you satisfied? Are you happy about it?"

"No."

"Then why, when I asked you not to," she sobbed, "when I tried so desperately to stop you!"

"Because I felt it was the only ethical thing I could do."

"By punishing everyone else? You had no right! You knew how he'd react. You knew it'd spoil everything. And yet you persisted. Even though I begged and pleaded, you had to have your wilful, stupid way!"

"What did I spoil? A gesture? A sentimental conversion that would have lasted a week?"

"How do you know?" she demanded harshly. "What right have you to assume? He was trying. You didn't give him a chance!"

"Why are you so upset about it?" he asked quietly. "Why is it so important to you?"

"I told you last night. For twenty years I fought and cajoled and turned myself inside out to have him accept you. And then, when he finally did, you had to rush in and reinforce every bigot idea he'd ever had about you."

"That isn't what bothers you. You managed to balance and reconcile no matter what he felt. You kept papa in one compartment, me in the other. What disturbs you now is that he's upset the balance by asking you to make a choice. Which is something you never did. Oh, you married me against his will. But you managed to keep the passage back clear. You had your Friday nights and Wednesday lunches and, after we moved, those frequent trips to New York. You kept up your cozy, snug relationship. And it never occurred to you that I might not like it, that I might be hurt—and I *was!* But you couldn't acknowledge that because once you did you'd have to acknowledge also that your first loyalty was to your husband and, if the one clashed with the other, then you couldn't have both. You couldn't face it then and you can't now, because you worship him and always have."

"I hate him," she sobbed. "I hate you both."

"No, you hate the idea that you can't have your cake and eat it too. The last thing in the world you want to do is break with him. Well, I'm not holding you. The passage back is still clear, the empty rooms still waiting. And so is he, with his arms open to embrace you."

"I'm not in love with my father, if that's what you're trying to say."

"He said he hated my guts. Do you know why? Not because he's anti-goy but because he's anti-anyone who'd go to bed with his daughter. All these years he's been jealous—and you liked it!"

She looked up, startled, as if he'd slapped her. "That's an ugly thing to say," she said, her lips trembling. "And maybe I deserve it . . . I did worship him when I was a kid. I always wanted his approval."

"And still do."

"Yes, and still do," she admitted. "Call it a father fixation if you want. It's true; even though I defied him to marry you, I didn't have the guts to risk an all-out break. I should have. I can see that now. Because it did hurt you, did affect our relationship. You probably wouldn't have left research if I had."

"Probably not. Fact is, I did."

"Not on my urging. *I* didn't want it."

"I'm not blaming you, I'm grateful! What I'm not grateful for is that you've thrown it up to me ever since."

"Because you talked yourself into the misguided notion that you were denying me and had to provide for me."

"Rather than have him do so, yes!"

"Did I ask for anything? I didn't need it."

"Why should you? You always wore the smartest clothes, served the best food. And if you weren't concerned with the source, I was. For all you say, you like living in style."

"And you don't!"

"I learned. It wasn't hard. Especially since *I wasn't* disinterested in money. And I liked surgery. Something you never recognized."

"A nice rationale for continuing to live in style, for turning your back on the work you were trained for and really wanted."

"I—or you?"

"Why do you keep insisting that you didn't care?" she demanded.

"Why do you keep insisting that I did? Oh, I did at first. But you simply wouldn't believe me when I discovered I preferred surgery. That was heresy. Why? Because you had some snobbish, romanticized image of Alex Frazier, the research man. Some exalted notion of wanting your husband 'on a pedestal' with Pasteur and Semmelweiss and Salk—yes, you actually used that phrase! Well, maybe I wasn't the research man you thought I was—or *I* thought I was!"

"You never gave yourself the chance to find out!"

"I have news for you. I was no Dick Lerner or I'd have stuck at it as he did. Dick never gave up. Not when they dropped him from Olive, nor when they pulled those grants out from under him. Oh, for a moment when they were lowering his body into the ground I indulged in the sentimental fantasy of picking up the torch. What nonsense! I'm a surgeon. A good one. And what's wrong with it?"

"Nothing. If you're content."

"I am, no thanks to you! Because you, in your superior way, have done your damnedest to chip away and denigrate, to make it unworthy, crass, a sort of plumbing of the flesh—which it is. And what greater gratification is there than repairing a leaky valve of the heart or rerouting the blood stream or removing the blockage of a malignant growth? What greater satisfaction than to see life returning to a failing body, to see the color of health restored? I'm not going to let you sour that satisfaction. I'm not going to let you make me feel guilty and inadequate by suggesting I sold out."

"Is that what I've done?"

"What else was your constant harping on research intended to mean? I didn't have to listen, of course. And I'm not any more. I'm not apologizing for saving several hundred lives a year. Nor for using my ingenuity to open up a couple of surgical techniques which are probably responsible for hundreds more. I've been talking about pulling out, running off. And I suddenly realize I don't want to and don't intend to. I won't find nirvana in Hawaii or in the aseptic cloisters of a research lab. I can't run. I can't escape. I'm going to stick it out, Bert or no Bert."

"I told you I thought you should."

"So I could cut down on my case load and take a couple of days a week to work back into research. No. I may take a couple of days in the hospital, but it'll be in the clinic with more surgery cases. Because that's my work. It's my salvation. It's the one thing that means anything to me, whatever you may think!"

"It doesn't matter. I seem to have been wrong about everything," she said wretchedly.

The despair and abnegation in her tone touched Alex. "I don't know why I'm taking everything out on you," he said just as miserably.

"Because I *have* been at fault. 'You have to face yourself before you can understand others,' Ike Press told me this morning. And I never have. I haven't been honest with myself, the folks, or you. A snob, you called me. And so did Dad."

"So easy to paste a label on someone."

"You were right. And so was he. Why is it that I wanted to marry a gentile? The simple answer is that I was in love. And I was. But I think I liked the idea, liked the sound of a gentile name. I'd lie in bed and repeat it over and over: Peg Frazier, Peggy Frazier, Mrs. Alexander Frazier. Why did it please me? Because I was so relieved it wasn't Lapidus or Shapiro? And wasn't that snobbery a form of anti-Semitism? So many things I'm beginning to discover about myself. So many things I don't like. What did you ever see in me? Why did you marry me?"

"For the Strauss fortune, according to Mr. Strauss. Isn't that what you've been thinking, too?"

She didn't say anything.

"I don't blame you," said Alex. "I've been pretty lopsided on the subject of money. It took a knock on the head like New Year's Eve to show me how badly." He sat down beside her on the sofa and, facing her, said, "I didn't marry you for your money, Peg. I'd like you to believe that."

"I want to."

"All I can tell you is that I knew I wanted to marry you a minute after you walked into the room on Cinco de Mayo that first night in Mexico. I knew before I found out your father was a dress manufacturer. Which didn't detract from your charms. But I'd have pursued you just as ardently if you were penniless. I can't prove it, but, if it were the Strauss fortune I was after, I'd long since have divorced you. There are a half dozen divorcees who come into the office, everyone of them loaded and dying to marry a Beverly Hills surgeon. I know that's a silly thing to say, but there's a logic to it—if you care to follow that kind of thinking."

"I don't. But I have. Because I happen to know one of them. And she's a lot more attractive and exciting than I am . . . It's occurred to me."

"Have I ever given you cause to worry?"

Peggy was silent.

"You know the answer," he said quietly.

The ring of the phone intruded from the study. Alex rose, went in to answer it. It was Ike Press, calling to express his concern over Bert's letter, which he considered utterly shocking and irresponsible. "I talked to Dan and Ted, and, I can assure you, they were as offended as I was."

"Ted dropped by to tell me," said Alex.

"And I'm sure you'll get a call from Dan."

Yes, Dan would call, and without any prompting from Ike. You expected it because of the damn fine human being he was. Just as you didn't expect it from Frank.

"I think it's unforgivable," Ike was saying. "And I know how disturbed you must have been. But knowing your good wife's attitude, I knew she'd dissuade you from acting impulsively. Not that I think you would. The whole thing was so outrageous that I don't see how—"

"My impulse *was* to leave."

"You're not going to, of course?"

"No. I've had second thoughts about it."

"Good. I wish Bert would have second thoughts. I talked with him too, you know. I'm afraid he hasn't simmered down enough to be rational on the subject. It's not a purely personal thing, I must say in his defense. It's an ideological crusade that goes back to the beginnings of Memorial, which was founded, as he points out, in answer to the discrimination and quotas against Jewish doctors. Bert's convinced himself he's fighting in defense of that original cause, and I haven't been able to persuade him that you don't correct one abuse by creating another. Dan's undertaken to talk to him when he calms down a little. He'll probably make more headway."

Whether he would or not, Alex knew he'd have to meet the challenge of Bert, learn somehow to cope and live with it. Whether he'd ever find ease, ever lose awareness of the Dark Presence here among these men who had seen its scabrous face, was problematical. This was his battleground, and he felt committed to it.

"Incidentally," said Ike, "did you resolve the problem of telling your father-in-law?"

"I resolved it. I told him. No need for worry on your part. He's all for giving the rest of his money to Memorial to keep it out of my anti-Semitic hands."

"I wouldn't take that too seriously. He'll get over it."

"It's fine with me if he doesn't."

"Would you like me to have a talk with him?"

"No. I'd actually prefer that you didn't."

"As you say. I'm sure it will work itself out in any case."

After he'd placed the phone back on the cradle, Alex asked himself why he'd been so quick to reject Ike's offer. Ike could be very persuasive. He might very well temper Joe Strauss's attitude. Which would make things easier on Peg.

It occurred to him that one of the underlying motives which had prompted the scene with Joe Strauss was the very need to precipitate the break. Perhaps because he *wanted* Peg to be confronted with the reality of her relationships to Joe Strauss and himself, wanted her to be faced with the choice she now must make. Perhaps, also, because he'd become so aware of the money-hunger in him that he needed to prove to himself that it wasn't an essential part of him, needed once and for all to extirpate it. That's why he wasn't jumping at Ike's offer to intercede. He'd rejected the appointment, been frank with Joe Strauss. It would have been easier to keep quiet, avoid the break, spare them the realities and the grief. But it would have been perpetuating a falsehood, living a fraud. He'd done what he had to do and was his own man. We are what we make of ourselves, Ike had said. What we will and do . . .

He sat in the stillness of the study, dark except for the spill of light from the living room, where Peg sat alone with her decision. He knew the struggle she was going through, sensed her anguish and bewilderment. Because in these last few days he'd pretty much demolished her world, pulled the props out from under the protective structure in which she lived.

He rose, walked back through the lane of light into the living room. She was sitting as he'd left her, staring with sightless sadness, looking so small and stricken and vulnerable that he felt a wrench of compassion. Sitting down beside her, he said: "I'm sorry I've been so rough on you, Peg. It wasn't very fair to lam into you because I was unhappy with myself."

"It wouldn't have been if you were entirely wrong. You weren't."

"I'm afraid I've pushed you into a corner."

"It's just as well. It's time I faced a few truths about myself. I failed you because I didn't years ago. I romanticized and glossed over and avoided. In a way, I'm grateful that you forced the issue. Because it brings it down to you and me and what we do from here on out."

"I don't want to push you on that, Peg."

She sighed. "I haven't been much help, have I? I can see now how I complicated things, gave you conflicts you should never have had. I certainly didn't help at San Vicente. I knew how upset you were, but instead of being understanding, I was impatient, made cracks I shouldn't have. And then I had to aggravate things further by my half-baked attitude toward Ted, had to get romantic about something that was twenty years dead. Where was I when you were getting drunk? Off dancing with my old beau, behaving like a moon-struck adolescent. Oh, you must have loved that in the state of mind you were in!"

"It didn't help."

"No, it didn't. I feel as though I provoked the whole thing."

Alex shook his head. "I'm afraid you can't take credit for something that was my responsibility."

"If I hadn't been so self-absorbed, I might have stopped it."

"So might I. I didn't."

"I let it happen and then fell apart when it did. My first impulse was to believe every horror that came out of you. I wanted to run. I did, at Palm Springs. I wanted to stay and never come back."

"I knew."

"But I did. I'm glad you were understanding enough to leave me to myself. I haven't slept much. I've tried to think things through. Ike helped. And so did tonight. As awful as it was, it clarified so much for me. . . ." She was silent. "God," she said with a break in her voice, "why are we so mixed up? Why are we so complicated?"

"We're human," he said.

She wilted suddenly, buried her face in her hands. "I didn't know I was making you unhappy!" she cried.

He put his arm around her, and she turned toward him, seeking the solace of his shoulder.

"I shouldn't have said what I did, because that isn't the story." Alex tried to find the words to tell her that whatever happiness he'd known he'd found in her. "I don't know what the twenty years have meant to you," he said fumblingly. "I know what they have for me. . . ." He gripped her arm, and for a long while they sat in silence.

Chimes from the grandfather clock in the hallway sounded the half hour.

"I'm so tired," she mumbled.

"I'd better go," he said reluctantly.

"No." She clung to his arm.

"You need to think it through, to know."

"Perhaps I do know," she said, after a pause. "I understand more now than I have in twenty years. And in some ways, I don't understand a thing. Doesn't make much sense, does it?"

From the street came the squeal of a car braking to a stop, then the sound of young laughter erupting in the night air. Probably the boy next door returning from a party with friends. For some reason it took him back to Vera Cruz and the days of their honeymoon, to their bedroom, the open windows looking out over a country road. The same laughter, young and uninhibited, of the earth and of the heart, would reverberate in the stillness of the night. In it was the unhoarded confidence of youth, the lusty yes to life. They'd shared it then, their low laughter echoing the shouts outside. Oh, to be back in that time, to have it all ahead, unsullied and good . . .

"I don't suppose it can ever be the same," Peggy was saying.

No, probably not. But there could be other things. A return to the forgotten yes. An understanding and compassion that might go deeper.

"I want it to work out," she said wistfully. "Do you think it can, Alex?"

"We can try," he said, and had to turn away to keep from breaking down. Her hand closed tightly on his. Weeping soundlessly, he returned the pressure of her grip. She guided him to her, cradling his head in the hollow of her shoulder. Softly, her finger tips stroked his hair. He let himself lie against her, surrendering the full weight of his weariness.

A NOTE ABOUT THE AUTHOR

GEORGE SKLAR, who has devoted himself to writing fiction since 1945, has been both playwright and screenwriter. He graduated Phi Beta Kappa from Yale in 1929, completed his studies at the 47 Workshop with George Pierce Baker in the Yale Department of Drama, and in 1939 won a John Golden Fellowship in playwriting. Mr. Sklar's plays, written between 1932 and 1940, are: *Merry-Go-Round, Peace on Earth, Stevedore, Parade* (all in collaboration), and *Life and Death of an American.* His novels (1945-61) are: *The Two Worlds of Johnny Truro, The Promising Young Men, The Housewarming,* and *The Identity of Dr. Frazier.* Mr. Sklar is married, has a daughter and two sons, and lives in Los Angeles.

June 1961

A NOTE ON THE TYPE

THIS BOOK is set in Electra, a Linotype face designed by the late W. A. Dwiggins (1880-1956). This face cannot be classified as either modern or old-style. It is not based on any historical model, nor does it echo any particular period or style. It avoids the extreme contrasts between thick and thin elements that mark most modern faces, and attempts to give a feeling of fluidity, power, and speed.

Composed, printed, and bound by

H. Wolff, New York.

Paper manufactured by

S. D. Warren Company, Boston.

Typography and binding based on designs by

W. A. DWIGGINS